GREEN DANGER

Part two of the Operation Jigsaw Trilogy

MARK HAYDEN

Paw Press
www.pawpress.co.uk

Copyright © Paw Press 2013
All Rights Reserved

Cover Design - Hilary Pitt, 2QT Publishing.
Design Copyright © 2014
Cover Images Copyright © Shutterstock

This edition published 2015 by Paw Press:
www.pawpress.co.uk
Independent Publishing in Westmorland.

ISBN-13: 978-1512332391
ISBN-10: 1512332399

In Memoriam

Kenneth Attwood 1921-2005
Joan Attwood 1927-2013

Together in Life, together at Rest

Acknowledgments

This book would not have been written without love, support, encouragement and sacrifices from my wife, Anne. She agreed to carry on full time work and let me step down so I could write. I also do the cooking and ironing, so it's not a one-way deal.

Thanks also to the tribe of readers who gave the thumbs-up to the books (with the occasional thumbs-down to certain sections): Jen Driver, Jane McQuillin, Martin Marriott, Mark Nicholson, Gail Sheldrick, Bob Smith, Martin Trent and Chris Tyler. Speaking of Chris, thanks also to the fellow members of Kendal Writers' Café.

A special mention has to go to former DC Nick Almond of Cumbria Constabulary for sharing his experiences with me (and to his daughter, Amy, for introducing us).

Finally, I am grateful for the professional services of the team at 2QT Publishing. Thanks are owed to Hilary Pitt for designing the cover and to Joanne Harrington for proofreading. It should be emphasised that any remaining errors are entirely my own and not Joanne's.

If you are thinking of publishing your own work, I can strongly recommend the services from 2QT.

GREEN FOR DANGER

Prologue

Earlsbury, Staffordshire
In the Black Country
Friday 12th June 1992

'*Sláinte.*'

Twelve glasses were raised, and twelve shots of Irish whiskey were downed in one. Some of the younger drinkers spluttered a little on the neat spirit, and most took sips from their Guinness to wash away the taste. At the head of the table sat Patrick Lynch: the toast had been in his honour. He rolled the whiskey around his mouth to savour it, before swallowing and smacking his lips.

'And why shouldn't a man have two birthdays, especially when he's forty?' said Patrick.

'No reason at all, Patrick, no reason at all,' responded his brother Donal.

'Thank youse all for coming. I know some of youse can't believe I'm forty, but it's true.'

'We thought you was fifty.' said the youngest man there – a second cousin. Probably.

'Less of your cheek, thank you very much. Who bought you that drink, eh? A proper man's drink, that is. Not like you get in that godforsaken hole The Frog and Parrot. That's just an outlet for chemical poison. A proper Irish drink in a proper Irish bar: you can't beat it.'

Patrick looked around him at the nicotine yellow walls, the frosted glass keeping out the June sunshine, and the little-boy-lost face of the Barley Mow's landlord, Dave. The Barley Mow was nothing like the Irish theme pubs that were springing up all over Europe. There was no stained glass, no weighing scales, no tricolours, no leprechauns and no smiling colleens behind the varnished counter. What it *did* have was the patronage of Earlsbury's Irish community and lots of Guinness taps on the bar. Random posters of long gone rock bands were framed on the walls – Band of Joy, Listen, The Diplomats: they were Dave's personal collection, and they were as faded as their owner. Thanks to him, it also had occasional live music. Thanks to a merciful God, there was none tonight.

'So why are you having two birthdays?' said the young cousin.

Patrick was lighting a cigarette, and Donal answered for him. 'Wouldn't you prefer to go out with your mates rather than have Sunday dinner with your mother?'

'It's not *instead of*,' said Patrick, 'it's *as well as*. Sure, your Auntie Fran will be putting on a big spread on Sunday. I'm looking forward to that one, too.'

'Yes, but who heard of an Irish birthday with nothing to drink?' said Donal. He took a long swallow from his pint and raised it to Patrick.

It was true enough. Patrick's wife, Francesca, wasn't keen on his drinking and had insisted that a big Sunday lunch would form the centrepiece of the celebrations, and that attendance at Mass beforehand would be expected. He couldn't handle the thought of church with a hangover, so tomorrow he would be watching England lose to France at the Euros. Well, he hoped they were going to lose after they'd knocked Ireland out in the qualifiers. He looked over to the bar. 'Bring the malt round again, Dave.'

The landlord hurried round from the bar with the whiskey bottle and asked who wanted a drink. Only half a dozen held up their glasses for a refill. Dave topped them up and returned to the bar, adding the drinks to Patrick's tab.

'A toast,' said Patrick. 'To absent friends of all shapes and sizes.'

'To Micky,' said one of the gang. 'To the boys in the Maze,' said another. Patrick didn't want talk of the IRA – not with his special guest here.

To cover it up, he raised his glass again and said, 'And especially to our Honorary Irishman, Solomon King. May God bless him and Theresa with a healthy baby.'

Drinks were taken and glasses replaced on the drip mats. 'Any news from the hospital yet?' said Donal.

'Not since this morning,' said Patrick. 'I had a call in the middle of the night to say she's gone into labour suddenly, and could I mind the stall for her. It's her third, so she'll be alright.'

Donal downed his whiskey and looked at the bar hopefully. *Now there's a man with a real drink problem*, thought Patrick, *it's beginning to affect his work*. He had stayed off the good stuff himself all day because of Theresa's unexpected admission. His market stall, with its general goods and miscellaneous special offers, was next to Theresa's sophisticated selection of vintage clothes. Patrick may have called Theresa's husband their *Honorary Irishman*, but Sol had been born in Jamaica and was only accepted by the group on sufferance, in part because he had married one of their own: sweet little Theresa Murphy.

'Speech!' said Donal.

Patrick was about to stand up and say a few words when Dave shouted from behind the bar. 'Telephone, Patrick. It's the hospital.'

He crossed the floor to where the frowning Dave held out the receiver, took the phone, and said hello.

'Patrick? Is that you?'

'Theresa! What are you doing on the phone? Is everything all right?'

'No it isn't. I've had a girl, but there's a problem.'

'What is it, love? What's happened? Is the baby okay?'

'Yeah, she's fine. A very healthy little girl with very pink skin.'

Patrick gripped the receiver so hard it nearly cracked. 'What are you saying?'

'It's yours. It must be, because it's certainly not Solomon's, and I didn't do it with anyone else.'

'Could there not be a mistake?' Patrick ran his finger round his collar to get some air into his lungs. The sweat was pouring off him. He and Theresa had only done it once after her husband had come out of jail, and they'd used protection. 'Maybe her colour will change as she gets older. It often happens like that.'

'Patrick, *the baby's got red hair.*' He could hear Theresa's breathing getting more ragged. She must have called shortly after the delivery, and he was surprised she hadn't fainted already. 'Listen,' she said, 'Sol stormed out of here in a rage. He knows where you are, and I'm scared he's going to come looking for you.'

'How does he know to look for me?'

'He's not stupid. He took one look at the kid and shouted, "Whose bastard is this? Is it Lynch's?" I wasn't in a position to deny it, was I?'

'Okay, Terri, get some rest. I'll...'

Before he could finish the sentence, the bar door slammed open, and Solomon King strode in. Patrick put down the phone and instinctively rejoined his group. Everyone was staring at the new arrival, massive and quivering with rage, his dreadlocks swinging as he looked around the room, hands jammed in his jacket pockets. All of his body language screamed aggression, but Donal Lynch didn't notice a thing.

He blithely stood up and said, 'Solly, my mate. Has she sprogged? What is it?'

King walked two paces towards the group. 'I want a word wid you, Paddy. Outside or in here, I don't care.'

'Easy, Solly,' said Donal and moved towards him. 'What's the problem, mate?'

'She rang here,' said Patrick. 'I know. I'm sorry, I'm really sorry. It was only the once after you came back.'

'After? After? What about before? I'm in jail and you're screwing my woman! You Irish…'

Donal had put out an arm to restrain him, but King pulled his hands out of his pockets and shoved Donal aside. Patrick could see a blade in his right hand.

King lunged forward towards Patrick and everyone froze in their places except the shortest member of the group. Big Ben swung his leg and kicked King in the kneecap, then shot out of his seat and chopped down on the wrist holding the knife. King tried to grab hold of the smaller man, but Ben was behind him and pushing him forward. He slammed King face first into a pillar, then grabbed hold of the dreadlocks. The little man had pulled out a knife of his own and used it from behind to slash open King's neck. Then, in the silence of the bar, they heard the giant Jamaican gurgle as his lifeblood sprayed out on the floor. By the time he had collapsed completely, the blood had stopped flowing.

Patrick's eyes flicked from the six foot corpse of Solomon King to the vibrant Big Ben. The killer picked up his whiskey glass and his pint of Guinness and placed them on the bar. 'Wash these,' he said to Dave. 'Now.'

The barman did as he was told, and Ben turned to Patrick. 'You'll not forget this birthday in a hurry.' In the silence, his harsh West Belfast accent contrasted sharply with the Dublin and Black Country voices that had been heard before. Ben picked up the bottle of whiskey and spat on King's leather jacket. 'That'll teach you, you black bastard.' Then he disappeared out of the door.

'Uncle Don, am you alright?' said the cousin, nudging Donal Lynch – who hadn't moved since King had pushed him over. 'Oh fuck, fuck! He's been stabbed.'

Patrick shook himself and moved over to Donal. He could see blood coming from underneath his brother-in-law and rolled him over. Right in the middle of his chest was the handle of a knife, wrapped in masking tape. It was the classic shiv: a short bladed prison weapon that King must have had in his left hand. Donal's face was already drained of colour.

Sirens sounded in the distance, rapidly approaching. Patrick was going to have a lot of explaining to do. And not just to the police.

EIGHTEEN YEARS LATER

Chapter 1

City of London / Earlsbury
Another Friday Night
5th June 2010

The City of London Police building has very few windows with anything that could be described as a view. Some lucky officers had rooms which overlooked the tranquil garden of St Mary Aldermanbury, with its bust of Shakespeare, but most did not. Detective Sergeant Tom Morton thought that the worst prospect was undoubtedly those windows which looked inwards to the courtyard. That was where his office was.

At least they had invested in air conditioning. Even so, Tom had had enough, and he shoved the papers on top of his desk into the drawer and shut down the computer. From the corner office, his boss could see him preparing to leave and came out.

'All set for tomorrow, Tom?'

'Yes, sir. No problem if I go home and relax, is there?'

'Of course not. You'll be fine.'

DI Peter Fulton, section head of the Money Laundering Investigation Unit, clapped his sergeant on the back and shook his hand. Tom picked up his briefcase and headed to reception.

'I know what you need, Sergeant Morton,' said the receptionist, Elspeth Brown.

'I hope you're going to suggest a long cold beer,' said Tom. 'I don't know if I've got the energy for anything else.'

'As long as you've saved some energy for tomorrow, that's the main thing.'

She fished in her handbag and passed him a small greetings card. 'Good luck, Tom,' she said. 'But I don't think you'll need it.'

He was too polite to stuff the card in his pocket, so he opened it in front of her: *Good Luck in your Exams!* exclaimed the little leprechaun on the front, dancing a jig and waving a four leaf clover. He flipped it open to see that she had signed it *with Love from Elspeth*, but hadn't put any kisses: that was a relief.

'Thank you so much, Elspeth,' he said. 'It's very kind of you to remember.'

'It's been on the duty roster for weeks, so I couldn't miss it, could I? Talking of rosters, have you worked out when you're taking your summer holidays yet?'

'Yeah. I've told the boss.'

'You must get away,' she said, placing a comforting hand on his. 'Somewhere completely new...'

'You mean where I can forget about Caroline?'

Elspeth blushed and took her hand away, shuffling some papers and looking down.

'Sorry,' said Tom. 'That came out wrong. It was kind of you to ask.' Marooned in his embarrassment, he tried to paddle out of it. 'As it happens, I am doing something new. I'm having a week on the farm in Yorkshire, then I'm going to a cordon bleu cookery school in Spain. I've eaten enough tapas, so it's time I learnt how to make it.'

She looked up again. 'That's lovely. I look forward to hearing all about it.'

He left the dry coolness of the building and found the warmth outside still pleasant, not too sticky to enjoy. It was only a short stroll to his flat down London's narrow lanes, some unchanged since the Great Fire. He liked to vary his route and discover new businesses or say goodbye to old ones that had shut down as the recession bit harder. Some of the narrowest lanes had A-board mazes of special offers to negotiate. He took the shortcut through Paternoster

Square, eyes on the pavement to avoid looking at the depressing concrete pillars, then casting his gaze up again when he emerged into St Paul's Churchyard.

Wren's masterpiece was almost white against the blue sky, and for a few moments the sun was able to fight its way through the concrete forest to warm the whole area. Looking up was a moment of respect for higher forces, but he had no idea what might be up there and whether they were looking down at him. His older sister would have gone in to the cathedral and said a prayer, just to be on the safe side, but Tom preferred to rely on hard work and making his own luck. Nevertheless, if there was someone watching over him, he had made his obeisance.

Offices were starting to empty out for the weekend as he cut through Dean's Court into Carter Lane, and finally turned into his own little piece of the City – Horsefair Court.

Tom lived in a studio flat at the top of the only building. From Carter Lane, he had gone under an archway into a dead end which had brick walls on three sides and a three-storey Georgian house on the right. The developer had started at the top of the property, and Tom's flat had been finished first. No one would buy into a building site, so the developer had rented it to him for a year. The fact that a policeman would be living there was probably a consideration, too.

It was his second return home today. Last night had been city-hot and had made sleep almost impossible, so Tom had left the house at five thirty to do some shopping. He was the only pedestrian on the Millennium Bridge (joggers didn't count) and quickly weaved his way past the Tate Modern to Borough Market. The City of London was well provided with restaurants and delis, but had few outlets for fresh food which was why he had crossed the river. The lemon sole were almost flapping at the Furness Fish &

Game stall, and he added a serving of their speciality – Morecambe Bay potted shrimps.

He hoped that by being out and active so early he would sleep properly tonight. With no aircon in the flat, he quickly got changed to start preparing the meunière sauce for the sole. He took the receptionist's card from his suit pocket, put it next to the kettle and switched it on for a cup of tea. He was reaching into the cupboard when the landline rang. That would have to be his mother – no one else used it regularly and certainly not on a Friday night. He was right.

'Have you called to wish me luck?' he said.

'What for? Don't tell me I've forgotten something.'

'Inspector's exams. Tomorrow.'

'Oh, you'll be fine. You got a first in law, so they can't be that difficult.'

'Thanks for the vote of confidence … I think. Well, it's been lovely talking to you, Mum, but if it wasn't to wish me luck, why have you called?'

Tom thought of her in the little sitting room in York, door firmly closed in case his father wandered in, her hair and make-up perfectly prepared for tonight's social event. There would be one because there always was on Fridays.

'We've had a bit of bad news, I'm afraid.'

'Oh?'

It couldn't be that serious: if there had been a real problem, she would have come straight out with it.

'Your Great Uncle Thomas's cancer has come back. They can't treat it this time, so he's gone on to a palliative care regime. They're quite good at that over there.'

'Sorry to hear that. Will Granddad go to the States and see him, d'you think?'

'Yes. He's already been invited – first class tickets paid for, so he's got no excuse.'

'That'll be nice for him. Well, as nice as it gets to see your brother dying, I mean.'

'Yes, but it's a special invitation – there's going to be a wedding.'

His mother paused for dramatic effect, and Tom tried to think who on earth might be getting married. His great uncle had gone to America during WWII in mysterious circumstances and hadn't come back. Well, he would come back for visits, but he'd settled down in Boston and become a Harvard professor of something to do with history. Tom had no idea of the marital status of any of his American cousins, nor why it should be of interest to Granddad, his mother, or him. 'Who's getting married? Is it whats-her-name with the funny voice?'

'Violet? No, Great Uncle Thomas is marrying Rebecca.'

'What? How can he marry his wife?'

'They never *got* married. They went through a religious ceremony, but the priest or rabbi, or whatever, wasn't licensed by the State of Massachusetts. They never got round to sorting it out, and he wants to put it right before he goes.'

'That's nice.'

'Don't you see what it means, Tom?'

'Hang on,' he said, and reboiled the kettle to make tea. It would infuriate his mother completely if she had to wait a second longer, so naturally he dragged it out. 'Sorry about that. What were you saying?'

'I said, don't you see what it means?'

'No. Sorry.'

'It means that Cousin Isaac isn't legitimate under the Letters Patent.'

As his mother had reminded him, he had a law degree from Durham University, but that was no help. He knew what Letters Patent were in theory, but he had no idea why they mattered to Great Uncle Thomas – or to Cousin Isaac.

His mother supplied the answer. 'Isaac can't inherit the title. Your father's going to be the third or fourth Lord Throckton – and you'll be the fifth.'

'Not for a long time, I hope. Anyway, isn't Dad due to get a knighthood next year?'

'Yes: but I was thinking of you, Tom. I wouldn't want you to make the same mistake.'

She had lost him completely now. He did feel a little frisson that one day he might inherit a title – even though there was no land attached to it, and he couldn't sit in the House of Lords any more – but why was she talking about mistakes? 'Sorry, Mum, who's made a mistake?'

'Great Uncle Thomas, of course. I wouldn't want you to have a child before getting married again and disinherit the poor thing. I suppose you're still going ahead with the divorce?'

'Given that we haven't spoken for months, it seems likely. And no, I'm not going out with anyone at the moment.'

'Oh well: I thought you'd be interested. Good luck tomorrow, but I'm sure you'll be fine.'

Tom ended the call and drank his tea. Before he could get out the frying pan, his mobile rang. It was Kate.

'You having an early night?' she said.

'Yes. I thought you'd be hard at it by now at the party.' This was Kate's last day as an officer in the Regular Army. From Monday, she would be unemployed for the first time in her life, and as far as he could tell, she still had no idea what she wanted to do.

'We're having a mess night first – Number One Dress uniform and all the trimmings – then party on. I just wanted to say good luck for tomorrow. You've worked so hard for this, Tom. Sock it to them.'

'Will do, captain.'

'They offered me a promotion today. Major Lonsdale, Military Intelligence. How about that, eh?'

'Did you take it?'

'Nah. It would have meant joining the liaison team and taking overseas postings. I've had enough of foreign lands to last me a lifetime, thank you very much. Anyway, I've got to go. I'm standing up in my room because I don't want to get my skirt creased. Oh, hang on: I meant to ask: how's the trial of Thornton and Co coming along?'

'Plea and Directions is on Monday. I'll fill you in at the welcome home dinner. Di's place, as usual.'

'Has she been dumped again?'

''Fraid so. Have fun.'

The small town of Earlsbury in the Black Country slopes down from a hill which boasts the Saxon church of St Oswald of Worcester on its summit. Patrick Lynch, as a good Roman Catholic, rarely crossed its Protestant threshold.

He drove down the High Street and forked right towards West Bromwich. While he waited at the lights, he turned to look at the Indian restaurant on the corner. *East of Earlsbury – Tandoori Cuisine at its Best* said the sign outside. He was one of the diminishing number of locals who still thought of it as the Barley Mow. He wanted a drink very badly, but there was no chance of that for now.

When he got home later, his youngest daughter would be celebrating her fourteenth birthday with a Harry Potter party – watching the films and looking forward to the first instalment of *Deadly Hobbits*. No, that wasn't it. *Deadly Hallows*? Something like that. Either way, Fran would expect him to be sober and help out in the background. Ach, wouldn't he enjoy it once he got there? All those kids running around in costumes and reading books. His own father wouldn't have believed it possible, but Elizabeth was a real bookworm.

The lights changed, and he drove down the road to his prior engagement. A left turn took him past the old football pitch and on to a track that headed towards the great concrete pillars of the M5 motorway that soared above him. At the end of the track was a turning circle and an access gate to the canal. There were abandoned and forgotten spots like this all over the Black Country – except that they weren't forgotten by the people who lived here. Whichever government body owned this little slice of purgatory may have lost track of it, but Patrick knew exactly where to go when he got the message. His visitor was already waiting.

Pat turned the car around and pointed it towards the exit. He was in no hurry to get out into the mud left behind by last night's rain – let the other fella come to him. After all, wasn't this their idea, not his? His phone pinged with a text and his new varifocal glasses came in handy. *Come here, Paddy. I'm not getting my feet wet.*

It was from the new number, the one he had been told to expect, the one who had chosen this meeting place. He cursed and dived out of the car and over to the waiting Range Rover. The bastard had locked the doors. Patrick had turned and started to walk back when he heard the central locking click open.

'Don't you ever pull a fecking stunt like that again with me, d'you hear?' he said to the man in the driving seat.

'Keep your hair on, Paddy. I forgot about the locks, sure I did.'

The interior light hadn't come on when he opened the door, and it was gloomy down here below the motorway. For June, it was very gloomy. He got a sense of bulk, of height and the voice, although not young, was much younger than his. 'My name is Patrick Lynch. No one calls me Paddy. Is that clear?'

'But you are a paddy, aren't you? A bog-trotter of the first water, no less.'

A Prod. They'd sent a fecking Prod from Belfast to deal with him. Could today get any worse? 'What do you want? Hurry up, I've got to be somewhere else.'

The other man ignored him. 'Do you have a SatNav in that nice Jaguar of yours, Patrick?'

'Yes. Why?'

'Before you go, turn it on. The wee machine will think it's on the motorway, you know. Possibly stuck in traffic 'cos we're not moving. This little space doesn't exist in the digital world. No one wants it, no one loves it. I love places like this, Patrick, where no one knows where you are.'

Patrick shifted in his seat.

'Down to business, eh?' said the man. 'I'm pleased to offer you a new opportunity. If you play your cards right, you could be even richer.'

Patrick said nothing. This man represented the Principal Investors in what they called Operation Green Light. He had made a lot of money from Green Light and he wasn't in a position to say no to their suggestions.

'Open the glove box. There's a sample in there.'

The glove compartment had its own courtesy light, and suddenly Patrick could see the other man properly. He was in his early forties, probably, and the smile on his face was even scarier than his ramblings about secret places. There was a brown envelope on top of the junk and Patrick picked it up.

'Holy Mother of God, what's that for?' Underneath the envelope was the biggest automatic pistol that Patrick had ever seen.

'Sorry. Forgot about that. Just ignore it and open your free sample.'

Patrick tore open the envelope and took out two bundles of twenty pound notes, wrapped in plastic, together with a smaller white envelope that contained something hard.

'Careful how you spend it. The ink's still wet.'

Patrick looked carefully at the notes and peeled one out from its wrapper. He had been offered counterfeit bills many times on the market, and usually he could tell just by the feel of the paper that they were forgeries. He tried to hold it closer to the light and ruffled it in his fingers. 'These look good,' he said.

'They're very good. Very good indeed. We've tested them extensively, and they pass any detector except the ones in banks. Something to do with the yellow dots on the back. Be very careful about leaving fingerprints – they do check them and if anyone's prints come up more than a few times, they'll be on to you. Apart from that, just be sensible.'

Patrick put the packet inside his coat and shut the glove compartment. He did not want that big gun staring up at him.

'Here's the deal,' said the man in the driving seat. 'There's a key in that white envelope. It fits a small van that we use. You'll be sent a text message forty-eight hours ahead of a drop-off. If you're on holiday or some shit like that, text back. You'll receive a second text with the location and exact time of pickup. And I mean the *exact* time. You, and only you, are to drive the van away. It'll have a different paint job and different number plates every time. Take it to a safe place, unload the goods, and return the van to the same spot exactly three hours later. Got that?'

'What are the terms?' he asked.

'A good question for once. We expect 30 per cent on future shipments, but the first one you might have to give some incentives. We'll take 25 per cent on that. Our cut has to go through Emerald Green Imports as usual, but paid into a different account. The Principal Investors on this job are different to your current bosses. All the details are in that wee envelope you've stashed away. I'm your contact, but I sincerely hope we never meet again.'

'The feeling's mutual. What do I call you? For reference.'

When the light had come on, Patrick had caught sight of brush cut ginger hair on his visitor's head, as well as the sharp features of his face.

'You can call me Red Hand. It'll remind you of Ulster. Out you get, Patrick, and don't follow me.'

As he climbed out of the vehicle, there was a final word from Red Hand. 'Oh, Patrick, if that tame copper of yours mentions the names Tom Morton or Kate Lonsdale, you be sure to let me know.'

Before he could reach the security of his own car, the Range Rover had sped off, covering him in muddy water from its spray. He was breathing hard and he could feel the onset of pain in his chest from the stress. He turned on the ignition and closed his eyes, breathing slowly and deeply until the pain subsided. By then, his SatNav had warmed up and orientated itself. He looked at the display, and Red Hand was right – the little icon was smack in the middle of the M5. 'Do not attempt a U turn on the motorway,' said the disembodied voice. 'Proceed to the next junction.'

The locker room at Earlsbury police station felt too small to contain the heat and smell of male bodies as they prepared for work. PC Ian Hooper strapped on the anti-stab vest, utility belt and other equipment designed to keep him safe on a Friday night. What a joke. With Birmingham so close, most revellers headed into the city for their fun, leaving a patchwork assortment of locals to frequent the pubs and bars. Because it had spare land at the back, Earlsbury division had been given a new custody suite, but the night-time economy in the Black Country was not exactly booming.

The duty sergeant threw him a set of keys.

'Hooper, you take the Incident Car and circle round from the east. There might be something going on in Elijah. Be ready to mop up anything else.'

It was a sign of trust – he was considered competent enough to work on his own and intelligent enough to make good use of his time even though this wasn't his shift – he had done a swap for a mate. Ian left the police station and climbed into the garishly painted Incident Car. There was always the possibility of a crash on the M5 and the summons to support Traffic, but otherwise, statistics stated that he could expect a quiet night.

He was glad that he wouldn't be doing night duty next week, especially if the weather stayed warm. Flags were starting to appear around the town as England geared up to begin their World Cup campaign in South Africa on Friday. The evening kick-off would see even Earlsbury's bars full to bursting. If he was lucky, there would be overtime through the evening; if not, he could enjoy the game himself. Then again, the chance of any enjoyment was remote with this England team.

The police station was halfway up Earlsbury hill, and to get round to his first port of call he would have to cut through the industrial estates or take the long route via the railway station. He took the latter option. The station itself was unmanned in the evenings, the old buildings had been converted to accommodate a taxi office where several cabs waited, their drivers clustered around a burger van with cups and cigarettes in hand. Ian slowed down and saw a woman on her own emerging from the station in a very short skirt and killer heels. He pulled into the forecourt and got out, meeting the woman as she arrived at the snack stop.

'Alright Erin? You been stood up again?'

'Story of my life. What you doing 'ere? I thought you was the community bobby now.'

'Fancy a cup of tea and a lift home? I'm on me way to Elijah.'

Erin King looked at the taxi drivers. The two white men carried on their conversation, but kept glancing at her. The three Asians stopped talking and stared. She stared back and they lowered their eyes.

'Go on then, twist me arm,' she said to Ian. 'Two sugars, love.'

Ian ordered two teas and asked how her children were getting along. Erin told him that they were both fine, and that the youngest had started school this term. Polystyrene cups in hand, they settled into the car.

Ian picked up the radio. 'Control? This is 4621 Hooper in Incident Car. En route to Elijah estate with civilian for information gathering.'

'Did you have to say that? Can't you just give me a lift?'

'No chance. I'm responsible for you while you're in the car. I didn't give your name, though, did I?'

Erin held her tea in her hands to warm them, and Ian took the Smethwick Road round the back of St Oswald's and pulled into the bay outside a parade of shops, all closed for the night.

'What was you doing in Brum?' he asked.

'I could say it was none of your business and I'd be right. Just 'cos we went to school together, it don't mean you're my brother or nothing.'

'We did a bit more than go to school together. And since.'

She sipped her tea. 'I wasn't in Brum. Believe it or not, I was in Kidderminster for an interview. Well, audition. I had to get the train back.'

'Pole dancing? I never thought you'd be back at that. Not since the kids, anyway.'

'If you've got it, flaunt it.'

Ian looked up and down the road so that he didn't have to make eye contact with her.

'Go on. Say it,' said Erin.

'Say what?'

'Say that I'm too old at twenty-eight, that I've had two kids and no one's gonna pay top whack to see me strut me stuff no more.'

'Erm…'

'You don't have to be nice. They said it, too. Can I smoke in here?'

'Sorry. If the day shift smell smoke they'll report me.'

Erin got out of the car and lit a cigarette. She came round to Ian's side and leaned on the roof. He lowered the window and she leaned in, thrusting her breasts through the gap.

'I could always go on the game. There's good money in that.'

'Give over, Erin. You said it: I ain't your brother *or* your boyfriend. If you want to sell your body, go ahead. I'll make the phone call to Social Services meself.'

She stiffened and pulled back from the car. 'You would 'n'all. You'd get me kids took off me.'

'Calm down, Erin. You're not going on the game, and I'm not calling the Social. What did they really say at that new club?'

A smile crept back on to her face and she dropped the cigarette. 'They didn't quite tell me I was over the hill, but I could tell they fancied the younger girls more than they fancied me. Thing is, these blokes might be great businessmen, but they're no judge of a dancer. It's okay being young and supple, but if you don't know what you're doing you can get tired out very easily, and if you haven't got any tricks, the punters soon get bored. I've got meself a job as choreographer. How about that?'

Ian had seen Erin perform when she was younger – when she was a kid, really. He still saw her as young. She had been very good at what she did, but he was struggling to see that it required a choreographer to do it. Wasn't that what they had at the ballet? He told her how pleased he was for her and asked her when she started. Erin went back to the passenger side and climbed in, telling him that they had asked her to start tomorrow by re-interviewing all the girls and sorting out the ones with stage potential, as she put it. Ian started the engine.

'Are you still going out with that teacher?' said Erin.

'Ceri? Yeah. We moved in together this summer.'

'Get you, Mr Conventional. First you join the cops then you settle down with a teacher.' She patted his arm as he drove over the junction and into the Elijah estate. 'I hope it works out.'

Ian drove slowly round the curves and crescents of the post-war housing estate. Originally built as council property, it was now a mixture of owner-occupiers and some social tenants. He looked at the parked cars but they were all dark, and no one was lurking in the entryways of the houses. At the back of the estate, built on to a small rise, was Ezekiel House – a 1970s low-rise block of flats. The police had more trouble from there than from the whole of Elijah put together.

'Listen, Ian, I heard something the other day.'

'Go on.'

'I heard that one of the gangs has been sniffing around.'

'Are you sure? People are always saying that Elijah's got gang problems, but it's just kids. There aren't enough of them to form a gang, and if they did, their moms would clip them round the ear.'

'It's not the wannabes; this is for real. There's a girl in Ezekiel House who has a brother in one of the Birmingham gangs. He's been round a lot lately, and I saw him at the corner shop this afternoon. I'm pretty sure he's gonna be there tonight and I think he's loaded.'

'You know what I'm gonna ask next, don't you?'

'His name, yeah.'

'No. His sister's name.'

'Oh. I thought I could just say I don't know him.'

Ian drove the car back round to Erin's house. 'Who's babysitting?'

'Theresa. You know, Rob's mother. It was her as told me about the new pole dancing club in Kidderminster.'

'I'd have thought that Mrs King would want you at home and waiting for her son to get out of jail, not heading off to Kiddie to go dancing.'

'You know Terri better than that. She wants her grandchildren to grow up in a house where people work and don't claim benefit.' Erin played with the straps of her bag. 'And she wants to see them. And she wants Rob to know that she cares.'

It was what had driven Ian and Erin apart ten years ago – first her friendship and then her relationship with Rob King. Rob had been arrested a couple of times, and Ian had been aiming for a career in the police. He had to distance himself from Rob, and that meant saying goodbye to Erin – who immediately fell into Rob King's arms. Erin and Rob had married, then they had separated when Rob's brushes with the law had turned into serious dealing of drugs. He was currently doing four years for intent to supply.

'When's he getting out?' said Ian.

'Monday.'

There was nothing more to be said.

'Thanks for the tea – and the lift,' said Erin as she got out of the car. She leaned over, and Ian thought she was going to kiss him; instead, she whispered a name and address into his ear.

He drove off and called Control. 'Message for CID tomorrow, please. Information received on supply of class A drugs on Elijah estate. Please contact for details. Over.'

'Received. I'll log it.'

He could have given them the name – but now they would have to see him, and he could try to get involved in the operation and follow-up interviews. It would put him first in the queue when they chose volunteers for attachment to CID work.

Patrick Lynch had the sense to keep quiet as the guests arrived for his daughter's birthday party. The last two birthday parties had been in costume, wearing Hogwarts uniforms and celebrating their love for all things Harry Potter. This year was different. They looked like they were dressed to hang out at some American diner. In fact, they looked like they had been hanging out there all night and were ready for bed – pale skin, red eyes and tousled hair. His daughter was wearing a disturbingly tight pair of shorts. He welcomed them to his house and took the first opportunity to ask his wife what was going on.

'Sure, Fran, I was expecting another Harry Potter party. What's with all the white faces?'

Fran checked on something in the oven. 'Where've you been, Patrick? Harry Potter's for little girls now. It's all Twilight at the minute.'

'Twilight? What's that?'

She gave him a look he had often been served over the years – *don't you know what your children are up to?*

'Haven't you seen the posters?' she added. 'All over her room.'

'You know I never go in her room. I've never been in the girls' bedrooms. It's not right.'

Elizabeth, fourteen today, had two much older sisters who had preceded her through the Lynch household, and one who hadn't. Patrick had tried to be firm with them, but he never went in their rooms unless Fran had been with him. Well, not after they were babies, anyway.

Fran put the oven gloves down. 'I know, and you do right, but there are other ways of keeping up with the kids. It's all about sex.'

'What? Our Elizabeth?'

'Calm down. You'll give yourself an attack.'

Fran leant against the worktop by the sink and enjoyed her moment. Patrick was sure that he had kept tabs on his daughter's interests. He hadn't missed a single one of her parents' evenings. He had taken her riding when she developed a passion for horses (now finished, thank goodness), and he had bought her almost anything she asked for, including the fees for St Modwenna's school in

Stourbridge. So what was Twilight and what did it have to do with sex?

'Vampires,' said Fran. 'They're the new wizards. There's these books about a girl who falls in love with a vampire, and now they're making films and all the girls have fallen in love with the star: Robert Pattinson. In fact, if Dermot doesn't turn up soon with tonight's main event, you're going to be in serious trouble.'

'Me? What? Why?'

'Don't you remember? She said that what she wanted more than anything for her birthday was to have *Eclipse* for her party.'

Patrick vaguely remembered something like that. He began to feel uneasy because he had done nothing whatsoever about it.

'It was at Easter,' said Fran. 'We were at Ma's for lunch and Dermot was there. He said he'd do his best.'

The gravel crunched at the side of the house, and Dermot himself appeared through the back door.

'I hear you're going to save my life,' said Patrick.

His nephew grinned and fished a DVD box out of his coat. 'There you go. I'll tell you how much it cost afterwards.'

Fran opened the oven, and the men helped her to put things on plates. There was a door from the kitchen into the through-room that made up most of the house, and she led the way with the food. When Patrick followed her, he found the girls were giggling, and some of them had draped themselves over the furniture in provocative poses. They all sat up when Dermot followed him, and the young man was riveted by nine pairs of adolescent eyes.

'Have you got it, Dad?' asked Elizabeth.

She was sitting cross-legged on the floor by the TV, not quite at the centre of her own party. That honour belonged to a blonde girl who had even tighter shorts than Elizabeth. Patrick didn't know where to look and he didn't remember seeing the girl before. The girls started crowding around the food while the queen bee unfolded herself from the settee and walked over to Dermot as if it were her house and not Elizabeth's.

'You must be Lizzie's cousin,' said the girl.

'That's me,' said Dermot with a neutral smile.

'I'm Pandora Nechells. I'm in Lizzie's class at school.'

Dermot's eyes narrowed and something clicked behind them. 'Your father wouldn't be David by any chance, would he?'

The girl flushed and stepped back. Lost for an answer, she went to the food. Elizabeth came over to Patrick and asked him again if he had the film. He beckoned her into the kitchen and pointed to the worktop. The box was plain, and she fumbled to prise it open. When she saw the disk inside, she gave a cry and threw her arms around him. Like her mother, Elizabeth was petite and barely came to his chest. He gave his little girl a big hug and wished her happy birthday again. She ran back into the other room holding her prize aloft and was instantly surrounded by her friends.

The three adults put pans in the dishwasher, and Patrick was finally allowed into the garden with Dermot for a smoke and a drink. After the heart attack, Patrick had given up cigarettes but couldn't do without the occasional cigar. Because he was driving some of the girls home later, he stuck to a small white wine. Dermot had a bottle of lager.

'I presume that film isn't on general release yet,' said Patrick as they sat down.

'It's not even released in America until the end of the month. I had to call in all sorts of favours to find that – and it cost me a grand.'

'A grand? A thousand pounds for a film? I could have made me own movie for that.'

'But didn't you see the look on her face? It was worth it.'

'Sure and all, you're right. Thanks, Dermot. Here you go.'

Patrick had taken the carrier bag outside and took out one of the shrink-wrapped bundles of counterfeit notes out. Dermot took the package and turned it over in his hands.

'Where's this from?'

'It's our new business opportunity. Don't open it. Here, look at this.'

Patrick handed over one of the sample notes and, while his nephew examined it, he explained what had happened when he met Red Hand underneath the flyover. Dermot nodded and smoked another cigarette while he listened.

'So,' concluded Patrick, 'I'm used to selling fake fags, but I can't see our regular clientele being able to shift much of this stuff without the filth breathing down our necks.'

Dermot nodded. 'We need to enhance our distribution network,' he said.

'I wouldn't have put it like that but … yes, we need more dealers.'

'What do you suggest?'

'It's time, Dermot. There's another birthday party a week tomorrow.'

'I'm not going. You know I'm not. I've got nothing against Hope – she's a good kid – but you know where I'll be on Saturday. At the cemetery, paying my respects.'

'I'm not suggesting you forget about your father, Dermot, but Theresa didn't call her Hope for nothing. It's her birthday as well as being the anniversary of Donal's death. After eighteen years, can't we let him rest in peace, along with Solomon?'

'Try telling that to Bobby King.'

Patrick walked slowly back inside. The DVD player in the lounge was linked to the TV in the kitchen as well as to the big screen that the girls were watching. He found Fran sitting on a stool looking at a pale young woman and a paler young man talking earnestly in the woods. The young man bore a passing resemblance to Dermot.

'Is it good?' he asked.

'If you're fourteen, I imagine it says everything there is to say about life, but no ... I'll switch over to *Eastenders* in a minute.'

Patrick took a bottle of lager for Dermot and a mineral water for himself. Fran had muted the sound, and he kissed her head. 'Thank you for bringing Elizabeth into my life,' he said. 'She's a very special girl, and I'm a lucky man to have had the chance to see her growing up.'

Fran waved him away, and he went back to the garden. His cigar had gone out and he relit it.

'Bobby's coming out of jail on Monday. He'll be there on Saturday, and so will Jim, apparently.'

Dermot looked up. 'Even more reason to stay away. I'm surprised Theresa's going to allow you anywhere near the house with both of them there.'

'She asked me, but no, I won't go. She also asked me to try and sort Bobby out. I mean Rob, that's what he calls himself now. She doesn't want him to go back to dealing. She thought that if I could get him in our game, he might stay away from drugs. Completely.'

'She asked me the same,' said Dermot. 'She also asked me to shop him last time, and even told me when he'd have the most gear on him.'

That was news. Patrick had been shocked when Rob King had been arrested with so much stuff on him and sent down for a clear four year stretch. To find that Dermot had been involved, even at Theresa's behest, was even more disturbing.

'It did us a big favour too, don't forget' said Dermot. 'It was breaking up King's group that got Griff his promotion. We've done very well out of Detective Sergeant Griffin.'

'So we have, so we have.' Patrick crushed out his cigar. 'If we play our cards right, we could keep Rob well away from Emerald Green, you know. We could just sell him the dodgy notes for 50 per cent of face value. That's a big enough margin for him to make a profit. We have to give

30 per cent to our suppliers so that leaves us one pound in five to make our money. Plus we can get rid of a bit ourselves from time to time.' Patrick leaned in closer to Dermot. 'And that man of yours in Blackpool – the amount of fags and vodka they're taking off us, they must be able to shift some notes as well.'

Dermot nodded thoughtfully. 'Could be, could be. Mind you, they only deal wholesale with us. There's no way they'd take the notes at 50 per cent.'

'Fair enough, but they can make money at 40 per cent, surely?'

Dermot stood up. 'I think it's a great opportunity, especially if Blackpool take a bundle, but I'm not keen on having Rob King involved. Keep me out of this. If you can work with Theresa to pass the goods along, I'll be much happier.'

'Theresa or someone else, possibly, but you'll have to come to Hope's other birthday party. The one we're having here.'

His nephew made a face but didn't argue. Patrick walked with him back to the front drive and remembered something Dermot had said inside. 'Should I know that girl's father? What's her name? Pandora?'

'You should know him. He's Deputy Chief Constable David Nechells.'

'Well, well. I hope his daughter doesn't tell him what she's been up to tonight. Watching pirate DVDs is very naughty.'

Chapter 2

London / Earlsbury

Sunday Night / Monday Morning

7th-8th June

Tom's cousin Kate Lonsdale and his younger sister Diana welcomed him with raised glasses and a toast.

'Here's to Inspector Morton.'

Tom raised his hand. 'Whoa! I don't get the exam results for ages, and then I have to actually get a job.'

'But you did all right yesterday?'

'Yeah. I think so. You have to know everything for the Inspector's Exam: child protection, custody, traffic, the lot. It's comprehensive so that all inspectors have to prove they've reached a certain standard across all aspects of policing. Don't worry, no one's going to appoint me to Territorial Support any time soon.'

'What's Territorial Support?' said Kate, thinking of the Territorial Army Reserve.

'Riot Squad,' said Di. Her brother went to object but she stopped him. 'Don't argue. No police politics tonight.'

'Do you want to stay with the City of London Police?' asked Kate.

Tom went to check the food in the kitchen before answering. He seemed satisfied with the progress of the roast. 'It's more a question of, "Do I want to stay in Economic Crimes?"… because that's where my experience is. It's possible to specialise too much. Like the Army, I suppose.'

'Smooth link,' said Di. 'So tell me, Kate: is Tom right to be worried about your future now you don't have anyone telling you when to get up and what to wear? Mind you, if this is your idea of smart casual, you probably do need someone to help you out.'

'What's wrong with this?' said Kate. She and Di had been lying at either ends of the sofa with their legs up while Tom did the cooking. Kate swung her legs down and stood up.

Tom raised an eyebrow. 'Don't look at me,' he said. 'My knowledge of fashion begins and ends at Marks & Spencer, or at least it does now I'm living in a box. Anyway, who's Di to give advice?'

Kate wondered what she was doing standing up so she picked up the bottle and topped up their glasses.

'Don't try and avoid the question,' said Tom. 'We *are* worried about your future. Well, I am. I don't want you cluttering up my flat, for one thing.'

'Your concern is so touching. I've got news for you two. Just before I got too drunk to remember, the Colonel gave me a contact. I'm seeing him tomorrow.'

'Great news. What's it all about?'

'Sorry, can't say.'

Her cousin and his sister stared at her open mouthed. 'You're joking,' said Di. 'Really?'

'Yes, really. It's in the private sector, I can say that much.'

She sipped her wine and made herself comfortable on the settee, pushing her feet into Di's ribs just because she could. The younger woman pinched her leg and shifted position.

'Another toast to the chef,' said Di. 'Here's to the next-but-two Baron Throckton.'

'What?' said Kate.

'Hasn't he told you? Due to a legal irregularity in America, the Lordship of Throckton is coming home to Granddad, then Dad, then brother Thomas.'

'Erm… congratulations?'

'Don't,' said Tom. 'I was quite happy before and I'm still quite happy. I hope that I'm very much older before I inherit the title, because I'm in no hurry to wish my father into his grave.'

Kate thought for a moment. 'Don't you fancy being an aristocratic detective? Like Lord Peter Wimsey and that other bloke.'

'No. As I said, I want Dad – and Granddad – to enjoy the title for many, many years before I do.'

'Don't forget that the first Lord Throckton was a detective,' said Di. 'As Tom will discover when Granddad gets back from the States with the Memoir.'

'The what?'

'Ah,' said Di. 'You're not a Morton so you don't know about the Memoir.'

Ouch, thought Kate, *Is Di worried I'm trying to displace her?* Kate's mother was the younger sister who had married the dashing soldier; the older sister had married the respectable lawyer. The lawyer and his wife had gone on to become Fiona, Tom and Diana's parents.

Kate was young when her mother died leaving her and her father alone. Her great aunt had given Kate shelter from boarding schools and military bases, and she had made her real home in Throckton.

The Mortons of Throckton in Yorkshire had seemingly been around since the Domesday Book, but she didn't remember them talking much about the title – most of the talk had been about the farm and who was going to run it.

Tom came to her rescue, as he had always done when her clumsy feet or clumsy tongue had got her in trouble. 'It's a family legend,' he said. 'Apparently, the first Lord Throckton was involved with something very mysterious at the turn of the last century – 1901, I think. He wrote it down in a Memoir and gave it to his heir: only the next in line to the title can read it. Cousin Isaac will pass it on to Granddad now that he can't inherit. I have absolutely no idea what's in it, though.' He turned to Di and said, 'And what about you? When are you going to give up the day job and concentrate on your Art?'

'Resolutions.' said Di. 'It's coming up to Midsummer, and we should make resolutions that we have to achieve before Midwinter.'

'What do you mean, Midsummer?' asked Kate.

'Diana's a bit of a pagan,' said Tom. 'She likes to celebrate the solstice.'

'Heathen,' said Di, 'not pagan. Let's meet up again on the twenty-first of June and make proper resolutions.'

They looked at each other and nodded. Kate asked Tom about the Plea & Directions hearing the next day.

'Are you doing anything tomorrow morning? Half past nine?'

Kate shook her head.

'Good. The Old Bailey is two minutes' walk from Horsefair Court.'

There are two ways into the grounds of Ezekiel House. One comes from the Elijah estate and leads to Earlsbury town centre; the other comes from the Smethwick Road and leads towards Birmingham. Concrete bollards had been placed in the middle to stop it being used as a rat run.

The police vans had taken the long route out and round to the Smethwick side because the target property was facing town, and they didn't want anyone to see them coming. At this hour on Monday morning it was unlikely that the target was out of bed, but one of the neighbours might see them and raise the alarm. The police were rarely welcome visitors to Ezekiel.

Ian Hooper knew that this was only part of the story. Most of the residents worked hard at minimum wage jobs to keep themselves afloat. Yes, a good number also claimed benefits illegally, but he found it hard to blame them. They wanted to keep their heads down and enjoy a quiet life –

they were no keener on drug dealers than were the police themselves, but when the boys in blue have so often been the enemy, it was hard to win their trust. Ian was glad that he would be part of a team and wearing a helmet.

His tip-off had borne fruit over the weekend, and he had been summoned to join the squad for the take down. They had assembled at 0500 for a briefing which Detective Sergeant Griffin gave after introducing the team.

'Thanks to information received, we have good intelligence that a known dealer from Birmingham has taken up residence in Ezekiel House. The flat is rented to his sister, but the Target has been seen entering the building on CCTV. We've checked the tapes from the lobby, and from Saturday afternoon onwards, most of our known drug users were seen arriving at Ezekiel House. Word gets around fast when there's a new supplier in town. Following that info, we used binocular surveillance, and yes, they all called at the door of flat 428. We also believe that the Target has not yet had time to reinforce the door – another reason for going in today.

'You've all done this before, so I'll cut to the chase. The Target has numerous convictions for dealing and two for wounding. There is no intelligence connecting him to firearms, but I'm not about to take that risk. Tactical Seven will lead the take down and make the arrest. The Earlsbury officers will secure the property and conduct a preliminary search while we wait for SOCO. Detective Constable Lindow and I will be waiting well out of sight to take the glory afterwards.'

At least he was honest and got the laugh he deserved. Ian had been on many raids, several take downs, two riots and even a hostage situation. He quite enjoyed them as a change, but he didn't want to make them his career. He wanted to be standing next to Griffin, and using his brains instead of his right arm to make arrests.

As usual, Ian was on ram duty. It was his job to break down the door and duck. The giant policeman next to him was the leader of Tactical Seven – one of the specialised support groups. This one was also armed. He would be the one who went through the door first. On the other side of that door could be a man whose grip on reality had been blown away by drugs, and the weapon next to his bed could be a submachine gun.

Tactical Seven took up positions beside flat 428 and their leader waved him forwards. Ian took a look at the door. It was fairly new and therefore not made of plywood like the older ones. It also had a decent lock. Even so, he reckoned he could do it with one blow and he took two steps back.

On the signal, he surged forwards and smashed the ram into the lock. Timing was everything to get the maximum force on the sweet spot. The door and the lock held firm, but the frame gave way. Before the door had banged into the inside wall, Ian had dropped the ram and rolled to one side.

Shouts of *armed police* and *on the floor* reverberated around the landing along with more crashes as internal doors were brushed aside. It took nine seconds for the squad leader to call them in. Two females were kneeling on the floor crying, and one male was face down and restrained. He was stark naked.

It was a good haul. There were enough drugs to get a conviction for possession with intent to supply, and a large roll of banknotes. There was also a knife. Ian hoped that he would never see the day when there was a gun on his patch.

Tactical Seven had left almost immediately, and DS Griffin had decided not to call in SOCO for a detailed search. They had their evidence, and the cost saved would go towards another raid in the future. He gathered them together in the living room before they left.

'Good job, well done. Thanks Boys.' Ian looked at DC Lindow (who was most definitely not a boy), but she smiled. 'It's not a coincidence that you four were asked to join us today,' continued Griffin, gesturing at the uniformed officers (who, yes, were all male). Angela gave me some news last week – it'll be round the station by lunchtime so she won't mind me telling you here. I'm pleased to announce that Earlsbury CID will be advertising for a temporary maternity cover from October.'

They congratulated the detective and were about to go when Griffin resumed. 'Three of you have applied to CID before, and I'm sure Hooper will be doing so soon. Just to let you know, I'm going to make sure the appointment comes from Earlsbury and not Birmingham or Sandwell. It won't be me who chooses between you – but the DCI will be listening to what I say.'

Ian glanced at the three other potential recruits. Two were younger than him and were graduates; the other had applied several times and not been successful. Neither of the graduates were from Earlsbury originally, and Ian reckoned that local knowledge might be his competitive advantage.

Kate was standing on the steps of the Old Bailey staring at the statue of Lady Justice, trying to work out if she were wearing a blindfold or not. Tom had already been into his office and came up to her wearing too much of a smile considering the amount they'd drunk last night. He escorted her through security and headed for the public gallery.

'Are we allowed up here? Should I be here at all as a witness?' she asked as they climbed the stairs.

'You aren't a witness in this case. You have nothing to say about Moorgate Motorhire. Your evidence was for R v Finch, and Mina pleaded guilty a few weeks ago.'

They arrived outside Court No Four and Tom peeked inside. 'We've got a few minutes yet.'

'What did they get her for in the end?'

'GBH with Intent. Her brief argued that there was enough evidence to support a plea of self-defence for the actual killing, but she confessed to shooting Croxton in the back. She pleaded guilty to money laundering as well.'

'Except she didn't shoot him in the back, did she?'

'I doubt it. There was definitely someone else there – I proved it when I read the report on that Nissan Micra. The fire burnt out all the forensic evidence, but one thing's for certain: five foot two Mina Finch did not drive that car into Croxton's Mercedes. The seat was too far back for her to reach the pedals. I reckon that whoever drove that car shot Croxton, and she administered the *coup de grace*.' He finished with a shrug.

'Is that it for her? Nothing that can be done to make her give up the other name?'

'No. Without a murder charge to threaten her, the CPS took the rational decision to focus on Thornton and Co. Especially the wife and son.'

'Why?'

'Money. Thornton never denied distributing the counterfeit notes or the money laundering, but he said that Adam and his wife had nothing to do with it. With Mina's evidence the CPS had enough to charge them. That means they can pursue all of his fortune under Proceeds of Crime Recovery. It's a tidy sum.'

Kate felt cheated again. She knew that compromise was important – she couldn't have functioned as an officer without it – but she had seen the casual violence that spread around Thornton's empire, and it was very frustrating that only those caught red-handed would pay for it. Tom glanced inside and waved her forward.

It was all over in minutes. It took the clerk longer to read the indictments than anything else. George Thornton, his wife, his son and eight others all pleaded guilty to a bewildering array of crimes. Kate lost track of the statutes referred to and wondered if Tom had been required to memorise them for his exams last week. The judge nodded at the end, and she was surprised to see him referring to a discreetly hidden computer when they discussed dates for sentencing. The other surprise came when the Crown's barrister asked if he could raise the question of Mina Finch.

'We're not planning to sentence her alongside these defendants, are we?' said the judge.

'No, my lord, but I have received a request from her counsel that sentencing be deferred for her to undergo a major medical procedure which will require inpatient treatment.'

'Of what nature?'

The barrister looked at the dock and raised an eyebrow. The judge dismissed the prisoners. When they had gone, the lawyer continued. 'You may recall that she suffered a significant facial trauma some years ago. She is now in a position to have corrective surgery.'

'The Crown is content?'

'I don't think it's in anyone's interest for this to happen while she's serving a prison term.'

'Very good. I'll cancel the hearing and you can let me know when you're ready to proceed.'

'All rise.'

Kate and Tom made their way downstairs, lost in their own thoughts. In the lobby, a bewigged woman was waiting for them. Kate heard Tom hiss when he recognised her. It was his wife.

'I was looking for you in the court, Tom: I didn't expect you to be skulking in the gallery. Now I know why. Hello, Kate.'

'Hello, Caroline,' said Kate. 'I'll see you later, Tom. Thanks for bringing me.'

As she left the building, Kate looked over her shoulder. Caroline was handing him a bundle of papers that could mean only one thing – divorce. She waited outside for a few seconds, and he came out still carrying the documents. It was already hot on the steps.

'Are you okay? That was a mean trick, ambushing you like that.'

Tom shrugged as if it were nothing, but the corners of his mouth were turned down and his eyes were half closed.

'She said that she didn't want to serve the papers before my exams, but couldn't wait any longer after that. That's Carrie for you: half thoughtful, half selfish.'

'Let's get a coffee before you go back.'

'No thanks, I shouldn't really have come here: it's not my job. How about we meet up at the Creed Lane wine bar tonight, and you can tell me about your interview with the Men in Black?'

It was Kate's turn to offer the wry smile.

James King had already been approached by two security guards outside the prison. He informed them that the sign on the car park entrance was very clear – it was not part of the prison premises. On the one hand, he told them, this meant he had to pay a fee to park there. On the other hand, they had no jurisdiction. He had bought his ticket and he was waiting for his brother; if he chose to sit outside his van and play music, he had every right to do so. If they didn't like it, they could call the council and ask for environmental health. Not even the police had jurisdiction here.

The van in question was mostly green with red and gold highlights. The words *King James – by Royal Appointment* were featured on each side along with a small illustration of him playing the bass. The picture was quite good, although it gave him more dreads than he actually had: James thought he might be going bald, which would be a tragedy of epic proportions. He blamed his mother for that, or at least he blamed the Irish genes which she had inflicted on him.

There was a much larger illustration on the van showing a black woman pouring her soul into the microphone. He wasn't allowed to put her name (Vicci's management company had wanted a huge fee), but people recognised her anyway; the *Royal Appointment* wasn't just a pun on his own name – he played bass for Queen Victoria.

James and Vicci had been backing musicians on a recording when he heard her voice one night in the studio. Stripped of the music, and the lead singer's pitiful efforts, he had listened to her pitch-perfect track through the headphones and fallen in love with the sound. He had stayed up all night to write her a song, and the rest was history.

They had played a couple of gigs together, and James had suggested that *Queen Victoria* was better than *Vicci & King*. Then she entered a TV talent show and made it to the Grand Final where the critics lauded her, and the Great British Public voted for the thin white boy.

James had been told to stay away during the competition because of his criminal record, but now they were back together and building up a head of steam. She was still officially signed to the competition's promotion company, but she was pressing for a renegotiation that would recognise his contribution. Two years after the competition, the Great British Public had forgotten the winner, but the name of Queen Victoria was on a lot of lips.

Gentle sounds came out of the van, a chilled out ballad he had been working on ahead of the summer festival season. The top notes were melodic, but the beat was his own: the beat that his father had taught him before he died. James had visited this same prison twenty years ago, and his father had used the table to beat out a rhythm that he said came straight from Kingston, Jamaica. When he was released, they practised together with an old bass guitar. James preceded every gig he played with a prayer *in memory of King Solomon and his wisdom*. No one in the band except Vicci knew that Solomon King was his father.

James relaxed in his camping chair, enjoying the warmth and thinking about where to take the melody when suddenly it went dark. He opened his eyes, and instead of another security guard, he saw his brother.

'What's this shit, man? You got no decent music?'

James stood and embraced Robert.

'Too long, man. Too long.'

Robert broke the hug and looked at the van. 'Nice. I like that. Who's the fat lass?'

'Have some respect. She started out with less than you, and she's got a lot more now.'

Robert shook his head. 'I don't know which is worse: Mom peddling vintage clothes and wearing them or you playing vintage music and listening to it. I think that jacket's seen better days an'all.'

James was wearing an olive green lightweight combat jacket, adorned with patches and badges. He put his hand on Robert's shoulder. 'Don't you recognise them? The coat 'n' the beat? Father bought this jacket in Jamaica and he wrote the bass line in that song.'

Robert started to twitch, but didn't pull his brother's hand off his shoulder. 'What about my name? It's usually my name next,' he said.

'And so it shall be. Father gave you the name Robert Marley King because he wanted you to remember it every day in your prayers…'

'… and Robert Nestor Marley died in the year of my birth. I know. It's Rob, by the way. Not to you or Mom, but to everyone else it's Rob. Can we go now?'

James had no desire to linger, and he packed up the chair and turned down the volume before they set off. Robert was even more impressed by the air conditioning in the van.

'You really are doing alright, aren't you? Air con don't come cheap, do it?'

It had been three years since James had seen his brother. In that time they had grown even farther apart, but Robert (not Rob – no, not Rob) still spoke like a child of the Black Country. It was good to hear; James had wondered whether his brother would come out of prison as a wannabe gangsta.

'I'm getting there. We're playing five festivals this summer. No main stage yet, but we're getting there.'

'Not I & I is getting there?'

'No. I'm not Rastafarian any more. A man has many roots, and he must draw sustenance from all of them. Including the Irish ones.'

Robert looked uncomfortable, but ignored the pointed remark. 'Listen, I'm glad you're doing well. I can't thank you enough for paying off my suppliers. That was more than I deserved. I'll pay you back with interest.'

When Robert had been sent down, he had left serious debts which James had paid off for him.

'Maybe. We'll see.' Before they left the car park, James handed his brother a box. 'As requested.'

The box contained a Pay As You Go mobile, and Robert asked if he could make a call. James turned the music off and then listened to a one-sided conversation which seemed to please his brother enormously.

After disconnecting, Robert told him that Erin was going to allow him access to his children, and that the police had made a dawn raid on Ezekiel House.

'And how is that good news?' asked James.

'Eliminating the competition. I don't want no Crew moving on to my patch.'

They met in a hired room in the City. On the way there, Kate started to appreciate why Tom had become so attached to the Square Mile.

Yes, the most likely thing to find round the next corner was either a building site or a brutal slab of glass and concrete, but the Ghost of London Past was never far away. Today the Ghost led her past the Drapers' Hall. She lingered outside the extravagant baroque entrance and peered at the photographs of the gilded dining room (available for weddings and banquets); there was even a courtyard garden, tucked away inside.

The meeting room was less impressive. Modern, clean and anonymous: it could have been anywhere in the world. Her contact had covered the table with papers and was making enthusiastic use of the free Wi-Fi. He introduced himself as Anthony and offered her coffee.

Kate accepted and then asked the most obvious question – who Anthony worked for.

'In any other line of work, I'd be called a headhunter,' he said, 'but that doesn't have positive connotations in the world of intelligence, so we'll settle on recruitment consultant. Quite simply, I keep track of people in our field and try to match them to opportunities as they become available. I do have an office, but I prefer first encounters to be on neutral territory. More secure that way.'

Was it? Kate wondered if it were just because he didn't make much money and couldn't afford a base somewhere. On the other hand, if his assets were all in his contact book and he had clients on four continents, it would make sense to keep on the move. The other thing she wasn't sure about was the designation *Our Field*. Kate saw herself as a soldier first and only by accident an intelligence officer.

'Your colonel tipped me off that you were leaving without any particular place to go. I guess that your presence here today sort of confirms that.'

'I've been in the Army a long time. I didn't want to rush into anything so I'm keeping my options open.'

'Great. I felt like that myself, so I can see where you're coming from.'

She looked at him again. He was older than her, but he didn't look like an ex-soldier. SIS? MI5? His natural and open demeanour was a good cover. She didn't know his full name, his real location or anything about him except that he was British. Or had a good dialogue coach. She decided on SIS: she could see him blending in with a delegation to the former Soviet Republics quite nicely.

Anthony leaned back in his chair and crossed his legs. 'So tell me, Captain Lonsdale, what did you offer to the Army that someone else could use? And you can leave out the loyalty and hard work; I'll take that for granted.'

Kate crossed her legs too and fiddled with her coffee cup. 'I did electrical engineering at Uni and I was going to join REME, but there was a big push on at the time for hardware engineers so the Signals grabbed me… and the next thing I knew, I was fitting up fibre optic networks and learning about interception. I did that for a while and then moved into Intelligence. I'm considered something of an expert on battlefield sigint, but we all know that Afghanistan's going to wind down soon, and I thought I'd get established outside.'

He nodded as she spoke and considered what she said. 'How important is public service to you? I could give you a very good introduction at GCHQ or MI5, but you don't really need me for that.'

'I honestly don't know. There's something to be said for the public sector, but if I went to Cheltenham I'd miss the field work. I'm not sure about MI5; I've not had much to do with them. Been too busy hunting the Taliban in their caves.'

'How would you feel about going back? To Afghanistan, I mean. The PMCs are getting a lot of work there, and a NATO trained officer could command a premium salary.'

It was the question she had been dreading. She knew all about the private military contractors, and they had often attended briefings. She had no problem with them in principle, but it was the thought of going back to Helmand that she was uncertain about.

'Have you got anything UK based? To start with, I mean.'

He locked eyes with her for a second and then picked up some papers. 'Have a look at these two. They're purely hypothetical, of course.'

Kate was shocked when she read the first sheet. It described an operation to gather information on two Islamic groups in England. There was no mention of the words *Warrant* or *Authorisation*. She put the paper down and turned to the second one. It described a white hat consultancy service which attempted to breach security at various organisations and then prepared reports for their management.

'I like the look of this. Are there many opportunities?'

'Yes and no. It tends to be a bit seasonal. Every time there's a serious breach in the press they get a flood of work. I couldn't guarantee you a steady income, but you could build up a good CV quite quickly. It helps that you're mobile.'

'Give me six weeks to sort myself out and have a holiday, then let me know what you've got. I'd be especially interested in anything happening in South Wales.'

Anthony gave her a business card. It was different from the one her colonel had given her because it had the man's name and a mobile number.

'Thank you, Mr Skinner,' said Kate as she stood to shake his hand.

James King was finding Earlsbury very quiet. In the back garden of his mother's house there was a little traffic noise and a distant lawn mower, but no music. At home there would be tunes coming from every window on such a day as this, and he would have his own music playing. Then again, he didn't have a garden. He had to grow his ganja plants on the balcony.

He had rolled two joints and given one to Robert and, with a beer, his brother was starting to calm down. Theresa brought a tray from the kitchen and put it on the table. 'Home-made lemonade,' she announced. 'Perfect for this weather.'

'I think I'll stick to the beer,' said Robert.

James accepted a glass and enjoyed the bitter tang followed by the sweet coolness.

'To freedom,' said Theresa. 'Long may it continue.'

The boys – men – raised their glasses and Robert finished his beer. He had a cold six pack under the chair and started on the third. 'There's going to be a lecture,' he said. 'I can feel it in the air.'

'I've lost track of how many times I've seen my men come out of prison,' said Terri. 'James promised me he wasn't going back and he's kept that promise. I don't care what you get up to, Robbie, but I can't face you going back inside. Nor can Erin. I had to work very hard to convince her that you were going straight this time – and not straight back to jail. If you want those boys in your life, you need to be there for them. She's not going to take them to visit you if you're behind bars, and that's a fact.'

'So what do you suggest?' said Robert. 'We're in the middle of a recession, and the only thing I can do well is sell stuff. I'm not going on the market stalls and, you know what, Land Rover aren't hiring black ex-cons. I think I'll stick to what I know.'

'I didn't say it had to be legal: I just said it had to be safer. Would you consider a change of product?'

James couldn't help himself. 'Product? Are we in the Mafia now?'

Robert turned to face their mother. 'Go on. What do you suggest?'

'Tell him about the party first,' she said to James.

'It's our sister's eighteenth birthday, and we're going to show her a good time, King style.'

'She's not my sister.'

Theresa banged the table. 'If Hope is my daughter then she's your sister. Is that clear?'

Robert squared up and his jaw twitched. His mother stared him down. 'It's not her fault your father got killed on her birthday, and you'll get her a present, too.'

'Hasn't she had enough presents from *her* father? School fees paid for, and university next year. She don't need no present from me.'

James showed a united front: 'Respect our mother, Robert. She has welcomed you back into her house like the prodigal son, and she loves you more for being a sinner.'

'Is that your Catholic school speaking, or is it Jah Rastafari?'

'It is the Bible. The wisdom of God is open to all who listen.'

Theresa raised her hand to separate them and turned to Robert. 'What if I said that you could get some business?'

'From who? What?'

'Dermot Lynch. He said he needs someone with your connections.'

Robert sat back in his chair. 'All right, I'll listen to Dermot, but if his poxy uncle comes anywhere near me, I swear I'll do to him what his psycho friend did to my father.'

James relaxed for a moment but he wasn't convinced. Until Robert could accept that their father had killed Dermot's father, he doubted that the peace of God would descend on his brother.

Chapter 3

Earlsbury / London

Monday Morning / Afternoon / Tuesday Evening

13-14th September

They used to call it *back to school weather*. September had brought the return of the rush hour in the mornings, and hordes of children wondering why they were stuck inside when it was clearly still summer.

Patrick left his coat in the car and unlocked the side door of Emerald Green Imports, a small warehouse on a busy estate of similar warehouses. It wasn't anonymous (a large shamrock on the side was not what you'd call hiding yourself), but it wasn't easy to find, either. You had to turn in from the Stourbridge Road at the garage, take the second left past the tile shop and then bear right at the electrical wholesaler.

Patrick whistled a jig as he put the kettle on and took the security bars off the big shutters ready for later. There was a rumble and clank from outside as Dermot arrived in his pickup. His nephew locked the side door behind him when he entered, and Patrick put down two mugs of strong tea. Both mugs were emblazoned with the Old Gold and black logo of their team, Wolverhampton Wanderers. Dermot had even pinned a poster of the current squad on the wall.

'How did we do at the weekend?' he asked Dermot.

'Do you mean me or the business?'

'Keep your depraved love life to yourself.'

'You're just jealous. Any road up, I did better than the Baggies.'

'Not difficult.'

They grinned and lifted their Wolves mugs in a toast. It was always a sweet day when the Baggies (West Bromwich Albion) lost.

'Two good results,' said Patrick.

'Four, actually. Wanderers won away, Albion got hammered at home, we made money, and I got lucky.'

'Dermot, enough. I'm surprised you could face going to Sandwell.'

The counterfeit cash was flowing steadily in from Red Hand's deliveries, and Patrick was constantly on the lookout for new places to dispose of it. He had already argued with Dermot about how much they could shift through their regular distributors, and he had set tough limits. It had been Dermot's idea to target the various borderline legal businesses that floated around local events, including the football.

'It was easy. Because Man United brought so many fans, there was a lot of trade outside the Away end. I went up to every scarf seller, burger van and ticket tout I could find and bought something – anything – with a twenty pound note. Then just before kick-off I went back and said, "If you didn't spot that dodgy note, who else will?" Then I offered to sell them some more.'

'Did no one call for the police? There must have been enough of them around.'

'That was the best bit. Most of the time there was a copper within ten feet of me. No, if they weren't happy I gave them a refund and they kept quiet. Most took some off me. One of the ticket touts took a bundle.'

'So, how did we do?'

'Ten grand cleared.'

That was good. That was very good for an afternoon's work. One thousand counterfeit notes exchanged for real ones to the value of ten thousand pounds, and they would crop up in Manchester instead of the Black Country. Even better.

'Is it secured?'

'Yeah. I stashed it on Sunday morning.'

Patrick put his mug down sharply. 'Why not on Saturday night?'

Dermot grinned. 'Well, Sky Sports had these two promotion girls up from London and they were staying over for the Villa game yesterday. I told you I'd got lucky.'

That boy. What could you do? Patrick chuckled to himself and remembered his own adventures at Dermot's age. 'Ma was asking after you again.'

Dermot shuffled in his chair. 'Sorry. I wanted to get rid of the cash, and by then it was too late for dinner.'

'Make sure you're there next week. She was asking when you're going to settle down with a nice girl. I told her there wasn't a nice girl in Staffordshire who'd touch you wid a barge pole. What about Blackpool? Are they ready to take more?'

'Possibly. My contact wasn't very keen on the percentage, but it's hard to tell with him. Every time we send them something he tries to renegotiate the price after the event. I get the impression that the bloke in charge is a bit more easy-going. Mind you, their local plod have been having a clampdown – they found half of the last shipment of vodka. I checked it out online, he wasn't bullshitting me. We might have to take a reduced payment from them – call it a gesture of goodwill.'

'Good idea. We need to keep them sweet. Drink up: time for business. I'll open the shutters.'

The legal side of their enterprise was stacked in crates around the warehouse. Patrick still rented two stalls on Earlsbury market and one of them was still next to Theresa King, but he didn't sell fancy goods any more. All his stock was now Irish crafts: quality goods from small suppliers. It made a small profit and covered his costs, but that was all. The real money-making side was carried out in a different warehouse altogether. That one wasn't just difficult to find, it moved around on a regular basis, wherever abandoned and empty properties could be secured for cash.

Patrick had carefully cultivated people over the years… people in shipping, law enforcement and trade. He knew ways of getting Chinese cigarettes and Chinese vodka into the country that others could only dream of. He was especially proud of the vodka because he'd seen a gap in the market for Chinese tractor tyres, and had designed a giant rubber ring which fitted inside the tyre. Each ring could hold a hundred litres of vodka. His longstanding contacts in the Black Country meant that he knew exactly who to approach to do the bottling.

There was a clear division of labour between Patrick and his nephew. Patrick laundered the money and sourced the goods; Dermot distributed them. He had come out of jail with some interesting contacts a few years ago, one of whom was a big player in Blackpool where they seemed to have an enormous appetite for all things illegal. Patrick hadn't been to the place for donkey's years, but Dermot told him it had a very poor side away from the Golden Mile. Sure … wouldn't the folks there be grateful for some help with the cost of booze and fags? The final link in the chain was Patrick's dividend to his Principal Investors. They guaranteed that all sorts of channels remained open to him, but they took a big percentage of the profits.

With the shutters open, Dermot backed his pickup to the doors and started loading.

'Would you not be better with a van?' asked Patrick. 'Sure, doesn't it rain as much in this country as it does in Ireland? Only a farmer would use an open truck.'

'Nah. It's flexible. We've got enough vans for the winter. Hang on.' Dermot pulled out his phone and studied it. 'That's Rob King. He had a good weekend, too. Twelve grand.'

The maths was simple for Patrick. It was the one thing he had enjoyed at school, and he rarely used a calculator.

Dermot had cleared ten thousand – six thousand for Red Hand and four thousand for them. Robert King had cleared twelve thousand: thirty-six hundred to Red Hand, eighteen hundred to them and six hundred left for Robert himself.

You can't do a huge lot with six hundred pounds these days, and if Robert was relying on the dodgy notes as his only source of income, he would be stretched. He might build up the business further or he might diversify. It was the latter thought that worried Patrick most.

Before Dermot drove off, he asked him if he knew what Robert's plans were.

'In what way?'

'You know … like is he still living with Terri?'

'Far as a I know. I think she wants to keep an eye on him. He's spending time with Erin and the boys as well.'

'That's good to hear,' said Patrick and patted his nephew on the shoulder. 'Perhaps he's trying to work an angle at that pole dancing club of hers.'

'I'd like to work an angle there. They're well fit, those birds. Classy too, most of'em.'

'I despair of you, Dermot, I really do.'

Some things still have to be done in writing. The Metropolitan Police may be increasingly paperless, but when it comes to witness statements, warrants, and exam results, only the printed page will do. Tom stared at the envelope for a full minute before opening it.

Did he want to become an Inspector? Did he have any choice? Most of the detective sergeants at the Money Laundering Investigation Unit (the MLIU) were happy doing their jobs and would carry on until retirement – and probably afterwards as consultants. They fitted the job and the job fitted them. Tom knew that wasn't for him, but he didn't know what was.

He had been forced to slow down when he joined the City of London Police. He worked just as hard, but the long, drawn out process of gathering small pieces of information, checking bank accounts, trawling phone records and compiling huge spreadsheets was very different from the work of a solicitor or a beat copper. He could do it and do it well, but it wasn't what he wanted to do forever. He wasn't sure that he wanted his boss's job, either.

DI Fulton had given Tom a case five years ago when he had joined the team as a detective constable. In a year's time he would have been working on that case longer than his marriage had lasted, and he wasn't much nearer a solution.

He came to a decision: if he had passed the exam, he would leave the City of London Police and take the first DI job that came up. Wherever it was.

He opened the envelope and, despite his nerves, he was now considered fit to be an inspector. The sun broke over his desk, and he agreed with the weather – this was actually a very good day. He picked up a file and carried it downstairs where he dropped it in the internal mail.

'I got my results,' he said to Elspeth.

'And?'

'I need to revise my knowledge of immigration law, but I passed.'

'Tom! Well done. Sorry, I mean: congratulations, Potential Detective Inspector Morton.'

'That somehow seems less impressive, but thank you.'

She looked over his shoulder at the security barrier and buzzed the door open. Only staff and known visitors were allowed through this entrance. 'Here's someone else who'll be pleased for you.'

Tom turned to see Frazer Jarvis from the Bank of England approaching. Much to his embarrassment, Elspeth insisted on telling the man his news straight away.

Jarvis shook his hand and then said, 'Have you got a minute, Tom? Something's come up.'

The visitor was issued with a pass, and Tom took him upstairs. Frazer declined coffee (always a wise move) and quickly got down to business.

'You can guess why I'm here, I'm sure.'

'*PiCAASA*?'

'That's right. The same notes that were being circulated by the Moorgate Motorhire gang have started turning up again.'

'Are you sure they're the same?'

By way of an answer, Jarvis took two evidence bags from his case and put them on the desk. 'You can open them and take a look,' he said.

Both contained £20 bank notes. To Tom, they looked not only identical, but also indistinguishable from the real thing. On the last case, he had left the counterfeiting side to Frazer and focused on the money laundering, but if he were going to follow this up, he would need to be certain.

He turned the two notes over and felt the quality of the paper. He examined the holographic seal and held them up to the light. A second portrait of the Queen looked back at him from the watermark.

'How do you know?' he asked Frazer.

'These are level eight forgeries.'

'Sorry, I must admit I haven't been on the counterfeiting course. How many levels are there and what do they mean?'

Frazer ticked the items off on his hand.

'Level one is the appearance. A good inkjet printer can make something that *looks* like a banknote.'

Tom nodded.

'Level two is the paper and level three is a basic silver strip. Anything less than quality rag stock just doesn't feel right in the hand. It's very rare for notes up to level three to get accepted in shops.'

Tom looked at the holographic strip on the forgeries. Alternating images of pound signs, the number 20, and silhouettes of Adam Smith flickered under the lamp.

'That's level five,' said Frazer, 'the images on the holographic strip. Level four is the watermark and level six is the raised print. And there's the problem. Anything up to level six can be checked by the naked eye. A few minutes' training with a shop assistant, and they can spot all of them. You need a machine to go higher than level six.'

'And machines are expensive.'

'Too right. To detect level seven, the notes have to be put through a security scanner. On the high street, only bookmakers and casinos can afford to check for level seven and above. Oh, and by the way, level eight is the little yellow dots. They have to be in a certain pattern. After that we don't tell anyone except our partners what the advanced security features are.'

'Am I a partner?'

'No. The partners are a select group of hi-tech scanner manufacturers. We don't even tell the banks who use them. A bank will scan every deposit over a certain figure and reject the fakes. If you're trying to run a pub or a corner shop, you can have your whole profit margin wiped out when you pay into the bank. It can ruin small businesses.'

The notes still looked real to Tom. There must be a very sophisticated press somewhere which was churning these out. 'Are you sure these are from the same forger?'

'After the *PiCAASA* operation was wound up, they changed the plates and the paper stock. These notes started turning up in June, and it took us three months to realise what was happening. It was only when we did a spectrographic analysis of the ink we discovered the similarities.'

Tom took one final look at the notes and slipped them back into the evidence bags. If Frazer said they were from the same source, that was good enough for him. Everything else was technical detail. 'So, where are they this time? Essex again?'

His colleague frowned and stowed away the bags. 'No, that was another confusing factor. They've been turning up all over the West Midlands in quantity; Blackpool and the Republic of Ireland, too.'

'All of the West Midlands or mostly Birmingham?'

'Not so much in Brum: more to the north west of there.'

'Aah. Yam Yam Land.'

'What?'

'I was a solicitor in Edgbaston. Brummies used to call the Black Country *Yam Yam Land*.'

'Erm… yes, Tom. I'll take your word for it. I knew you'd want to know about this, but because it's so far out of London, I don't know what you can do about it.'

'Can you send me the reports?'

'Of course. Soon as I get to the office.'

They stood up, and Tom escorted him out of the building. Back at this desk, he sent DI Fulton an email asking for a meeting to discuss something personal.

There is a small parade of shops on the Elijah estate which has kept going despite the existence of two major supermarkets in Earlsbury. On one end is an Indian takeaway and at the other end is a hairdresser. In the middle is a minimarket which all the locals refer to as Derek's. The eponymous former owner died in the 1970s but the name lingers on. Derek wouldn't have known what a cappuccino was if it had been poured over his head, and had only eaten croissants on holiday, but Ian Hooper was munching one and slurping the other outside Derek's and enjoying the sunshine. He didn't count it as a break because someone would come and talk to him sooner or later. He didn't expect it to be DS Griffin, however.

'Awright, 'Ooper. Awm ya doing?'

'Bay 'arf bad, sarge.'

'That's what I like about you, Hooper. You're not ashamed of your roots.'

Griff was notorious for testing new recruits by *talking broad*. If they didn't get what he was saying, they were likely to be the butt of jokes for some time.

'You here on business, sarge?'

'I need a favour, Hooper.'

Ian tipped the dregs of his coffee down the drain and threw the packaging in the bin. He dusted crumbs from his hands and tried to look competent. He didn't want to be too keen, but it didn't hurt to be helpful.

'I've had intelligence about one of the lock-up garages being used as a store for stolen bicycles,' said Griffin.

'Sounds about right. There's barely half of those garages used for legit business.'

'I know. I also know that it's impossible to put surveillance on 'em because they're wide open and there's no CCTV. We can't get a warrant until we know which garage.'

'I'll see what I can do.'

Griff went into the shop, and Ian walked off towards the garages. The detective was right. There was a large rough space outside the garages which ended in allotments. There was nowhere to mount a surveillance that wouldn't get spotted in seconds. Three kids with BMX bikes were messing around. One of them looked familiar and his suspicions were confirmed when the lad shot off in the opposite direction as soon as he clocked the uniform.

Ian took out his mobile and scrolled down to *Earlsbury High School*. There were four direct numbers listed, and he chose the one marked *Attendance & Welfare*. Who knows? This could be the second step on his road to CID.

Tom's boss always kept a pile of rubbish on his only spare chair. When DI Fulton wanted to talk over a case, he always came to see you, not the other way round. When Tom was summoned after lunch, the chair was cleared and ready for him.

'Congratulations, Tom. Well done with the exams.'

'Thank you, sir.'

'You don't need to tell me your plans; just give me the heads-up when you're off to pastures new.'

'Don't you want to keep me?'

Fulton laughed and leaned back in his chair. 'You don't need me to put a stamp of approval on your career. You're a good detective and you'll make someone a good DI. That's if we're still around once this new lot get started with the cuts.'

It was true. The coalition government were making a lot of noise about deep cuts in all sectors of public spending. Unusually for the Tories, the police and the Army seemed to be in their sights along with their perennial targets in local government.

'Something else has come up,' said Tom. Fulton nodded for him to continue. 'Jarvis from the Bank of England has been to see me. Those counterfeit notes have surfaced again. In the West Midlands.'

Fulton weighed up the news. 'How much?'

'More than last time and spread over a wider area.'

'Have you alerted Midland Counties police?'

'Not yet. I don't want this going through normal channels.'

Fulton leaned forward and pushed his face towards Tom. 'If you say the M word, I'll get annoyed. My team – *your* team – is solid. There are no Moles in Economic Crimes.'

Tom held up his hands in surrender. 'I agree. No question. Everyone is whiter than Persil. Even you, sir.'

Fulton's mouth twitched and then he laughed: his was the only black face on their floor of the building. Tom continued, 'There may not be a mole, but I believe – I really believe – that there's a leak from somewhere in London. I want the chance to track down the big players behind this operation, and I don't want them tipped off again.'

'You want to go to Birmingham? Didn't you get enough of it before you joined the Force? Sorry, Tom, that's a non-starter. You've got four active cases that won't wait. Sometimes you've got to learn to let go.'

'You didn't.'

The two men stared at each other. Fulton had been nearly killed by drug dealers and had risen from his hospital bed determined to track them down. He did it by following the money and had earned himself a place in MLIU. Tom was determined not to blink first.

'Give me a good reason that's not connected to *PiCAASA*, and I'll think about it.'

Ian Hooper planned his attack carefully, first gathering intelligence on when the target would be at home. It wasn't in the same league as the raid on Ezekiel House, but trying to track down a teenage boy is a challenge in itself.

He knocked on Carol Davis's door and the target himself, Finn Davis, answered.

'Hello, Finn. Does your mother know you weren't in school today?'

The young lad gripped the door and looked around him. In the films the lad watched, the suspect would slam the door in the policeman's face and run away. Ian Hooper was about three times Finn's size, and had already taken a step over the threshold. Finn let go of the door and walked upstairs instead, leaving Ian to find Carol in the kitchen.

'Why have they sent the police? Couldn't they have texted me after registration?'

'He was there for registration, but skipped off afterwards. The attendance officer told me they're going to put in some new system for taking the register every lesson. You know what this means, don't you?'

'It means that crime must be very low in Earlsbury if they can send a policeman round to chase up every truant. Are you going to follow him around every minute? Check when he goes to the toilet? If the school looked after him properly, he wouldn't bunk off so much.'

'It's not the truancy I'm here about. It's what he does when he's off that worries me.'

His tone of voice struck something in Carol's conscience, and she turned off the grill to give Ian her full attention. 'What do you mean?'

'I saw him hanging around the yard with two people who never went to school, either. That red BMX of his is very distinctive.'

'It's green,' said Carol automatically. 'His dad bought it for him last year. Are you sure it was Finn you saw?'

'Go out the back and have a look. If it's not red, I'll go home for my own tea and leave you in peace. Otherwise, I think we both need a word with him.'

'Do you want a brew?'

Ian allowed her the delaying tactic. He wasn't going away without some answers, and if Carol needed time to face up to the issue, so be it. When the kettle had boiled, and the teabag was floating around a Best Mom in the World mug, she wiped her hands and went out the back door. Seconds later she marched silently through the kitchen and up the stairs. Ian finished making the tea while shouts and then sobs came from Finn's bedroom.

By the time he had drunk it, his notebook had three names, a garage number and a confession for theft.

'It's your last chance, Finn. Next time I'll have to arrest you.'

Carol was shredding a tissue; she had done most of the crying. 'Are you sure you can keep his name out of it? If those boys ever think he's grassed them up, they'll kill him.'

'I won't say anything if he doesn't.' Ian fixed Finn with a stare. 'If we raid that lock-up and it's empty, I'll know that you've tipped them off. Got that?' Finn nodded and Ian left them to it.

On the way home he called DS Griffin with the news.

'Bloody hell, Hooper, that was quick. Where did you get that from?'

'You know, sarge, just asking around. It's good, though. I wouldn't hang around if I were you, this tip-off has a short sell-by date.'

'Very good, Ian. Protecting a source. I like that. Fair enough. What shift are you on tomorrow?'

'Early.'

'I'll get the warrant and meet you outside Derek's at eleven o'clock. I'll make the arrest, but we'll need someone to go through all those bikes. If they're there.'

Griffin strikes again. Ian had found the stash but CID would get the glory, and he would be up to his armpits in stolen bikes for weeks. On the other hand, his application for Angela Lindow's maternity cover would shine even brighter now.

DI Fulton examined the file that Tom had presented to him. It was the thickest folder in Tom's in-tray, and by far the biggest lost cause in Fraud since Bernie Madoff.

'Are you serious, Tom?'

'It's the only way I can make progress on the Islamabad case, sir.'

'It's a snake pit out there. And I don't mean Pakistan.'

Three years ago, the Bank of England had notified them of several large transactions that had been routed to Islamabad, and that were linked to Islamic fundamentalists. Sums of money like this clearly pointed to groups in Britain who, if not engaged in terrorism themselves, were almost certainly promoting it. Somewhere. Over the years, Tom had added hundreds of pieces of evidence which might or might not be linked until the file resembled something from a CID car boot sale.

It was also like one of Nostradamus's prophecies. Looked at the right way, it could mean almost anything.

Tom had selected four pieces of evidence that pointed to Birmingham and written a summary. On the other hand, he knew what Fulton meant. The complex multi-agency unit in Birmingham which came under the heading *Counter Terrorism* was indeed a snake pit. Shadowy representatives of MI5, MI6, GCHQ and for all he knew the CIA, would slip in and out of the offices near the Bullring in an attempt to forestall active terror plots.

'You can have a week in Birmingham on two conditions. First, have you got a mate with a spare room? My expenses budget is way over.' Tom nodded. 'Second, you've got to find this bloke before I'll let you go.' Fulton tossed the Islamabad file back to Tom and pulled out one of his own.

There was a Post-it note on the cover which said *Lord Lucan*. Tom peeled it off to reveal the name of a serial conman who had absconded from an open prison, much to their embarrassment. Fulton clearly didn't expect Tom to be going anywhere in the near future.

He studied the file on the way back to his desk and came across the list of visitors to the prison. There had been various attempts to locate these men, but Tom had another idea.

The job offer from Anthony Skinner had come suddenly, and Kate would soon be on her way up north. Pembrokeshire would have to wait. She wasn't leaving town for a couple of days, but Diana Morton had been insistent: it was the autumnal equinox on Tuesday, and that's when they had to get together. As well as saying goodbye to Kate, they would be reviewing their Solstice Resolutions.

'So can you tell us where you're going?' asked Di.

'Of course. I'm not working for SIS, you know. I'm going to Tyneside, but I can't tell you the client or the target.'

'Why you? I get that you're a white hat hacker but I thought all hackers, no matter what colour their headgear, were spotty boys who need to get out more.'

'We do have a couple of those on the team. In fact one of them works exclusively from his bedroom in Swindon. I don't do hacking.'

'Yes, you do,' said Tom from the kitchen.

'Well, not much. It's my job to try and attach gadgets to their network. Makes the real hackers' jobs a lot easier if they can physically get inside the system.'

Diana's expression was starting to glaze over so Kate didn't go into packet sniffing and Wi-Fi intercepts. 'I've got a job, so that's my Midsummer resolution completed. What about yours? Have you finished three pieces for your exhibition?'

'Yes, I have. Do you want a look?'

'Dinner,' said Tom, and he served them one of the dishes from his summer cookery course.

Di waved a fork at him and said, 'Did you make this for Ingrid?'

'Lay off him, Di,' said Kate. 'He's entitled to a bit of fun in the sun.'

'I know. It was the resolution I made for him – get laid and forget Caroline for five minutes. Well, however long it took. I didn't tell him to get revenge by shagging a married woman.'

'I didn't know she was married.'

'That's what they all say.'

'She made a point of telling me afterwards – so I knew she wasn't looking to get together again after the course was over. She took off her wedding ring at Oslo airport and went on the cookery course to get laid.'

'Yeah, right.'

Kate believed him. It was good to see Tom a little less frustrated. She kept quiet about what she'd been up to for the last four days: a spontaneous dirty weekend in Edinburgh with a canoeing instructor from Oban.

After dinner, they looked at Di's paintings. Kate thought that Diana had cheated by doing a triptych and trying to pass it off as three separate pieces, but they were good. Kate would never look at sheep in the same way again.

While Di loaded the dishwasher, Tom whispered to Kate. 'How did you get on with that favour?'

She opened her bag and passed him a piece of paper. It was the printout from a hotel register in Spain showing three of the names from the visitors' log with an asterisk next to a known alias for Tom's missing conman.

'You were right,' she said. 'Your colleagues *had* missed the big picture. In fact it was literally a big picture – on a social media website. Four of them at a bar in Spain. Some criminals really are stupid.'

'What are you two plotting?' said Diana.

'Tom's just won the booby prize,' said Kate. 'He gets to go to Birmingham.'

Despite the late hour, Gatwick Airport was busy, and Conrad Clarke found it difficult to secure a table in the café. He was gasping for a cigarette already, and it would be a very, very long time before he could have one. A woman in black robes, headscarf and veil approached him, and he was about to tell her that the other seat was taken when he recognised the eyes and stood up to greet her.

'Have you converted to Islam?' he said.

'No, Conrad, I haven't,' said Mina. 'I can see the attraction, but I don't plan on becoming a Muslim just so that I can wear a veil.'

She sat down, and he asked her if she wanted anything from the café. 'No thanks. I can't eat solids for another few days and if I have any more coffee I'll burst.'

'How is it?'

Mina turned away from the crowded departure lounge and carefully unhooked one side of her veil. She showed him the wound. Dried blood and stitches lined her face where the surgeon had rebuilt her jaw. 'I'm not just wearing the veil for anonymity. I don't want people looking at this.'

'My God, you're beautiful. You do know that. I can't believe what a difference it makes.'

She hooked the veil back on and told him to stop flattering her.

'But it's true. I always thought you were stunning, but now you've got your jawline back it's completely different. Did they do the dental implants as well?'

'No. Too much for one operation. I'll have to wait until I'm in prison before I can have them – and the cosmetic work on the scars. But I can chew on the left side from Wednesday. That's the day after the sentencing hearing so I get my first solid meal for six years inside a prison.'

Clarke reached under the table and took hold of her hands. He massaged her fingers and stroked her nails and felt the tension in her palms receding. 'If something happened to me, would you wait?'

She gripped his hand and locked her eyes on him. 'What's happened, Conrad?'

'Nothing. Nothing at all, but if they ever tracked me back to what happened in Essex or if something happened in the future…'

She lowered her gaze, and he could see only the veil but her hand was still in his. 'For what you did before,' she said, 'all has been washed away. What you do in the future is different. By the time I come out of prison, we will both be different people. I cannot promise anything until I have paid my debts.'

'Our *atmans* will still be the same.'

She took her hand out from under the table and punched him on the shoulder. 'Stop winding me up. You don't believe that for a second.'

'And if I didn't believe it – would that make it any less true?'

'Go and get me a diet Pepsi – and a straw.'

Clarke heaved himself out of the seat and wondered why the change of mind. Half way to the counter, he remembered. She hadn't seen him since his own operation to remove the pins from his leg. Well, to remove the ones sticking out. He was left with a rod in his tibia and no matter how hard he worked in rehab, he now had a limp. She was checking out his walk.

'It's so funny to see you without crutches,' she said when he got back with her drink. 'What did you call running on them?'

'Cromping.'

'That's right. You could move faster on one leg and two crutches than my mother can move on two legs.'

'It had its moments, but I'm glad to be off them. It doesn't hurt most of the time, either.'

'No heroics in Afghanistan, do you hear me? If I'm going to dump you when I get out of prison, I want you to be alive, so that you suffer.'

Clarke grinned at her. 'You can't dump me unless we're an item. And you've never said that before.'

She looked down again, and he thought that she might be blushing. 'I do want you to take care, though. Please.'

'I'm going to teach the Afghan Air Force how to fly large helicopters. It's not completely safe, but it's a lot safer than Helmand.'

The delayed BA flight to Manchester is now boarding at Gate 14, came the announcement.

'When you get back,' he said, 'start developing a serious interest in cricket, especially the Indian Premier League. I'll explain why in a letter.'

She reached into her niqab and pulled out a small box. 'Here, I have something for you.' He opened it and inside was a Zippo lighter with a garish purple image of Ganesha, the Hindu elephant god.

'Look on the back.'

He took it out and turned it over. There was a custom engraving of a little fish. Her name – Mina – meant little fish.

'Ganesha will watch over you, and so will I. Now give me your other one. You won't be wanting it now.'

He pulled a similar (if more tasteful) lighter from his pocket and took one last look at the inscription: *To Conrad, with love from Amelia*. He tossed it on the table, and Mina – equally casually – picked it up and tossed it into the bin.

Clarke gripped his new lighter in his palm and leaned over to unhook her veil. As the final call for her flight was announced, he brushed his lips against hers.

Chapter 4

Earlsbury

4th – 17th October

The custody sergeant at Earlsbury division was beginning to lose patience. Ian Hooper had filled one of his cells with stolen bicycles two weeks ago, and there were still four left in it. Ian promised the sergeant they'd be gone by Wednesday. Perhaps Ceri's school could 'borrow' them for cycling proficiency practice. That would get him a bonus point for community engagement.

The recovery of stolen bicycles and the arrest had tipped the balance in his favour, and Ian was now an acting detective constable. He went back to the CID room and asked Angela what was new. Her bump was now very large and she wasn't going to be doing much field work for the next two weeks. Then her maternity leave would start, and Ian would have six months to prove himself.

'Get us a cup of tea, love,' she said. 'We've all been summoned to an eleven o'clock briefing. I'll see you in the conference room.'

Ian did as he was bid and slipped into the back of the room five minutes later. Angela was next to the door because anything longer than half an hour was likely to be interrupted by a visit to the Ladies. She'd given up on coffee but didn't seem to realise that tea had much the same effect.

At the front of the room, Griff was talking to an unknown suit with a temporary security pass. The visitor was pale, thin, and had hollows round his eyes. The hunched shoulders suggested a man with an intimate knowledge of computer screens.

When DCI Storey – the head of Earlsbury CID – appeared, Griff moved to a seat on the front row, and their senior officer addressed the group. 'Morning all. Sorry to drag you away from operations, but you all need to hear this. I'll say no more except to introduce our visitor.' Storey consulted a piece of paper. 'This is Detective Sergeant Tom Morton from the Money Laundering Investigation Unit in the Economic Crimes section of the City of London Police. Have you all got that?'

'I got the "Tom" bit,' said Griff and the others laughed.

Blimey, thought Ian. *If that's what happens to you when you join the Fraud Squad, I'm avoiding it like the plague.* The visitor stood up and straightened his jacket.

'Thanks. I'll be very brief. Earlier this year we uncovered a major counterfeiting and money laundering ring in London and Essex. We cleaned up the distribution network, but we got nowhere near the actual forgers. Now they're back in action, and they're on your patch.'

While this was sinking in, DS Morton took some twenty pound notes out of his pocket. 'These aren't in an evidence bag because we've got so many of them. I'll leave them here for you to have a look at afterwards. I'm not going to try and tell you about the economic damage caused by counterfeiting, because life's too short.' Morton paused and put the notes on a table. 'But I will tell you this. When we closed down that gang, one man was stabbed to death, one man was shot and a young girl was beaten up so badly it took months for her to recover. There's a network around here somewhere, and I need your help to root it out. Preferably with a solid lead back to the printing presses this time.'

He sat down, and DCI Storey stood up. 'I endorse everything DS Morton has said. He has to go back to London in a week, and I want you to put maximum focus on this while he's still here so we can pick his brains. If we get a result, it'll be to our credit. DS Griffin, could you take over?'

The DCI shook hands with the visitor and left. Griff replaced him. 'We're going to have a full Ops meeting on Thursday at nine o'clock when I've worked out the details.' He turned to the visitor. 'In the meantime, DC Hooper will introduce you to Earlsbury. Where are you staying, Tom?'

'I'm at the Holiday Inn in Birmingham - at my own expense.'

'We can't have that, mate: it's too far away and I want you to sample some Black Country hospitality. You've got a spare room, haven't you Ian? Good. You can show our guest the highlights and lowlights of Earlsbury, and book it down to expenses. Any questions? No? Right, off you go.'

The room cleared, and some officers took a sample from the pile of forged notes. Ian went up and looked at them. They were stamped FORGERY in red letters. He shook hands with the visitor.

'Has DS Griffin told you I'm only acting DC, sir?'

'Yes, and it's "Tom", not "Sir".'

'Righty-ho, Tom. Shall we start with a walk down the High Street?'

The Lynch family were used to compromise. Patrick was very lucky that Fran had accepted him back after Hope's birth had exposed his infidelity. When you've a bastard in the maternity unit and two dead bodies in the Barley Mow, it's a special woman who's willing to forgive. Patrick had promised to keep his flies zipped, and eighteen years later (and eight years after his heart attack) he reckoned that their marriage was at its happiest since its beginning. Tonight's compromise was a family send-off for Hope, conducted midweek instead of round the Sunday dinner table. Since Rob King had come out of prison, Hope's house was out of bounds for him, and so the assembled Lynch clan were making polite conversation in the conservatory.

The guest of honour was leaving tomorrow for university in St Andrews after a good crop of A Level results. She was leaning on an armchair, talking to her grandmother. Elizabeth, who idolised her older half-sister, was standing on the other side. Patrick and Fran watched from the living room.

'At least she's not doing the four year course,' said Fran.

'What do you mean?'

'It'll save you a few bob not having to pay for the extra year, like most of them do in Scotland.'

'The fees are cheaper than at St Modwenna's.'

'And how much will her living costs be?'

'I told her mother that it was fees only from now on.'

'Maybe she'll pick up a prince. That seems to be the main reason for going to St Andrews.'

'It has a tremendous reputation. So I'm told.'

'It's a long way off, and that's the main thing. So long as we aim higher for Elizabeth.'

'Higher?'

'Oh, yes, Patrick. If our daughter doesn't get into Oxford, I'll want to know the reason why.'

The doorbell rang, and Fran went to answer it. Dermot should be here by now, surely, but if that was him, why didn't he use his key? Fran took her time and came back with a sour look.

'It's your golfing buddy. I told him this was a private function but he said it was urgent. I told him to wait outside.'

Putting down his glass of wine and soda (urgh, but at least it still had wine in it), Patrick went through to the hall and peered out of the glass. Shit. What was Griff doing here tonight? He opened the door and almost yanked the detective sergeant through the kitchen and into the garden. They paused by the garage, out of sight of the conservatory.

'Nice to see you, Griff. You've not brought a present for Hope, then?'

'Give over,' snapped Griffin. 'This is fucking serious.'

DS Griffin squared his shoulders and took half a step closer to Patrick. 'How long have you been shifting dodgy notes, eh?'

Patrick ran his finger round his collar. It suddenly felt very warm for October. 'I don't know what you mean.'

Griffin took another half step, and Patrick backed into the wall with a bump. 'You said you wanted a tip-off if someone called Morton appeared. Well, he appeared this morning with a big bunch of counterfeit twenties and an action plan to find the distributor. That would be you, wouldn't it? He said this is the second time he's been on the gang's trail and he's not going to give up until they're all in jail and he's closed down the printing press. Last time there were two murders. I looked it up. The people behind this are psychos.'

'Jesus, Griff. I had no idea about this. Honest. I'll admit to playing a part in distribution, but I had no idea it was connected like that.'

'You're on your own. I won't help him, but I won't shield you, either. I've palmed him off with a rookie until Thursday, but after that…'

'Don't worry. I'll sort it.'

'You better had.' Griffin walked off. 'Enjoy your party,' he said over his shoulder.

'It's very kind of you to invite me into your home.'

'Don't be daft, Tom. We're getting a free meal out of it.'

Tom started to remove the lids from a huge selection of Indian takeaway cartons. After their tour of Earlsbury, Ian had insisted that a good curry from *East of Earlsbury* was exactly what they needed. Instead of a menu, the acting detective constable had simply phoned the restaurant and asked for *A Special for three please, Ali, on the CID account*.

There was barely room for all the food. Tom had scanned the flat, and the coffee table in front of the TV was the closest the young couple had to a dining area. Where Tom would have put a proper table, there was a desk and computer. The kitchen didn't look much used, either.

When they arrived with the Tandoori Banquet, a young woman was sitting at the desk and busily typing, surrounded by exercise books. 'Lesson plans,' she said, as if that explained everything.

'So how did you two meet?' he asked while Ian opened some beers.

'Rugby,' she replied. After a day of Black Country accents, Ceri's Welsh was strikingly different. 'Ian played for the Midland Counties police team – still does – and they had a Police Cup match against South Wales Police. My brother was on the winning side, of course. I took pity on the losing Number 8.'

She looked up at Ian (most people had to look up at Ian) and gave him a smile. Then she tweaked his misshapen nose. 'We texted each other for weeks after, and when I finished college, I applied for a job here. Easier for me to start here than for Ian to get transferred to Wales. He doesn't speak Welsh too well.'

Tom put down his plate and excused himself. Ceri pointed to the bathroom, and he locked himself in. The food was excellent, so why did he feel sick? Looking at the two of them had turned his stomach: not with revulsion at them, but at himself. They had bought this flat, about twice the size of his own, and they had made it a home. Together.

He was only seven years older than Ian. For goodness sake, man. Pull yourself together. He washed his face and stared in the mirror. When his father had paid a visit to London in August, he had taken one look at Horsefair Court and said, 'Mr Bleaney lives here.' When Tom had asked what he meant, his father said, 'Philip Larkin. *A hired box*. Look it up.'

Tom returned to the room and found them watching TV.

'Are you alright, Thomas?' said Ceri.

'I'm fine. It must have been the CID coffee. Ian must be immune.'

She patted his arm and offered him the biryani. 'Put a proper lining on your stomach, that will.'

'Gorra build your strength up for tomorrow,' said Ian. 'We're going to a pole dancing club in the afternoon.'

'He's not joking, either,' said Ceri.

They met up at Sandbach services in Cheshire. Patrick parked on the north side and walked over the bridge. After buying a coffee, he went to the petrol station and waited by the exit. Dead on time, an anonymous white van filled up with diesel and stopped next to him. The driver wound down the window. It was Red Hand himself.

'Are you sure you want to do this, Paddy?'

'Patrick.'

'Same question.'

'Yes, I am.'

'Well get in, then.'

Patrick went round and climbed into the van. There was a big slot on the dashboard for his coffee carton, and he put on the seat belt. Red Hand drove on to the M6.

'Right then, *Mr Lynch*, what's this all about?'

'It's about bad faith. And I don't mean your heathen religion, either.'

'Very funny. What's the problem? Remember who's driving this thing. I know a few secluded spots round here where they'd never find your body.'

'Stop being a fool, man. I've just heard all about your last distributors – George Thornton and his pals. He got sent down for six years last week.'

'He chose his friends badly. I'm sure you won't make the same mistake.'

'You didn't ask how I knew about him.'

'Because I don't care.'

'You should care, because his nemesis is sniffing round my patch right now.'

'Morton? From the Fraud Squad?'

'The very same. Arrived yesterday.'

'That's unfortunate for you.'

'Not for me it isn't: it's unfortunate for you. I've put out the word to stop all distribution immediately. And don't try and threaten me, okay?'

They had arrived at the next junction, and Red Hand (who looked older in the daylight) turned off the motorway and took the third exit at the roundabout. A short way along, he pulled into a lay-by.

'And what if I threaten your wife and daughter instead?'

Patrick had seen this coming; he had even taken an angina tablet with the coffee while waiting.

'This is my world, not yours. You can put me in a ditch if you like, but if you do anything, *anything* to hurt my girls, I'll be after you. And not just me.'

'I have a target to meet, Paddy, and you're going to help me meet it.'

'How about a change of direction? I have a contact in another part of the country who can shift more notes than I can. He's already taken some. How about I take double the quantity at 10 per cent instead of 30 per cent? I'm sure your bosses would rather have an ongoing deal than another body to explain.'

The other man drummed his fingers on the steering wheel for a moment and stared through the windscreen. With no movement of air in the vehicle, Patrick could smell fish coming from the back.

'How about 20 per cent?' said the Ulsterman.

'Fifteen per cent is my final offer. It's double the quantity, remember, and I'll still be doing the money laundering for youse.'

'Okay. It'll be with you in a fortnight. Now get out.'

'Don't be an eejit. Just drop me at the Northbound services; it's only a couple of minutes up the road.'

'I'm not having this van's number plates on any other CCTV today. If you walk up the road for a bit there's a garage. They'll tell you the best taxi firm to call. Or you could hitch a lift.'

Patrick swore at him and climbed out of the van. As Red Hand drove off, he realised that he'd left his cup of coffee behind. Ah well, never mind. He'd have been willing to settle for 20 per cent, so all in all it was a good day.

'This used to be The Bird in Hand,' said Ian as they pulled into the car park of a large pub on the outskirts of Kidderminster. It was a classic 1930s roadhouse, built to service the growing business from motorists on their way south west to Bristol, Wales and beyond.

Tom looked at the intersecting roundabouts which had cut off the passing trade some years ago. It clearly had no future as a pub, and he wasn't surprised that someone had taken it over. Ian had explained to him that a whole raft of pubs had come on to the market a while back and had been bought as a job lot by a local property developer.

He said that most of the pubs got converted for housing but this one, The Bird in Hand, had been designated as commercial premises only by the planners. It stayed closed for a bit, and then it was leased to this guy from Birmingham. It had been open as a pole dancing club for a few months now.

There was a thirty foot high silver stripe running down the gable end of the building, which had neon letters announcing *The West Pole*. A longer name probably wouldn't have fitted.

Inside the club, there was no trace of the former bar, lounge or dining room for hungry motorists. One long room was split by a raised walkway. On either side were tables and chairs, nestling up to the stage like insects swarming up to a fallen tree. There were seven poles spaced evenly apart, and a young lad was spraying them with disinfectant; an older woman was Hoovering the carpet.

'I'm sorry that I couldn't bring you when it was open,' said Ian.

'Don't apologise,' said Tom. 'I'm sure that neither of us wants to be clocked at a pole dancing club when it's open. Unless we're raiding it.'

'This is a respectable club, Sarge. See, all the poles are at least five feet from the tables, so no touching. It's just a place to unwind.'

'Have you brought Ceri here?'

'Well, no. It's a bit out of the way for us.'

Tom said nothing. Their relationship was none of his business, and if DC Hooper chose to do his unwinding in front of dancing girls, then that was Ceri's lookout. He peered at a poster. 'I see they do hen nights, with the Worcester Vikings to entertain the ladies. You'll have to get her a ticket.'

Ian turned red and shouted over to the disinfectant monitor. 'Is rehearsal on this morning?'

The lad nodded and shouted back, 'They'm just waiting for me to finish off.' He gave the last pole a vigorous rub and walked back along the stage to a glittering beaded curtain where he disappeared. The cleaner with the vacuum also finished and disappeared after offering them a cup of tea. Tom was amazed. Not only was Ian familiar with the premises, he seemed to be a regular visitor. He winced as dance music assaulted his ears, got louder and then much softer. The curtain parted, and five women walked up the stage in a line.

The first four were wearing cardigans and leg warmers above bare feet; each was carrying a pair of high heeled shoes. The fifth was carrying notebook and gave Ian a wave and a smile when she noticed him.

'All right girls, five minute warm-up, then we're going to synchronise if it kills us. I'm just going to help the police with their enquiries.'

She hopped down from the stage and gave Ian a kiss. He blushed again and introduced the woman as Erin King, resident choreographer. 'We've known each other for years,' he added.

'I can see that,' said Tom. He held out his hand, and the woman seemed surprised. 'I'm Detective Sergeant Tom Morton from Economic Crimes in London.'

'He means the Fraud Squad,' said Ian. Erin had shaken Tom's hand as if she were out of practice.

'Sorry,' said Erin. 'I thought you were off duty, Ian.'

'Hadn't you heard? I got that secondment to CID. It's Acting Detective Constable Hooper now.'

The women on stage had started to stretch and swing to the music. Tom turned around so that his back was to the dancers.

'DS Morton's come up from London to look into some counterfeit twenty pound notes,' said Ian. 'I wondered if you'd heard anything.'

'From the management here, you mean?'

'Here, there … anywhere. You know, has anyone started complaining that they've been given dodgy notes? Or have you heard anyone talking about having some for sale?'

'You mean Rob, don't you?'

'Including him, yeah, but anyone.'

The dancers on stage had all been evenly tanned on the parts that Tom could see, but Erin was much paler. Their hair was loose but hers was pulled back in a ponytail; she seemed to be about the same age as Ian – a good five or six years older than the others. When she mentioned Rob, she had placed her hands on her hips and stared up with defiance.

'I told you, Rob's clean and has been clean since he came out of prison. I know the signs better than anyone.

He hasn't touched anything stronger than dope since he was busted, and I know you're not going to persecute him for that.'

They locked eyes for a second until Ian turned to Tom and said, 'Tell her about the Essex gang: I want her to know that these people are serious villains.'

Tom gave a brief summary of the *PiCAASA* story and watched Erin's reaction. When he got to the double murder, her eyes widened and they flicked involuntarily towards the back of the club, behind the scenes. Ian's attention had been taken with the dancers and he hadn't noticed.

'So if you do hear anything,' Tom concluded, 'give Acting DC Hooper a call. I'm sure you've got his number.'

It was Erin's turn to blush. 'We was at school together. It was a small school, and everyone knew everyone else. Ian's got a proper girlfriend, you know.'

'I do know,' said Tom. 'I stayed at his flat last night. She's very nice. And so are you.'

'C'mon Tom,' said Ian. 'Erin's got a job to do.'

He practically pulled Tom away from the stage and whispered in his ear. 'She used to be married to one of the local dealers. Probably still is on paper. They had two kids before he got nicked for Class A distribution. She's one of my best sources of information, and I don't want you creeping her out.'

The cleaner appeared with two mugs of tea, and Tom was appalled at the prospect of standing around watching the rehearsals, especially because Ian was right. What was he doing flirting with this woman? He was never going to see her again, and this was most definitely not his patch. To his relief, Ian took the tray and led Tom behind the scenes to the manager's office to ask about counterfeit notes. Along the corridor, a man was leading a toddler by the hand to the outside door. Tom gently pressed Ian's arm and pointed, but the door had swung closed, and Ian couldn't see anything. Tom couldn't help wondering if he'd just spotted Rob King doing his parental duty.

The invitation had said *Party Like It's 1978!*

James King could think of no earthly reason why anyone except his mother would wish to do this. The fact that Theresa King had celebrated her eighteenth birthday in that year was a feeble excuse to make her fiftieth birthday a carbon copy of the decade that taste forgot.

'It was the night she met our dad,' said his brother when James expressed his horror at the prospect.

'I know that,' he replied, nodding his head. That made it worse.

In September 1978, the newly minted adult, Theresa Murphy, had gone out with her friends for the day to Birmingham. After some shopping, they had queued at the Odeon to see *Grease,* and then gone for Theresa's first legal drink in a pub.

None of the girls had had a camera to record what happened, but James had pieced it together over the years in conversation with his mother – starting, of course, with the music. Birmingham was awash with new sounds at that time, if you knew where to listen. Punk rock was making the headlines and reggae was coming out of Handsworth and into the mainstream; Motorhead were pioneering a new brand of heavy metal and all of these musical tribes looked down their noses at the most popular form of all – disco.

Theresa had been planning to go to the Madison nightclub after the pubs had closed, but one of her new friends from college had talked her into going to an alternative club instead. Before she was violently sick (isn't everyone on their eighteenth birthday?), the bass player from the support band at the club had given her a ticket for the Bob Marley concert at Bingley Hall in Stafford. The rest was family history.

The fiftieth birthday had been planned for some time. Theresa had pestered James to get Queen Victoria to perform – and she would have done, if he'd asked her, but when James saw the songs his mother wanted to include in the set list, he gave her a very firm *No*. Vicci was no diva, but he knew she'd draw the line at *You're the One that I Want*.

'She hasn't got that sort of voice,' he'd told his mother. 'I'll get a friend to DJ, then we can all be family together.'

Theresa had patted his cheek and moved on to other subjects; James had breathed a sigh of relief. Even his brother had seemed quite positive about the event, especially when Robert learnt that *family* meant *Hope has gone to university and isn't coming back for mother's party*.

The evening had been split in two: the first half was a chance to remember the old days. Various relatives and old school friends caught up with each other and got slightly drunk. James wasn't surprised to see Erin there with his nephews – Theresa's grandchildren. What did surprise him was how much Erin had taken Robert back into her life. They arrived looking like a family and behaved like one. What surprised him more was that Theresa – resplendent in a bouffant 1950s dress from her stall – was being squired around the room by an old rocker, complete with denim jacket.

James knew that his mother was seeing someone (and why not?), but had no idea that it was Dave Parkes, aka Dave the Rave, owner of Music & Memorabilia, a shop on the High Street. Food was served, and Theresa adjusted the seating on the table for close family to accommodate everyone. Robert seemed completely unfazed by it all.

James and Dave got up to go to the buffet at the same time, and James said hello. 'I hear your shop's doing good business,' he said.

'Not bad, thanks. There's always money in nostalgia if you get the gear right. The shop does okay, but that's almost a store room, really. I do most of my trade online.'

They loaded their plates, and James asked if he had any reggae vinyl from Solomon's era.

Dave's eyes flicked back to the family table. 'Sorry. No I haven't. I don't mind reggae, in small doses, but you have to specialise if you want to corner the market: srictly heavy rock and metal, that's my trade. It's what I grew up with, and how I got started.'

On closer inspection, Parkes looked a lot older than the image he projected. His hair was mostly white and his face was wrinkled all over. *He must be a good twelve or more years older than my mother*, thought James. 'Did you start by selling your own stuff?' he asked to try and keep the conversation going.

'Oh yes. I tried running a pub once upon a time until someone told me the posters were worth more than the rest of the fixtures put together. I had some old Robert Plant stuff from the sixties, before he joined Led Zeppelin. I surrendered the lease on the pub, and sold two of the posters for a fortune. I've enjoyed every minute since then.'

James had no interest in rock or metal, just as Parkes had no interest in reggae. He changed the subject. 'Which pub did you run?'

'Oh, you wouldn't know it. Closed down years and years ago. Are you all right for a drink? It's my round.'

James spent most of the meal talking to his grandmother and trying to explain that just because he didn't go to Mass, that didn't mean that he was a Rastafarian – nor a Muslim – and, yes, he was allowed to drink and no, he wasn't getting married any time soon. He had gone to get some more of the cheesecake when his uncle stood up and asked for silence. Theresa's brother gave a very short speech saying that their father would have been proud to see his daughter grow into such a fine woman, and would they all raise their glasses? James was about to rejoin the table when his mother stood up to speak. He stopped dead in his tracks. Why hadn't she warned him about this?

'Thanks, Tony,' she began. 'I'm not going to make a speech, really, more of an announcement. Do you like my dress?' She paused and there were cries of "Very sexy" and "Not very 1970s, is it?" from around the room. 'As you know,' she continued, 'This item and others like it are available from my stall on Earlsbury market (Audience groans). But not for much longer. It gives me great pleasure to announce that I'm going into a special partnership with my good friend Dave the Rave.'

James's mouth dropped open and he relaxed his grip on the plate so much that cream began to run from it on to the carpet. *Damnation. Double damnation. What on earth is the woman doing?* He looked around for a serviette to clean up the spillage as someone called out, 'Are you going to make an honest woman of her, Dave?'

'It's not that sort of partnership.' continued Theresa. 'Well, not yet. I am pleased to announce that David has just taken the lease on the double unit next door to Black Country Bargains. From next month, we'll be sharing the same premises and working together to create a joint online business. No more standing about in the rain.'

There was spontaneous applause and cheers from around the room; Robert seemed especially happy, for some reason. James knelt down to scrub at the carpet, and his mother finished off by announcing that the disco would begin shortly and that unfortunately, for licensing purposes, the under-eighteens would have to leave in ten minutes. Next time he looked up, she had disappeared.

He said goodbye to Erin (who took the children with her) and was searching for his mother (and Dave the Rave) when the room suddenly went dark. A spotlight from the DJ's area picked out the dance floor, and James's world lurched on its axis again. His fifty year old mother strode into the middle of the room, having been away to get changed: the dress was gone, and in its place was a pair of wet-look jeans, red shoes and an off-the-shoulder top. There was thunderous applause and the music started.

Just when James didn't think his day could get any worse, Dave the Rave appeared in a John Travolta wig.

James had chills, all right, and they appeared to be multiplying...

Tom had gone back to London over the weekend. The operation that DS Griffin had put in place on Thursday had produced some drugs, some smuggled cigarettes and a small quantity of counterfeit notes, but had taken them no nearer to finding the distributors. All suspects claimed that they had been the victims of other people's malfeasance and that they wanted their lawyers. He had been promised something bigger on Monday morning.

When he arrived at Earlsbury division, they had already made the arrest. A grubby middle-aged man was sitting in the interview room alone, with his arms folded. Tom was watching via CCTV.

'Where's his lawyer?' he asked Ian.

'This is one of Griff's top snouts,' he replied. 'We pick him up every so often with something dodgy in his possession, and then Griff puts the screws on him.'

Tom wondered whether the training course for detectives now included *The Bill* for dialogue purposes.

'What did he have today?'

'A pile of blank V5C forms from the DVLA.'

Tom remembered that there had been a big theft of vehicle registration documents. It was so big that every car in the country was being issued with a new one, but until they could be rolled out, a perfect forgery could be produced for any stolen car.

'What would he have to do before you actually charged him? Drugs? Child porn?'

Ian laughed as if Tom had made a joke and offered him a cup of coffee. Tom opted for tea, and Ian returned a few minutes later with four teas and DS Griffin. Ian handed them round, and Griff took one mug for himself and one for the man inside the interview room.

'Morning, Tom. Good journey?'

Tom nodded, and Ian left them alone. Griffin continued, 'You're the expert here, not me, but I know this witness. Don't hold back if you've got any questions, but let me start off, okay?'

'You're treating him as a witness, then?'

'Of course I am. Kelly has been registered as a CHIS on numerous occasions. All done properly when necessary, but not today, I don't think.'

There had been so many scandals about the way that the police used Confidential Human Intelligence Sources that an elaborate code of practice had been introduced. In reality, most police officers carried on as before and only filled in the additional paperwork if a significant arrest was in the offing. Inside the room, Griffin made the introductions. Tom detected a light Irish accent when the informant said hello.

'Where've you been, Mr Griffin? Haven't you kept me here for ages. I'll miss me lunch.'

'Give over moaning, Kelly. Those V5Cs could be used for all sorts of mischief. Count yourself lucky that we've stopped them falling into the wrong hands. We're doing you a favour by catching you out.'

'That's one way of putting it. I might have said something different meself.'

'Let's cut to the chase, eh? My colleague has come all the way up from London to talk to you, Kelly, so don't hold back. DS Morton, could you show him the money?'

Tom took a bunch of the counterfeit notes from his pocket and spread them in a fan on the table. There was silence while all three men stared at them. Kelly sniffed and reached out to the notes, taking one and examining it.

'You've missed the boat on this one, gentlemen.'

'What do you mean?' said Tom.

'They've gone. The guys that were selling these have moved on to pastures new.'

The two policemen looked at each other and then back at the witness. 'Tell me more,' said Griffin. 'Tell me all of it.'

'Eastern Europeans, they were. Turned up a while ago and started selling these in a couple of the bars. It was nice and easy work for us – you give them a ten pound note and they give you a twenty. So long as you're careful where you spend it, you can't go wrong.'

Tom took out his notebook and clicked his pen. Griffin took the hint and prompted Kelly to give descriptions and dates:

According to Mr Kelly (witness), two men of foreign extraction (poss. Albanian?) had appeared with counterfeit notes to sell. They had turned up occasionally over the summer, but had now moved on. One man was tall and heavy and wore a leather jacket; the other was short and did most of the talking. They would only sell a maximum of £100 at a time. They didn't appear to have any local partners.

When Tom had finished writing, Griffin took him outside. 'That fits,' he said.

'With what?'

'Haven't you checked your email since you got here?'

'No.'

'That bloke from the Bank – Jarvis – copied me into an email he's sent you. Apparently a large amount turned up in Manchester at the back end of last week. Looks like we were just too late. Sorry.'

Tom put his notebook away carefully. 'Thank you, DS Griffin. That's been very helpful. And could you pass my thanks on to DC Hooper. I think he'll fit nicely into your team: you've trained him well.'

The irony of Tom's remarks seemed lost on Griffin, who clapped him on the shoulder and promised to keep an eye out for the distributors coming back. 'That's if you haven't caught them first.'

Tom handed in his badge at reception and stood on the steps. The few shoppers on the High Street were wearing heavier coats and the older residents had already dug out their winter scarves.

It was bullshit, all of it, but Tom had no idea who the bull might be.

There was no way that some Albanian gangsters from Central Casting had started to run the distribution. Thornton's gang in Essex was 99 per cent White British (with Mina Finch as the 1 per cent). Whoever had set Thornton up in business wouldn't stray too far from what had worked the first time, but they had been tipped off. Yet again – as soon as he started to follow a lead, the thread was whipped out of his fingers. Maybe the operation had moved to Manchester, but the timing was no coincidence: as soon as Tom had arrived in Earlsbury, the money had left.

There was no way that DI Fulton would let him go further up the M6 to hunt them down. He would have to hope that South Lancs police were more on the ball than Midland Counties. He called the Holiday Inn to cancel his reservation and then called Elspeth at City Police headquarters.

'Tell the boss I'm coming back early,' he told her. 'I'll see him tomorrow morning.'

Kate's team was at a holiday cottage in Scotland which would also be their home during the operation. *It's very nice*, thought Kate, *though it might get rather cold*. Should that bother her now? Afghanistan could get *very* cold in the winter, but she wasn't a soldier any more.

It was a completely different team from the one which had taken apart the firm on Tyneside: this one was older, quieter and much more expensively dressed. Their hacker actually wore a hacking jacket: perhaps he thought it was ironic. One thing that hadn't changed was the gender balance – Kate was still the only woman.

Their previous target, in Newcastle, had been a specialist manufacturing company who wanted a security report to clear them for Defence work. The first job had been so easy that Kate had deliberately spun it out for two weeks because she wanted to do some shopping and try out a new look.

After two days' surveillance, Kate had got herself a job as a cleaner with the contractors who covered the target's offices. Their resident hacker was only nineteen, and it had taken him precisely nineteen seconds to access the computer and change the roster to put Kate on duty.

In two days, she had found several passwords, installed several snooping devices and picked up a bunch of flowers from one of the engineers who liked to work late. If he hadn't been married…

So now they were in Aberdeenshire, and Kate's new look was about to be road-tested for the first time. They had been told to unpack and unwind until fifteen hundred and then meet in the dining room. That was too long. If she'd not had time to think about it, she would have just grabbed the first thing that came to hand and gone downstairs, but with time to think, every item had been spread on the bed or hung from the chairs.

Her hair had been cut to shoulder blade length (that hurt sooo much), but she couldn't decide whether or not she was a skirt person, especially as the weather dictated thick tights. The only skirt she really liked was a tartan – everything else that suited her shape was in black, and she'd vowed only to buy one black item (which was the trousers). Was she allowed to wear a tartan skirt in Scotland? Would she look like a div? She texted Diana, the only civilian she knew well enough to ask:

K: Can I wear Tartan skirt in Aberdeen? Shd I stick to trsrs?
D: Send pic of skirt
K: Sorry. No camera on phone. Long Story. Trsrs make me look like army dyke
D: Go naked or wear jeans on first date
K: Am at work not on date
D: Trsrs + heels. Don't argue.

It was ten to three. Kate spent five minutes walking up and down the room in her only pair of heels and then changed into her jeans.

The reason why Patrick Lynch went to jail for the first time was because he had been caught red-handed with the stolen goods. After that mishap, he tried to make sure other people handled the goods, and he was very careful about using the telephone. The trouble is, when you're running a business people have to be able to get in touch. On Earlsbury Market, it was easy. They would come up to him, have a chat and place their orders: he knew everything about everyone that way.

Although he still owned two market stalls and visited often, Patrick had to find other ways of doing business. One of them was Dermot. The lad was going to take over the business one day so it was in his best interests to make it as successful as possible – and not to double-cross the old man. His other means of keeping in touch was the golf course. It wasn't as good as being back on the market, but it was the next best thing.

His opponent today was a property developer who liked cash business, and Patrick always had a bet with him. There was a third person on the greens with them, but he wasn't a good enough golfer to join in. Like Patrick, Griff enjoyed his golf, but didn't have the time to practise properly. Not only that, Griff had joined the club under a false name and never went in the clubhouse. A man in Griff's position couldn't be seen associating with a convicted criminal.

Patrick had a thing about the number thirteen, and rarely played that hole well. Griff said that it had nothing to do with luck and everything to do with the slope on the green.

The property developer had already played straight and long down the fairway. Before Patrick could place his own tee, Griff stood in the way.

'Fifty quid says that I can beat you on this one.'

'I wouldn't take your money, Griff. It may hurt your pride, but I'm a better golfer than you.'

'I know, but this is number thirteen. Fifty quid says I'll beat you by one stroke. A hundred if either of us wins by two strokes: bet's off for a draw.'

Patrick was about to argue when his phone rang. Only Dermot and Fran were allowed to interrupt the game: he saw his nephew's name on the screen so he took the call.

'Make it quick. I'm about to take a hundred quid off DS Griffin. The man doesn't know when he's beaten.'

Griff could hear every word and shouted, 'Tell the old man to quit, Dermot.'

'What is it?' asked Patrick.

'I've just had a message from Red Hand. He said that because the next delivery is going to be so large, he wants additional security. All types of security – including Griff to head off any other police interest.'

'That's good timing. Thanks.'

Patrick ended the call and looked at Griff. 'If I let you win this hole, will you do an extra job for me?'

'What's that?'

'I've done what you asked. I've cut out all distribution of counterfeit notes in Earlsbury but we're still acting as wholesalers. I need your help keeping an eye on a transhipment in a couple of weeks.'

'No.'

'Obviously, you'd be in for a cut of the proceeds.'

'No. If you're going to branch out, fine, but it's nothing to do with me. Now are we playing this hole or not?'

It's all about connections, thought Patrick. Griff is under the impression that he has a choice in this matter, but there's a man who knows different. Whoever Red Hand was connected to would have a word with someone else. Patrick didn't know who that was, but he was fairly confident that someone would have a word with Griff in due course.

Patrick placed his tee and addressed the ball. He relaxed his shoulders and looked at the distant flag on the green. Then he raised his club for the swing and gave it his best shot.

Mina was spending some quality time with her new jaw. She could go out on to the wing and talk to the other prisoners, but she liked to spend time after lunch feeling her way around the stitches with her tongue, testing their strength and pushing into the firmness underneath. For years she had kept her tongue out of the right side of her mouth, but now it could go where it liked. There would be plenty of time for talking later.

When she was sentenced, her barrister had said, 'Don't think of it as four years. Think of it as eighteen to twenty-four months.'

That was good advice, but it didn't help. Mina was still in prison and she wasn't going anywhere for a long time. Good God, she would be getting on for *thirty* when she was released.

The tannoy announced the start of visiting, and she wrapped one of her two scarves around her face. They were plain but soft; nothing that might stir up jealousy among her sisters in crime. Four gates and two sets of searches later, she was admitted to the family room.

As each prisoner was admitted, one more table would become complete, and their heads would turn away from watching the door.

Her brother had said he would visit, 'The next time I'm in England, okay?' So not at all, in other words. Her father and her other brother were ashes in the Ganges; her mother had disowned her when she married Miles, so there was only one person who could visit her: the priest.

'How are you bearing up, little one?'

The old man embraced her gently to protect her face, but she buried it into his shoulder and sobbed until one of the officers separated them. While she dried her tears and rearranged the scarf, the priest talked of nothing and made observations about the other families.

'Tell me, little fish, is the large lady over there also newly arrived?'

Mina glanced over and looked away. It was not a good idea to make eye contact with Shelley. 'No, she's one of the longest serving. Don't ask what for.'

'I see. It's just that her hair is so black, I assumed that she must be new. Surely it would go grey in here?'

'They let us dye it, you know, but there's a limited range of colours. You can't go wrong with midnight black. Suits me well enough. I might get new teeth in January ... if I'm good.'

'Ganesha is watching you. And so is someone else.'

His eyebrows rose and fell with a smile, and he went to the senior officer, who handed over a package. Crossing back over the room, Mina realised just how old he really was; the limp had become more pronounced since they had last met.

'Have you been to the doctor, Baba-ji?'

'I am not your father, Mina. You must not forget him or try to replace him. You can call me uncle, if you wish. That's what I put on the visiting order.'

'Have you been to the doctor, *Uncle-ji*?'

'Yes. He says I need a new hip. So there. Now, I have two presents for you. You must promise to read both of them properly.'

'I promise.'

The priest, Mr Joshi, handed the package go Mina, but only after removing a folded piece of paper and putting it in his pocket. He gestured at the package. 'Look at this while I get us some tea.'

Mina would have saved him the pain of walking to the hatch, but only visitors were allowed to have money. She opened the package and a stonking great book tumbled into her hand – a well-thumbed copy of the *Mahabharata*.

Great. She'd been tricked into giving her promise to read the longest holy book in the world. Her mother said that was her biggest problem – twisting older men around her little finger to get things from them and then doing whatever they asked in return. Mother had been thinking about her father when she said that, but it could apply equally to Miles or the priest. She was turning the pages when he returned with two teas.

'I expect you to have read many pages before my next visit. I will ask questions.'

Mina looked up, and he met her eyes. He was very rarely serious, but when he was, Mina could feel something tingling in her face. She looked down. 'Yes, Guru-ji.'

'Good. Now for your other present.'

The folded piece of paper reappeared, and he handed it over. It was the printout from a website called *The IPL Review – Full Scorecards and Analysis*. It was full of details from cricket matches. She turned it over and looked again. Two of the scorecards were in a slightly different layout. What had Conrad said about *developing an interest in cricket*?

'That young man of yours is very clever.'

'He's not my man and he's not so young. That's part of the problem.'

'From a great distance, two points may seem close together. When you get to my age, everyone under fifty is young. He's definitely yours, though, and he's definitely clever.'

Mina remembered one of the few details about Conrad's family that he had let slip: his mother worked for GCHQ. Was there a code somewhere here?

'I see that you've already spotted that he has altered two of the scorecards. Starting with chapter thirteen, look at the batsman's score – then count in that number of words. The next game is chapter fourteen. The messages won't be long, or frequent, but I'll bring them in when I can. I'm afraid there's no mechanism for you to reply. Yet.'

It was thrilling, but Mina didn't know whether she wanted to be thrilled or not. Conrad was ten years older than her. Was she repeating the same cycle again? Whether she was or not, if Conrad's letters meant that Mr Joshi would keep visiting her then she was all in favour of it. Even if it did mean reading the *Mahabharata*.

She stood up and kissed the old man.

'Last warning, Mina,' said the officer. 'Next time you touch him, you'll be sent back to the cells.'

Chapter 5

Earlsbury / London / Aberdeen
Wednesday / Thursday / Friday
20-22nd October

When Patrick, Fran and Elizabeth had arrived for the St Modwenna's parents' evening, there was a large sign in the foyer which said:

Parents and Girls must switch their mobile phones OFF inside the school.

Typical of St Modwenna's, thought Patrick. Although his middle daughter was ten years older than Elizabeth, when she had gone to the local Catholic comprehensive they had always referred to *Parents & Guardians*, and the kids were always *Students*. That's what he was getting for his money – a school which expected their girls to have both parents still in tow, and if there had been a messy divorce along the way, you were expected to turn up together.

His money was also buying access to the beautiful Victorian buildings, small class sizes, fast track to Oxbridge (could his daughter really go to Oxford?) and the habit of mixing with girls whose parents would never otherwise have anything to do with him.

'I haven't seen Pandora round the house since your birthday,' he said to Elizabeth. Fran gave him a sharp look and Lizzie looked down at the parquet floor.

'Have you had a falling-out or something?'

'I don't think they ever had a falling-in,' said Fran, coming to her daughter's rescue.

'Mom's right,' said Lizzie. 'She more-or-less invited herself to the party when she heard that I was getting the Twilight DVD.'

'Let me guess,' said Patrick. 'Ever since then she's been embarrassed to have known you.'

Lizzie's face turned crimson, and Fran gave her husband a sharp dig in the ribs. Patrick leaned down and whispered to his daughter. 'She's a stuck-up bitch, that one. You're worth ten times what she is. Now, let's see the appointments list.'

He was rewarded with a half smile from his daughter, and he was pleased to see that her eyes were dry. He would be very worried if she cried over someone like Pandora Nechells. He scanned the list of appointments with Lizzie's teachers.

'Now aren't you the smart one?' he said.

'What d'you mean, Dad?'

'We start with PE, Scripture and ICT, and then move swiftly through maths, science and technology before the humanities ... and then art, Latin and English to finish. Now would that be the exact order of your place in class, by any chance? Bottom in PE and top in English?'

'It's a fair cop.'

'What have I told you? If you want to be a chip off the old block, never confess to anything unless there's a deal on the table.'

'I think she's aiming a bit higher than being a chip off the old block,' said Fran stiffly.

'Right. Where's the dreaded Miss Jackson? In the gym?'

Shortly later, Lizzie was trying to explain to her mother about not getting on with Mrs Soames the science teacher, but Patrick wasn't listening. Miss John, the head of maths, had tugged at his sleeve following a perfectly satisfactory report delivered in front of Fran and Lizzie. She had told Patrick that she believed Lizzie to have great potential in maths, but that she was refusing to show it.

'None of her friends are mathematicians, I think, and she's just not willing to show them up,' Miss John had concluded.

He was still mulling this over when his pocket vibrated. He never turned his phone off on principle, especially if it were a school rule. He glanced at the display then took the call.

'Make it quick, Dermot. I'm at St Mod's.'

'There's been a cock-up. The shipment's already here, and I haven't told Blackpool. They're on their way down but it will be a couple of hours. We need Griff onside. When will you be free?'

'I can't. This goes on for another two hours at least, and then I have to get back to Earlsbury. You can handle it, son. I'll sort Griff out. Let me know how you get on.'

He had been given a mobile number. He wasn't allowed to call it, just text. From the entrance to the science labs, Fran and Lizzie were giving him evil looks, and Patrick put the phone back in his pocket. He didn't get a chance to text the number until the queue for the history teacher gave him a chance to slip away.

Red Hand had assured him that if he texted the time and place of the handover to that number, the person on the other end would ensure that DS Griffin turned up to keep an eye on things.

The first thing that Ian Hooper had done when Angela Lindow cleared her desk was to find himself a new chair. Occupational Health had provided her with something suitable for a heavily pregnant woman and they had beaten him into the office on Monday morning to take it back; Ian had to make do with a cast-off from the civilians. He filled out a request for his own chair and emailed it to Resources.

The second thing he did was start to work through her bulging in-tray.

By Wednesday evening he was bushed. Ceri was preparing something for school which involved witches hats (Halloween, apparently), and all he wanted to do was watch the football on TV.

'Will it disturb you?' he asked.

'I'd rather you watched it here than go down the pub. At least I can keep an eye on you that way.'

Ian raised an eyebrow at her and settled down for the warm up. Ten minutes later she passed him a roll of Sellotape and some scissors. Manchester United had taken an early lead against some Turkish team, and Ian found the problem of turning square paper into conical hats to be more interesting than the game. While he was getting another beer, his mobile rang. It was Griff.

'Ian, can you get in now?'

'What's up, Sarge?'

'Can you come in? There's something on.'

'Yeah, sure. I'll be there in ten.'

'Make it five.'

He gave Ceri a kiss and picked up his coat. Their flat was less than ten minutes' walk from the police station, and Ian jogged most of it. Griff was waiting by the main entrance. Ian could smell the drink on his breath from several feet away; knowing Griff, he'd probably been watching the same match as Ian.

'Are you okay to drive?' asked Griffin.

Ian nodded, and Griff jerked his head towards the back of the station. In the car park, he handed over the keys to his private car (a very nice BMW). Ian hesitated for a second. 'You haven't brought me out to give you a lift home, have you?'

'Don't be stupid,' said Griffin. 'Something's come up. Get in and drive us to Sharrow Road.'

Definitely not home, then. Sharrow Road was a mixture of old houses and half demolished factories out towards

Dudley – under the M5. Neither spoke until Ian had turned off the main road.

'I've had a tip-off that something might be happening in the old goods yard. We're going to do a spot of surveillance.'

Ian pulled up the car. 'Do you mean the Great Western Yard? That's over the other side, isn't it?'

'Yes, and it's huge. There's nowhere we can observe from over there so we're going to watch from this side. You can go down Raleigh Street. It's on the right.'

The terraced houses gave way to a couple of small factories and then a gap where one unit had been pulled down. Just after that, the last streetlight was broken, and before the road disappeared into a dead end, there was a small turning on the right between two blank faced structures. Ian turned into the opening and drove down at walking pace. After two hundred yards, the street ended at a small lane running cross ways. On the other side of the lane was a stout metal fence with razor wire on top.

'Lights off,' said Griffin. 'I'm going to go in and see what's happening.'

'Where do you want me?'

'Here. You can't be too careful these days – it's my car you're driving, and I don't want some tosser coming along and breaking in.'

Ian looked around the deserted street. The chance of anyone else coming here was remote in the extreme.

'Pop the boot, will you?' said Griffin. 'It's a handle just by your right calf. The big one.'

Ian felt down and there were two levers by his leg. He pulled the bigger one and there was a subdued thunk from behind. Griff got out of the car and went round the back. The fresh air blew away some of the beer fumes, and Ian realised how cold it was outside. He fiddled with the controls until he could lower the driver's window. There was a louder slam as Griff closed the boot and came back with something wrapped in a blanket.

'Are you sure there's backup for this?' Ian asked.

'Already in place. I'm just there for observation. You look after the car, and I won't forget this. I'll owe you one, big time'

Griff pulled up the hood on his waterproof coat and crossed the lane to the fence. He peered through the gaps in the metal and then went along to his right. Ian's eyes were adjusting to the darkness, and he saw a gate set into the fence.

They were at the back end of the old Great Western Railway Goods Yard. The trains had stopped running there before Ian was born (except for the through line to Stourbridge), and the site had become first a warehouse, then a distribution depot, and finally a white elephant. The railway goods depot had been squeezed into a gap between the tracks and the canal. The main entrance required waggons to cross a hump-back bridge. When lorry weights exceeded thirty-two tonnes, the bridge had been declared unsafe, and the haulage company moved to somewhere more accessible. The site was now awaiting redevelopment (when someone paid for a new bridge).

He looked back over his shoulder. There was a clump of terraced houses that were seemingly built at random, like many of the houses in the Black Country. All over the area, houses had been built to serve coal mines, small furnaces and other centres of employment. Often, town centres like Earlsbury had seen little growth during the Victorian period because the action was elsewhere, near the mines and foundaries. These houses, off Sharrow Road, had been built by the Great Western Railway, giving the workers their own entrance to the goods yard. It was only when you dug deeper that a pattern emerged. It had been his special project for A level geography – growth and development in South Staffordshire.

By the time Ian had finished recalling his geography project, Griff had disappeared through the gate. Very carefully, Ian got out of the car and went up to the fence.

He could see nothing inside except a long shed with another to its left, end-on. Griff had already disappeared. A small plop of rain hit his face, and a gust of wind blew down the lane. Ian shrugged and returned to the car.

When the rain started sluicing down the windscreen, he became completely isolated. With nothing else to do, he fiddled with his new toy – an iPhone 4. According to the BBC, there had been no further score at Old Trafford. One day, he supposed, you would be able to watch live games on your phone. But not yet.

He was about to send a text message to Ceri when he saw lights to his right. Another vehicle was coming along the lane behind the factories and approaching the gate into the goods yard. He had parked Griff's car quite a bit back from the road end, and the oncoming vehicle stopped short. They hadn't seen him. Ian left the car and ducked over to the corner. Peering round, he saw the lights go off and the engine died. A man got out and tried the gate, clearly expecting it to be locked. When it opened easily, the man went back to the car and lifted the boot.

An automatic light came on and shone into the man's face. Ian recognised Robert King, bending down to find something; Robert stood up and stood back. In his left hand was a gun.

King closed the boot and was gone through the gate while Ian was still taking it in. His boss was inside the compound, and behind him was a man with a gun. Ian knew that whatever was going on tonight was unofficial. No police officer goes on a surveillance operation without a radio and without telling Control where he is. The problem for Ian was deciding just how unofficial the action was. It could be unauthorised unofficial – police business without police procedures. Or it could be illegal unofficial – something that Griff was doing all on his own.

It took Ian about five seconds to decide that calling for backup was going to get both of them in trouble and get him in trouble with Griff. He also decided not to ring Griff – if his boss was in a concealed position, giving away his location could be fatal. Ian had picked up his baton from the hallway at home and dropped it on the back seat of the car. He went back to collect it then followed Griff and Robert King through the gate.

He cut round the corner of a shed and along its short side. It was darker here, and he could only just make out the end. He edged along and crouched down to peer round the corner. There was a short space and then a gap in the buildings: from inside that gap he could see lights but could hear nothing because of the rain.

A shape separated itself from the darkness and went out of sight into the gap. It was Robert King. Ian started to cross towards the building, then he heard voices shouting. Out of the light came a figure he didn't recognise: a man in a green coat, hood up, running for his life.

Ian snapped open his baton and caught the man on his shins, sending him flying into some long grass. Ian landed on top and whispered into his ear.

'Police. What's going on in there?'

'Some fucker's gone mental with a gun.'

He had his baton and his warrant card, but Ian didn't have the other equipment he was accustomed to carrying on the beat. No radio, of course, and no handcuffs or taser. He didn't recognise the man under the Manchester United hat, but surely, if there was something nasty happening, then the guy must have a criminal record.

'Take cover but don't go very far,' he said, and took his weight off the man's back.

Ian started to move along the wall and then he saw Griff reveal himself.

When his boss emerged into the light, Ian could see him holding up his baton with his coat wrapped round the handle. It looked a bit like a gun, he supposed. Ian took two steps closer to the corner, and he could see the side of a white van with its lights on. Robert King was standing in front of it, pointing his gun at someone else, off to the right.

'Armed police! Drop your weapon.' shouted Griffin.

Whether King thought the baton was a gun or whether he just panicked, Ian didn't know. Either way, the result was the same. Rob turned on his heel and shot straight at Griff. One round in the body. His boss collapsed.

King turned back towards the gap. While he had been shooting at Griff, whoever he'd previously been pointing the gun at had disappeared. He looked wildly around and realised he was trapped between the van and the warehouse, fully illuminated by the headlamps. Ian could see panic twisting his face.

'Put your gun down, Son,' came a voice from beyond the van. It was not Tactical Seven.

Robert King ducked and ran round the van and started to head towards Ian. Should he try to trip him like he tripped the other bloke? Rugby tackle? No, if Robert was going to shoot him, he wanted it to be a deliberate act. Ian stepped out of the shadows.

'Robbie! It's me, Ian Hooper.'

King stopped in his tracks and stared, but he didn't shoot. From round the corner of the van came a stocky man in a balaclava. He took one look at them and raised a rifle with a curving magazine. Just before he opened fire, Ian recognised it as an AK47.

'Robbie. Duck!' he shouted and started to dive away to his left, but it was too late. Robbie pitched forwards, and Ian felt like he'd been kicked in the guts by a prop forward.

He tried to breathe, but all was pain. Pain in his chest, pain in his legs, but above all, pain in his guts. He curled up and it got a little easier, and he dragged in a breath. Then another. He knew his biology. He knew that endorphins were doing their best, but they wouldn't last long. He had a few moments to get help before shock and pain took over, and his brain shut down to deal with the trauma. He reached into his pocket for his phone and tried to swipe it into action. All of a sudden, his fingers were swollen like black puddings, and the icons on the screen meant nothing.

And then a hand reached down and took it off him. More hands rolled him on to his back and lifted his coat. Something was pressed into his stomach.

'Can you hear me, Son?' It was the same voice as before, the one that told Robbie to put down the gun. Ian groaned.

'Don't go to sleep on me now, will you? Are you there?'

'Shit,' was all Ian could manage.

'Good. We'll call an ambulance for you when we've gone, but you need to know something. Wake up.'

'Oh shit, shit, shit.'

'Better. Now listen here, PC Hooper. We know where you live. We know which school your wee girlie teaches at and we know your mother's phone number. So if you live, you're going to have a terrible memory. Terrible. You remember nothing. Got that? You especially don't remember that twat Robert King.'

The message got through to Ian all right. So did the man's Irish accent. To reinforce the message, the Irishman slapped him hard on the face.

'Let's hear you. Do you understand?'

'I understand. Now get lost and call me an ambulance.'

'Good.'

Ian felt the Irishman take his hand. He tried to pull away from the grip but his strength was going. The man guided Ian's hand to where the pain was worst. He could feel fabric.

'Press down, son. Press down as hard as you can and you might make it.'

Ian rolled to his left and pressed on the fabric, trying to hold himself together.

In the background, engines started, and then it went dark. He focused on the pain. If he could think about the pain it would give him strength enough to hold on. Hold on to the compress and hold on to life. He gripped himself and that made it hurt worse. He gripped tighter.

The parents' evening had gone very well in the end. When Patrick was Lizzie's age, no one at *his* school was fighting to get him in their O Level groups. The school and Patrick had both known that he'd be leaving at the age of fifteen, and they put him on the General Course in fourth form.

It was called Year 10 now, and everyone did GCSEs. There wasn't a lot of choice in the matter, but the geography, history and Latin teachers were all fighting to have his daughter in their class. The English teacher had almost purred with pleasure and predicted great things for her.

He was worried about the maths, though. On the way back to Earlsbury, Fran and Elizabeth had chatted about a trip to Birmingham they were planning for next weekend, and Patrick had mulled over the fact that his daughter would rather do just okay at maths than be seen to leave her friends behind. He was also thinking about Dermot.

The boys from Blackpool should have been and gone by now, but he had heard nothing. There was a lot of money at stake here – Dermot had agreed a deal for two million pounds in counterfeit twenties, which meant collecting eight hundred thousand in exchange, all to be laundered in a hurry.

Back home, Fran went into the kitchen to make them all some supper, and Elizabeth went to change out of her uniform. Patrick had difficulty swallowing the sandwiches, and he could feel his chest starting to tighten. When Lizzie went to bed, Fran took his hand.

'Are you alright? Is something going on?'

'It's been a long day, love. Could you get me a tablet and some water?'

As his wife went into the kitchen, Patrick's phone rang, showing an unknown number.

'There's been a problem. The van will be in the Wrekin Road lock-up tomorrow morning. Deal with it properly.'

Before he could ask any questions, the caller disconnected. Patrick tried calling Dermot's number. It was switched off. The caller's voice had been northern English, male and obviously under some strain. Fran was standing in the doorway with a glass in one hand and the other cupping a tablet.

'I think I might need your help in the morning,' said Patrick.

Francesca had lain in bed and listened to her husband pacing around downstairs. At two o'clock she had made him take a mild sedative and lie down on the couch to avoid putting even more strain on his heart. Fran herself had only dropped off to sleep at about four.

She put on the usual brave face in the morning. Last night's rain had left the air feeling damp, and she had had terrible trouble with the straighteners. Then she had to face a bleary-eyed daughter who was in danger of missing the train and demanding a lift to Stourbridge.

The deadline for the train was five past eight, and Elizabeth made it out of the door with thirty seconds to spare. Patrick had surfaced from the couch and gone upstairs to shower leaving Fran to catch her breath in the kitchen with a cup of coffee.

Her husband went up in a rumpled suit but came down looking like he was dressed for gardening. She gave him a level stare.

'What's going on?'

'I don't know,' he replied. 'Dermot was on a job last night and I can't get hold of him. Can you come with me to Wrekin Road?'

'What's on Wrekin Road, for goodness' sake?'

Fran knew that much of Patrick's business was carried on in hiding, but Wrekin Road had never been mentioned before: it was a name she hadn't heard since she was a girl, when her father worked there in a foundry. The road had been cut in half a long time ago by one of the motorways; the grimy, smoky building where her dad had spent two thirds of his life was pulled down overnight to be buried and forgotten.

'I just need a lift there. You'll still be in time for work.'

'There's no rush. I don't have to be anywhere until ten o'clock, and it's only Dudley. I want to see you eat something healthy first.'

'Of course, love.'

Fran made him a cup of tea, and Patrick ate his way mechanically through some muesli and yogurt. She made sure he had taken his morning medication, and went to get changed herself.

Fran had failed her eleven-plus and anyway, her parents wanted her to go to the Catholic school in Earlsbury rather than the state grammar in Dudley. In those days, 'careers' were for girls who went to university; the likes of Francesca Whelan had a choice of office work or factory work, and after seeing what her father's factory was like, she enrolled at the Tech for shorthand and typing.

They did placements at the college, and Fran was introduced to a vast barn of a room full of women and typewriters: the typing pool. Was it any wonder, then, that when she visited the market one day, and Patrick Lynch asked her out for a drink, that she said *Yes Please*? She could see through his patter all right, she could see that he might be trouble one day (and he was), but he had a good heart and he loved all three of his daughters.

Well, he loved all *four* of his daughters, of course, and Hope King was always going to be there in the background. Maybe it was the strain of being nice to so many women that had put him in hospital. Patrick's real heart, the one in his chest, hadn't been so steady.

It was partly worry about his health and partly boredom that drove Fran back to work. Her older daughters had taught her a lot about computers, and she was ready for it. What she hadn't realised was that the tech revolution had led to a shortage of skilled shorthand-takers. Digital recording machines were all very well, but nothing beat having a smart woman in the room who could get everything down and produce the transcript by the end of the day. Fran was in demand.

She went downstairs to find that Patrick had moved his Jaguar off the drive and was in the garage, changing the number plates on her car. Her Ford Fiesta was the most common car on the road, and Patrick kept a series of false registrations in a drawer. Every time he needed to travel without leaving a trace on the vehicle cameras, he put on a different set of numbers. This was the first time that he'd made her go with him, though.

He told her to pull into a lay-by before they hit the first camera.

'Put your hair up and slip this on,' he said. In his hand was a baseball cap.

'You're joking.'

'I wish I was. Pull the peak down.'

'If someone gets a good picture through the windscreen, they'll be looking for a woman in a Jaeger suit and a Wolves cap. There aren't many of them.'

'You're right. I've got this as well,' he said, reaching into the back seat.

Fran muttered at him under her breath but put on the padded training jacket he gave her. It made her feel like the Michelin man. Looking like that, she was more worried that one of her friends would see her, and she took every detour she could think of. When she crossed over the Smethwick Road, she could see several police cars heading north, and she lingered at the junction until they were long gone. In ten minutes they were turning into Wrekin Road and Patrick hadn't said a word.

Two hundred yards ahead, the road ended in concrete blocks and a motorway fence. There was a shabby building on the right, and Patrick told her to drive round the back.

'Dad used to work in the foundry up there,' she said, pointing to the motorway.

'Dirty, horrible place,' said Patrick.

'It was, but he got a good living out of it.'

'He got arthritis and tinnitus as well. Drop me by those doors and you get off home and change the number plates before you go to Dudley.'

The front of the building had a disintegrating sign for Earlsbury Double Glazing, and around the back was a workshop with roller shutter doors. Glass was strewn over the small car park except for a section in front of the doors which had been swept clean. There were a lot of nooks and crannies like this in Earlsbury as businesses grew and moved on or faltered and died. If this recession ever ended, someone would put up a new building here and start all over again.

Patrick got out and walked towards the doors and looked over his shoulder to make sure Fran had left. She started to drive round towards the front, but stopped, counted to ten and reversed back. When she came in sight of the doors, Patrick was looking at the back of a van inside the workshop. Boxes and some pallets full of cigarette cartons were stacked around it. Fran put the car in first gear and gave one last glance at her husband.

He was staggering away from the open van doors. He turned towards her, clutching his chest then took a couple of steps before collapsing on to the floor.

Fran killed the engine and dashed over to him. He was still breathing, but it came in short shallow gulps, and he was going into shock.

'Pat, where's your pills?'

She shook his shoulder roughly. This wasn't the first time she'd found him like this, and it was quite simple – if he took a nitro pill he'd be okay. If he didn't, there probably wouldn't be time for an ambulance. She felt his pocket and came up with an empty packet. He'd put the wrong one into his old clothes. She knew there were none in her car so that left the warehouse or the van.

Fran jogged towards the doorway as best she could in her heels, checking the ground for obstructions and not looking up until she was almost on top of the van. Her stomach punched up towards her throat, and she heaved – but held on to her breakfast – turning away from the van and trying to take deep breaths.

Spread out in the back of the van were two bodies, one white and one black.

She looked back at Patrick. There was no way that she was going to let him die now, the useless bastard. No way was she going to deal with that mess on her own. She slammed one of the van doors closed and worked along the side. There was a small area at the back with an empty workbench. Nothing. A door led through into the main building, and she stuck her head through into a storeroom with more crates. At the end she could see another door into an office – it was in there or in the van and she didn't want to touch the van again.

In the office, she started tossing jars and packets aside to look for medication. Tea, coffee, milk powder and sugar spilled over the floor and there, behind a Christmas biscuit tin was a curled up strip of tablets. She grabbed it and felt the blisters. One left.

The effect on Patrick was almost instantaneous as the nitroglycerin dilated his arteries and allowed blood to flow round his lungs. His shoulders relaxed, and he started to breathe more easily. She stepped back from him and realised that she was panting and sweating worse than the man on the floor having an angina attack. She peeled off the padded coat and put it on top of him. Patrick started to cry.

'Jesus, Mary and Joseph, Patrick. What in God's Name has happened?'

He rolled on to his side and levered himself into a sitting position, clutching the coat around him.

'It's Dermot. The bastards have killed him. Oh my God, Fran, what am I going to do?'

Fran couldn't help but look back at the van. Dermot! Patrick had been so relaxed lately – business seemed to be going so well. Another realisation hit her.

'Who's the other one with him?'

'Robbie King.'

A shiver ran all the way down her spine, and she could feel cold sweat on the nape of her neck. Theresa King was a dirty slapper, but she didn't deserve this. Even Dermot's useless mother didn't deserve this.

'How do I get the doors down?'

'What?'

'How do I lower the shutters? We're going home.'

'I can't. I can't leave them there.'

'Yes, you can. No one else is coming, are they?'

'No, but…'

'But nothing. I'm taking you home and going to work. We can deal with this later.'

Patrick said nothing, and she waited. A small breeze found its way through her suit, and she could feel the blouse sticking to her back as it dried. She looked down and saw that there were stains on her skirt and a ladder in her tights. She would have to get changed as well. Patrick looked up at her.

'There's a box on the left hand wall, outside the doors,' he said. 'Press the red button and wait until the shutters are down then take the key out.'

She lowered the shutters and blocked out the sight inside. Patrick had climbed to his feet, and she held his arm as he got in the car. His face was as grey as her suit.

On the way home, she spotted two more police cars and she turned on the local news. The reporter said that a body had been discovered at the old Goods Yard, and that a man was critically injured in hospital. More killing? She looked across at Patrick. He had gone from grey to white.

She gritted her teeth and helped him inside the house. Thank God the next door neighbours were away and the one across the road was at work. She rooted through Patrick's medication and found a stronger sedative. He didn't ask what it was as she gave him a glass of water to wash it down. He just lay on the couch and slipped into a deep sleep. Fran got changed and took the Jaguar to Dudley.

The details on the morning news were sketchy – a shooting near Birmingham. Tom barely noticed it, and when his local news for London came on, it was all about Arnold Schwarzenegger's visit. He went to work.

There was a substantial fraud case on Tom's desk which DI Fulton had given to him on Monday morning. Sitting next to the file were the final papers from Caroline's solicitor. All he had to do was sign them and drop them through the firm's letter box: two weeks later he would be divorced. She had tried one last time to get him to take on some of the negative equity in the Guildford property, but he had stood firm, especially when his father had heard about it. He blamed Diana for telling him.

If he signed the papers, he would be consigning several years of his life to the box marked *failure*. His mother had tried to get him to see the positive side – *Weren't you happy with Carrie at first? Didn't she change your life? Remember that, Tom, and forget the last year.*

He pushed the divorce papers aside and opened the fraud case. With one finger on the list of names, he started to transfer the information to a spreadsheet. This was the seed from which his investigation would grow – addresses, aliases, bank accounts, company records, wire transfers and land registry entries would all be painstakingly added as his team built up a picture of the suspects' financial position.

After an hour, he had entered the same name four times because he couldn't concentrate. He looked from the screen to the divorce papers and back again. Did he really have anything to thank her for? He had been making a good name for himself in Edgbaston and was already on the ladder to a partnership at the firm of solicitors. Then Caroline had been retained as a junior barrister for one of his clients.

Her boss was a well-known silk who had breezed up from London as if he were visiting the colonies. On the first day of the hearing, Tom and Caroline had been forced to smother their giggles when he described Birmingham as a Great Northern City that would benefit from his client's inspiring designs for regeneration. Tom spent that night in her hotel room, and two weeks later she turned up at the office Christmas party.

He still shivered at the memory of her coming towards him and leaning over the table. 'Dance, Tom,' she had said. Then she grabbed him by the tie and pulled him on to the dance floor while the senior partners stared at how short her skirt was. That night she had asked him what he wanted to get from being a lawyer.

'To help people find justice. To be on their side,' he replied.

She wagged a finger at him. 'Wrong job, Tom, wrong job. You should be a copper. The way you represented that shyster made it very clear that you didn't believe a word he said. If you can't fake it, get out before it's too late. With your background, you'll be in CID in no time.'

And here he was at the Economic Crime Unit, putting numbers into a spreadsheet, about to be divorced and living in a hired box.

By lunchtime, the Midlands shooting had become the death of one police officer, and the location had moved from 'near Birmingham' to 'Earlsbury'. A second police officer was in a critical condition. There had been no arrests and Tom was taking a closer interest.

He liked to get out of the office every day, at least once. Most of his colleagues ate in the canteen, but Tom liked to get out. The canteen food was okay, but there were so many options if you were willing to experiment. Within ten minutes' walk of the station he could sample food from more countries than he had even heard of.

Tom signed the divorce papers and put them in his overcoat pocket before heading out into the rain. Unless the sewers backed up, the City always smelled fresher when it was raining. He breathed deeply and cut through between two office blocks. He could drop the papers at Caroline's solicitor and pick up something from Taste of Scandinavia to remind him of Ingrid. Carrie would call it wallowing, but he preferred to think of it as ironic counterpoint.

The trees in the square beyond were losing their leaves, but people still sheltered under them, mostly smoking. Tom was about to give them a wide berth when one of the group called out to him. He looked up to see a couple huddling together for shelter under the man's umbrella. The woman had her hand around the man's waist, inside his coat. It was Caroline and Nikolai.

He marched up to them and fished out the papers. Before she could object, he stuffed them into her half open handbag. 'That'll save me a trip,' he said.

Nikolai had taken two steps back and turned round to light a cigarette, withdrawing the protection of his umbrella from Caroline. She tried to hand the papers back to him, but he stuffed his hands in his pockets.

'Stop behaving like a spoilt child, Tom. These need to go to my solicitor, and you need a receipt.'

She was right. Only an adolescent would do something like that but he was tired of being grown up. 'Not my problem. If you lose them, It's no skin off my nose.'

'For God's sake. Oh, all right, it's on my way. Why you couldn't have got your own lawyer to handle it, I have no idea.'

'Because I *am* a lawyer. Why should I buy a dog when I can bark myself? And bite.'

She laughed. 'You can take the boy out of Yorkshire, but you can't take Yorkshire out of the boy. You Mortons are all tight-fisted.'

Is that how she saw him? A boy to be pushed aside when a man like Nikolai came along? She looked around the square and pointed to an anonymous glass building. 'You'll have to take a different short-cut if you want to stop bumping into me,' she said. 'Nikolai's office is up there.'

'I'll make a note of that. In case my colleagues need to visit him.'

'Grow up, Tom. You've got what you wanted. A clean break so you can get on with what you call a life – cooking dinners for your sister, taking your cousin out for dates, catching sweaty men who hide VAT money under the mattress. It obviously gives you a great deal of satisfaction.'

'Thank you.'

'What for?'

'For reminding me why I became a copper. I'd almost forgotten.'

He turned and walked back to the office, hungry and burning with embarrassment.

Fran didn't know whether or not she was in shock. The pace of the meeting was fast, and once she'd got the first few lines down in shorthand, she'd had to concentrate so hard her hand stopped shaking. When the chairman closed the meeting and invited all the Members to lunch, Fran quietly asked if they could wait for the minutes until Friday.

'We can wait a week, can't we?' said the Chairman. The other Members nodded, and she slipped out. When she tried to unlock the Jag, her hands started shaking again. She took a deep breath and drove slowly back to Earlsbury.

There was a police car at the entrance to Sharrow Road, and Fran remembered that there was a back way into the Goods Yard from there. She tried to think what an innocent person would do, and so she gazed curiously down the road as she waited for the lights to change. The news bulletin had no further details of the shooting at the Yard, and on impulse she pulled into a side road and went into the corner shop where she bought cigarettes for the first time since … the 1970s, she reckoned.

'Have you heard what's being going on down Sharrow Road?' she asked the shopkeeper.

'Only what's been on the news,' he replied. Then he lowered his head and whispered, 'I think that one of the men who was shot might be a police officer.'

'Blimey.'

'I know. It's a terrible thing. They must be waiting to inform his family.'

The image of the back of the van flashed through her mind. Should she go to Theresa King's house and tell her? What about Maria Lynch? Would either of them have missed their sons yet? Would they be worried about them after hearing the news? Fran thanked the newsagent and went back to the car.

She lit a cigarette and coughed deeply, the smoke filling the car and making her eyes water. She threw it out of the window and tried to dab her eyes. The smoke took her back eighteen years, to the Barley Mow. Robbie and Dermot had died together, just like their fathers, and now Robbie's boys were without their dad, too. Fran started the engine and headed home.

Patrick was still asleep – unconscious, really. She stripped off her suit and wiped the smeared make-up off her face and then sat down on the bed in her dressing gown as she realised something else. Not only could Patrick end up in prison, his business would be destroyed. Instinctively, she looked around at the house they'd lived in for twenty-five years and which they'd extended twice. That was secure: paid for with legitimate money and registered in her name. But that was all. Everything else would be up for grabs if Patrick were arrested. These days, the police seemed to think that confiscating assets was more important than catching criminals. She shuddered and went downstairs to get a cup of tea.

She felt her husband's pulse and checked his forehead. The angina attack seemed to be over for now, and it could be either the pills or exhaustion that was keeping him asleep. Suddenly hungry, she made a sandwich and ate it at the dining table, watching him breathe steadily and snore slightly. Three people had lost children: Theresa and Maria, obviously, but also Patrick. He had never once said that he wanted a son, but he didn't have to. When he gave Dermot a safe haven after prison, Patrick was adopting a son to take over the business. Now that was gone, too.

She got dressed into her running gear and put the kettle on again. Then she gently started to massage her husband's hands until he groaned and twitched awake.

'How are you feeling, love?'

'What? How long was I asleep?'

'Doesn't matter. Have you got any chest pains?'

He tried to sit up, but she pressed him back down. 'Just lie there for a minute. If you move suddenly you might faint. I'll get you a cup of tea and another nitro pill.'

When she returned, he was staring at the large family picture on the wall, taken at their oldest daughter's wedding but featuring only the Lynch clan (which still annoyed her son-in-law every time he visited). Patrick and Francesca were either side of their three daughters. Ma Lynch stood beside Patrick, and next to Fran was Dermot.

'It's time to tell me what's going on, Pat.'

'I don't know.'

She sat down next to him and put his tea on a side table.

'I know you was with me all night, and I know you wasn't there, but I didn't ask what happened. I asked what's goin' on. And I'm certain you know that much.'

He coughed and took a sip of tea.

'Dermot was doing a big handover last night to some boys from up north. I don't know who they are or what happened or what the connection is to the other death on the radio.'

'I've heard that the other one might be a police officer.'

Patrick sat up straighter. 'Griff. What about Griff? Why hasn't he been in touch? D'you think it might be him?'

Fran couldn't stand Griffin. He was always giving her daughters the eye, and more than that, he was bent. A policeman should stand up for the good things in life, like priests. They weren't supposed to be the bad guys. She ignored the comment.

'What was Robbie King doing there?' she asked.

'I don't know. He shouldn't have been within a mile of the place last night. He's been doing some work for us, bits and pieces on the distribution side, but nothing on wholesale.'

'Were they handing over those fags I saw?'

'No.'

Patrick hung his head.

'If it was drugs, I'm going to get a knife and stab you myself.'

'God, no. I'd never do that. It was counterfeit money. Twenty pound notes.'

Where on earth had they come from? she thought, *this is way out of Patrick's league: he's basically a smuggler, not a villain.*

'That's not important. What are we going to do with...' She took a deep breath. 'What are we going to do with that van?'

'We?'

'Yes. We. If you go out on your own, you'll have another attack, and I'm not going to lose you today. Tomorrow, maybe, but not today.'

'We've got to burn it. Completely.'

That was a relief. She was afraid that Patrick would insist on transporting the van somewhere and digging a grave.

'Do we need some petrol or something?' she asked.

He gave a sharp bark of a laugh. 'We'll not be short of stuff for a fire. What do they call it on the telly? Accelerant. That's it. There's enough accelerant in the warehouse to give them a proper send-off.'

Patrick got up and steadied himself on the back of a dining chair. 'I'm okay. I'm okay. We don't need petrol, but we do need some cigarettes, matches and a rubber band.'

Fran had dumped her coat on the armchair and she felt inside the pockets. 'These do?' she said, offering him the new packet.

Patrick took them and examined the packaging. 'You want to watch out, Fran. I imported these from China. They're bad for your health.'

When it came to opening the roller-shutter doors, Fran baulked. She couldn't turn the key and open up the nightmare again. If the shutters stayed down, she could try to forget about it.

'Can't we just leave them?'

Patrick shook his head and took the key off her. 'They'd be found soon enough, and so would lots of juicy forensic evidence. Including your fingerprints, I'm guessing.'

He put the key into the control panel and pressed the green button. The shutters rolled up and the van was still there. Thankfully both doors were closed.

Patrick ripped open one of the cases and revealed a dozen bottles of vodka. He twisted off the caps from two bottles and handed them to her.

'Go to the office and tip these out. Work backwards and cover everything with as much vodka as you can. Use at least ten bottles.'

She went through the back towards the office where the tea things were scattered over the floor. From the warehouse, she could hear the van being opened. When she came back for more vodka, Patrick had removed the petrol cap and stuffed a rag inside it.

'What were you doing in the van?'

'Closing his eyes. Saying a prayer for them both. Looking. Robbie was shot four times, I think, but they shot Dermot in the back of the head. He must have brought them here.'

He moved around to the driver's door and leaned in to release the handbrake.

'Nearly there,' he said, and went round to the back of the van. Together, they pushed it further into the warehouse. 'I've got to leave the doors open,' he said.

Another case of vodka went around the van, and Fran started to feel giddy with the fumes. Patrick started to fiddle with the cigarettes and matches.

'How are we going to ignite it?'

'My dad taught me this. It works with petrol and it should work with alcohol, too.'

He wrapped several matches around a pair of cigarettes and secured them with a rubber band so that the match heads were halfway down the tubes of tobacco. He examined it and grunted and then made two more. Finally, he got some more rags and soaked them in vodka and made three little heaps by the door.

Fran stepped back, outside and away from the building. 'You'll kill yourself,' she said.

Patrick shrugged. 'If it doesn't work, I'll either go up with the evidence in a big bang or I'll have to think of something else.'

She didn't argue. Patrick took each little bundle of match-wrapped cigarettes and lit the tobacco, inhaling once to get them going. He placed one on each heap of rags and jogged towards the car. Fran bolted after him and started the engine.

'Let's go,' he said. 'I know that both of us would like to see it burn, but we'll have to miss out on that.'

Fran drove off without looking back.

The fraud case was still on Tom's desk when he got back from his encounter with Caroline and Nikolai. There were plenty of victims here, not just Her Majesty's Revenue & Customs. It was work, but it wasn't much more than that. If the Coalition went through with their plans for cuts to the police, there would soon be a lot of people who would be glad of an excise fraud. But it wasn't enough for Tom.

The next case might be different, though – the sooner he finished this one, the sooner he could pick up something more sympathetic, like the boiler room fraud he'd done last month. Call centres in Spain had identified vulnerable old people and pestered them until they bought worthless shares. Each case was a small fraud to the police, but a massive loss to the victim. The only way to stop it was to hit the perpetrators where it hurt – in the wallet. Tom had insisted that letters were written to every victim (after all, they had them on their database) informing them of when the trial was taking place. A group of thirty senior citizens had watched the judge give the villains lengthy custodial sentences. He was good at his job, and that *was* enough. He unlocked his computer and went back to work.

He had filled in most of the spreadsheet (without mistakes) when the hunger became unbearable. He got up to head for the canteen. There was always someone around in the canteen because the operational units of the City Police were housed in the same building, and uniformed officers need regular sustenance. Tom nodded to the man in front of him in the queue and considered the sandwich option.

'Have you heard about the Birmingham thing?' said the officer

'Which one?'

'That shooting in Earlsbury.'

Tom couldn't be bothered to argue about whether or not Earlsbury was in Birmingham, so just asked what was new.

'One of ours dead and one in hospital. Sounds like a gunfight.'

Tom grabbed the nearest sandwich and a bottle of water then gave the officer a tenner. 'Tell Rosie to put the change in the charity box.'

He hurried back to his desk and logged on to the BBC website. The officers were named as DS Griffin (deceased) and DC Ian Hooper (critical condition with gunshot wounds). On the same page was a report that fire crews were attempting to bring a serious blaze under control in a disused building.

Tom stared at DI Fulton's door and started munching the sandwich. When his fingers had stuffed the last crust into his mouth, he brushed off the crumbs and checked the online directory of serving officers.

The man he wanted was still with the same department in Lambeth, and he seemed to have had a promotion. Even better. Social climbing had never been a vice with his mother, more of a hobby. She used to say that *I have a friend in the Close*, meaning the Cathedral Close in York. Tom had occasionally responded by saying *And I have a friend in*

Lambeth. He needed to act and he needed to act now. He grabbed his coat and headed for the tube.

After setting fire to the Wrekin Road building, Patrick had gone home and gone to bed for a couple of hours. He felt like he was wandering around someone else's house, and either the pills or the shock or the angina attack made it impossible to think. Fran had said nothing on the way home, either.

He woke up feeling worse but better. He could feel the loss inside him. Whether it was his arteries clogging up – or grief – didn't matter: either way it hurt. He lay on his back and said another prayer, his second of the day, and two more than he could remember saying in a long time. The first had been for Dermot's soul, but this one was for Fran: a prayer of thanks to God for sending her to him and for giving her the strength to help him through.

He took a shower and got dressed. Downstairs, Fran was waiting for him. She was still wearing her gym kit, a thing he had never seen before. Well, it was a day for changes all round. She made a great cup of tea, did Francesca, as good as his mother's (though he tried to convince both women that theirs was the better). The leprechaun tea cosy was keeping the pot warm on the coffee table, and she had pulled up a dining chair. The last time she had set out the room like this was when he came back from the police station eighteen years ago and she wanted to interview him about Theresa King's baby.

He went over and kissed her forehead. 'Thanks. Thanks for everything.'

'It worked,' she said. 'The fire. It's been on the news all afternoon that they can't get it under control.'

She bent her head and poured him some tea. For this interrogation, she had chosen his least favourite mug: the one that said *Old Golfers never die, they just lose their Balls*.

'Thanks for letting me sleep. Have there been any calls?'

She shook her head. 'How's your chest?'

'Fine. It's drama night for Elizabeth, isn't it?'

'Yes, and it's her turn to have tea at Amanda's. She'll get dropped off about eight o'clock so we've got time.'

'How much time have any of us got?'

She reached over and squeezed his hand. 'I know you're going to miss him ... probably more than his mother will. And I know that Theresa will miss Robbie. He was always her favourite.'

Patrick nodded, and Francesca withdrew her hand and then folded her arms. His moment of sympathy was over.

'What's really going on, Patrick? Really. The whole truth, this time.'

He drank some more tea and met her gaze. Of course, he wasn't going to tell her everything, but if he wanted to stay alive and stay out of jail there was no one else he could turn to. A man shouldn't have to rely on his wife: it just wasn't natural.

When she had threatened to throw him out after Hope was born, he had reflected on what his father would have done. First of all, his mother would never have given his Da an ultimatum. Second, if she had, his father would have got drunk and hit her. Then she would have hit him back. Patrick had never struck a woman in his life.

'It started when Dermot came out of jail and joined the business.'

'Go on.'

'He knew a man who knew a man in Blackpool, and I knew a man who knew a man in CID. I started bringing stuff in from China and Dermot sold it on. I laundered the money, and Griffin made sure we didn't get too much attention from the police.'

'So what went wrong?'

'The perils of diversifying. That man I knew, the one who…'

'Stop. Stop talking about A Man. Tell me who it is.'

'I don't know. I really don't.' He paused. 'You know Dermot was arrested for the murder of that football fan?'

'Yes. You said he was fitted up by the police.'

'He was, he was. And he was going to sue their arses off when it came out that the police had tampered with the evidence.'

Francesca frowned at him. Was 'arse' a swear word? No matter. He'd avoid them from now on.

'We were about to issue court papers,' he continued, 'when I got a phone call from a guy.' Patrick held up his hands to ward off Fran's intervention. 'No more lies, honest to God. I really don't know who it was. He had a posh voice, though, and he said that if we dropped the court case in return for a cash payment, he'd see we were all right.'

His wife frowned. 'How could he do that?'

'They've got very good connections. That's all I know. I agreed to the deal, and the next day DC Griffin turned up with twice the amount of money they'd offered. Said it was an investment, and if I did business in a certain way, they'd watch my back. All I had to do was pay them a percentage of the profits. That's how we could afford to start up Emerald Green Imports. Have you got any biscuits? I'm starving.'

Fran poured some more tea and brought a slice of Ma Lynch's cake. Now that was one thing that his wife couldn't compete on – nothing could beat his mother's baking.

'You were saying about diversification.'

She was relentless. Patrick chewed his cake slowly before continuing.

'Do you remember Elizabeth's last birthday party? I had to go out for a meeting.'

Fran nodded.

'I actually met one of the guys. Their enforcer, I suppose. He told me we were going to start shifting the forged notes.'

'Couldn't you have said *No?*'

'He was driving around Earlsbury with a great big gun in his car. I wasn't inclined to argue. Not only that ... he was from Belfast.'

Fran gave him a sharp look. She had always known that Patrick sympathised with the IRA, and that he had taken those sympathies as far as active support. 'Does all this go back to when Donal and Solomon were killed?'

'No. I severed my ties with the Boys on that night, and I've had nothing to do with them since. This fella was from the other side: called me a Fenian and worse. He was itching for a fight, and besides, we got a good deal out of that money. For a while.'

'What went wrong?'

'We weren't the first to get the contract. They started off-loading the cash down South. It went ...' He was going to say *it went tits-up*, but he stopped himself. 'It all went wrong and people were killed. One day a copper from London turned up here, and Griff told me to stop.'

'But you didn't.'

'I was between a rock and a hard place. Griff threatened to arrest me and this Prod was threatening all sorts if I didn't carry on, so we did a deal.'

'We?'

'Okay: *I* did a deal. I said I'd offload the counterfeit notes wholesale to Blackpool. That was what was supposed to happen last night.'

'What was Griff doing there if he was against it?'

'Orders. I insisted that we have someone to protect the exchange, and he was ordered to keep an eye out.'

They sat quiet for a moment. Fran had unfolded her arms and her gaze had moved to the wedding photograph by the TV.

'What about Robbie King?' she said.

'I don't know. D'you remember that he came out of jail in the summer? He'd been given a long stretch for dealing.

Well, Terri was desperate to find him some way of making money that didn't involve drugs. She's always had a good idea of what I'm up to and …'

Fran frowned and folded her arms again. Patrick cringed. He could have expressed that better.

'You see, with her having the market stall, she can't help but know what's going on. She asked if I could put some work Robbie's way, and I thought it was a great way of offloading some of the counterfeit cash.'

It was Patrick's turn to frown. He just couldn't work out what had gone wrong. 'The thing is, Darlin', our Dermot didn't trust Robbie King: wouldn't have involved him in last night's shenanigans. I just don't know what happened. But there is one thing I do know – the money's gone.'

'What do you mean?'

'Last night was an exchange. Dermot was supposed to collect the forgeries and swap them for a percentage of real money. Both have gone, and I can only imagine that the boys from Blackpool got greedy and took the lot.'

He shrugged, and put his hands in his lap.

'But your suppliers will want paying anyway, won't they?' said Fran.

'You'll have to leave that to me. If I can't sort them out, I need to keep any payback away from you and Elizabeth.'

'We're finished, aren't we?' said Fran, and Patrick wondered what she meant. She gestured around the room. 'All this is finished … the lifestyle, the holidays, the cars … Elizabeth's school fees. Hope's tuition fees at St Andrews … all finished.'

Patrick stood up and opened his arms. 'Since we've been married, I've gone to prison twice, been bankrupt twice, and had heart surgery. So long as it keeps beating, I'll bounce back.'

She hesitated, and then stood up to let him fold her in his arms.

He whispered into her hair. 'D'you think I'm too old to learn shorthand? That seems to pay well.'

Later that evening, Fran went for a run: she was dressed for it and her stress levels were high enough to blow out the walls of the house. Patrick had insisted on going to the golf club, which she had at first vetoed. When he told her that it was the most likely place for his suppliers to get in touch, she reluctantly agreed. In the half hour before Elizabeth was due home, Fran headed out into the rain to get a few miles under her belt.

She was soaked through, her hair plastered to her head and water dripping from her nose when she got back. Sheltering under an umbrella on the doorstep was Theresa King.

To buy some time, Fran bent double and put her hands on her knees. She breathed as deeply as she could and then turned round and walked back to the pavement. She turned again and walked slowly up to Theresa, who hadn't moved from the doorstep.

'He's out,' said Fran.

'I guessed. Do you know where Robbie is?'

'No. Do you know where Dermot is?'

Theresa grimaced. 'There's something going on, and Patrick must know about it. I can't believe you haven't got it out of him.'

'I thought that was your speciality.'

'Lay off, Fran. This is serious. No one's heard from Robbie since yesterday afternoon. Erin's going frantic with worry after that shooting. We don't know what to think. Is he on the run? Have he and Dermot done something stupid?'

'Not likely. Robbie's the one with the criminal record. If anyone's going to do something stupid, it would be him. We're just as worried about Dermot, you know. That's what Patrick's doing. Looking for him.'

A pair of headlights could be seen through the trees along the drive, and a car door slammed. Elizabeth dashed along the drive towards them with her coat over her head and then pulled up short when she saw her mother standing in the rain.

'Mom! What are you doing? Oh … Hi, Terri. How's Hope getting on?'

Theresa stepped away from the door. 'Great. She's having such a good time that I only know what she's up to by logging on to Facebook. You probably know more than me. I'll see you later, Francesca.'

Theresa walked off up the drive, and Fran wiped as much rain as she could from her face.

'Have you got your key, love?'

'Yeah.'

'Let yourself in and get me dressing gown, will you? I'm going to strip off in the porch.'

By Friday morning, thirty-six hours after the shooting in Earlsbury, it was front page news across the whole of England.

The injured officer was in a critical but stable condition in hospital and heavily sedated. Pictures of DC Ian Hooper and his attractive girlfriend outnumbered those of the deceased DS Griffin many times over. Journalists had found it very difficult to come by pictures of Griff, and crime correspondents had taken about five minutes to figure out that something was rotten in Midland Counties police.

Their first question to the media relations team had been this:

What were two unarmed officers doing at an abandoned distribution centre at ten o'clock on a Wednesday evening … and where was the backup?

When they received no answer at all to that question, they smelt a dead rat. After much delay, the MCPS Media

Relations had put out a statement appealing for witnesses. When that happened, the journalists knew that something had gone seriously wrong.

And then there was the fire. The evening news had featured dramatic pictures from Earlsbury showing a supposedly empty building being consumed by flames. The police had no comment when asked if the blaze was linked to the shootings.

Tom had left the office on Thursday afternoon and headed to see an old friend in Lambeth. The old friend had told him exactly how badly wrong things had gone in Earlsbury and he had made Tom an offer.

At nine o'clock on Friday morning, Tom hung up his coat and took a ring binder out of his briefcase. He knocked on Fulton's door and went straight in, holding up the ring binder as a shield.

Fulton scowled, focused on the cover of the binder and scowled more deeply.

'Don't even think about it, Tom, I won't let you,' he said. 'Now get out and get on with your job.'

Fulton's tone was so curt that Tom wondered if he'd brought the right folder. Half expecting to see a collection of recipes, he looked at the cover himself. No, it was the right one. The title was writ large:

Handbook of the Central Inspectorate of Professional Policing Standards (CIPPS).

Fulton grimaced and said, 'You're still here.' He sighed and pointed to the door. 'Shut it. I'll give you five minutes of my valuable time to explain why you are not going to join CIPPS, and why this is the wrong reaction to what's happened.'

Tom shut the door. He hadn't been invited to sit so he awkwardly held on to the binder. First he held it in front of his groin, and when he realised how stupid that was, he put it under his left arm. It weighed two pounds and the spine was about three inches thick. It was hard to stop the slippery plastic from descending towards the floor.

'I do read your reports, you know,' said Fulton. 'I know that you worked with both DS Griffin and DC Hooper in Earlsbury. I even remember that Hooper took you to a lap dancing club. Hard to forget that bit.'

'It was a pole dancing club, sir, and it was closed at the time. I also stayed one night in Ian's flat and had supper with him and his girlfriend.'

Fulton shook his head. All trace of anger was gone from his face. 'That's a bugger, Tom, and no mistake. I can see why you want to help out with the investigation, I really can, but this isn't the way to do it. I also know that you think the counterfeiters are involved too, but no. I am not letting you join CIPPS. You'll never be welcome in any CID office again. Ever. I like you too much to see you join the Gestapo.'

Tom put the ring binder down on Fulton's desk, and his boss twitched back away from it.

'Thank you, sir, I respect your opinion, but I have to ask: is this careers advice you're giving me or is there a personal reason for wanting to keep me away from CIPPS?'

The corner of Fulton's mouth twitched. 'Not like you to go on the offensive, Tom. Go on, sit down.'

When the files had been cleared from the chair, Tom sat down and made a point of removing the CIPPS handbook from Fulton's desk and stowing it out of sight. He said, 'I know the Assistant Director of CIPPS, Samuel Cohen, from my Birmingham days. I went to Lambeth to see him last night, and he said I could transfer as detective inspector. Not acting DI, but permanent. They're a bit short staffed at the moment.'

'This moment and every bleeding moment. No one wants to work for them – I'm surprised they didn't offer you a DCI's job. For the record, I have had dealings with

CIPPS before, but they weren't investigating me. I reported an officer from Thames Valley once, and they came calling. He retired two weeks later.'

Tom nodded but said nothing. Fulton folded away the newspapers and asked Tom what he had learnt about the Earlsbury shootings from Cohen.

'Apart from the fact that Midland Counties Police are in meltdown, not a lot. The reason that there are so few details in the media is that they have nothing. No witnesses, no CCTV, no record of activity – nothing. With Griffin dead and Hooper unconscious, they're going to be reliant on forensics. Or a tip-off.'

'What about the fire? Is there any connection?'

'Probably. The fire service gained access in the early hours of this morning, and discovered two more bodies in a burnt out van. It can't be a coincidence. I got an email on the way in to work.'

Fulton nodded as he digested this development.

'And what's going to be your role?' he asked.

'The chief constable of MCPS wants to cover his backside on this – he wants to tell the press that an independent investigation will look into the irregularities at the same time as their Major Incident Team investigate the actual killings.'

Fulton leaned forward. 'If you were my brother, I'd nail your hand to the table to stop you leaving this office and wrecking your career ... but you aren't my brother and CIPPS don't need my permission, so off you go. There's just one thing to sort out first.'

The DI went to his filing cabinet and pulled out four folders. He looked at them and put two of them to one side. 'Right, which one of these two is going to become acting DS when you leave tonight?'

Fulton placed the folders in front of Tom, who looked at the names and then sat back: it was a difficult question. He guessed that Fulton had pulled the files on all four of the team who had passed their sergeant's exams and rejected two of them for being too old or too limited in their approach. He would have done the same. That left Megan and Maxwell.

'Do you really want my opinion, sir?'

'You'd be offended if I didn't ask. Whether I listen depends on what you say.'

'In that case, it has to be Maxwell. He's much better looking than Megan.'

'Harsh, but fair. Send them both in then sod off and start to prepare your handover report.'

Thursday night's rain had turned into the occasional shower with strong gusts of wind. Patrick knew this because he was standing on the sixth green, and if he completed the round, it would be his worst ever score at Earlsbury Park. The mature trees around the course were shedding their leaves at a rate of knots, and he had already lost one ball in a drift of leaves. He was also losing the feeling in his fingers.

He had learnt very little the night before. He had made small talk in the bar for a couple of hours, and eventually Craig Butler, the steward, had come in with a message. According to the note, *A friend from the Old Country would like to catch up over a round of golf in the morning.* Patrick had worked on the driving range for an hour and then headed out on to the course. When he finally sank the ball into the sixth hole (three shots over), a figure detached itself from the trees and sauntered across. He was wearing a knitted cap and a scarf over his face but Patrick could see red sideburns.

'Hard going,' said the man.

'If we're going to talk out here, we need to pretend to know each other. I'm not calling you Red Hand in public.'

'Pick a name – any name.'

'How about Adam Gerard?'

The other one burst out laughing. 'As in Gerry Adams? I'm glad you've still got your sense of humour, Paddy. You're going to need it.'

'It's Patrick or Pat, if you must.'

'And I'll be Adam Paisley, if you must.'

Patrick shook his head and pushed his golf cart towards the seventh tee. 'If you've no clubs, you'll have to share mine, though it pains me severely. Let's get down the fairway then we can talk. Have you ever played this game?'

'Ha! Do I look like I have the time for golf? Just hit the bloody thing, and I'll copy you.'

Patrick played a conservative shot off the tee and passed the driver to Adam (first Red Hand and now Adam – did the man enjoy all this cloak and dagger nonsense?). The Ulsterman took a mighty swing at his ball and missed. He tried again and smacked it into the woods. Patrick sighed and fished out another ball.

'Take this and we'll pretend you landed close to me.'

'What does it matter where the fockin' thing landed? Christ, it's only a game.'

'It's golf. Golf is not a game, it's a martial art.'

Patrick strode off towards his ball, and Adam came up to his shoulder.

'Cut the crap, Pat. What the fock's been going on down here? It's like the Wild West, so it is.'

'I wish I knew, pal, I wish I knew.'

They stood over Patrick's ball, and Adam leaned in close to his face.

'I know one thing, Pat. I know that we sent two million pounds to you, and we expect three hundred thousand in return.'

'Back off, Adam,' said Patrick. Adam didn't move so Patrick took a step back and raised his club to stop the other man coming nearer. He thought Adam might grab it and attack him, but they heard voices coming from the tee. Adam stepped back and frowned.

'Put your ball there,' said Patrick, gesturing a few yards towards the green. Adam tossed it down, and Patrick placed two markers. He retreated to the tree line and waved at the newcomers for them to play through. Adam slipped behind him when the golfers started to tee up.

'I'll tell you this,' said Patrick. 'I'll tell you what I know, all right? I know that my nephew went out on Wednesday night to meet his man and he didn't come back. I know that I got a phone call from some fecking eejit telling me to pick up the van, and I know that when I went there it had two more bodies in it. One of them was my nephew, and I had to set fire to the whole damn place. I burnt one of my own family like a piece of evidence to be disposed of. The Blackpool mob did for them as well.'

Adam watched the following golfers work their way past them and head for the green.

'That's bad news right enough. Bad news for you, but not my problem.'

'It'll be your problem if the police start digging. *When* they start digging. If we don't work together on this, they'll hang us separately.'

'And what about our money?'

'What money? Those counterfeit notes weren't real money. If you're that bothered, I'll give you five hundred for the cost of the paper and the ink. You can always print some more.'

'I heard about those bodies in the fire on the radio. The other one wasn't one of theirs, was it?'

'No. He was the son of a good friend of mine. I'll be having to answer for that as well.'

'Here's how it is, Pat. Your nephew obviously got himself in bad company. I need to speak to my associates and see where we go from here. If you're lucky, they might decide not to see you as a loose end. Here, take this and don't ring me from anything except a Pay As You Go mobile.'

Adam handed over a piece of paper with a phone number, and Patrick shoved it in his pocket.

'Enjoy your game,' said Adam as he disappeared into the trees.

Patrick had bitten his lip when Adam started on the threats. He doubted that the Principal Investors would act without warning – Patrick knew too much about how the money was laundered, and they would want to cover their tracks. Staring back at the course, he realised that he was looking at something very valuable.

He went back to where the balls were lying and fished a plastic bag out of his golf cart. Adam had taken off his gloves to play the stroke, and they were still off when Patrick had given him the new ball. He used his shoe to nudge Adam's ball into the plastic bag. It would have a nice set of fingerprints on it, he was sure, and he would be very surprised if Mr Adam Paisley didn't have a criminal record somewhere.

It had been a late night for James King. Queen Victoria had played a session in Manchester at a private club, and they had lingered afterwards to talk to the movers and shakers who were organising the promotional tour for Vicci's forthcoming album. Everyone who might have wanted to call him was at the club, so James hadn't even taken his phone with him.

There was a burger van outside the club, and the band enjoyed an early breakfast at six am before taking a taxi back to their hotel and crashing out. James was getting too old for this.

When he finally surfaced in the afternoon, it was to answer the room phone.

'Is that Mr James King?' said a male voice.

'Yes. Who wants to know?'

'This is Police Sergeant Chandler from South Lancs Constabulary. I'm in reception and I'd like to come up and see you in ten minutes, if that's okay.'

This was worrying. He could have handled a raid because he was always clean when they were on the road. A policeman who was being nice and giving him a chance to dispose of his stash obviously had something serious to discuss.

'Can you make it fifteen minutes? Then I can have a shower. You woke me up.'

'Sorry, sir. Just call reception when you're ready, but don't be too long.'

Sir? They called him sir? This was getting worse. James headed for the bathroom.

He threw on some clean clothes after the shower, but didn't attempt to dry his hair. When the policeman came up to the room, he was in uniform, but had a woman trailing behind in plain clothes. This was getting serious and it got worse when they insisted that he sat down in the armchair. The sergeant introduced his woman as Detective Constable Smith and they both sat down on the bed, moving apart when the sergeant's weight nearly pitched them together.

'I'm sorry to say this, Mr King, but I've got some bad news. A body was found this morning which we have reason to believe may be your brother. Have you heard from him since Wednesday?'

'Wednesday? It's Friday now. Anyway, how did you find me and what do you mean by *We believe it may be your brother*?'

James rocked back and forward in the chair. The woman was about to speak when James remembered his phone. He made a grab for it but the sergeant, a big man, took hold of his wrist. James flinched but the man wasn't hurting him, just trying to slow him down.

'It's switched off, isn't it?'

James nodded, and the man let go of his wrist. They all sat down again. This time the sergeant took the chair by the dressing table instead of risking another go at the bed.

'That's why it's taken so long,' said Chandler. 'Your mother's been trying to get hold of you, and she told Midland Counties police to try Queen Victoria's management company. They pointed MCPS in this direction and MCPS asked us – me – to come and see you. DC Smith can answer some of your questions, and I'll leave you with her if that's okay.'

'Yeah, thanks,' said James, and the sergeant let himself out.

DC Smith was young and chubby and pale. James was surprised they hadn't found a token black officer for this job. With PS Chandler gone, she gave him a diffident smile.

'Tell me what you know,' he said. She lost the smile and looked at her notebook.

'Your mother reported your brother as missing this morning. She was especially concerned in light of the events on Wednesday and the fire.'

'What you talking about? I've been on the road for three days, and we don't get newspapers.'

Smith flicked back another page. 'On Wednesday evening there was a shooting in Earlsbury, and two police officers were injured. One of them died at the scene and the other is in a critical condition. On Thursday afternoon a serious fire was started in a warehouse. When Fire & Rescue gained access, they discovered two bodies. No one has heard from your brother since Wednesday. We're conducting tests to determine whether one of the bodies is Robert.'

James's foot started tapping maniacally on its own. He looked down and wondered what the noise was. He put his hand on his knee to try and stop it, but his other foot started tapping instead. He leaned forward and wrapped his arms round his knees.

'Robbie, Robbie, Robbie. What have you done, man? What's happened to you?'

He shot a look at DC Smith. 'He was murdered, right?'

'Almost certainly.'

'And who's the other one? The other one found with him?'

'Midland Counties police have reason to believe it may be a Mr Dermot Lynch. Do you know him?'

'Together? They were found murdered together?'

'I can't give you any more details, I'm afraid. I just don't know.'

James picked up his jungle jacket, the one his father had left him, and took out some cigarettes. He didn't care whether or not the hotel fined him. DC Smith pulled open a window and gave him a saucer from the tea tray, then she picked up the hotel phone and muttered something to someone.

'I've ordered some tea and coffee,' she said, and opened her notebook again. 'So you do know Mr Lynch, then?'

'Of course I know him. The Earlsbury filth – sorry, the Earlsbury police, know that I know him, too. Look, DC Smith, you've been very kind, but I'm going to go home as soon as you've left, and I'll present myself at the station if they don't get me first. Is there anything you really need to know?'

She looked at the list of questions and snapped her notebook closed. 'Not really.'

There was a knock at the door, and she let in the room service porter with the tray. Before she finally left, she gave him a card. James smiled and thanked her.

He had been desperate to get rid of them ever since Chandler had grabbed his wrist. He knew that Robbie was dead, but he had just remembered the last text his brother had sent on Wednesday. It had said simply this:

Payback time, Bro.

Now he wanted answers. Payback for what? James had always suspected that Dermot Lynch had played a part in his brother's arrest for dealing, and if Dermot had been found dead, it would have been a disappointment rather than a surprise. But both of them? Together? All he had thought when the text arrived on Wednesday was that Robbie's English teacher would have been pleased to see him using a comma in the right place.

Chapter 6

Earlsbury

Saturday Morning

23rd October

There was no leaving do at the MLIU, no presentations of single malt, or hastily arranged parties. At three o'clock on Friday afternoon, DI Fulton had gathered the team together, and the chief superintendent had come downstairs and hovered at the back. Fulton began by announcing who would be acting DS, and then looked over at Tom's desk where a police issue cardboard box was sitting with his personal possessions.

'This is gonna be brief,' said Fulton. 'I just wanted to have it said, on the record, that Tom Morton is a good copper. More than that, he's been one of the best sergeants I've ever had. Mortgage fraudsters across Europe will sleep easier in their beds tonight. Yes, my children, the Force is strong with this one. It's just a shame he's going to join the Dark Side. Thanks, Tom, and good luck. You'll need it.'

Tom didn't know what to say. He hadn't expected anything to be said, but to be so publicly praised and damned in the same speech had wrong-footed him completely. He stood up and cleared his throat to give himself thinking time.

'Thank you, Yoda,' he said, and got a small laugh. 'This is either the best thing I've ever done or the most stupid. Either way, it was the only thing I could do, given the circumstances. The guv'nor will tell you why, if you're interested. If I've done good work here, it was only because I had a good boss and a great team. I'll miss you.'

The chief superintendent led a round of applause, and by the time it had died away, Fulton was back in his office. Tom shook hands with his replacement and picked up his box. Fulton had taken his warrant card off him at five to three, and that left one more duty to perform.

Elspeth Brown looked very put out. She folded her arms and refused to accept his security pass and locker key.

'I can't believe it, Tom. You're going to *Professional Standards*?' She shook her head. 'All my dreams are shattered and my heart is broken.'

'But we were star-crossed lovers from the start. It could never happen.' He put the pass and key on the ledge in front of her. 'Besides, you haven't heard who my replacement is. It's Maxwell.'

She snatched the pass from under his nose. 'Ooh, good. I do like a challenge. If the lottery syndicate wins anything, I'll donate your share to the benevolent fund: it'll make up for what you're doing to us.'

Tom left the building and hailed a taxi. On their way to the off-street garage where he kept his BMW, Tom stared at his new warrant card, hand delivered from Samuel Cohen. The cover showed the generic Metropolitan Police crest, and the interior identified him as a detective inspector. If he held his fingers over the designation *Central Inspectorate of Professional Policing Standards*, some people might think he was an ordinary copper. Who was he trying to kid?

The Friday afternoon traffic was foul, all the way from central London to Earlsbury. After handing over his active caseload in the morning, he had scoured the Internet for a decent hotel. The best deal he could get was just to the west of the town at the Earlsbury Park Golf and Country Club. That would make a change, he supposed.

The room was okay, and had a decent-sized desk with a view of the golf course. The food was less appealing but at least he was fed. He took a glass of wine back to his room and started up his laptop. Tom wasn't as good with computers as his cousin Kate (who was?), but he knew his way round most of the standard programs. He logged into his new CIPPS email address and found three messages. One was a standard message from the IT manager, one was a *Welcome aboard* email from Samuel Cohen, and the third was from the Assistant Chief Constable of Midland Counties Police Service. Well, he wasn't hanging about, was he?

I understand that CIPPS have assigned you to conduct the investigation into DS Griffin.
Please see me in the Station Commander's office, Black Country South Station at 0800 tomorrow (Saturday).
Malik Khan
ACC Operations
MCPS

Tom had once visited the old Dudley police station, opposite the Courthouse pub. He didn't know whether it was still there or not, but much of the work was now done from the new Black Country South Station (BCSS), next to the M5 motorway. Tom had read about it in the newspapers – it was a Private Finance Initiative project. The taxpayer would be forking out millions of pounds every year to pay for a police station without any cells. That was a design error, apparently.

The PFI contractor had been asked to quote for providing a custody suite and had quoted a figure so high that the police authority had decided to build its own cells at the back of Earlsbury division. When the cuts came in next year, there were going to be several officers facing redundancy because of this extravagance.

Tom shook his head and consulted the hotel guide. They didn't start serving breakfast until eight o'clock on Saturdays. Tom shut down his computer and went to bed.

The BCSS building looked good, all right. It was brick faced and solid without being brutal. Tom was issued with a pass at reception and shown up to the Station Commander's office.

ACC Khan was standing by the window, talking on his mobile. The station commander himself was absent, but a second officer, an Afro-Caribbean woman in plain clothes, was seated in the corner, on her own and far from the desk. Khan waved him in and pointed to a chair much closer to the seat of power. Tom smiled at the woman, but she barely flicked her eyes up and didn't acknowledge him. She appeared to be sending a text message and was hunched over her phone.

Khan finished his call and welcomed Tom to the Black Country.

'Sorry to drag you in so early, but I needed to see you before the main briefing at 0930, and I've got my own session with the Senior Investigating Officer in half an hour.'

'No problem, sir. I came up last night so I'm ready to go.'

'Good. Now let's get things straight, shall we? The Chief Constable asked for CIPPS participation in this enquiry because he wants to know if we've got one rotten apple or a whole barrel. That's all. Your role is to investigate DS Griffin's professional conduct and what connections he may have had with criminal elements. Okay?'

Tom nodded and glanced at the woman in the corner. She still hadn't looked up from her phone.

Khan continued. 'Was Griffin acting alone within MCPS, or are there other officers who need to be investigated? That's the question you have to answer while we concentrate on finding who shot him, who shot DC Hooper, and who killed those two in the van.'

'So, in other words, I'm not part of enquiry team.'

Khan tapped the desk. 'Consider it this way: you're conducting a specific part of the enquiry, with clearly defined elements and boundaries. It would be difficult for you to operate without having access to the main enquiry's resources and discoveries.'

It would be ruddy impossible, thought Tom. To Khan, he said, 'So I'm okay to join the briefing. Who do I report to?'

'You plough your own furrow, Tom. If you need anything or discover anything relevant to the main enquiry, hand it over to the SIO. Everything else you discover comes to me. Routine reports by email, but if you discover anything that needs further investigation, give me a call.'

Khan handed over a business card, and Tom slipped it into his pocket.

'We're also providing you with local support,' said Khan. 'Can I introduce Detective Constable Kristal Hayes? She's between teams at the moment. She'll show you where the canteen is. See you at half past nine, Tom.'

Before Tom could stand up and offer his hand to the woman, she swept out of the office without acknowledging him or ACC Khan. By the time Tom had picked up his laptop bag and coat, she was disappearing through the doors of the Command Corridor.

He found her waiting for him at the next turning. Now that he could look at her properly, he that realised she was younger than he thought – perhaps no more than twenty-four or twenty-five. Her hair was pulled back in cornrows and she was wearing a blue trouser suit with a white blouse: Caroline had referred to this style as *plain clothes for women detectives 101*. It didn't suit DC Hayes. Tom approached and held out his hand. She gave him the fastest handshake ever and continued to block the door with her other arm.

'You can tell who likes me round here very easily, sir,' she said. 'Anyone who calls me Kristal doesn't like me. Anyone who does like me calls me Kris, okay?'

'And what about people who've only just met you, and haven't formed an opinion yet? People like me.'

'Hayes is fine. What do I call you? Sir? Guv'nor? Boss?'

'*Boss* implies a team of more than two, and we're not in London now so that rules out *Guv'nor*. You can call me *Sir*. However, unless I eat some breakfast soon, you'll be calling me an ambulance.'

She didn't smile, and Tom felt his heart sink. Humour was his leadership style of choice, but it looked like he might have to try a different approach – such as giving orders, perhaps. He followed her to the canteen.

The family home where Francesca's husband had finished growing up after the move from Ireland was on the Elijah estate, and his mother, 'Ma' Lynch still lived there in her eighty-third year. Even though Fran's home was bigger, the family seemed to gather instinctively at Ma Lynch's ex-council house in times of celebration or crisis.

Ma was making her way slowly from the kitchen with another plate of bacon sandwiches as more relatives arrived, and Fran jumped up to give her a hand. Her mother-in-law waved her away and went over to the corner where Elizabeth was pretending to do some homework. Lizzie shook her head when offered a sandwich, and Ma put them on the table then returned to the kitchen to fetch the teapot. Ma's daughter, Janet, had already started on the washing-up. Daughters were allowed in there, but daughters-in-law were not. Fran picked up the plate of food and offered it to Maria, Dermot's mother. She had just finished crying.

'Come on, Maria. You've got to eat something,' said Fran.

'They were his favourite. Ma's bacon sandwiches. He'd find any excuse to come here for them.'

Fran smiled at her sister-in-law. Flaky. That was the word Pat had used to describe Maria. It summed her up perfectly.

A car drew up, and Fran breathed a sigh of relief – it was her eldest daughter, Helen. She found it hard to comfort Maria and didn't know how to comfort Lizzie (because Lizzie didn't know she needed it yet), but Helen was a different story. Her husband had been on one of the fire tenders which had been called to Wrekin Road. He was back on duty now.

As she went to open the door, she looked around Ma Lynch's house at the four women. Ma, Janet and Maria were widows, and there was a good chance that she might join the club herself.

She let Helen in and the first question was, 'Any news on Dad?'

'He's still at the police station,' said Fran.

The walk to the canteen gave Tom a chance to ponder the woman who marched four paces ahead of him with a chunky-heeled clatter that announced her to the whole division. What were her parents thinking? *Kristal Hayes?* It could have been worse – they could have called her Purple. *Black women don't often have it easy*, he thought, and to be saddled with a name like that must have been an extra handicap. In the horse racing sense, of course.

Tom queued for hot bacon rolls and a mug of tea in the busy canteen. There were an awful lot of officers for a Saturday morning. Kris did the same and they found a distant corner.

She sat as far away from him as she could while still being on the same table and took out her phone while she tucked into her food. She had also chosen to put her back to the room. Tom left her alone and savoured his breakfast, then wiped his hands as noisily as possible; she didn't look up at him. He pushed back his chair and moved next to her.

'Have you ever been posted to Earlsbury?' he asked.

She put her phone down, but only shook her head. He stared at her, and she shifted uncomfortably in her seat.

'What? Sir.'

'If you haven't been posted to Earlsbury, where *have* you worked?'

'Uniform in Sutton Coldfield for five years, and then detective. Six months.'

'In Sutton?'

'No.'

Tom drank some tea. The background noise in the canteen was rising as more officers arrived ahead of the briefing. Hayes played with a serviette for a second and tried to give him a smile.

'Where are you staying while you're here?' she asked.

Okay, thought Tom. *I'm not allowed to ask any questions about her background. Not to worry, I can always find out. That's what makes me a detective.*

'Earlsbury Park,' he replied. 'I got a special rate but the food might kill me if I'm there too long. Are you travelling from Sutton?'

'I'm staying at my Mom's in Dudley. It's not far from Earlsbury Park.'

He checked his watch. Half an hour to go. 'I've heard something about the enquiry, but not much apart from what's been in the papers. What have you heard that I should know about before the briefing?'

'Nothing. I've been on leave until this morning.'

Her eyes narrowed when she said that. Another subject to avoid for now.

'Then I guess we'll have to adjourn this exciting conversation until after the briefing. You need to go to the Ladies.'

'What?'

'You've got brown sauce on your blouse. Serves you right for texting and eating at the same time.'

She looked down aghast at her front, and then did the worst thing possible by smearing it with a tissue. Tom thought she was going to cry. Instead, she grabbed his laptop case from the empty chair and stood up.

'You go to the briefing, yeah? I'll go to IT and get them to sort your laptop out for the BCSS Network.'

Before he could point out that his notebook was in there too, she had gone.

There were no bacon sandwiches in Grasmere Gardens: James King was munching through a packet of Jaffa Cakes and drinking instant coffee. His mother's kitchen looked over the small garden to the house behind them, and all he could see, apart from fence and roof, was a small piece of sky. It looked certain to rain again soon.

James had dossed down on the couch because the house only had three bedrooms. His mother had gone to sleep in one of them at three o'clock that morning when James had convinced her to take the sleeping pill left by the doctor. The smallest room was Hope's; she was due back from St Andrews tonight, and James didn't want the hassle of changing the bed. The other bedroom was Rob's. That one was barred by blue and white tape, announcing that it was a crime scene. It wasn't a crime scene, of course, but the police didn't have special tape that said *You may not enter your dead child's bedroom because we think he was a drug dealer.*

The biscuits made him feel a little less light headed and he went outside for a smoke. Through the house, he heard a diffident knock on the door. Not the filth, then.

James dropped the roll-up into a plant pot and went to see who it was. He opened the door to find Erin, alone and shivering. They had hugged and embraced yesterday but somehow, the day after, it seemed worse. Night had not brought Robbie back to them, nor would it ever again. He wrapped his arms around her, and she sobbed into his shoulder. James steered her into the living room and closed the door behind him to stop the sound waking his mother.

He sat next to her on the couch and waited until she had blown her nose before pulling away.

'Terri's asleep. She's taken a tranquiliser.'

'I thought she might. Anyway, it was you I wanted to see. I stayed at Mom's last night and she's looking after the boys. I can't tell them what's happened because it doesn't make sense in their little worlds. They think he's gone back to the big house. You know, the prison.'

'Tell them he's with God, Erin.' She looked at him uncomfortably. 'It doesn't matter if you don't believe it. Little kids can't tell the difference between prison and heaven, but they're both places. You can say, "Daddy's in Heaven", and they understand you. They don't understand the idea of death until later.'

'Bit too philosophy-cical for me, James, but thanks.'

'Do you want a cup of tea?'

'I daren't. I've done nothing but drink tea since yesterday morning. Listen, there's something I wanted to talk to you about. It's the police. You know they asked me some questions yesterday, yeah?'

James nodded. Theresa had said that detectives had accompanied the family liaison officers who had come to break the news. The detectives had asked some preliminary questions as well as searching both houses.

'Well,' continued Erin,' they want me to go in and make a statement. What shall I say?'

'There is only one thing you *can* say. The truth.'

'But…' Her voice trailed off.

James took her hand. It was small and cold and rough. 'Don't speculate. If they say, "Where was he?" … then tell them you don't know. If they say "Who did this?" then don't give them any names because you don't know. If you only tell them what you know to be true then you can do no wrong.'

Erin patted him on the knee. 'You sound like the Priest at school. Remember? Father Stockton. I'm sure he was there when you was there.'

'He was.' James wasn't flattered by the comparison. The whole school knew that Stocky Stockton had been shagging a parishioner for years before the Church forced him to resign from the priesthood.

Erin seemed to have found his words some comfort because she stood up and smiled. She gave him a peck on the cheek and headed for the front door. 'Thanks, James. I'd better go 'cos Mom'll be going mental with the boys.'

James showed her out and stood with his back to the door. Robbie had told her nothing about his business, he was certain of that. On the other hand, James had a shrewd idea that Theresa knew a lot more than she was giving away. When his mother surfaced, he was going to have to have a completely different conversation with her.

Tom found his way to Conference Room 1, and there was a note pinned to the door that the first briefing was for Team Leaders Only. He supposed that Kris Hayes counted as a team, and he pushed his way through.

The walls were unadorned, and the only paperwork visible was whatever each officer had brought with them. A laptop had been plugged into the data projector and the screen was showing the MCPS Screensaver (motto: Protecting All). A top table had been formed at the front, and five empty chairs awaited. Tom couldn't sit at the back because about thirty officers had beaten him to it. On the front row was a woman with a large notepad. Cascades of dark brown hair were being held in check by a cream coloured knitted scarf. She hadn't taken her bright red coat off, either. He had never seen a detective dressed like that before, certainly not at the start of a murder enquiry. Tom sat behind her.

'Sorry to bother you, but could you give me a couple of sheets of paper?'

She jumped and turned round, then raised a severely plucked eyebrow.

'Long story,' said Tom.

She ripped off a couple of sheets and handed them over. 'Are you up from Coventry?' she asked.

'No, but you might send me there in a minute.'

The eyebrow remained raised. What was it with people round here? Had they had a sense of humour bypass? He held out his hand before introducing himself, just in case she refused to shake it when she knew who he was.

'Thanks. I'm DI Morton from CIPPS.'

Tom felt a short spasm transmitted through her fingers, but she didn't snatch them away. On the other hand, the plastic smile she gave him wouldn't have been out of place on a minor royal asked to open a sewage farm.

'Nicole Rodgers, Deputy Media Relations Manager.'

She was wearing a lot of make-up. The effect was probably good on television, but at a conversational distance it made her look even more out of place among the police officers. Underneath her coat and scarf, he couldn't help notice a rather tight black turtleneck stretched across her chest.

'From London?' she asked.

'That's where I'm based.'

She handed him a card, and Tom gave his own number for her to write down. After that, he sent a text to Cohen in Lambeth which asked his friend to get some business cards printed urgently and couriered up to him. They could afford it.

He was putting his phone away when he recognised Kris's footsteps. She accelerated as she came to the front then squeezed in beside him. She was now wearing a black blouse which she must have borrowed because it clashed horribly with the blue jacket. The elegant Nicole Rodgers had turned to examine the new arrival and gave a disdainful look before turning back to the front.

Hayes plonked his notebook down on the table and gave him a half-smile. The room went quiet from the back, and Tom whispered into her ear, 'Thanks. That means a lot.'

Patrick had spent the night in the cells at Earlsbury after being interviewed in the brick outhouse they called Black Country Station South. As everyone knew, it had no custody suite. They released him in the morning.

'Can I have my phone back?' he asked the custody sergeant.

The man riffled through some notes and handed him a piece of paper.

'What's this?'

'A receipt. Your phone has been taken for investigation and will be returned in due course.'

'For God's sake,' muttered Patrick.

'You are being released on police bail under Section 47…'

'… of the Police & Criminal Evidence Act 1984. I know. When do you want me back?'

The custody sergeant handed over the paperwork. 'Monday. Ten o'clock.'

That was quick. Police Bail meant that they could play cat and mouse with him if they wanted. They could break down their allowance of twenty-four hours of interview time into blocks and release him on bail in between.

The sergeant unlocked a drawer and pulled out Pat's medication. Another five minutes were spent ticking it off. When the sergeant had seen it all yesterday, he had called a doctor to double-check that Patrick was fit to be interviewed.

'Of course,' the medic replied. 'He's got a heart condition, that's all. But just you make sure that he takes every tablet on time and gets his meals at exactly the time specified.' Patrick hadn't been arrested for a lot of years, but this regime was quite civilised. Made it a lot easier to say 'No Comment'.

After the pills were returned, his shoes, belt, and other bits and pieces were handed over. There was enough money for a taxi to his mother's.

He was released at the back of the nick, well away from the Victorian building that fronted the High Street. He took a couple of turns and emerged next to the market, busy as always on Saturday mornings. From an alley corner, he slowly scanned the stalls from one end to the other. They had been his world for over forty years since he had got his first job at Toddy's veg stall, cutting and trimming the veg at the back, and stocking up the boxes. Toddy's grandson still had the same stall and didn't need a trimmer because that was all done on the farm by Bulgarians or some such.

As well as giving himself a moment to feel normal again after the cells, Patrick was also looking for surveillance. They would be there somewhere. Well, they were welcome to him. When he passed the newsagent on the corner, every front page featured Earlsbury.

His own two stalls were in the middle, pride of place on Earlsbury Market, and in between them was a gap: Theresa wouldn't be opening her stall for a while, if ever, and unlike Patrick, she had no one to run it for her.

It was getting late. Patrick crossed the road and made his way through the market with his collar pulled up and tried to keep a low profile. A few people nodded at him, but they left him alone with his thoughts.

He kept the stalls partly out of sentiment and partly because they were a good fit for his business. One sold Irish produce and the other sold Irish crafts: between them, they absorbed a lot of laundered cash, and he was careful to make sure that none of his part-time stall holders could see too much of the picture. Today, a young married couple were taking one stall each. Patrick approached the husband, Dan.

'Hey, Pat. Are you okay? I'm so sorry for your loss. We all are.'

Patrick wrapped his hands around the young man's and shivered. 'It gets worse. I've just got out of the nick, and they want me back.'

'Bastards.'

'I know. Tell me, Dan, have you seen Kelly this morning?'

'Arr, I 'ave. Paid his respects about half an hour ago and said he was going in the George.'

That sounded about right. Dan's wife came over and gave him a kiss and a hug. Patrick thanked her and asked if she could manage both stalls on her own for a bit. She nodded, and he drew Dan aside.

'Take a hundred out of the float. Make it a hundred and fifty. Go and find Kelly. Tell him to get me two of those Pay As You Go phones, and tell him to take them to Ma's house. There's police following me somewhere: probably taking a picture of us right now. They'll follow you too if you go straight away, so give it a few minutes.'

'No problem, Pat. If there's anything else, just let me know.'

Patrick patted him on the shoulder. Kelly knew the score, and Patrick could rely on him when he wasn't too drunk. In other words, only in the morning.

He headed for the taxi rank at the top of the High Street and a trip to the Elijah estate. He had lost many people over the years – His Da, his brother, his brother-in-law, and friends, too. Dermot was the best of them and deserved to be mourned. Patrick owed him a good wake, and the sooner he opened a bottle of Irish whiskey in the boy's memory the better. But Dermot wouldn't want him to go to jail or get killed for no reason: the Jameson's would have to wait.

Pat was over the shock now and had survived the first twenty-four hours intact. It was time for action.

Chapter 7

Earlsbury

Saturday (continued)

23rd October

'I've got to get out,' said Kris Hayes to Tom, but it was too late. The Command officers filed into the briefing room, and she was trapped. As he passed their table, ACC Khan gave her a stare which clearly said *team leaders only*. She shrank in her seat and lowered her head.

Of the five men who filled the chairs at the top table, the three in the centre wore uniform. The Chief Constable was flanked by Deputy Chief Constable Nechells on his right and ACC Khan on his left. At the end nearest to Nicole Rodgers was the senior media relations man, and at the other end was the SIO, Detective Chief Superintendent Nigel Winters. The Chief stood up and ran his eye round the room.

'On Thursday afternoon I told you that we had lost one of our own and had one in hospital. Since then the picture has got messier and more complicated. Earlsbury was front page news this morning, and will be again tomorrow. I will be holding a full press conference this afternoon. When a policeman is murdered, it's the Chief's job to be our public face. It's your job to catch the bastards who did for him.'

There was a long pause.

'When I say that they did for him, I don't just mean that they shot him. I mean that someone put DS Griffin and DC Hooper in that Goods Yard on Wednesday night. Why those officers came to be there is as important as what happened afterwards – and may be a harder question to answer, but I know you won't rest until you've answered it. Midland Counties Police Service has a high reputation for major enquiries. I like to think it's higher than that of the Met. DS Griffin and DC Hooper deserve the best, and DCS Winters will have the resources to ensure they get it. Nigel, over to you.'

Rather than upstage the SIO, the three Command officers rose from their seats and left the room. The media relations man moved to sit next to his deputy, and Winters went to the laptop.

The SIO must be close to retirement, thought Tom. He was the most senior detective in MCPS, and had been pulled off a major terrorism enquiry to lead the hunt for Griffin's killer. He was grim and grey and his eyes glinted behind his glasses.

'After the Chief spoke to you on Thursday afternoon, I had the job of telling you we had nothing to go on, but I had to dress it up. Well, there are over a hundred new officers assigned to this case today and I'm going to go back to the beginning so you can bring all your team members up to speed.'

He logged on to the laptop and put up the first slide of a Powerpoint presentation. It showed a timeline from Wednesday night.

'We received a 999 call at 21:50 on Wednesday evening from a man with a local accent saying that there was an injured officer at the old goods yard. His exact words were, "There's a shot copper in the old Great Western Yard. This isn't bullshit. You need to get to him fast. He's behind the second shed on the left." The caller than rang off, and the control centre notified the nearest unit. In some ways we were lucky it was raining because there was nothing else going on and they went straight to the scene. Those officers were able to staunch the bleeding enough for the paramedics to save Ian Hooper's life. We didn't even know that Griffin was dead until the Territorial Support van started to search the area.

'The bad news is that the rain was heavy and prolonged. It washed away every piece of forensic evidence that might have been left behind. All we have are the bullets that were removed from Griffin and Hooper. I'll come back to them later.

'Ian Hooper is still under heavy sedation and critical. According to the chief surgeon, he will need further surgery no later than this evening, because all they did on Wednesday night was stop the bleeding. There's a lot of damage in there that needs detailed repair work. The good news is that he's recovered enough for them to attempt it. Virtually the whole surgical team is on standby for this afternoon. They're going to do it in relays.'

Tom thought of Ceri, Ian's girlfriend, and what she must be feeling. Had she moved from his bedside since Thursday? Were they allowing her into Intensive Care to sit next to him, or was he in isolation? And what about the armed guard which would surely be near the doors to the ICU? Ceri was a bright young woman, and Tom was sure she'd be strong for her big man, but would she realise what people were already saying behind her back: that Ian and Griff had been in something together and that they had brought this on themselves. The Chief Constable's coded message couldn't have been clearer to the officers present: *Someone corrupted Griffin and probably Hooper. Take them out before they do it again.*

Winters continued. 'Since then, we have scoured every known associate of both officers in an attempt to answer one simple question: What were they doing there? As yet, we don't know. According to Ceri Jones, Hooper's partner, he received a call on his mobile from Griffin at 20:20 and left the flat. Griffin was in the George pub in Earlsbury from around 18:00 until he left after making that call to

Hooper. His drinking buddies say that he was enjoying the game on TV and they have no idea why he disappeared.

'When we discovered Griffin's car off Sharrow Road, we also found another vehicle, close to the back entrance of the Yard. That vehicle was stolen on Wednesday afternoon, and we had no idea why. We think we now have an answer.'

Tom knew most of what he'd heard so far because Sam Cohen had given him the initial summaries of the case that Winters had prepared. The presentation was now moving into new territory.

'Whoever set fire to that building on Wrekin Road knew what they were doing,' said Winters. 'And they were helped by several hundred litres of vodka. The only thing we got from *that* crime scene were more bodies and bullets. But those bullets tell a story. The forensics people were up all night testing them, and we are now certain that Robert King was shot by the same weapon that hit DC Hooper, and that Dermot Lynch was shot by the same weapon that killed DS Griffin. The positioning of the bodies also suggests that they were killed elsewhere and then transported to Wrekin Road.'

There were too many officers in the room for Winters to allow a discussion, but Tom was already jotting down questions. When he wrote *Type & Calibre of gun* he realised that he wouldn't be allowed to ask that question because it had no bearing on DS Griffin. The more Tom learnt about what was going on, the more he realised how out of the loop he was going to be.

Winters changed the Powerpoint slide to give a list of names that Tom had never come across before. The slide was in two columns with police officers' names on the left and suspects / witnesses / innocent bystanders on the right. Winters lingered for a second and showed two more pages of the same.

'Now we know that Dermot Lynch and Robert King were involved, we have a lever. It's up to you to use it to crack this case and bring things into the open. Naturally, the first person we pulled in was Lynch's uncle, Patrick. Turns out he was at his daughter's parents' evening on Wednesday, and he offered us the DCC's wife as an alibi.' Winters' smile was as grey as the rest of him, but he made the effort.

'However, we know that Dermot and his uncle were in business together, and we know that the Wrekin Road premises were full of cigarettes and alcohol. One of our first tasks is to turn over every rock and stone in Earlsbury until we find a connection between Patrick Lynch and that warehouse. In addition, the body of Robert King points towards a drugs connection. He was released from prison this summer after doing time for dealing class As. Was King dealing again? Was Dermot Lynch? Someone has eliminated both of them – who stood to gain from their deaths? All the obvious questions.

'These here,' he pointed to the screen, 'are the names given to us by Earlsbury division as people we should talk to, and that brings me to the most delicate point.'

Winters pressed a key to bring back the screensaver.

'The CID team from Earlsbury is focusing on other issues. You and your teams are not, repeat *not*, to approach them for any reason. All liaison with them will go through me. Everything. The only exception to that rule is the Professional Standards enquiry being led by DI Morton from CIPPS.'

Winters pointed at Tom, and he felt as if the Mark of Cain had just been placed on his forehead.

'This is a major enquiry. You in this room have all been on the HOLMES 2 course, but most of your teams don't know the ins and outs of the Home Office Large Major Enquiry System: that's why I'm relying on you to ensure that everything you turn up today is entered into the system before you go home. That's what the overtime is for – to get this enquiry up and running, not to pay for your

Christmas presents. Until Monday morning, only Team Leaders are allowed in the Major Incident Room. If you have any questions, contact the MIR manager.

'Now go and tear these bastards apart.'

The sound of thirty chairs being scraped across the carpet was followed by the bang of swing doors and voices disappearing down the corridor.

'What's that?' said Hayes, pointing to Tom's notebook.

Tom wasn't an inveterate doodler, but during Winters' presentation he had drawn a large £20 note on his pad. In place of the usual text, he had written:

Bank of Toytown. Pay <u>Kelly</u> on demand.

'I was up here a couple of weeks ago,' said Tom. 'It's funny, neither Mr Kelly nor the outbreak of counterfeiting was mentioned in the briefing. I'll fill you in later; right now, I need access to HOLMES 2, and I need to find out where the evidence seized from Earlsbury division is being kept. I'll meet you in the canteen in twenty minutes.'

Hayes's eyes flicked from the notepad to Tom and back again. She nodded and pushed her way out of the desks. Tom slipped away behind her and headed for the Major Incident Room.

There were no whiteboards covered with theories and flow-charts in the MIR: it was really just a communication and co-ordination centre, and the information was all on computers. It was busy, though. Tom paused at the only significant display – a large scale map of the southern Black Country with a variety of pins and annotations. In the space at the side were four pictures: DS Griffin, DC Hooper, Dermot Lynch, and Robert Marley King. Had Tom caught just a glimpse of King when he was at the West Pole? There was one other list: Significant Witness Interviews for Saturday. Tom scanned it.

Erin King
Theresa King
Francesca Lynch

James King

Three women and one man. These crimes were professional all right, and women make the best professionals – but the crimes were also vicious, heavy and casually committed. Tom could almost smell the testosterone, along with the smoke and fire.

At that moment, Nicole Rodgers came into the room with DCS Winters, who called for quiet. When he had it, he handed over to Rodgers.

'Sorry, everyone,' she said. 'The media circus is going to be even bigger now. One of the Sunday tabloids has made the connection between Robert King and James King, and from him to Queen Victoria. For those of you over thirty, she's a singer from the telly, and James King is her bass player / songwriting partner. If the Chief Constable can't give them something else this afternoon, that's what's going to be on the front pages tomorrow. Just so you know.'

The room dissolved into animated discussion, and Tom racked his brains. Queen Victoria? Well, if James was a musician, he was unlikely to be a violent criminal.

Tom collected a printed list of evidence that had been logged from the initial search of DS Griffin's desk and personal effects. He took the list down to the Exhibits Manager and signed out one item. Then he headed back to the canteen.

It was fairly easy to spot the surveillance because only one car followed Patrick's taxi on to the Elijah estate. When he lingered a few seconds to pay the driver and catch up on some gossip, the car had no choice but to go past them. He waited a minute by the front door, and it reappeared up the road. He gave the officers a wave. This was only the start. By tomorrow they'd have the experts on the job, and there would be no point in looking for them – always safest to assume they're there.

Janet opened the door and gave him a wordless hug. He took off his coat and went into the airless lounge.

Maria was sitting on her own, dabbing her eyes and probably wondering why Dermot's brother hadn't turned up from London yet. Fran was on the couch with two of their daughters. Elizabeth was leaning on her shoulder, and Helen was trying to get a conversation going. Ma was where Ma always was: in her chair by the fire. Janet had already disappeared into the kitchen to make tea, and the hiss of the gas fire was slowly replaced by the thunder of the kettle.

Fran stood up after lowering Elizabeth gently to the couch. The poor little one had drifted off to sleep.

'They came round not ten minutes ago,' she said. 'They wanted me to go in and give a statement there and then but I told them to arrest me or come back in an hour.'

He folded her in his arms and whispered in her ear. 'You're the best, love, and you know that. You'll be fine.'

He heard a theatrical sniff from behind him, and realised that he hadn't actually spoken to Maria. He placed a dining chair next to his sister-in-law so that he could put his arm around her. 'I'm so sorry, love. So sorry. He was such a good lad, and a credit to you and his father.'

Maria started crying again, and Patrick gave her another tissue from the box on the table.

'Is it because of what happened to Donal?' she said. From across the room, Fran shot him a look. 'You know, with Dermot and Robbie being found together ... is it because of what happened to Donal and Solly?'

'That was eighteen years ago, love. Whatever happened, it's because of what they got up to today, not what their fathers got up to last century.'

Maria pushed his arm off. 'Dermot didn't get up to anything. It was *you* who got up to things and *you* who got Dermot involved in the business. What was he doing there, Pat? What was he doing in that warehouse?'

He treated it as a rhetorical question, and tried to comfort her again. At first she resisted, but she took the comfort of his arms, as she had done when Donal was knifed in the heart. Francesca and Helen were both staring at her, mother and daughter united in their contempt for a woman who would accept comfort instead of a straight answer.

Pat hoped that his son-in-law would never test Helen's patience in the same way that he had tested Francesca's. He doubted that Helen would be as forgiving as her mother.

He patted Maria on the back and turned round. Ma's eyes had been on him since he entered the room, and now it was time. He slipped off the dining chair and knelt in front of her.

'I'm sorry, Ma.'

They had the canteen to themselves this time. All the officers were off in their teams being briefed, and only the occasional junior admin worker scurried in with orders for their bosses. Tom and Kris took the same table, but this time she sat opposite him. She booted up his laptop and showed him how to log in to the BCSS network and get into HOLMES 2.

'Sorry about that, sir. For showing you up by going into the briefing.' When he waved away her apology and drank his tea, she pressed on. 'Can we go back to the beginning? I mean, can we have our own briefing so I know what's going on?'

He leaned back in his chair and looked at her carefully. 'Have you ever heard the expression *Tilting at windmills*?'

'I've heard it. Sort-of means something pointless.'

Tom brought his chair back down to the ground. 'There's a book called *Don Quixote* where this old bloke thinks he's a knight and goes off to attack these giants with his lance – that's the tilting part. Except that they're not really giants, they're windmills. Everyone laughs at him. My my ex-boss accused me of doing that. Tilting at windmills.'

Hayes shuffled back in her chair. *She thinks I'm mad*, thought Tom, *and I don't blame her.*

'Ex-boss?' said Kris. 'What do you mean?'

'This time yesterday morning I was a DS in the London Fraud Squad, more or less. I took this job with CIPPS because I think there are giants out there who need to be brought down. Here, look at this.'

Tom took out his phone and scrolled through to the picture of Tanya Sheriden in hospital, her face ripped open by Joe Croxton at the beginning of the *PiCAASA* investigation. Kris Hayes flinched away from the picture then looked back again.

'That girl brought a small piece of a jigsaw to me,' said Tom, 'I told her it was like a bit of blue sky – a start, but only a small one. I've got another piece of the jigsaw up here in Earlsbury.'

They leaned towards each other, and Tom told her what had led up to the events of Valentine's Day, when Miles Finch and Joe Croxton were killed, and when the big picture – the pattern on the lid of the jigsaw box – had melted in the Essex snow. The only bit he left out was the part played by Kate.

Hayes blew out her cheeks. 'Blimey, sir. You've given up a job in Fraud to join CIPPS and chase around here?' She shook her head and finished her tea. 'But we've got no authority, really, have we?'

'It's like this. The Chief Constable really wants to know whether he can trust the rest of the Earlsbury CID team. That's all. But before we can answer that question, we have to work out the extent of Griffin's corruption. Effectively, I'm betting my career that I can find a lead from Griffin to the counterfeit distributors, and from them to the printers, and from them to whoever created this whole bloody jigsaw in the first place.'

Hayes tapped her fingers on the table and played with the ends of her hair where they emerged from the cornrows on her scalp.

'Where do we start then?'

'Have you got some wellingtons in your locker?'

'No. I haven't even got a locker.'

'You're a bit shorter than my cousin, but I've got some that should fit. Right, DC Hayes, lead me to the Great Western Goods Yard.'

Ma Lynch didn't often give orders, but when she did, they were law. After Patrick had apologised, his mother had announced what a terrible, terrible trial he was to her, and he had been allowed to sit down and enjoy his cup of tea. Helen told him that her husband would be off shift at two o'clock, and an idea started to form in his mind.

'Will he be going straight to bed?' asked Ma of Helen.

'Probably not. He did get a little sleep last night, so he should be okay.'

'Then he can join us for six o'clock Mass. We'll all be there to support Maria.'

Maria looked worried. 'I'm not sure I'll be well enough to go tonight,' she said.

Fat chance, thought Patrick: *she'll be more worried about missing The X Factor or whatever show is sucking out the nation's brains through the TV.*

Ma was not to be gainsaid. 'All the more reason to be there. All of us who are back in Earlsbury will go and support each other tonight, just like we will afterwards.'

As well as being an order, it was also a code. 1950s Dublin was a very different place from twenty-first century Earlsbury. What people did then was *show out*. Pat knew that the purpose of tonight's visit to Church was to show the community that the Lynch clan still stood strong and had nothing to hide. Word would get round.

The second part of Ma's statement had been addressed to him. When the funeral was over, Ma expected Patrick to contribute financially to Maria's future. She'd be lucky. There were going to be a lot of cutbacks, whether he went to jail or not. He'd bounce back in time, but not soon. Not this time.

'I'll pick you up,' said Fran to Maria. 'Pat can bring Ma and the girls.'

He wouldn't be surprised if Fran told Maria, in the privacy of the car, that she would find some work for her to do. Paid work, that is. Every penny that Pat earned from now on would have to be accounted for. Subsidies to Maria Lynch were somewhere at the bottom of Fran's list, below the golf club subscription and the winter break in Portugal.

A flash of light through the windows caught his eye. The unmarked police car that had followed him on to the estate pulled up, and a woman got out. Their controller must have given them the order to bring his wife in for the interview. He touched her arm and pointed. Seeing the policewoman, Fran set her mouth for action and got up to go, giving Ma a kiss on the way out.

Once her mother was out of the way, Helen excused herself to go out for a cigarette and Patrick joined her.

'Could you lend us a tab, love?'

'No, Dad. Your heart can't stand it, and if Mom smells smoke on you, it'll be me that gets it in the neck for supplying them.'

He shook his head. 'They'll keep her for hours yet. Besides, I don't think I can get through today without one.'

She hesitated then handed one over and lit both their cigarettes.

'Listen, love, you know what I felt about Dermot, don't you?'

Helen nodded and sucked on her cigarette. They had only been a couple of years apart at school, and Dermot had always had a soft spot for her.

'Well,' he continued, 'things are going to be bad for me for a while – perhaps for a long while. I had no idea of the people he was mixing with, and I need to be careful.'

Helen's eyes narrowed. 'You don't owe nobody nothing do you? No one's gonna be coming after us?'

As she started to speak, he shook his head vigorously. 'No, not at all, nothing like that, but they've pretty much wiped out the business and the cops will be all over me. I need to get in touch with people. Discreetly. They'll be monitoring everything for a while – including you.'

Helen looked around the garden, half expecting to see a pointy hat appear above the rhododendron, and Pat thought she might have a point. Didn't they have those fancy microphones now that could pick up conversations through glass? He drew her aside and turned his back on the other houses, whispering in her ear.

'I'm expecting another visitor. Can you do me a favour tonight?'

Kris Hayes looked dubiously at the wellington boots that Tom had passed out from the back of his car.

'Did you say your cousin was male or female?' she asked.

'Definitely female. Mind, she was in the Army for a long time. Back home, they used to call her *a strapping lass*, but not to her face.'

'Don't tell me you're from Yorkshire.'

''Appen I am, lass. Grew up on a farm an' all.'

'Oh. Sorry, sir.'

'Don't worry. It only comes out when I'm at home. My father is actually a circuit judge, and I used to be a solicitor in Edgbaston. We all have our crosses to bear.'

Hayes gave him a sideways look and pulled on Kate's socks before plunging her feet into the boots. Tom put his hands in his coat, and they walked through the gates into the Great Western Goods Yard.

The large apron in front of the buildings was potholed and disintegrating, remnants of the railway ballast from an earlier era peeking through the dissolving tarmac. *This is where trains would have lain idle*, thought Tom, *ready to be fed back into the network, and where lorries would have done the same.* On the right hand side of the open area, the surviving tracks were separated by a well maintained steel fence. A passenger train rattled its way towards Birmingham.

At the back, an older brick building with huge wooden doors was showing its roof trusses and leaning to the side. He pointed to it. 'Loco shed.'

'Sorry?'

'That brick one. It's a locomotive shed. You can tell from the height: there's room for the smoke to escape and for the hoists to take bits off the engines.'

'A Yorkshire trainspotter who used to be in the Fraud Squad.' Hayes shook her head in sad contemplation of the boss she had been given.

'My school in York was near the railway museum. It was something to do. The museum, that is. I have never stood on a station platform collecting train numbers.'

The other buildings were more recent but in no better repair. Tom led them through a larger gap where the tarmac gave way to mud, and they soon came across police markers where Hooper and, later, Griffin had been found. They were surrounded on three sides by sheds, though there were gaps between them, and Tom could see houses beyond which must have been where they gained access on the night.

'Okay, detective,' he said. 'What are your thoughts?'

She did look around a little, but not much, and she seemed to focus on the floor. 'I can't see anything that SOCO missed.' She looked at where Griffin had fallen. 'I know this: I wouldn't want to die here.'

'He didn't come to die here, did he? Look around you, Hayes, and try to imagine the night it happened. How much light would there be? Where is the nearest viewing point? You could hold a rave in one of these sheds, and no one would notice.'

'A rave? How old are you?'

'I'm trying to teach you something. Think about it. Griffin and Hooper came in from the back, and they *must* have known something was going on. They didn't stumble into this place by accident. We even know that Griffin was dragged away from the football and Hooper was dragged away from Ceri.'

She gave him a sharp look when he mentioned Hooper's partner by her first name. Perhaps she was paying attention.

'Then, when they got here, something went wrong. Whatever was happening here was definitely illegal, that's obvious, but did Griffin come to spy on them? To join in? To disrupt whatever they were doing?'

'He can't have been coming to arrest them. No way would he have come here without telling Control.'

'I didn't say he'd come to arrest them. I said he might have come to *disrupt* them – to stop them doing whatever it was they were doing for reasons of his own.'

Hayes looked around again. Then she walked back a few paces towards the entrance.

'If you want to avoid being seen from those houses, you'd have to be here,' she said. 'That's quite a way from where Griffin was shot, and Hooper was found round that corner, even further away. Griffin was an experienced detective. He wouldn't have been seen unless he wanted to be. He must have made himself known, and someone must have unhappy about that. Either they recognised him or they were so jumpy they were willing to shoot first and ask questions later.'

'Good. I agree.'

Tom turned and started walking back to the car. Hayes clumped behind him, the rubber of Kate's wellingtons slapping against her feet.

'I hope the next place is indoors, or at least has tarmac,' she said.

'It did the last time I was there. We're off to Earlsbury nick.'

On the short drive, Tom's hands-free phone went off. He couldn't reach into his pocket to check the caller so he just pressed Answer and announced himself by rank and name.

'Tom. I thought you weren't an inspector yet.'

'Hello mother. I've got a colleague with me in the car. She can hear you.'

'Oh. Hello. Can you call me when you get home?'

'I'm in the Midlands again on a big case. Don't know when I'll be finished tonight.'

'Oh dear, well, I'll have to ring Diana myself. It's Great Uncle Thomas. He passed away last night.'

'Sorry. I'll call you later. Thanks for letting me know.'

'Take care.'

Hayes was studiously looking out of the window and trying to pretend that his mother's polished vowels hadn't been assaulting her ears.

'Sorry about that,' said Tom. 'My great uncle has been ill for some time. He lives – lived – in America, and I only met him a dozen times.'

She turned towards him. 'Still hurts, though. I don't know how to put this, sir, but you've just gone the wrong way down a one way street.'

Tom swore. He looked frantically around and started a three-point turn. After a nervous moment with a delivery van, he reoriented the car and piloted them safely to the back of the police station.

There was a notice on the door of the custody suite saying *No Shortcut to Station. Walk round you Lazy So-and-Sos.* Nice welcome. He took the long route and presented himself at the desk. A civilian was behind the glass screen.

'DI Morton and DC Hayes to see CID. We're on the Griffin case.'

'Thanks. Can I check your ID?'

Tom hesitated then gave the woman his BCSS pass instead of his warrant card: the fewer people who knew exactly who he was the better. She kept his pass and made a phone call. Finally, she asked him to wait, saying that DCI Storey would be with them shortly. Tom sat but Hayes stood and started reading the notices. Anything to avoid being the first person that people saw.

Storey didn't look any older than when Tom had seen him earlier that month, but he had become a lot more dishevelled. Where once there was a crisp shirt, now there were creases. He buzzed them through and took them upstairs. As they entered the CID room, he said, 'Have they brought you up for your economic expertise, Tom?'

'In a way.'

'It's a big mess, so I can see that they'd want help from the ECU.'

Tom was about to correct him when they stopped in the almost empty room. Only one other detective was on duty that Saturday – Imran Hussein.

'Imran, you remember DS Morton, don't you?'

'I'm sorry,' interrupted Tom, 'but it's DI Morton now. And I'm with CIPPS.'

Storey winced and bit his knuckle. Hussein had half risen from his chair, but stopped and sat down again, the half offered handshake withdrawn.

'Come inside,' said Storey.

As they passed through, Hussein spoke to Hayes. 'I'm surprised you aren't on holiday with your pay-off money, Detective Constable.'

Tom stopped but Hayes marched past him, ignoring Hussein. From behind, Tom could see her spine stiffen in response. She arrived at Storey's office ahead of him and stood outside, following him in and sitting in a chair by the door. At least she got her notebook out.

'What do you want, Inspector?' said Storey.

It was neutral. Neither fawning nor hostile. Tom could work with that.

'Very simple, sir. I want to clear as many of your team as quickly as possible.'

'Good. Now what do you want from me?'

'Two things. First, I want to see where Griffin would have put the stuff he was working on.'

'Winters's team cleaned all his stuff out on Thursday.'

'I know, but that was his personal stuff. I checked. I want to see where he would have put something work-related if it weren't on his desk.'

Storey nodded. 'What's the second?'

'A question. You can say "Don't Know" or "No Comment" if you like, but I'd rather have the truth.'

Storey's mouth twitched a little.

'The question is this: do you think Griffin recruited Hooper to CID because he was already corrupt, or because Griffin saw his potential for corruption?'

Storey didn't even think about it. 'No Comment.'

Tom turned to Hayes. 'Have you got that, Constable?'

'Yes, sir.'

'Good.'

Storey stood up and went to the door of the office. He shouted across to Hussein, 'Show DI Morton the pending cases area,' and then he stood aside until Tom and Kris were out of the way. Behind them, he slammed the door.

Hussein stood waiting for them and then walked up another flight of stairs to the attic of the Victorian building. At one end of the low corridor, an even lower door was padlocked shut. Instead of a key, the lock was a combination. Hussein hid the tumblers from them as he released it then pocketed the padlock.

'How could you spend the night in Ian's home and then investigate him for corruption?' said Hussein. 'How could one officer do that to another. You might as well have slept with his girlfriend.'

Tom took half a step back. To his left, Hayes bristled and stuck out her jaw. Her eyes flicked between the men. Tom's armpits prickled with sweat, and then Hussein walked away.

To his retreating back, Hayes shouted, 'He stayed with Hooper because Cousin Malik didn't have any room.'

Hussein stopped for a beat then went downstairs. Tom let out a big breath.

'I'm not going to be your Sancho Panza,' she said to him. 'Yes, that's right. I looked up Don Quixote on the internet while you were talking to Storey. I'm not going to run round cleaning up after you.'

Tom leaned against the wall and rested his head on the sloping ceiling. He had expected it to be bad, but not this bad. He hadn't thought that CIPPS' reputation was quite so terminal until it was shoved in his face. But that wasn't the worst thing. It was the fact that he had let Hussein walk away. That was his fault, not CIPPS'. Hayes was about to say something else, and the anger was making her dark brown skin almost orange. He held up his hand and closed his eyes for a second.

'Give me your notebook, Kris.'

'I'm sorry, sir, I'm really really sorry about that. It's just that...'

'Stop it. Stop apologising and stop lashing out and give me your notebook.'

She handed it over, and he tore out a sheet from the back (so as not to disturb the page numbers). Leaning against the wall, he wrote:

Bring the largest evidence bag in the station. Now. DI Morton.

'Give that to Hussein. Don't say anything to him, just hand it over and come back. Not a word, okay?'

She snatched the paper and disappeared. He could hear her feet going down each step then back up again.

'Now we wait,' he said.

And wait they did. After a couple of minutes, Tom said, 'Is he really ACC Khan's cousin?'

'Yes. Sort-of. Something to do with an uncle marrying Khan's younger sister, I think.

It took Hussein nearly five minutes to return with a very large, laptop-sized evidence bag and a huge, dining chair-sized version. Tom examined them and put the enormous one on the floor. He offered the other bag to Hussein.

'Put your head in that, Constable.'

'What?'

'Put your head in the bag. It's evidence of your stupidity and needs to be catalogued. It may not be a crime, but it's certainly not good on your record.'

Hussein gave him a look of contempt and opened his mouth.

'Now give me the padlock.' Tom held out his hand, and Hayes stepped to her right, blocking the way back down. Hussein fished it out of his pocket and dropped it on the floor. Hayes stepped aside, and he walked away.

'Try not to take so long to think about it, next time before you put them in their place,' she said to Tom.

'I will, if you try to take *longer* to think about it. So it's us and them now? You said *put them in their place*.'

'It's always been us and them for me. Did you ask for the bag just to have a go at Hussein or is there a real reason for this?'

Tom scooped up the bags, the padlock and his briefcase, and gestured for Hayes to open the door.

'We're looking for blank V5C forms. You know: vehicle logbooks. A bundle of them. And when we've found them, look for anything in an evidence bag that you think someone might have been offered for sale in a pub – stolen, illegal, counterfeit. Use your imagination and keep going until we've filled the bag.'

'The big bag or the huge one?'

'Let's not beat about the bush. The huge one. We've a slippery fish to catch, and the more bait the better.'

'Talking of fish, do I get lunch on this job or not?'

St Andrew's Hall was having its afternoon nap. The house was quiet except for the background creaks and groans as the Edwardian radiators warmed the stones. The fire was laid, but not lit. Lady Jennings would be gone for the afternoon, and Sir Stephen left the house to its slumber, taking his dogs and his shotgun with him.

He went down the drive, over the lane and then into his woods: they weren't huge but they did contain a variety of wildlife. Jennings knew exactly where the rabbit warrens were located in relation to each other and to the open pasture on top of the hill. After letting the dogs run loose for a while, he called them to heel and told them to stay next to a big oak tree, then he moved slowly along the track for the last hundred yards before the woods ended and he got a clear view of a mound. The rabbits were feeding, and right on the path were two bucks. He got one of them with his first barrel.

Calling the dogs, he picked up the rabbit and went to the top of the hill. Will Offlea was waiting for him.

'Nice shooting, Sir Stephen. You've not lost your touch, so I see.'

'Hmph. Only got the one, though. Scarcely worth making a pie from.'

Offlea's names were legion, and his choice of name depended on who he was talking to: Red Leader, Barbarossa, Red Hand and now Adam Paisley. *For goodness sake*, thought Jennings, *whatever next?* Today, his man was dressed for fell running and had obviously arrived from some distance away.

He sat down next to the Ulsterman and put his shotgun carefully over his knees. The threat of rain seemed to have moved north but it was cold and little whips of wind found their way around the woods and under the collar of his Barbour. Offlea passed him a hip flask.

'Why on earth did you suggest meeting *on a golf course?*' said Jennings.

'I'm thinking of taking up the game, so I am. That's where our man Lynch does his business. Great for privacy, and you can wear any disguise you want.'

'I wouldn't have described Pringle sweaters as a disguise; I'd never be seen dead in one. You could always tell which officers didn't have a future in the Army: they took up golf when they made captain.'

'We don't all have our own estate to wander around, you know. Some of us live in cottages. At the moment.'

'One wood and a couple of pastures doesn't make an estate. Anyway, what's going on up there?'

'Duck and cover time, sir. Everyone's gone to ground and no one knows anything. I had a wee chat to our Principal Investor there this morning and the news gets worse. The police standards people in London have sent up their new recruit – Tom Morton.'

'Damn and blast. That man doesn't take no for an answer, does he? What's he doing?'

'He's looking into Griffin who, as we know, had no link to the counterfeit money, but he's shown us before that he can find things out, given time. Have you any news on that cousin of his? Morton wouldn't have cracked open Blue Sky without her, and we need to keep her well away from Earlsbury.'

'She's in Scotland. We're going to try and get her out of the country completely after that. Skinner reckons that with a little more prodding, she could be a valuable recruit for us.'

'Wouldn't that be a turn-up for the books?' He paused. 'Morton's not the reason I asked for a meeting: I've had contact from the men who walked off with our money and left a trail of corpses in their wake.'

'I see. Are you sure it's them?'

'It's them, right enough. They used the mobile we gave to Patrick Lynch. They must have taken it off his nephew before they shot him.'

'What do they want?'

'To do business. They say they want to pay us for the two million they took on Wednesday and carry on afterwards. I said I'd need to talk to you about it.'

'If this had happened last year I'd have said it was too risky. I've heard from Clarke in Afghanistan – the Red Flag shipments are starting up again next week. They are the priority and always will be. But that's not the point.'

Jennings took another swallow from the hip flask and passed it back to Offlea.

'Have you heard what this new government are proposing? They want to cut the Army by up to 20 per cent. Not just the budget, but the number of actual men. Probably more by the time they've finished. There's only one way they can do that: pull out of Afghanistan as quickly as possible. We'll never be able to keep Red Flag going without a substantial presence on the ground. And if the Army is cut by that much, Operation Rainbow will be needed even more.'

Jennings stood up. The cold was seeping through his coat and his hips were getting stiff. He set off to walk round the boundary of his pastures and check the fences.

'That's not all,' said Offlea. 'The man from Blackpool said they were in the market for other stuff as well – booze, fags, pills.'

'No drugs. Never. And without Lynch to source the merchandise, how are we going to get our hands on any more of the other stuff?'

Offlea waited while Sir Stephen checked the barbed wire fence and grunted with satisfaction.

'How many Principal Investors have we got?' asked Offlea.

It was a blunt question. Offlea knew most of the nooks and crannies of the Operation Rainbow portfolio. He knew who dealt with whom, and he knew about the flow of money and goods, but he didn't know many of the backers or the people who arranged things. Only Jennings knew that.

'Apart from you and I, there are four. Two in Red Flag, one each in Blue Sky and Green Light. Why do you ask?'

'If Red Flag closes, what's going to happen? Green Light relied on Patrick Lynch, so it did. Blue Sky is nothing without a distributor, and I don't think our return on the investment was good enough. In my opinion, sir, Operation Rainbow needs a long term replacement for Red Flag and, if you don't mind me saying, some of those Principal Investors are holding us back.'

The next post in the fence was a little wobbly. Jennings gave it a tug and made a mental note to point it out to the farmer who leased the pasture in winter for some ewes. Unfortunately, he had to agree with Offlea. There were just too many people taking a percentage from all these deals and putting very little back into the pot in return.

'It's not just the freeloaders,' said Offlea. 'It's dealing with some of these people. Thornton in Essex, Lynch in Birmingham. They're hard to keep hold of. These new boys – the ones with our money – they're based in Blackpool. It would be a lot easier for me to keep tabs on them as I'm round the corner, so to speak. If we consolidated all our operations in one part of the country, we could reduce the risk.'

Jennings nodded. 'And what about the money laundering? Who's going to do that?'

'If you cut back on the number of Principal Investors, we could put it all through the downstream side of Red Flag.'

'Are you up to this, Will? Can you work with these people in Blackpool and get the sort of returns we need?'

'Have I ever let you down, sir?'

'Let me think about it. It would mean a big shift in direction.'

Offlea dug his hand in his pocket. 'All change. We need to move the mobile numbers around.'

He handed Jennings a new phone and took the old one in return. Sir Stephen wondered where they all ended up – would some future metal detectorist come across a deeply buried hoard of discarded phones, or did they end up in Africa with various illegal goods?

Offlea jogged away alongside the fence then vaulted over the gate. He accelerated away along the ridge, then disappeared down the other side of the hill. Jennings felt the October wind ripple his jacket and thought of the fireplace in St Andrew's Hall – it was becoming a refuge that was harder and harder to tear himself away from. Operation Rainbow, in all its aspects, was going to need a new leader soon. Not Offlea, of course, but someone who could give it strategic direction and control.

He summoned the dogs. One of them had a second rabbit in its jaws.

Tom and Kris were sitting in his car, sharing a helping of fish and chips. Neither of them had fancied a whole one after they saw the size of the portions. His BMW would smell of vinegar for days.

'What next?' asked Hayes.

'I need to find someone – and I need his mugshot for that – so I think we'll go and have a look at Griffin's house first, then print off some pictures when we go back to BCSS.'

'Fair enough.'

Tom tore the remaining battered haddock in half and ate one of the pieces. He left the rest to Hayes who started picking among the scraps to see if there were any juicy chips left. Tom wiped his hands.

'You won't be going to America for the funeral?' said Hayes around the last of the fish.

'No. Great Uncle Thomas had sort-of converted to Judaism, and they'll hold the funeral tomorrow, in line with tradition. My Granddad, his brother, went over in the summer to say goodbye.'

Hayes wrapped up the newspaper and stuffed it into a carrier bag, then left the car to look for a bin. That was thoughtful of her. She came back and offered him a wet wipe from her well-stocked bag. That was even more thoughtful.

'My dad will have to go to the States, of course,' said Tom, mostly to himself. Then he remembered his passenger. 'Because Great Uncle Thomas didn't get married properly, Granddad is now the Third Baron Throckton.'

'You're joking me.'

Tom started the engine. 'I wish I were. As well as being a white public schoolboy, I'm also going to be a Lord. If I outlive my father.'

'I'm not bothered about the white part, sir. It's the rest that bothers me.'

'Pardon me for being born. Now, do you know the way to Griffin's house?'

Hayes directed him out of the town and on to a small estate of executive homes.

'A bit posh for a detective sergeant, don't you think?' said Tom. 'Check the file, will you? Was he ever married? Any kids to support or alimony to pay?'

'Neither,' said Hayes without looking. 'Forty-eight years old, never married. At one point a woman was named as beneficiary on his pension records, but she was deleted.'

The murder team had searched the house on the morning after Griffin was killed, but they had taken nothing because nothing illegal had been found, and they had left the rest for him to sort through. Tom was fairly certain that whatever Griffin was involved in would leave few physical traces.

They contemplated the brick facade and snapped on latex gloves. 'What are we looking for?' asked Hayes.

'Anything which looks or smells like a financial record.'

'I'll have to defer to your experience, sir. I don't know what a financial record smells like.'

'Clearly a gap in your education. Consider this case as a masterclass in financial crime from the man who broke open the Wimbledon Mortgage Fraud.'

'You're being serious, aren't you?'

'I'm always serious about money.'

Tom opened the door and walked into the house. It didn't smell of anything. Griffin was obviously a self-sufficient bachelor who liked to keep his own nest clean. Either that or he had a good cleaner. Tom wouldn't have minded living there. It was a big step up from his hired box in the City.

'What do you think?' he asked.

'About what?'

'His taste. If you moved in here, how long before you wanted to give it a makeover?'

Kris looked around the combined sitting room/diner. 'Apart from the TV, I'd insist it was all put in a skip before I took the keys, and I'd send in the decorators before I crossed the threshold.'

That's clear, thought Tom: *bachelor policeman is a not a style I should aspire to.*

'You start downstairs, I'll do upstairs. One more thing, if you see anything you think is worth more than five hundred quid and is small enough to fit in your pocket, take that, too.'

For half an hour, they meticulously emptied drawers, lifted furniture and checked for loose corners of the carpet in case there was a stash under the floorboards. The results were piled on the dining table.

'Loft or garage?' said Tom.

'Garage. I've had to stand on three spiders already, and you can't see them in the dark.'

Apart from empty boxes, the loft yielded nothing. Hayes came back with nothing from the garage.

'Before we go, I want to pat you down. And I want you to do the same to me,' said Tom.

Kris gave him a very wary look, but lifted her arms and spread her feet. He gave her a very quick search, avoiding all sensitive areas. He stood back, and she did the same to him. When she'd finished and shrugged her shoulders, he lifted up the sleeve on his jacket and pointed to his wrist.

'I could have walked out with this. It's one of Griffin's Rolex watches.'

He slipped it off his wrist and put it with the evidence on the table. 'This one was in his dressing table, and there was one on his body, but I found *four* Rolex boxes carefully preserved in the loft. What's the betting that the search team on Thursday walked off with the other two?'

They bagged all the evidence, including a laptop, and set off for BCSS.

'Did you leave your car there this morning?' asked Tom.

'I haven't got one. Mom had to give me a lift in.'

'If you wait for me to finish, I'll run you home.'

'Thanks. You don't have to.'

'No problem. Look, Kris, is there anyone at BCSS who would do you a favour? A small one?'

She breathed out and looked away. 'I can't think of anyone.'

Tom left it there, and when they got back, he told her to commandeer a computer and start entering all the items they'd taken from the house on to the HOLMES 2 Exhibit

Log. They would have to be checked in with the Exhibits Manager and then checked out again so Tom could make a start on the bank statements and other paperwork.

While Hayes got typing, Tom floated around the MIR looking for a friendly face. He settled on a busy looking female civilian.

'DI Morton,' he said, flashing his pass. 'Are the pictures I requested ready?'

She looked around her desk and lifted some files to check. She didn't find them because Tom hadn't requested anything. He pointed to the printer.

'Could you do me a really big favour, and print four copies of a mugshot? Bloke named Kelly.'

With a little teamwork, they tracked down Mr Kelly on the system, and Tom walked off with his pictures. Because they'd been done live, there was no electronic record, and no one would know he was looking for him.

It was getting dark as Tom drove them back towards Earlsbury. On the way, Kris put their mutual numbers into their phones then Tom asked, 'Do you want a lift in the morning or shall I meet you in town?'

'What time do you want me?'

'I doubt we'll find Kelly up and about too early. Unless you want to come to the hotel and help me work on the financials.'

'I'll pass on that. I want to go to church with Mom. I can meet you outside the Congregational Church at eleven.'

'Fine. See you tomorrow.'

The Roman Catholic Church of Our Lady, Earlsbury, is modern and intimate: the bishop had a sense that congregations were going to dwindle over time rather than grow, and until recently, he had been correct. However, there was now a graph on the diocesan computer somewhere that showed attendance levelling out and then growing in the last five years, as the number of Polish catholics swelled the Church's ranks – and some souls that had been lost were saved when they came to consider which school to send their children to.

Word had also got round that the Lynches were turning out in force, and the six o'clock Mass that night was the best attended service since Easter. Patrick didn't find it comforting. He never did.

Ma insisted that Maria accompany her on the way out of the church. A lot of the congregation had stayed behind to sympathise, and Ma made sure everyone knew her opinion. According to Patrick's mother, there were dark forces at work who would make sure that Dermot's death remained a mystery. Although she knew absolutely nothing of the circumstances, Patrick thought she was right on the money. As usual. He waited in the porch.

Almost the last people out of the church were Helen and her husband. She sent her man ahead into the rain and gave her dad a kiss.

'I've had a phone call,' she said. 'From James King. He's going to be at Erin's this evening. Says he'd like a word.'

'Right. Are you okay to nip out on that other errand?'

She nodded.

'Thanks, love. You're an angel, as always.'

He took his mother back to the Elijah estate and found a parking space outside her house. He helped her inside and settled her by the fire.

'What have you got for your tea?'

'There's one of those shepherd's pies in the freezer. I'll pop it in the oven.'

'Shall I do that for you?'

'Please, son. You'll be getting off, no doubt.'

'Sort of. I might nip out and nip back. Over the fence.'

'Aren't you a bit old for that?'

He kissed the top of her head and went into the kitchen. The pie would take an hour, and he suspected his mother would be asleep by then, so he set the timer and placed it next to her. She was already nodding over the paper.

Patrick swapped his coat for an old one in the hall and slipped out the back door. He climbed over the low fence into next door's garden and into the garden behind. He went down the entry between the terraced houses and unbolted the gate. In seconds, he was on a parallel road and checking the parked cars for occupants.

Two minutes later, he knocked at the door of Erin King's house, and James King answered it. He had never had much to do with James. Sol King's older son looked more like his mother than his Jamaican father, if you stripped away the dreadlocks. He was wearing a tatty green combat jacket that Patrick dimly remembered seeing at the market when Sol used to help out.

James stepped back and pointed towards the living room.

Patrick checked the curtains (drawn) and looked around the room. Pictures of Erin and her children were thick on the walls. Over the fireplace was a recent one that included Robbie. After the near sauna conditions at Ma's, the house seemed cold, barely warmer than outside. James followed him into the room and remained standing.

'Erin's at her mother's,' said James. 'I got problems with paparazzi, believe it or not.'

'What on earth for?'

James dismissed the topic with a wave. 'Read about it in the morning. I just wanted somewhere we could meet without the press knowing.'

'And the cops. They've got me under twenty-four hour surveillance.'

'Quite right. I hope they arrest you and send you down for a looong time, Mr Lynch.'

'Is that so, James? I hope for your sake they don't do that because they'll have put the wrong man in prison. On

Wednesday night I was at my daughter's school. I wasn't within ten miles of Earlsbury.'

'Are you telling me that Rob would still be dead if you hadn't got him involved in your business?'

Patrick pulled his lip and looked more closely. Under the combat jacket, James was thin as a reed. Unless he had a weapon somewhere, James hadn't called him round to do violence. 'And are you telling me that Dermot would still be dead if Robbie hadn't got involved?'

A shadow passed over James's face and his mouth twitched in a spasm. 'It was *your* business. Yours and Dermot's. Rob was just a bystander. Your business got him killed whether or not you or Dermot pulled the trigger.'

'That's another thing, James. It wasn't any of Robbie's fecking business what happened that night. He should have been at home with Erin, not out at the Yard.'

Patrick took a step towards the other man. 'Robbie didn't have an invitation to that party, and he shouldn't have crashed it. In fact, I'm beginning to wonder whether he wasn't involved with the other side. Or with the cops. What about you?'

Patrick stepped forward and grabbed hold of James. The younger man struggled, but Patrick's weight pushed him back against the wall. Patrick quickly ran his hands round inside the jacket then stepped away.

'Just checking to see if you were wearing a wire.'

After the buffeting, James had shrunk back. Patrick was not a violent man at all. He hadn't been in a fight since he was at school. Well, not many, but things were desperate. He couldn't afford to have James King on his back as well as the police and Adam fecking Paisley.

He grabbed the picture from the mantelpiece and thrust it towards James. 'See those boys? And Erin? What was your brother doing that night? Why was he out there? If you're going to be throwing accusations around, I'd look closer to home first. I gave Robbie a job because your mother asked me to. I wanted to keep him out of trouble, not get him into it. Whatever he was doing that night had nothing to do with me. You might start with his old friends. The ones that got him banged up for dealing.'

Patrick replaced the picture and fastened his coat.

'His name was Rob, not Robbie,' said James. 'And I would never, ever, do Babylon's dirty work.'

Patrick stopped in the hall doorway. 'Listen, James, I'm sorry for your loss, and even more for Theresa's. If you find out anything I should know, pass a message through Helen like you did today.'

He left James in the living room and went back into the rain. He got back to his mother's in time to take the pie out of the oven and serve it to her on a tray. He left her to eat it in peace.

The chair in Tom's room at Earlsbury Park was comfortable enough, but the level of lighting in the room was appalling. He moved the furniture around a little and managed to get the standard lamp close enough to the desk to actually see Griffin's financial papers. Having arranged the room, he took a shower and went to the hotel lounge. He needed some food before attempting a spreadsheet.

A young woman in a severe black suit was standing at the entrance to the bar. Tom assumed she was the duty manageress and asked her for a menu.

'Sorry. I'm just visiting,' she said. The embarrassment rushed up her fair skin all the way to her blond roots. Before Tom could offer his own apology, she went ahead of him into the lounge. Tom followed at a safe distance and grabbed the nearest empty table.

Earlsbury Park was both golf club and hotel. Signs on the wall pointed to function rooms, and there were several displays of happy brides showing how much it had to offer for your wedding. Tom wondered if they did divorces, too. The woman in the suit walked through the hotel lounge and entered the Nineteenth Hole. Tom could see her stop just inside and have a conversation with someone. She didn't look like a golfer, he supposed, and she was unsuccessful in gaining admittance to the Members Only part of the complex.

She retreated from the forbidden entrance and went up to the bar, where she leaned forward and whispered in the barman's ear. He nodded in return. The woman stepped back then walked back out to the lobby, and Tom went up to the bar

'Excuse me, sir' said the barman. 'I'll be back in a second.' He disappeared through the service door, and Tom browsed the specials board. A handwritten note at the bottom was offering a happy hour where double vodkas were available at a price that meant they couldn't be making a profit. In smaller writing, it said *cash only*.

When the barman returned, Tom ordered food, a glass of wine and, on a whim, the happy hour double. Instead of going to the optics, the barman reached under the counter to fetch out a vodka bottle which Tom studied carefully while it was being poured into a double measure. He charged the food and wine to his room and gave the man a fiver for the vodka, telling him to keep the change.

Walking back to his table, he saw through the arch into reception where the woman in the black suit was lurking. A man came through a service door and joined her. Tom hadn't seen him before, but he was wearing a jumper embroidered with Earlsbury Nineteenth Hole. Probably the golf club steward.

While waiting for his food, Tom sketched a rough approximation of the logo on the vodka bottle into his notebook and wrote the name underneath. When the barman wasn't looking, he left the glass with its untouched contents on another table.

Chapter 8

Earlsbury

Sunday

24th October

Fate did not intend that Tom should enjoy the Earlsbury Park breakfast just yet: he had been summoned to another early briefing on Sunday morning. At nine o'clock he signed in to Black Country South Station and made his way to the Major Incident Room after grabbing yet another bacon bun from the canteen.

In the police service, overtime is paid to constables and sergeants only. Tom was already beginning to regret becoming an inspector as he looked around the MIR. Winters was preparing for the briefing, and four other police officers were present, all at DI level or above. They pulled up chairs, and were joined by the civilian managers (who weren't on overtime, either). Winters didn't even thank them for coming in; he just got straight on to it.

'First the good news. DC Hooper came through last night's operation successfully. He is no longer in a medically induced coma, but he is very heavily sedated and will remain so for at least twenty-four hours. Off the record, the doctors think he's unlikely to remember anything from Wednesday night because he was basically dead when they got him into surgery. Apparently that doesn't help the brain form short-term memories.

'Now the bad news. We covered a hell of a lot of ground yesterday for very little reward. Over four hundred and sixty interviews were carried out, and we even had two arrests, but no one was willing to say anything except the obvious – that Dermot Lynch was selling Chinese cigarettes and that Robert King used to be a drug dealer. There is some evidence that King may have been trying to sell skunk, but that's not conclusive. No one reported any whispers of him dealing class A substances. Thoughts?'

Tom's notebook was still open at yesterday's page. No one had mentioned the counterfeit currency – again – and a quick check of the HOLMES 2 log had shown that no one had interviewed Kelly. Or if they did, it wasn't logged. Something was starting to smell off about this.

One of the DCIs from Birmingham put up a hand and said, 'My lads reported a lot of plain denials from people who should have known something. Quite simply, they've all closed ranks.'

'I found the same,' added another.

Winters was playing with a whiteboard marker as he looked at the group. He tossed it in the air and snatched it like a drum major. 'Okay, what's missing? Which dogs aren't barking?'

'Sir,' said Tom, putting up his hand.

Winters pointed at him with the marker pen. 'DI Morton from Professional Standards. You may have noticed he's working with DC Hayes.' The distaste in Winters' voice was obvious to everyone. What surprised Tom was that it came when he mentioned Hayes's name and not his own.

'We all know that this was a big operation of some sort,' continued Tom. 'The people that carried it out have disturbed the status quo in some way. Why is no one talking about that?'

'Exactly,' said Winters. 'I can think of three possibilities. First, they're so powerful that everyone's afraid of them. Trouble is, no one gets that big without us hearing about it first or without making enemies who want to grass them up. Second, could this be a takeover bid from outside? If so, they'll need to show their hand soon. There is also the possibility that this had nothing to do with the Black

Country and that they'll disappear. I don't think that's likely, so we're going to focus on option two.'

Tom disagreed profoundly with this assessment. If the murders at the Goods Yard were connected to the counterfeit money, this is exactly what he would expect – that they would move on.

From the background, Winters wheeled a portable whiteboard which had all their names on it (including Tom's, in small writing at the bottom). 'We are moving into a different phase now. The overtime budget is just about shot out, and I've only brought in a fifth of the officers we had out yesterday. I've concentrated on those who are going to be continuing on Monday morning. The plan is simple – we need to be laying traps, making contacts and getting to know the area that Lynch, Griffin and King were operating in. When the takeover starts, I want to know about it. That's part one.'

Winters wrote *Intelligence* next to two of the names on the board. 'Part two is preparation for the interviews tomorrow morning with Patrick Lynch and Theresa King. Patrick is a long term distributor with a record going back to the last century. I want two teams here building up a picture. Basically, everyone who nominated Dermot Lynch as a villain should be seen as knowing something about Patrick, too.'

The name *Lynch* was written next to the other two local officers and *Griffin* was written next to Tom's name. Winters didn't seem to think it merited a comment. They were dismissed.

Three of the team in Aberdeen liked to keep in shape properly, and they had more-or-less forced Kate to join them. Sunday morning to them was a chance for a cross-country workout with running, circuits and a final dose of sparring in various martial arts. Kate had never gone beyond basic self-defence so she left them to it after the run and headed into the holiday cottage for a shower. She could already smell Sunday brunch wafting up from the kitchen when she got dressed and went to check her monitors – not that she expected them to show much activity overnight. Their team leader was waiting for her in the dining room which doubled as Kate's communication centre.

'Skinner's been on the line,' he said. 'Asked me how you're getting on. I told him very well – so well that we could do without you.'

'I'm not sure about that,' she replied. 'The contract was a fixed fee until the job's completed.'

'And will be honoured in full. That doesn't stop you taking the next job if necessary.'

That was a shame. Kate was enjoying this job. A good team, challenging work and no one shelling her at night. Much better than Helmand.

'It depends on the job,' she said.

'We've got a lot of work in Pakistan at the moment, but I don't think you're our best asset for that. It'll be a long time, if ever, before white women can move around the country with the sort of freedom we need.'

'Good – because I wouldn't go.'

He gave the hint of a frown. 'The same can't be said of China. Contract for GCHQ. How's your Mandarin?'

Kate got the feeling that this was in or out – the two jobs they had given her so far were relatively straightforward and well paid. The look in her team leader's eyes suggested that the gravy train would be coming to an abrupt halt if she didn't agree to this job.

'How much and how long?'

He nodded and handed her a USB drive.

Tom was early enough to find a parking space with a good view of the approach to the George Hotel. He locked his car and left it, heading off into town in search of the Congregational Church.

He had passed St Oswald's on its hill several times and discounted it, but the A to Z of the West Midlands showed a road leading off the High Street with two little crosses marked. Tom stopped at the paper shop to pick up the *Sunday Times*. While waiting in the queue, he noticed that two of the tabloids were leading with the same story: *Queen Victoria in Earlsbury Link*. He picked up the *Sunday Mirror*, stowing the papers and a bottle of water in a carrier bag. He went round the corner and paid a visit to the custody suite of the police station. He didn't mention CIPPS when he asked the sergeant whether there would be an interview room free later. After that, he cut through to Earl's Hill.

The road sloped down and he could make out some of the Birmingham skyscrapers in the distance. As it twisted to the right, he saw a cluster of people hanging around the entrance to a church. He crossed over and soon spotted the long lenses of paparazzi. The church was modern, and Tom doubted it was the Congregational – a judgement confirmed when he saw the Roman Catholic display board outside. An older man was standing back from the scrum. Tom had plenty of time and sidled over to join him.

'Who are they waiting for?' he asked.

The man gave him a sour look. 'Bloody leeches, they are. Can't leave a family to grieve in peace. Mind you, they'll be lucky if they see anyone today. Jim King hasn't been to Church in years and it's family communion this morning.'

This might as well have been in Latin for all the sense it made, so Tom just nodded. He suspected the answer would lie in the *Mirror*. A newish Jaguar drew up to the kerb, and all the paps rushed over, then backed away when they saw who was in it. The last of the rain was forming little streams down the highly waxed bonnet. Three women got out of the car and huddled close together. The older woman put her arm protectively around a fragile looking teenager before she propelled them towards the throng of photographers. Tom heard a few shutters popping, but no one approached them.

The third woman who had got out of the car was between the other two in age and had changed her blouse since Tom had asked her for a menu last night, but she was wearing the same suit. He turned away in embarrassment and noticed that the Jaguar driver hadn't emerged to join them, but had sped off while the women were still adjusting their coats. The next vehicle down the hill was a satellite TV van. Not a news truck, but an engineer's vehicle with a film promo on the side.

He'd seen that film nearly four months ago, and he'd seen the same advert for it on an identical van this morning. The van was parked in the secure car park at BCSS. Who was in the Jaguar and why were the surveillance team following it?

He turned to the old man. 'Sorry to bother you, but I'm meeting someone at the Congregational Church. Is it down here?'

The man gave him an appraising look. 'No, mate, that's the United Reformed down there. Congs are back over the hill, by Elijah.'

Tom remembered his trip round the Elijah estate with Hooper and the small building at its entrance. He thanked the man and headed back up the hill.

The Congregational Church of Earlsbury was built from the same bricks as the Elijah estate which sprawled behind it. The doorway was mean and promised little in the way of architectural grandeur. When the congregation emerged at eleven o'clock, Tom could see why the old man of Rome had given him such a funny look. The worshippers here were about 90 per cent Afro-Caribbean.

Kris Hayes emerged in the middle of the throng, smiling and relaxed. There were far more women than men in the group, and she was being fussed over by motherly figures.

Tom kept well back on the pavement, but he could sense one of the women making for him.

'Excuse me, are you Mr Morton?'

'Yes. Mrs Hayes?'

'That's right. I'm Kris's mother.'

A handshake was followed by an appraising look. 'She says to tell you that she needs to get changed and she won't be long. She says you been good to her yesterday.'

'She's got the makings of a good detective.'

Mrs Hayes nodded. 'Of course she has. Shame on them, shame on them.'

Before Tom could ask what she meant, Mrs Hayes was walking back towards the church. A few minutes later, she reappeared with her daughter, who was now wearing trousers instead of a skirt. Mrs Hayes locked the doors behind her.

'Morning, sir. You met my mother, I see.'

'Yes. Is she an elder or something?'

'Sort of. Let's go before she invites you for lunch.'

Tom thought that lunch was quite a good idea, but fell in beside his DC. At the turning into George Street, he pointed at the pub, 'Which one of us is going to stand out most in there? You or me?'

She considered the building and pointed to the two blackboards outside. One offered *Traditional Sunday Roast* and the other promised *Three Live Games* with Stoke City vs Manchester United as the opening attraction.

'Both of us.'

Tom handed over the carrier bag with the newspapers and his car keys. 'I'm going to have a quick look round. When I get back, I want to know who Queen Victoria is and what on earth is her connection to Earlsbury.'

Kris gave him a deadpan look. 'Apart from her visit here in 1884, you mean.'

'Did she?'

'I've no idea. Sounds like the sort of useless information you should be telling me, though.'

Tom laughed and headed into the pub.

He avoided the room where sounds of Sunday morning TV were emerging and headed into the restaurant. A waitress told him that they wouldn't be open for food until twelve. Tom was about to leave when he spotted something behind the bar. He flashed his warrant card and told the waitress to get the manager. It took a couple of minutes before a man in chef's whites appeared.

'I thought you lot were finished with us,' he said. 'Make it quick. I've got two sides of beef to keep an eye on.'

'I think the other officers might have been asking the wrong questions,' said Tom. 'They were probably asking what happened last Wednesday night … and do you know anything about what was going on.'

The manager nodded cautiously. 'What did you say your name was?'

'DI Morton, special investigations.' It was near enough. 'The question that should have been asked is this: Why are you selling Dermot Lynch's knock-off vodka?'

'No, we're not,' said the manager, but his eyes had already flicked to the optics where the same brand of vodka that was kept under the counter at Earlsbury Park was on display.

'That beef's gonna burn. What do you want?'

'Two things: co-operation and Kelly. Will he be here?'

'You're welcome to the old bastard. Of course he'll be here. About half past twelve. He'll be making a book on the Man Utd game, too. If you arrest him, make sure you arrest the bloke on his left as well. He keeps the records.'

Hayes had spread newspaper all over his car, throwing the various components of the *Sunday Times* in the back and disappearing behind its Sports section. The *Sunday Mirror* was folded up on the driver's seat and she had helpfully put a ring around three paragraphs. Tom scanned the highlights:–

Queen Victoria – Pop Sensation – Competition Finalist – Bass Player – James King – Drugs Conviction – Both their fathers murdered…

He stopped reading. 'What's this about Lynch and King's fathers?'

'Looks like you an' me are the last to be told – because everyone else knew. Solomon King and Donal Lynch were killed in a fight in Earlsbury. King killed Lynch, and an unknown assailant killed Solomon King. It happens.'

'Surely it can't be a coincidence.'

'Why not? Dermot and Robert were in the same class at school. Earlsbury's a small town, and it was a long time ago. They were only little.'

'Is there more?'

'Try the big paper. There might be something in there.'

'It's called a broadsheet.'

'After the size of the paper, I know. We did all that in media studies. Doesn't make it any easier to read in the car though, does it?'

Tom ferreted about in the back until he came up with the relevant section. He learnt that Patrick Lynch had fathered a child with Solomon King's wife, and that the cuckolded husband had been killed in a brawl at a pub which no longer existed.

He was wondering what this could mean when his phone rang. For the second day running he had had to introduce Hayes to one of his relatives. This time it was Kate.

'Oh. Sorry. Can you talk?'

'Up to a point. I'm on surveillance in Earlsbury.'

'Aah.'

'Quite. I'll tell you all about it later. And why I'm not with the MLIU any more.'

'Oh. I'm afraid that *later* might be a while. I'm done up here and I'm off abroad.'

'Surely not back to Helmand?'

'No. Never. The food's much better where I'm going, though you might not agree.'

'Well, take care.'

Hayes had made no pretence of not listening this time. 'That sounded like you were talking in code.'

'We were. Kate's just left the Army and now she's off to China, apparently.'

'How d'you know that?'

'Old joke. I prefer Indian, she prefers Chinese. Which is your favourite?'

'Jamaican. Nice change of subject, by the way. What's the plan?'

'Drive off, come back in an hour or so and arrest Kelly. In the meantime, you do have a choice – Earlsbury Park or BCSS canteen.'

'If you're paying, it's Earlsbury Park.'

James stared around the room. His brother's room. He had rung the police yesterday and told them he was breaking the seal on the tape at six o'clock unless they came and stopped him. They didn't.

When he crossed the threshold, he expected it to be the room of a teenager, covered with posters and smelling of dirty laundry. Except that Rob was a father of two boys. At the end of his life, his little brother had become more of a grown-up than James might ever be. His mother was still raw with grief and shock. James wasn't cut out to hold the family together.

He sneaked a look through the curtains. Some of the paparazzi were still there.

He had convinced his uncle to bring some food round yesterday, but his mother needed more than packets and tins. That had been something else Rob had done – cook his fair share. If something didn't change, they would all go mad.

He went downstairs and found Hope tapping away on her computer.

'You busy?'

'Not specially. Just telling everyone what's going on.'

'If I can organise for someone to bring lunch, can you help Mom to get dressed?'

She looked a little queasy and brushed some of the red hair away from her face. 'Wouldn't she be better getting some rest?'

James jerked his head towards the ceiling. 'She's not resting, she's festering. The police will arrest her tomorrow because I get the feeling they've got jack shit going on, and you know what happens next: blame the black man.'

'What are you going to do? For dinner, I mean.'

'I'm going to ring Roots Kitchen in Dudley and get them to do a big spread. Then I'm going to ring Dave Parkes and get him to collect it.'

Hope shifted uneasily in the chair. 'I'm not sure that's a good idea. I don't think he was very supportive on Thursday or Friday and he was away in London yesterday.'

'It's about time he got his fat arse round here, then. She can shout at him instead of you and me.'

'She hasn't been shouting at anyone. I wonder if that's the problem: you're so angry, but Mom's just turned in on herself.'

'What about you, Hope? How do you feel?'

She shrugged. 'I don't know. Rob wasn't around much until this summer. First he was with Erin, then he was in that flat and then he was in jail. It felt like having a new brother when he came out, and that the old Robbie is still out there somewhere.'

He patted her on the shoulder. 'Go and help Mom. Don't tell her about Dave – just get her up and dressed and wearing something smart.'

Parkes took a lot of convincing. James had to lower his voice to swear at him properly, but he caved in and turned up at the appointed hour with the food. Theresa stood up when he came in and then fell into his arms with deep sobs, wrenched from the bottom of her pit of grief. For only the second time since Friday, James felt his eyes brimming and put his arm around Hope. She started crying, too.

They all managed some of the food, and for once Parkes didn't try and eat it all himself: like reggae, Jamaican food wasn't his first choice. Theresa had made an effort to talk about something else during the meal, and a brittle calm descended on the family until James noticed that Dave wouldn't meet his eye. James started to stare at him, and Parkes's end of the conversation flagged until Hope gave him a fierce dig in the ribs. He asked her about life in St Andrews, and she started to tell them about the Honourable Amelia and what she did with a live python during Freshers' Week. At the end of the meal, Theresa excused herself and Hope started to clear the dishes. James stood up and put his arm through Parkes's.

'Let's go for a smoke, Dave. The police have been very good. They haven't taken my stash. Yet.'

Parkes started to pull away, but James twisted his elbow and pushed him forwards. Hope stood open mouthed as her half-brother dragged her mother's boyfriend through the kitchen and out the back door.

James released the older man and pushed him against the garage wall.

'What the fuck's going on, man? You fucking know something, don't you?'

Sweat broke out on Parkes's forehead and his eyes flicked up to Theresa's bedroom. 'Leave off, James. Look at how your mother is – she's in bits.'

James poked his finger into Parkes's chest. 'I don't give shit about what you mean to her. That's her problem. If you don't fucking tell me what you know, I swear I'll gut you.'

He reached into his pocket and took out a very old flick knife. It had been in his father's toolbox. 'Talk, Dave, or I'll stick you like a pig.'

'All right, all right, but not here. I can't tell you unless Paddy Lynch is there, too.'

'Now is good. Tell me now.'

Parkes shook his head. 'I can't. I can't. Not without Lynch.'

James put the knife away. Patrick had a right to know, too, and Parkes had called his bluff. James would no more stab the fat rocker than he would stab himself. 'I'll set it up for tonight at the church. Seven o'clock. Now, let's have a smoke and chill out … eh, step-father?'

James went to retrieve his stash from the barbecue and saw Hope watching him from over the kitchen sink.

They opted for the Earlsbury club sandwiches in the bar rather than dine in the restaurant. This was the fourth time in two days that Tom had eaten a meal with bacon, and he wondered whether his blood phosphate levels were going to become critical. There were too many people around to talk about the case in comfort so they made small talk about Tom's life in Yorkshire and Kris's guilty pleasure in watching *Strictly Come Dancing* with her mother. She told Tom that they had to be finished in time for the Results Show that evening.

On the way out, she pointed to the Nineteenth Hole. 'Do you play?'

'Not many golf courses in the City of London.'

'You should have picked up Griffin's clubs instead of his Rolex. From what I hear, a good set is worth far more.'

Tom stopped in his tracks. 'What clubs?'

'They were in the garage, by the door. Looked like they were ready to load up and go – either that or he'd just got back.'

Tom started walking again and when they were outside he said, 'Golf's an expensive hobby. I saw no indication in his finances last night of any membership or fees or any charges on his credit cards. That's another avenue they haven't looked into.'

Earlsbury was busier when they got back to the town centre, though few of the shops were open. Tom drove carefully through the archway at the George which said *No Entrance* and parked next to the skips.

He led them into the kitchens and found the manager wielding a wicked-looking carving knife. 'Is that an I.O.Shen?' he asked him.

'Yes. Get out. This is a food preparation area.'

Kris stifled a giggle.

'One last thing,' said Tom. 'I want a plate of soup and a chef's coat.'

The manager waved his knife towards the pass, and Tom picked on a female commis chef and repeated his request, this time showing his warrant card. The woman hurried into a storeroom and threw a white jacket in Kris's direction, then ladled out some soup and got back to work.

'What am I supposed to do with this?' said Hayes.

'Put the jacket on, take the bowl and go into the lounge. Say *One Soup* very loudly, then walk around looking for Kelly. When you find him, stand behind him and look lost. When I go to make the arrest, make sure you liberate a notebook from his friend.'

Kris struggled into the smaller woman's jacket, gave Tom a dark look, and set off into the pub. Tom followed her into the lounge bar. It was still half an hour to kick-off, but most of the clientele were flicking their eyes back and forth to the big screen TV. Kris had disappeared around the corner, and Tom followed her.

A wave of silence preceded him through the bar and washed around the corner. As he turned to see into the nook, Kris dropped the soup down a man's back and Kelly leaped out of the way.

The punters pushed back their chairs to get away from the flying liquid and shouted in horror. The man with the soup was in pain and reached around to wipe the burning liquid off his neck. Kris leaned forward and lifted a notebook out of his pocket. He grabbed her arm at the same moment as Tom grabbed Kelly.

Kris broke the bag man's hold and pushed him away. Kelly looked up and flinched when he recognised the man who'd just put him in an armlock.

'Police!' said Tom. Half a dozen punters stood up and formed a ring. The soup man looked from Hayes to Tom and was about to start a fight to retrieve the book when Tom said, 'Mr Kelly's coming for a chat. Aren't you?'

'Okay,' said Kelly. 'Leave it. I'll sort it out at the station.'

The other man backed off, and Hayes stripped off the chef's jacket. Tom released Kelly and they backed out of the bar. Once safely outside, Tom issued the formal caution.

'That's no way to start a relationship,' said Kelly.

Patrick waited in the golf club lounge until he could talk to the steward in private. The man confirmed that Helen had dropped off one of the phones which Kelly had delivered to Ma's house. Patrick retrieved the phone and found one message:

Will call at 1300.

Pat had taken the phone into the locker room (mobiles were banned in the lounge) and found an unoccupied corner. It rang dead on time.

'Yes?'

'Good afternoon, Mr Lynch.'

'You're a grand mimic, Adam, so you are.'

'This isn't Mr Paisley, it's his boss. I thought you deserved to hear it from me. Operation Green Light is over,

I'm afraid. We're pulling out and going into business with your friends from the North. They're going to pay for what you lost, so don't worry about that. You can do what you like from now on – no dividends to pay, no obligation. But no tactical support, either, I'm afraid. I'll be destroying this phone after we've spoken, but I just wanted to say *thanks*.'

'What about the cops? They're swarming all over me.'

'I'm sorry, you'll have to fight that battle on your own. Just remember the initial contract, that's all. If you mention our involvement, we'll have to silence you. And your family. All of them. We've done it before. Goodbye.'

Patrick's hand was shaking when the screen went dark. He'd dealt with thugs like "Adam Paisley" plenty of times, but this was something different. He could hear the distant thunder of guns in that man's voice, and was glad to be shot of him. He took a deep breath and massaged his chest for a few seconds then went back into the lounge. He palmed the phone to the steward and walked out.

It took less than two minutes to get from the George to the custody suite by car; Kelly spent the whole time trying to get Hayes to hand back his book.

'Can I not give you some good odds on the boys today? United to beat the Potters at five to one. You'd be robbing me. And if you're not a sporting lass yourself, your man at home could place a bet for you.'

Hayes gave him a hard stare.

'Or your woman. I'm not prejudicial at all. If they place the bet, no one knows it's you, see?'

Hayes took out her handcuffs and waved them in Kelly's face as Tom waited to cross the High Street.

'Now let's not get off on the wrong foot. Your boss was bad cop last time we met and you can't both do it. Why not start again, and you be good cop, eh?'

Tom spoke up, 'Hayes, you take him inside. I'll bring the evidence.'

Kelly looked from one to the other. 'What evidence. You've no evidence of anything. Hey, if you're going to fit me up I want a lawyer.'

Hayes jerked him out of the car and frogmarched him into the custody suite; Tom collected the large evidence bag he'd stored in the boot overnight and followed along. When he arrived at the desk, he could feel a sudden drop in temperature. The sergeant, so friendly in the morning, was glaring at him.

'Good afternoon, Detective Inspector, or is that Oberleutnant?'

'It's Hauptmann, actually. I'm more senior than an Oberleutnant.'

The sergeant opened his mouth and closed it. Tom's friend in Lambeth had warned him about comparisons with the Gestapo. 'Front it up,' he'd said. 'Make them look a fool.' Tom had to swallow to get the next line out.

'Have you booked Mr Kelly in?'

'I need to check whether this other officer has authority.'

Tom went up to the desk. 'This "other officer" is DC Hayes. You know she has the authority, just like you know I have the authority to put a note on your personnel record. Hurry it up.'

Hayes's eyes were pinched and she was pulling Kelly's arm far too tightly. Tom hoped it wouldn't show up on the booking room video.

'Sign here,' said the sergeant to Hayes and Kelly in turn.

The door to the main station opened, and DCI Storey appeared, looking even worse than yesterday. It was all very well leading your battered team by example, but the man wouldn't be fit for Monday morning at this rate. At least his presence explained the change in the custody sergeant's attitude.

Storey led them through in silence and pointed to Interview Room 1. Tom looked at it and said, 'Do you have a family room here?'

'Yes. Why?'

'We'll conduct the interview there, thank you.'

'It's locked.'

'DC Hayes will escort Mr Kelly back to the cells, and I'll help you look for the key.'

'It's with the DVRA team. Domestic Violence, Rape and Abuse – they're based in BCSS. They're only on call at weekends.'

'Sir,' said Hayes, 'I think…'

'Thank you,' interrupted Tom. 'If you could take Mr Kelly away.'

She wheeled the prisoner round, and Kelly looked utterly bewildered at the sight of two coppers tearing strips off each other.

When the door slammed behind Hayes, Tom said, 'No station commander has off-limits areas in his building. There must be a key.'

Storey's voice rose in pitch and volume. 'I've told you, Morton, it's locked. Use the other room or sod off back to London and take the Squealer with you.'

Tom had had enough. He pushed Storey against the wall and lifted his finger, but Storey grabbed hold of his lapels and head-butted him. Tom turned away a fraction, and the DCI's forehead missed his nose. Instead, it landed on his eye socket, and he staggered away in pain with lights flashing and then Storey kicked him in the stomach.

He collapsed on his side and curled up. From above, he heard a scream as Hayes launched herself over his body to crash into Storey. Tom struggled for breath, and the other two fought briefly on the floor, but Hayes soon had Storey on his front with his arms pinned behind his back.

'You okay, Tom?'

'Heeurgh. Ow, shit. I think so.'

'I was trying to say that I know the head of DVRA and she told me it's not a key, it's a combination. I can text her.'

Tom climbed to all fours and tried to stop his club sandwich coming back up. 'I deserved that. Thanks.'

Hayes climbed carefully off Storey's back and stepped aside. The DCI got up and and straightened his tie. 'Do you often let girls fight your battles?'

Hayes turned her back on Storey and looked at Tom's left eye. 'I'll make the call to DVRA and put you in the custody suite medical bay. That eye needs attention.'

There were still stars winking across his vision, and Tom knew he needed a time out. He let her guide him to the medical bay and waited with his head between his knees.

'Have you done First Aid?' he asked when Hayes pronounced that his eye was not seriously damaged.

'No, just been an older sister. You learn a lot that way.'

'I think my vision's cleared now. Let's get Kelly.'

'Why did you want the family room?'

'All the other interview rooms have video feeds that can't be turned off. The family room is the only one with an independent system, and I don't want Storey eavesdropping.

'Neat. I'll remember that.' She stood back. 'Sir, what would you have done if I hadn't come along?'

'You know my cousin, the one that rang up when we were in the car?'

Hayes nodded. 'Kate, yeah.'

'Same thing happened to me at school once. She got me out of that one as well. Told me afterwards that I shouldn't start something I can't finish.'

He went to the Gents and checked first to see if Storey was there. In the mirror, a black eye was already forming. 'Last time,' he said to his reflection. 'That was the last time I let that happen.'

He took a deep breath and went upstairs to meet Hayes.

He cleared away the children's toys and chose the squashiest armchair before ordering Kelly to sit in it. The man's small frame was almost swallowed, and he had to struggle to sit up.

Hayes pointed to the microphone on the coffee table and gave the Caution.

'Why are you doing this?' said Kelly. 'Turn the tape off.'

'So you don't want a solicitor,' said Hayes.

'No, let's get this over with, and let me get back to the pub. They'll be kicking off in a minute.'

Tom dragged the enormous evidence bag over to the settee where he and Kris were sitting. They had filled it with a variety of desirable items from the CID storage room: mobile phones, perfumes, a couple of laptops, several cheque books and other miscellaneous examples of shady merchandise. Each item was in its own evidence bag, but the preprinted forms on the outside of the bags were blank – no one had logged these items or made any official record of their existence. He took out the bag containing the V5C forms from his last encounter with Griffin and Kelly.

'I am showing Mr Kelly Exhibit 10/539422/01. This consists of a number of DVLA Log Books with serial numbers that are known to be stolen. Mr Kelly, do you recognise these?'

'What? Are you mad? That's all been sorted.'

'DC Hayes, could you pass me DS Griffin's notebook.'

Kris rummaged in her bag to give herself thinking time, and then handed over her own police notebook: the HOLMES 2 Exhibit Log was strangely quiet about the real thing. Another loose end.

'I have an official entry in the late DS Griffin's notebook which says these forms were found in your possession after a search of your car. As DS Griffin is no longer with us, I am pursuing this investigation for him.'

Tom placed the V5C forms in the middle of the coffee table and put the microphone on top of them. Kelly's eyes followed his hands as he went back to the Santa Sack of stolen goods and pulled out four items at random, placing one at each corner of the table. He watched where the other man's gaze fell and where it tracked back. Kelly ignored the phone and chequebooks, but kept straining his eyes at the other two. When he had finished, Tom reopened Hayes's notebook and pretended to read it.

'I have a note here relating to anabolic steroids and a lady's diamond bracelet. Would you like to comment?'

Kelly licked his lips and moved in the armchair. 'You can't use that notebook.' he said with a note of triumph. 'It's tainted.'

'Why is that?'

'Because Griffin was a corrupt officer. None of his evidence will be admissible.'

'How was he corrupt?'

'I paid him five hundred a month, so I did.'

Hayes snorted and tried to turn it into a cough. Tom tried to keep the triumph from his own voice when he said, 'There's two of us.'

'I can give you two grand this morning, and the same as Griff every month if you can look the other way. I can't afford any more, this online betting is eating into my trade something terrible.'

He passed Kris her notebook. 'DC Hayes, could you make a note of this: Mr Kelly, I am arresting you for conspiracy to bribe a police officer and for conspiracy to pervert the course of justice. You are still under caution. Before I offer you a lawyer, answer me this question. How much did you lose the last time you played poker?'

Kelly took a clean handkerchief from his pocket and wiped his face. He took a dirty one from the other pocket and blew his nose. 'Why?' was all he said.

'Why what?'

'Why have youse gone to all this trouble? Why have you dragged me up here, gotten yourself into a fight, and done all this when there's murderers out there running amok. What harm have I done to youse lot that I should be locked in here?'

Tom looked at Kelly, and Kelly looked from Tom to Kris and back again. Kelly pointed to the microphone on the table and made slid his fingers across his throat. *Kill the tape* was Tom's guess though with Kelly it might mean *They'll slit my throat if I talk*. It was time for a gamble of his own.

'We'll need to arrange for forensic analysis of these items. Interview suspended at 12:45.'

Kris went into the family room's kitchen to turn off the tapes and the red light on the microphone winked out.

'Give me the counterfeiters and whoever was distributing the notes,' said Tom. 'If the tip off is good enough, I'll put in a word with the CPS.'

Kelly had started shaking his head before Tom finished speaking. 'No chance, brother. Their protection goes much higher than your man Griffin.'

'What do you mean?'

'You're right about the poker. I never could get the hang of it, but I know me odds. Stoke City have no chance against United this afternoon, and you have no chance of catching these guys.'

Kris shifted in her seat and tapped her pen. She was itching to have a go at him. *If this were a game of poker*, thought Tom, *Kelly is holding a very strong hand*. He put on his most reasonable voice – the one he used with defence lawyers.

'Look, Mr Kelly, the chances of getting a conviction for handling stolen goods probably isn't great. I'll let that slide. You have to remember, I've got you on tape offering us a bribe. That's guaranteed jail time. I can get you for bribing Griffin as well, even if he isn't around to testify. We can forget all that if you give me the counterfeiters.'

'I'll take me chances, thank you very much. When you lot were fighting in the passage, the custody sergeant told me who you are.' He nodded towards Tom. 'He says you're up from London and you'll be going back soon. As for you, DC Hayes, he told me why no detective in Midland Counties will be keen to follow up on your work. My brief will have a word with the CPS and say that as Registered Informant, I was just testing you. They'll argue a bit, and I'll get a suspended for pleading guilty. They'll fine me too – and I can pay that out of the money I save from not having to pay you off.'

Kelly didn't push his luck. He sat back in the floppy chair and let the detectives mull it over.

'Pass me his betting book,' said Tom to Hayes. He flicked through the pages and saw that it only related to today's games. The book was cheap paper, and Kelly probably used a new notebook every time he went out. Not enough for a conviction under the Gaming Act. Although…

'You're right about one thing, Mr Kelly. I am going back to London, but DC Hayes isn't. It only takes the word of one police officer to get an ASBO.'

'An ASBO? You're joking, aren't you? They're for teenage hooligans not old men like me.'

'According to the newspapers, they're being used more and more for older, persistent nuisances. Like you. An Antisocial Behaviour Order can be used to ban people from all licensed premises within a ten mile radius. That would cramp your style.'

'That's below the belt, but I still won't say anything.'

'How about this: I'll leave you alone to fight the CPS if you tell me, in perfect detail, exactly what happened in the George last Wednesday night.'

'I can't remember too well. It's the drink, you know.'

Tom slammed the betting book on the table. 'Drop the act, Kelly. You wouldn't last five minutes as a bookmaker without a decent memory. You can remember exactly what happened, and if you give me one detail, just one thing that turns out to be a lie, I'll stay in Earlsbury and follow you for a month until you're barred from every pub this side of Coventry.'

Kelly shrugged. 'There's not a lot to tell. It was a busy night and I took a lot of bets. I wasn't giving any odds on United to win because that Turkish side are rubbish. Griffin had twenty pounds on United to score in each half, and he was on to the third pint that I'd seen him drink. He was there before me as well.'

'Who did he talk to.'

'Just some of the lads. There's a couple of boys who work at the bakery and start at ten o'clock. They always have a couple before work.'

'Did he look as if he was settling in for the night?'

'Oh, sure. He was pissed off when he got the call.'

'Describe it. Exactly. Every detail, starting with where you were sitting.'

'Where you found me today. Griff sat across the way, but he was waiting to be served when his phone rang. He stepped away from the crush to answer it, and he blocked my view.'

No phones had been found on Griffin's body. The records of his official phone had been checked and rechecked.

'Describe the phone.'

'It was his private one and before you ask, I don't know the number.'

'I guessed that. What make and model was it?'

'How should I know? I can tell you that it wasn't one of them new smartphone thingies. It was silver and it had buttons on it.'

'What happened?'

'It wasn't a long conversation. Griff only said two things. He said, "I've told you once, I'm not doing it," and he said, "I'll need to get someone to give me a lift." Then he swore and rang young Hooper, but you'll know about that because he used his other phone.'

That left one question. 'How closely involved was DC Hooper in DS Griffin's business?'

'I don't know about that at all.'

Tom raised an eyebrow at Kris, and she shook her head. They just didn't have enough leverage on him. He started to shuffle his papers. 'I'm just surprised that Griffin didn't drink at the golf club.'

It was only a fraction of a second, but Tom saw Kelly's eyes contract. The bookmaker pulled out his clean handkerchief again and mopped his face.

'Take him back downstairs and charge him. I'll sort out the tapes and start to put the paperwork together.'

'Will you be releasing me on bail?'

'No chance. It's a night in the cells and off to the magistrates in the morning.'

Instead of pursuing the counterfeiters, Tom was now going to have to spend his afternoon preparing a case against Kelly. When Hayes returned, he sent her home. There was no point in both of them losing their Sunday afternoons. By the time he returned to Earlsbury Park, his eye was a vivid sunset of purples, blues, reds and an emerging black.

King's message had been oblique and abrupt: *Parkes wants to talk. Meet at Evening Vigil.* Patrick had no idea what this was all about. He hadn't spoken to Parkes in years, and had only heard about Dave's relationship with Theresa when he handed over her fiftieth birthday present and she told him that she thought she had found her soulmate in the ageing rocker.

This time he couldn't use his family as cover – he had to call in several favours to get himself dropped off at Our Lady without the police surveillance following him. There were three priests who worked the circuit around Earlsbury, one Irish, one Polish and one English. The Polish Father did the family services because there were a lot of young kids who'd come over with their parents looking for work, just like his own father had crossed over in the 50s. The Irishman, their family favourite, had taken last night's Mass and dispensed solidarity to the congregation. No one liked the Englishman. 'Too holy for the Church,' was Ma's verdict, and he had to agree. The man was prone to holding public meditations on the Name of Jesus. Now where was the fun in that?

He went inside and saw Dave Parkes looking lost at the back and James King sitting proudly at the front. Patrick cuffed Parkes on the shoulder and whispered, 'You can't sit here on Sunday night. Get up the front.' Parkes edged out of the pew and went to follow him. 'Cross yourself, man. You'll have to learn all about this if you've got designs on Theresa.' Patrick genuflected and crossed himself before sliding into a seat next to King. Parkes bowed instead of genuflecting and crossed himself from right to left. Typical.

Most of the worshippers were across the way, close to where they would be led in meditation. They looked as earnest and serious as the balding priest who emerged from the vestry.

The meditation was done through repetition of simple prayers, and it became kind of hypnotic after a while. In the space for silent reflection, Patrick prayed for Griffin and Rob King, for Dermot again, and finally for himself. When it came to that bit, he faltered because Patrick could think of nothing to ask that any merciful God would be likely to grant him.

'Our regular Bible study group will start in the parish office in ten minutes time,' said the priest at the end. 'All are welcome to join.'

Patrick edged towards him and said, 'Thank you Father. Very uplifting. I can't join you for Bible study but my friends and I would like to use the sacristy for some … personal prayer.'

The priest frowned, but didn't say no. He wouldn't have dared. 'Let me get changed, and I'll leave you to it.'

There were only two chairs in the sacristy, and James King insisted that the older men sit down. 'I think you've got something to tell me,' he said to Dave.

Parkes licked his lips. 'I've got something to tell both of you. I don't know what you're going to do about it, but I'm sorry. I'm really sorry.' He drew a deep breath. 'Pat, it's about the Barley Mow.'

He paused and looked Patrick in the eye. God in Heaven, what on earth was he on about? Dave Parkes was giving him puppy dog eyes and asking for Pat to shut him up, but Pat wanted to hear this.

James looked utterly mystified and asked, 'What about The Barley Mow? You mean the Tandoori restaurant?'

'No,' said Patrick, 'this was before it changed hands. He means the pub where your father died; the pub he used to own.'

'When did he own it?'

'Eighteen years ago. He was there when it happened.'

'You! You were there when my father was murdered and now you're sniffing around my mother.' James put his hands on his hips and squared up to Parkes.

Patrick was nonplussed. Why was Dave dragging all this up now? 'Go on, tell us.'

'Am you sure?'

'No, I'm not, but James here is going to beat it out of you anyway.'

Parkes exhaled a huge sigh of relief. 'Honest, Pat, I didn't know you wasn't in on it. I kept me mouth shut in case you was part of what happened.'

'You're talking in riddles, man. In on what? Start at the beginning.'

Parkes gave a humourless snort. 'How far back do you want me to go?' For the first time since they sat down, he looked James in the eye. 'What have they told you, Jim? About what happened to your Dad and Donal Lynch?'

'Why do you want to know? So you can decide which bits of the truth to tell me? Just spit it out.'

Parkes held up his hands. 'Okay, okay. It was Pat's fortieth birthday, and all the boys were there to celebrate. Your mom was in the hospital with your dad...' his voice trailed off and he looked from one man to the other.

'Rob used to call her the redheaded cuckoo,' said James, 'but I've always tried to forgive Patrick and my mother for what they did because it wasn't Hope's fault.'

Parkes looked relieved. He continued. 'When the phone rang, your mother asked to speak to Pat. She tried to warn him that Sol was on his way over, but she was too late. That was before mobiles, and she had to drag herself down the corridor to use the phone. Anyway, Sol came into the bar and started shouting the odds. He was like a madman. I've never seen someone so wild.'

Pat opened his eyes. He hadn't realised they were closed as Dave told the story. A story he had buried very deeply inside himself even though he'd been living with the consequences for eighteen years. Parkes was right, the look in Sol's eyes that night was a glimpse of Hell.

'Donal – Dermot's dad – stood up. He tried to act the peacemaker, but Sol just lashed out and stabbed him. No one realised at the time what had happened except for one bloke.'

Parkes paused again and looked at Patrick. He was giving him one last chance to stop the story. One last chance to keep the genie in the bottle. Patrick didn't stop him and didn't encourage him. If Dave was meant to tell the story, so be it.

'What bloke?' said James. 'They told me it was a big brawl and my father was stabbed in the fight. That's what they said – no one knew how it happened..'

'No,' said Parkes. 'That's not how it went down. There was one bloke, a little bloke from Belfast that I'd never seen before. He knew what was going on and he knew that Sol was going to gut Patrick like a fish. Your dad had a huge knife with him. This bloke stands up and takes out a knife of his own. He cut your father's throat like he'd done it before. Then he finishes his drink, spits on your dad's body and walks out.'

James turned to face Patrick. His eyes were cold, but his lip was twitching with rage. 'Who was it?'

'I don't know, James, I really don't. He was over from Belfast to see one of the units in Birmingham. I was just looking after him.'

'Units? What units?'

'He was IRA.'

James's eyes widened in shock. Before he could say anything, Patrick continued. 'He was the last one. I swear it. He saved my life because Dave's telling the truth: I was in shock, and Solly would have stabbed me and goodness knows how many others. Don't forget, your dad had already killed Donal when Ben stepped in. I never saw him again.'

'But I did.'

Dave was looking at the floor, but his voice carried around the little room like a gunshot.

'When? How?'

'A few weeks ago. Talking to Dermot.'

'Jesus, Mary and Joseph! Are you mad? What are you talking about?'

'It's true. I went to see Dermot at the Wrekin Road place, and he was there. He faded into the background when I appeared, but I'd recognise him anywhere. I didn't ask Dermot who it was because I was shit scared he'd recognise me, and I turned me back on him. It was Dermot who said the other bloke was a friend from Blackpool.'

A silence descended on the sacristy, a silence born of shock and grief and memory. It soaked into the multi-coloured robes hanging in the wardrobes and it pushed up against the crosses and candles stacked in the corners. It was Patrick who shattered it.

'Who did you tell? I know you must have told someone or we wouldn't be sitting here tonight.'

'Rob. I told Rob that the man who killed his father was doing business with Dermot.'

'Why in God's Holy Name did you do that?'

Parkes raised his eyes from the floor. 'Because Dermot was ripping me off with those dodgy notes. Some mate of his came into my shop and bought a signed vinyl copy of *Made in Japan*. He paid five hundred quid for it in fake notes. I was round at Terri's and I told Rob about it. He told me that Dermot was distributing them and I should ask for a refund.'

It was starting to make sense. Pat didn't think Dave was telling the whole truth, but it made sense. Dermot had come out of prison with new connections in the North. These people were well set up and well protected and could handle large volumes of business. He never asked, but he wasn't surprised that an ex-IRA man should be behind it. And then along comes Dave the Rave, big fat Dave who wants to get into Theresa's knickers and wants her son to accept him as one of the family. So what does he do? He drops a fecking hand grenade into things by telling Rob what happened to his father. God, what a mess.

'Just one question, Dave' said Patrick, 'how did Robbie get from hearing about his father over dinner to a bloody great shoot-out in the Goods Yard?'

'I don't know. I really don't. I just know that Rob said he was going to sort it.'

'I have a question,' said James. 'Who the fuck is this bloke? You called him Ben.'

'Ach, that was just a nickname.,' said Pat. 'He was the shortest terrorist I've ever met, so the boys in the Maze called him Big Ben because he was little and had a round face like a clock. We didn't do names in those days, just word of mouth.'

There was a timid knock at the door. James opened it a crack. One of the bible study girls was waiting outside. 'Sorry to interrupt,' she said, 'but you're James King, aren't you?' James nodded. 'I just wondered if you could get me Queen Victoria's autograph? I'm like a massive fan of hers.'

Patrick was desperate to get out of that room and think. He went up to the door and pulled it open a little. 'I'm sure your mother's waiting outside, isn't she?'

'Oh, hello Mr Lynch. Yes, she is.'

'If she were to do the Christian thing and offer Mr King a lift home, I'm sure he can arrange the autograph for you.'

'I don't think we're finished,' said James.

'I think we are for today. I've got an appointment tomorrow morning, but we can continue the meeting in the afternoon if I'm free. I'll get my daughter to give you a call.'

Patrick edged into James's personal space and gave him a smile. James backed off, then walked towards the front doors of the church without looking once at the altar. The girl scampered after him.

There was nothing he could say to Parkes that wouldn't make him want to smash the eejit's face in, so he waited until James had got into his lift and then hooked his thumb towards the doors. Parkes opened his mouth to say something but changed his mind and left.

Patrick walked towards the altar and knelt down. He didn't want to pray, but he did want a moment to think. Parkes hadn't made it up, of this he was certain. Through some horrible coincidence – or divine intervention – his nephew had set up a business with the man who had avenged his father's death, and then Rob King had gone looking for vengeance of his own. Now there was James.

The older brother may have had his brushes with the law, but he wasn't a villain like Robbie. Sure, he could intimidate a useless lump like Parkes, but James King wouldn't be heading up the M6 with a shotgun in the boot to start shooting. More like to get himself shot and end up in the back of a van and probably next to Patrick himself. What a mess.

The priest came out of his office, and Patrick got wearily to his feet and crossed himself.

'Thank you, Father,' he said, and passed a twenty pound note to the priest. 'I'll let you choose which box to put it in.'

He left the church and stood on the kerb for a moment. Out of divilment he waved at the satellite TV van that had tracked him down, then headed up the hill to face the music.

Chapter 9

Earlsbury

Monday

25th October

Everyone stared at him. It's not unusual for police officers to arrive at work with obvious injuries, but Tom's shiner was a standout attraction. When he picked Hayes up in Dudley, she had taken one look at him and, instead of sympathy, she had said, 'Can you see out of that eye to drive properly?'

On the way to BCSS, he told her what he'd decided last night: they would pursue the golfing angle for a day or two while he finished work on Griffin's finances, by which time, hopefully, DC Hooper would be sufficiently recovered for an interview under caution.

They got as far as the Major Incident Room without Tom having to answer anyone's questions about his eye, but he was stopped at the door by ACC Khan. 'I got your email, Tom. That's great work. Let's have a chat about this.'

'I'll start on the phones,' said Hayes, and Tom was led away to a small meeting room. The fifth man from Saturday morning's briefing was already there.

'Tom, I don't think you've met Niall Brewer, our Media Relations Manager. This is DI Morton from CIPPS.'

They shook hands, and Khan took a seat on the other side of the table next to Brewer.

'Congratulations, Tom, that was excellent work. We didn't actually expect you to track down who was paying off Griffin.'

'One of them,' said Tom. 'Kelly said he was paying five hundred a month to Griffin. I'll assume he was understating it – say, seven hundred and fifty – but that still doesn't explain some of the things I'm seeing in Griffin's financials. It's a start, but he was getting a lot more than that from somewhere.'

Khan nodded his head as if expecting the answer. Tom had obviously passed some sort of test. 'Kelly is going to be released on bail this morning. Do you think the Major Enquiry Team should interview him about last Wednesday night's events?'

'No. I don't think he had anything to do with it. I would have alerted DCS Winters if I thought there was a link.'

'Of course. Niall? Any comments?'

The media relations manager was Scottish and had the sort of smooth voice you'd expect from someone used to the cameras and microphones. 'I think that achieves the Chief's objectives nicely. We can show an early arrest which identifies Griffin as a bad apple, and we can demonstrate that the Chief hasn't swept anything under the carpet. Nicely done, Tom.'

'But this is only the start,' said Tom. 'I need to follow up a number of lines of enquiry, and DC Hayes is following one as we speak.'

Khan gave him an encouraging smile. 'That's great, that's really great, but we have to think about resources. Because the Chief invited CIPPS on to this enquiry, he's paying for your services. And for DC Hayes. He's even paying your bill at Earlsbury Park. So we have to think about whether your time is a good use of resources. Once you've written up Kelly's arrest, you can wrap things up here and finish your report into his financials when you get back to London.'

Brewer was nodding along to this and giving Khan his earnest unspoken support. It stank.

'There are two lines of enquiry that I can't pursue from London that I really think deserve to be followed through. Or at least one of them should.'

Brewer drew back away from him. Khan frowned and took the bait. 'What are they?'

'First of all, how's Ian Hooper?'

'Conscious, but only just. We can't speak to him until this evening, and then only if he continues to make progress during the day.'

'That's one line. I can't categorically confirm or deny his involvement with Griffin until I can interview him under caution. The Chief wanted to know if the corruption was widespread. I don't *think* that Hooper was bent but I'd rather clear him than leave a nasty smell hanging about.'

Brewer looked alarmed at this prospect and started to interrupt until Khan raised an imperious hand. 'Carry on, Inspector.'

Tom turned his attention to Brewer. 'I'm sure you'll appreciate this, *Niall*, that it's better to have a fully exonerated hero than a press release from CIPPS pointing the finger at him and saying there was "insufficient evidence".'

The media man shuffled in his seat, but kept his mouth shut.

'What was the other thing?' said Khan.

'It's a choice, really. I could carry on with the lines of enquiry that Hayes and I are pursuing, or I could revisit the officers who searched Griffin's house on Thursday morning.'

'What on earth for?'

'I've clear evidence that they walked off with two Rolex watches. I could get warrants for all their houses and get the Tactical Support Group to carry out some dawn raids.'

Khan pressed his lips together. 'Is that true? About the watches?'

'I don't lie to senior officers, sir.'

'Very well, you can have the rest of the week. It was budgeted for anyway. Keep me posted about all the lines of enquiry and don't speak to any police officer except the Earlsbury CID or the MIT without my permission.'

Tom pointed to his black eye. 'I've already spoken to DCI Storey.' Brewer looked like he was going to explode or have a fit of the vapours when he realised that two officers had been fighting.

'That's all, thank you Tom,' said Khan.

'One more thing, sir, is that I can't continue until I know why Hussein called my DC "The Squealer". If someone else does it, Hayes might give them more than a black eye.'

Khan put his hand on Brewer's arm and pushed down hard. 'I'll get you a coffee, Niall. Shall we go to the canteen, Tom?'

They went two paces down the corridor, and Khan checked in both directions before leaning into Tom and saying, 'I'm surprised you haven't asked that question to her: you must be scared. It's very simple. Something happened at her first CID posting. She interrupted her colleagues having a private party in a pub and instead of bringing it up with a senior officer, she reported it externally. Two officers retired early, one resigned and two had to be disciplined. She was put on garden leave, but she said she wanted to come back to work. I gave her to you so she'd realise something. I hoped she'd realise that her only hope of a career in the police is to join the Gestapo.'

'Thank you, sir. That's good to know.'

Hidden away in corner of the MIR, Hayes looked content. She had notebooks, phonebooks, and the remains of breakfast spread around her, and she was busy talking to someone on the phone. Tom didn't want to ruin the mood so he tried to forget what Khan had just told him in the corridor.

'What have you got, Kris?'

'Nothing, but in a good way. I've tried every golf course within driving distance of Earlsbury and none of them have a record of a Mr Griffin that matches our late DS. He's not a member, and they all have computerised systems for guests, so if he's been playing golf, he must have been doing it under a false name.'

'That was quick. Good work.'

'And I've checked and double checked all the HOLMES 2 entries; none of them have thrown up a connection.'

That was less good. Although Hayes had acted entirely within the procedures for major investigations, Tom was uneasy about the connection between Griffin and golf being broadcast throughout the system.

'What did ACC Khan want?' she asked.

'Oh, something and nothing. After I finished with him, I went down to eavesdrop on the interview with Patrick Lynch. I think Winters is on to something there – he was Dermot's uncle, and Dermot worked for him. It beggars belief that Lynch doesn't have a clue what his nephew was up to. I watched them for half an hour, but they didn't get anywhere. I think they're going to leave him dangling for a while and try to dig up something from his financial records. That's what I'd do anyway.'

'What's next then, sir?'

'Can you remember what make of clubs he had?'

'Sorry, no. Football's my thing, not golf.'

Well that answered one question about his DC. 'Pity. I thought we might try to track down where he bought them. I'll go and get the key to his house, and we'll take a look this afternoon. Until then, I'm going to ring some banks, and you can dig into Griffin's family. Often the money isn't hidden very far away – a sister, a parent, a grandparent. Get as much information as you can on Griffin's relatives so that we can start to widen the net further.'

Hayes smiled and turned back to her computer. It was a warning to him: she had found a comfort zone where neither her reputation nor her gender and her race were a barrier to police work. He had done the same with the MLIU – although he was a middle class white boy, he now realised that he never had the authority as a copper that someone like Hooper carried as easily as he wore his utility belt. It was why Storey had dropped the nut on him.

'Do you want a cuppa?'

'If you're going.'

'I'll hand in the Kelly paperwork first.'

Tom called into the CPS liaison office and had a depressing talk with the case officer. He agreed with Kelly's assessment of the situation – the confession was good, but without supporting evidence of the length and detail of Kelly's relationship with Griffin, it was unlikely to lead to an immediate custodial sentence.

Tom decided to call on the Exhibits Manager before going to the canteen. It would save time later.

'Hi, I'm DI Morton. I wondered if I could have the key to DS Griffin's house again?'

'Ooh, that eye looks painful.' Well, she was only saying what everyone else was thinking.

'It was at the time, but it only hurts now when I touch it. I try not to.'

'I won't ask about the other bloke. I hope he's in a worse state.' Tom said nothing. 'It was mad in here on Saturday, and I couldn't come in yesterday so I haven't caught up yet. You handed the key back on Saturday afternoon, didn't you?'

He nodded, and she picked up a cardboard box marked *Logged Items for Return*. 'It's in here,' she said as she rummaged through the evidence bags. She paused and rummaged again. Then she looked into the box marked *New Items* and then she hunted around her desk. Finally she logged on to the computer and checked the index.

'Sorry, sir, I can't find it. Perhaps it's gone back into store without being logged back in. Do you want it now or can you wait until later?'

Tom had grown increasingly alarmed as her search turned up nothing; by the time she finished, he was tapping his foot. 'Can you make a note of my request and the time, please.'

She took immediate offence. 'What for? I'm sure it's in the Exhibits Store.'

'Maybe. If it is, then you can throw the note away, but if it isn't, I want a record of when it went missing.'

He headed over to Hayes's corner and picked up his coat. 'C'mon, Kris, we need to get over to Griffin's house before it's too late.'

'Whatever they were doing in that private party you interrupted must have been pretty awful,' said Tom. He was driving as fast as he could towards Griffin's house. He thought it would give Hayes a chance to respond without turning it into an issue.

'You've heard. Who told you?'

'Does it matter?'

'Not really.' She paused for a second. 'The police station was next door to a pub where you could book the upstairs room for evening meetings and stuff. One of the guys had a big birthday. They got loaded and booked a stripper. Except it wasn't a stripper, she was a working girl who was giving them all blowjobs. I was on duty that night, and one of the stupid idiots called the front desk on his mobile, and thought it would be funny to report a crime in progress so that it would be me who went round to the pub. They were all drunk, and they wanted me to see what a great band of brothers they were.'

Ouch. That was tough. He hated to admit it, but the story had the complete ring of truth. All over the country there were groups of police officers who bonded together and who promoted loyalty to the group over loyalty to the Force as a whole – and from there it was often a short step to the sort of corruption that had taken over Griffin.

Tom thought that Hayes had said enough, but she had something to add. 'I would have left it alone, but I honestly thought the girl was under eighteen.'

There was nothing that Tom could say, so he concentrated on driving.

He knew what was happening at Griffin's house. Someone, somewhere connected with the investigation didn't want him to go through Griffin's golf clubs. He only hoped that he wasn't too late. There was no car in the drive and no sign of one nearby, but whoever it was wouldn't have needed that long inside.

'What are we going to do without a key?' said Hayes.

That was a good question. He had no idea so he ignored it. 'Let's glove up and get the camera out before we go any further.'

Hayes gave a half smile and fetched the digital camera from the boot with a couple of evidence bags as well. Tom snapped on his gloves and went up to the front door. The key was in the lock.

'Bugger me, Kris, look at this.'

'I'd rather not, sir. Bugger you, that is. I thought you were above profanity.'

Double ouch.

Hayes examined the key from several angles and asked with some irony, 'Would you like me to photograph it?'

'Of course I bloody would. Do you think *I* left it there?'

'Sorry, sir. Yes, I did, actually. It was you who locked up.'

'And I handed the key back in to the Exhibits Manager. Trouble is, I haven't got a receipt for it – she wrote my name on the evidence bag, and I signed it, but whoever stole that key this morning has taken the bag, too. I wonder if they'll try to convince her to "forget" that she saw me.'

Hayes said nothing and got to work with the camera. When she'd finished, Tom opened the door and went straight through to the garage. The golf clubs were leaning against the wall next to the up-and-over door. He pulled the release handle and opened the door to let the light in.

'Can you remember if they've been moved?'

'Sorry. They were here, in this corner, but whether they were leaning in exactly that way, I don't know.'

'Fair enough. Right, Hayes, this is what we're going to do. I'm going to strip that bag apart, and after every stage, you're going to take a picture.'

'Sir.'

And that's what he did. Club by club, pocket by pocket, he emptied the bag on to the drive, and Hayes took pictures while he jotted down details about each item removed. He was hoping for a used scorecard, matchbook, napkin or anything which would point to where Griffin had played his golf. There was enough rubbish in the pockets of the bag to show that items like that *should* be there. Someone had definitely beaten them to it.

With all the items spread over the floor he looked at them again. It had taken them nearly an hour to do this. There must be something, somewhere.

'I'll put the kettle on. You come at it with fresh eyes.'

He went inside and checked in the fridge – there was an unopened four pints of milk, still well within its date. He was making the tea when Hayes burst through from the hallway.

'Sir, look. On the back of this presentation pack there's a price sticker that says *Earlsbury Park Pro Shop*. Then I checked all the balls individually; ten out of the thirteen in his bag are stamped with the Earlsbury Park logo.'

Tom squeezed out the tea bags and chucked them in the bin. 'I think that counts as a hole in one, don't you?'

Patrick and his daughter were in Helen's car, on their way to pick up Maria for a visit to the Coroner's office – and a meeting with James King.

'It was a stroke of luck,' said Helen to her dad 'Aunt Maria had a phone call from the Coroner's office, and she went into a panic. You and Mom were both busy at the time, so she rang me. I said I'd sort it.'

She went on to explain that because Dermot and Robbie King had been found together, there had to be a joint inquest, and so Erin King would be there as Robbie's widow. Helen had arranged it so that the other family would go first, and that James King would wait behind. Patrick told her that her mother would be proud of her for being so devious.

'I thought you were the devious one in our family,' she responded.

'Ha. Deviousness is a female trait in this family. I'm just dishonest.'

Maria Lynch wobbled down the path on her heels. She was head-to-toe in black as if this were the funeral and not a bureaucratic visit. Patrick got out to open the back door for her, and she climbed inside.

'Where's the Jaguar?' said Maria. *Charming,* thought Patrick, *one minute she's ringing her niece and unable to cope, the next minute she's complaining about the same niece's offer of transport.*

'It's more convenient this way,' he said. 'Helen can take us to West Bromwich and leave us there. Francesca will collect us afterwards. In the Jaguar.'

Maria sniffed but said no more. Patrick explained that the next of kin were being invited to discuss the inquest and to be told what could and could not happen.

The rest of journey was conducted in silence, and Patrick escorted Maria into the building. He directed her towards the family liaison office and told her that she was bearing up very well and that Donal would be proud of her.

That seemed to flatter her vanity, and she attempted to glide towards the office. From behind, it was easy to see that she had let herself go when compared to Francesca. He scanned the foyer and spotted a room marked Private – *Family Only*. James King was inside, and so was a young couple he'd never seen before; James was telling them something about music but stopped abruptly when Patrick walked in.

'I'm sorry for your loss,' said James to the young couple. 'I think I'd better go.'

Patrick held the door open, and James whispered to him, 'There's a smoking area out the back. See you there in five minutes.'

Patrick smiled at the young people and pretended to be sending messages on his phone. They talked to each other in low voices, and after a few minutes he pretended to get a phone call then excused himself.

James was standing well away from the Designated Smoking Area and pointed upwards to a CCTV camera when Patrick appeared. They both looked around carefully, and Patrick spoke first.

'Last night must have been a terrible shock for you, Jim. It was for me.'

'James. Call me James; it's only Dave Parkes who thinks I like being called Jim.'

'And we both know what a tosser that man is. Sorry, James, but like I said, last night was a complete bolt from the blue.'

'I could tell. But that doesn't mean you weren't keeping things from me before. Time to stop, Patrick. Tell me what's going on and how we're going to find that bastard.'

'We're not. He was Dermot's contact, not mine. And it gets worse – my suppliers have cut me off without leaving a forwarding address. I couldn't find them if I wanted to and, to be honest, I don't.'

'Are you telling me that you have absolutely no way of getting in touch? I don't believe you.'

'James, I've got nothing. Nothing at all. If the police can't find them, what chance do I stand?'

'The police will find them if we give them a little help.'

This was very disturbing. James hated the police, probably even more than his brother had done. To Robbie, the coppers had been an occupational hazard, but to James it was political. What had he called them once? That's right *Babylon's Footsoldiers*.

'I'm surprised at you, trusting the police,' said Pat. 'If I give myself up to them, I won't add anything to their knowledge of the crime because I wasn't there. They know all about the counterfeit money, or they should do. If I give myself up, all that will happen is that I'll go to prison. Who will that benefit? I don't need Babylon's punishment when God has punished me already.'

James took a step back. 'Cut the bullshit, Pat. You're just trying to save your own skin.'

Pat took a step towards him and leaned his head inwards. 'I thought you knew me better than that. I care about Dermot as much as you care about Robbie, perhaps more because I had to fill in as his father. I reckon the scores are settled. I don't think Dermot would be dead if Robbie hadn't interfered, to say nothing of Griffin or that poor lad Hooper. The police don't need my help.'

James stood his ground. 'Don't you lecture me about responsibility. If you and your friends had told the truth from the beginning, none of this, none of it, would have happened. And that goes back eighteen years.'

Patrick laughed. 'I remember a song. You're a musician, perhaps you know it. Ever heard of a band called Stiff Little Fingers?'

James jerked his head up but said nothing.

'No? Not your cup of tea, perhaps. Well, not musically. I thought they were a terrible racket, no tunes at all, but their hearts were in the right place. They had a song which said that we Irish are treated like green wogs.'

'What do you know about it? You and your golf club and your private schools for Hope and Elizabeth. You don't know nothing about prejudice.'

'Talk to your mother. Ask her what it was like to be Irish during the Troubles. I've done my time inside, James, longer than you, and every time the police arrested me, I was guilty, even if they couldn't always prove it. Except once. They arrested me for being in the IRA just because I took out an Irish Passport. They used the old Prevention of Terrorism Act, not this new one.

'In those days there was no tape recorders, no access to lawyers, nothing except a bare cell and three days of interrogation. If I'd even *hinted* to the cops that there was a man from Belfast in the pub the night your father was killed, I'd have gone down for life, so help me God.'

He drew back and measured the impact of what he'd said. He'd knocked some of the bluster out of James, but there was a core inside that he couldn't reach. It was enough for now. If only he still had his own policeman – he hadn't realised how much he'd come to rely on Griffin's ability to pass on information about all sorts of subjects. There was someone higher up, he was certain, because who else would have ordered Griff to go out on that foul night and get shot for his pains?

If James wouldn't let the dead bury the dead, then so be it. He needed enough time to come up with a convincing plan, that's all, and he thought James was about to agree with him.

'There's something that came to me last night,' said James. 'Something I could do on my own that wouldn't *necessarily* come back on you.'

'Careful, James, these are some very murky waters. You don't know what sort of sharks are swimming around in there. I've dipped me toe in a few times and nearly had it bitten off.'

'It was something Parkes said about what happened. See this?' James fingered the tatty jungle jacket he always wore. Okay for Jamaica, but a trifle cold in Earlsbury. 'My father put this in my wardrobe when he went in prison. He liked me to wear it on visits and I liked it too, even if it was so big it came to my knees. When he came out, he bought a nice leather jacket for himself, something a bit classier as Theresa would say.'

'She would that. Look, there's someone come out for fag. We'd better get moving.'

James took hold of his arm and held him back. 'Wait.' Patrick stopped and James released him. 'I asked mother what happened to Dad's effects. She said she never got them back. That jacket would have been covered in blood, and I'll bet it's still in a warehouse somewhere. Your friend spat on it. I bet they could get DNA off that with all this new science.'

That was a shocker and no mistake. Pat couldn't deny it, the boy was right. There was every chance that Solly's jacket had Big Ben's DNA on it. Had the little psycho been in trouble since then? Would they have a sample of his DNA for comparison?

'Hold on, hold on. That's a desperate thing to contemplate. Information like that could blow up in our faces if we don't handle it carefully. Your Da's jacket isn't going anywhere, so why don't we think of the best way to approach this. Listen, have the paparazzi left you alone?'

'Yes, but that doesn't matter. I have to get back to work. Vicci cancelled the gigs last week, but her management won't let her do it again. I've got to go back to London on Wednesday, and I won't be able to come again until ten days later. How about we meet on Wednesday morning, and you can explain to me what you're going to do.'

Two days. It wasn't long, but it was enough. He hoped.

Tom asked Hayes to call BCSS and speak to the Exhibits Manager to inform her about the discovery of the misappropriated key. It was clear from Kris's expression that she wasn't getting the reaction Tom expected. Ah well, it could be sorted out later; he wanted to get to the golf club and ask some questions.

He walked through the door into the Nineteenth Hole that the blond woman had tried to pass on Saturday night. He found that he had crossed a metaphorical as well as physical threshold.

The golf club lounge was decorated more expensively and (possibly) more tastefully than the hotel whose buildings it shared. It depended on your point of view. There were the expected honour boards with roll calls of captains, champions and other worthies; there was a trophy cabinet and a display of products available in the Pro Shop, but mostly it was understated quality. Tom could see why people lingered there. Hayes was less impressed.

'It's a bit different from the Castle Women's FC clubhouse,' she observed.

'I suspect this is a bit more feminine,' he replied. 'Let's see what we can dig out.'

Before he could ask the barman any questions, he accosted them with an offer to help followed by an instant reminder that this section was a private members club.

'DI Morton and DC Hayes. We're investigating last week's shootings.'

'Oh.'

Tom took out the picture of DS Griffin. 'Do you recognise this man?'

'Yeah. That's Jack Kirkstone, one of the members. Is he alright? I haven't seen him for a few days.'

'How long has he been a member?'

'Couple of years. Longer than I've been here. Works in security, I think.'

'Does he have any particular friends? Colleagues who come in?'

The barman immediately sensed the move from fact to speculation and looked over his shoulder to the back of the bar. 'I'm usually too busy to notice that sort of thing. You'd be better off speaking to the steward.'

The man had already taken a couple of steps backwards but Hayes leaned over the bar and took hold of his arm gently. 'Excuse me, sir, but we haven't quite finished.' She let go as soon as he'd stopped moving.

'This is a serious enquiry,' said Tom. 'If you recognised this man quickly, I'm sure you recognise the people he normally talked to or played with.'

'I don't know what happens out there, unless people tell me,' he replied, pointing to the picture windows. 'When they do, it's usually about their own game, not who they played with. Golfers are a bit self-obsessed like that.'

Tom put on his best smile. 'My colleague will take your details and ask a few more questions. I'll just go and see the steward.'

It was the barman's turn to put out his arm. 'You can't go behind there without a warrant. Health and Safety.'

Tom weighed up his options. He patted his pockets theatrically. 'Damn, I've left my phone in the car. Carry on Hayes.'

The barman was torn between running after Tom and leaving Hayes unsupervised in the bar. He decided to remain behind, and Tom went straight to hotel reception where he asked them to call the golf club steward and summon him from his office.

Tom chose a discreet table in the corner and waited. The man he'd seen last Saturday was indeed the steward. In the ten steps from the Staff Only door to his table, Tom had a choice – a head on charge or a flanking manoeuvre. So far he'd been outflanked at almost every turn by the men behind this operation (and Mina Finch). He remembered something that Kate had once said – *Assault without intelligence is another name for suicide.* He decided to gather some intelligence first.

'Thanks for coming out,' said Tom as he flashed his warrant card. 'My colleague and I want to talk about Griff. Shall we go to your office for privacy?'

The man nodded and turned on his heel. On their way through the Nineteenth Hole, they collected Hayes, and left the barman looking worried. They were given chairs in the steward's office, and he introduced himself as Craig Butler. Hayes took out her notebook.

Tom studied the steward for a moment. He was about forty, and looked like he'd never properly recovered from an undernourished childhood. If Tom were running any sort of club, he doubted he'd want this man looking after the books – or the spirit cellar.

'Can you start by telling me how the club works and how it relates to the hotel?'

'Earlsbury Park Golf Club Ltd is a private company which leases the course, the changing rooms, and part of the buildings from the hotel. They employ me to run the Nineteenth Hole and administer the golfing side. Obviously, there's a greenkeeper who looks after the course.'

Tom nodded his head in understanding. 'I believe that golfers are pretty red hot when it comes to scores, statistics, and green fees. You must keep records of when people play and so on.'

'It's complicated. The club has a Secretary; he's elected by the members and organises the matches, competitions, and so on, but whenever someone goes out, they have to be entered in the book.'

'Is that a physical book or a computer one?'

The steward began to move in his seat, and as he swivelled on his chair, he glanced at the computer on his desk.

'A bit of both. There's a fee every time you play, and non-members' names have to be recorded. I have to account for them.'

In not answering the question, Butler had given himself away. It was time for the Assault.

'Do you know what Conspiracy to commit Misconduct in a Public Office is all about?'

'No. I'm not in a public office.'

'Aah. No. But Detective Sergeant Griffin was. You knew that he was registered here under a false name, and I'll bet that he gave a false address so that he could have his post sent here, too. By allowing a policeman to operate in this way, you are guilty of allowing him to commit Misconduct. The offence also covers bribery.'

'Are you arresting me?'

'Not yet. I presume the Golfing Committee aren't the most tolerant of people, and that they won't take kindly to having you arrested, the records seized, and the Nineteenth Hole shut down. With you gone, they'll have to close the changing rooms as well until a replacement can be found.'

Butler folded his arms. 'I'm not a grass.'

Tom reached into his pocket and took out a USB drive. He never went anywhere without it, which was a sad commentary on his life. He put it on the desk and rested his finger on top.

'I'm not asking you to be a grass. Just let me copy a few files; you can tell anyone that asks you had no choice.'

The steward stared down at the USB drive. Tom kept his finger still and added, 'Unlike your barman, you *knew* this was a murder enquiry. That Goods Yard was a bloodbath. The next step could easily be a Molotov cocktail through the window.'

'There's no spyware or nothing on that, is there?'

'No. If I wanted to hack your computer, I'd get my cousin to do it – you'd never know she'd been there until I came back with a warrant.'

He started to slide the drive towards Butler until the other man gave in and snatched it up.

'If I give away the membership list without a warrant, they'll sack me.'

'No. Just copy the daily journals over. Now that I know that Griffin called himself Mr Kirkstone, I'll sort the rest out.'

The two police officers sat in silence until Butler handed the drive back. Tom slipped it into his pocket. 'Thanks. Just a few more questions that I can find out from Companies House if I want – who owns the Hotel, who owns the Golf Club Ltd company and how much profit did the club side make last year?'

Tom had noticed that Butler was listed as the Licensee. It was almost impossible to get a liquor licence with a criminal record, which meant he wouldn't be that familiar with interview techniques. Now that Tom had the files on his drive, he could probe a bit further; the habit of disclosure is hard to break, and the steward was beginning to realise that he had already given away too much.

'Some finance company owns the Hotel, not sure who.' That was easy. 'The golf club doesn't make a profit as such, I don't think. It's like a surplus and I don't know where it goes.' That was harder. Tom waited for the final revelation. 'The shareholders are the members. Not sure how that works legally, though. Might be more your sort of thing.'

Damn. Tom had hoped that some local villain would have been revealed as the beneficiary, but no, it was all cosy and communal. Well, he would have to see what the data threw up.

'Do we need to go back to BCSS?' asked Hayes on the way out. 'You could analyse those files here in your room, couldn't you?'

'Your shift's nearly over. I'll drop you at home then go into the office myself. Earlsbury Park is okay, but I don't want to spend any longer in that room than I have to.'

When he arrived at the Major Incident Room, the Exhibits Manager gave him a sour look.

'I've come to sign your report into the unauthorised removal of Griffin's house key,' he said.

'You'll have to make it yourself. I can't say for certain that you handed it in – especially given that it was discovered at the property. You should have just brought it back, and I would have forgotten about it.'

Tom nodded and looked around the room. There were no senior officers present, and all the others were putting on their coats.

'If you're looking for DCS Winters, he's gone to the hospital to talk to Ian Hooper.'

The USB drive was comfortingly solid in his pocket. Suddenly he was unwilling to allow *any* of his observations on to the system when he didn't know who might be looking. He turned on his heel and headed back to Earlsbury Park.

The trauma unit at Queen Elizabeth Hospital in Birmingham is world famous. Despite being on the other side of the world, injured service personnel from Afghanistan were routinely shipped there for surgery and recovery. Ian Hooper was beginning to appreciate what a mess he was in, and not just from the gaping wound in his abdomen which had been lightly stitched for easy access in a further operation tomorrow.

As the serious anaesthetics wore off, he started to become more aware of what had happened and of some of the choices he would have to make. The first one was whether to talk to the Major Incident Team.

'You don't have to,' said Ceri. 'The doctor was very clear, you must only talk to them if you're up to it.'

He didn't remember much about recovering in hospital, but he could remember feeling Ceri's hand every second he was awake. When he finally got to focus on her, he asked what had happened to her.

'What do you mean?'

'What's happened to you? You look terrible.'

She gripped his hand. 'I've spent one hundred and twelve hours in this hospital waiting for you to talk to me, and the first thing you say is that I look terrible. Ian Hooper, you'd try the patience of a saint, you would, and I am not a saint.'

Tears rolled uncontrolled and uncontrollably down her face. She gripped his hand as if she needed to stop him slipping away. There was so much morphine in his system that he could barely feel her touching him.

'Marry me, love.'

'Oh my God – you're delirious. I'll have to call the doctor.'

'No. Call the priest. Get him to marry us before it's too late.'

A look of horror washed over her face. 'Don't say that. You're not going to die. Not now you've woken up. You're going to get better, and then, only when you're better and not before, you can marry me. But that will take months, and I'm going to plan every detail. Everything.'

There was so much water running down her face that she had to use her free hand to wipe it away. Ian was *fairly* sure he wanted to marry her. It would do for now. His heart had speeded up slightly, and with it had come an ache in his side like a thundercloud – getting bigger every second and clearly about to discharge a lot of pain very soon. He had to ask her something else.

'What happened?' If he kept it simple, she might tell him something he didn't know.

A big shadow passed across her face like an echo of the clouds building inside him. She looked around the intensive treatment unit. He was in a semi-private bay in what reminded him of a milking parlour: it had a desk in the middle which was always busy with staff and a dozen bays around the edge of the room.

'It's like this, see,' said Ceri. 'They told me that I can't discuss what happened with you. We're even on CCTV.' She pointed to a camera above the bed that he hadn't noticed before. 'Nigel made me promise. Said that if I wanted to be here, I had to give him my word that I wouldn't say anything to you. It was that or put a guard on your bed.'

The ache in his side was turning into actively hurting, mobile and stabbing pain. He would have to ask for drugs soon. 'C'mere, love,' he said, and tugged her a little towards him. She bent her head down to his. 'I can't remember properly. I just want you to let me know what happened after I was shot.'

She gripped his hand again. 'No, Ian. I don't know what you were doing there, and I don't want to know now, but it's going to stop here. You tell them the truth, all right? If you want to marry me, you have to start by being honest.'

He nodded his head. That was the easy bit; he'd do anything to stop her walking away right now. 'Who's Nigel?' he asked.

'Superintendent Winters. He's been here twice a day or more since Thursday morning.'

'Oh yeah, what day is it?'

'Monday afternoon.'

There was a spasm of pain and he tensed his muscles in response. That turned the spasm into a full on seizure. He screamed.

Before Ceri could even stand up, a doctor and nurse were halfway to his bed.

At half past six, they allowed him to drink some water but told him that it would be a long time before he ate anything. Ceri had reluctantly agreed to go back to their flat with her mother, and he was waiting for the doctor to allow DCS

Winters in for *a short chat*. All he'd got out of the medical staff was that he was unconscious from the moment they loaded him into the ambulance. Well, at least he hadn't given anything away so far. He had tried to ask if Griff were in one of the other beds. He might have been seriously injured too – the ambulance was there quickly enough, so maybe they'd picked Griff up before it was too late. The nurses just gave him a blank look.

Two of them came, DCS Winters and a DS he'd never seen before. The doctor told them he would be watching from the desk, and made sure that Ian had his call button in his hand. It was a lot less comforting than Ceri's fingers.

'I'm not going to ask how you're feeling,' said Winters. 'I can see that for myself. Nor am I going to ask why you were at the Yard – you'll be asked that under caution at some future date. I just want to know who shot you.'

'So do I. I've never seen him before. Ever.'

'Description?'

'Tall. Thin. Wore a mask.'

They weren't taking notes. Ian made a point of labouring his breathing.

'How many altogether? Was there anyone you *did* recognise?'

He was in real pain but not so much that he couldn't have concentrated if he wanted to. Ian gave in to the demon eating away at his guts so they couldn't read his face. He mustn't give anything away. *You never saw that twat Robert King.*

'Two of them. Apart from Griff, that is. Maybe more. Didn't recognise any of them. How is he? How's Griff?'

'I'm sorry, Ian. DS Griffin was found dead at the scene. We've reason to believe that two people who were known to you were also at the scene – Robert Marley King and Dermot Lynch. Did you see either of them?'

Ian moaned and shook his head at the same time. Another wave of pain followed on, and he didn't notice the officers getting up and walking away.

Chapter 10

Earlsbury

Tuesday

26th October

There had been a very peremptory message at reception. *DI Morton and DC Hayes were expected at morning briefing and afterwards.* The briefing itself was short. ACC Khan had been joined by DCC Nechells at the back of the room, but Winters took the lead.

'The good news is that I spoke to Ian Hooper last night, and he's at the beginning of a long recovery process. The bad news is that he could tell us nothing about what happened. He said something about a tall thin man but that's not very helpful. Looking around the room, I could arrest the DCC and ACC on that basis.'

No one laughed. Khan managed a smile, but Nechells (who wasn't very thin, in Tom's opinion) just pursed his lips in disapproval.

'We had been delaying the broadcast of the 999 call because we were waiting for Hooper to regain consciousness. He does not remember seeing Lynch or King, so you may have heard the tape being broadcast on local radio this morning. Within five minutes we had twelve people positively identify the voice as Dermot Lynch.'

Winters paused to let the news sink in. Tom was surprised that no one had spotted this before – but if they were keeping things hidden from the Earlsbury CID, then perhaps it wasn't so unusual.

'This places Dermot Lynch at the Goods Yard which is progress of a sort, and we will ask Patrick Lynch about it in due course. The mobile number that Dermot used to call 999 was only ever used for that one call, another item for his uncle to account for. As for today, we have twelve names still to track down for Trace, Interview and Eliminate, but the bulk of the work will be reviewing CCTV. The technical team have now tracked down every camera we asked them for, and two of the groups today will start to analyse and cross-reference using the major incident protocol.'

If anyone groaned at the news, they kept it to themselves.

'Finally, and you don't need me to tell you this, the investigation is now entering a new phase. Because we didn't get a breakthrough from Hooper last night, we're going to have to do it the hard way. There are still three murders and one attempted murder to solve. I doubt we'll do it today or this week, but do it we will. Now let's make a start.'

The group dispersed. Tom and Kris made their way up to Winters, and he jerked his head towards the empty office in the background. 'Just you,' he said to Tom. 'This doesn't concern her.'

'She has a name,' said Tom.

Winters' mouth twitched and a flush started forming. He walked off, and Tom followed. By the time they were both in the office, his face had turned from its usual grey to an angry red. Neither of them sat down.

'Look, Morton, we all make mistakes. You left Griffin's house key behind and you found it later. Problem solved. What in God's name are you playing at with my exhibits manager?'

'I'm sorry, sir, but someone removed that key from the Exhibits section. It wasn't me'

'What for? Why on earth would someone want to go round to Griffin's house?'

'That's a CIPPS matter, sir.'

'Then you leave me with no choice but to report you for losing evidence.'

'I handed that key back in. If you report me, I'll have to report the exhibits manager for failing to issue receipts properly.'

It was stalemate. If Tom followed through with his threat, there could be serious consequences. Anyone charged for these crimes would have Tom's complaint handed to them in the papers disclosed to the defence. A good barrister would use it to undermine the chain of evidence.

Winters looked about to explode. 'On the other hand,' said Tom, 'ACC Khan has made it very clear that I have a limited amount of time left in Earlsbury. If we could both sit on this for a few days…'

'Get back to work, Inspector. Oh, and don't expect to be interviewing Hooper any time soon. He's only held together with string and stitches.'

'Sir.'

Tom let out a long, deep breath as he walked back through the MIR. He headed for the canteen and found his hand shaking when he carried his mug of tea to the corner.

He had given Hayes a job, and told her not to use any of the HOLMES 2 computers to complete it. She was a lot longer than he expected.

'All right, boss?'

'Don't ask,' he said. Hayes had enough pain of her own without burdening her with his experiences.

She frowned at him.

On the other hand, she had also been shut out by too many people in the past. She deserved more. 'Get me another tea and I'll tell you about it.'

When she returned, he said, 'You know I'm only here on sufferance. The minute that either Winters or Khan can get rid of me back to London without upsetting the Chief Constable, they'll come over to Earlsbury Park and pack my bags for me. It was just more of the same. Cheer me up – tell me that you found something.'

She put a set of printouts on the table and pointed to a couple of places. 'Your hunch was right, sir. The Earlsbury Park Hotel isn't part of some multinational chain – or rather, it's *operated* by a national hospitality company, but they don't own the premises. The land and buildings are all owned by an overseas bank. Both the Hotel and the golf club lease their facilities from it.'

'A bank? That's unusual. I would have expected a property company at least, not a bank.'

'You might be able to dig a bit further into that, but I think the bank took it over a couple of years ago when the developer went bust. I didn't know where to look in the time I had.' She took a sip of tea. 'There is one more thing, though. I found a company called Nineteenth Green Ltd and the directors are Craig Butler, Jack Kirkstone (aka DS Griffin), and a man I've never heard of. They receive a facilities fee from the golf club every year – their only client.'

'Good work. I'm going to take a punt on this – let's go and put the third man's name into HOLMES 2 and see what pops out.'

They went through to the MIR and felt the temperature drop by several degrees. The central briefing area had been squeezed by the installation of a bank of specialist equipment on each side of the room. Both sets had a group of detectives and civilians working through CCTV and Automatic Number Plate Recognition data. It looked like a video arcade for grown-ups.

There were a couple of regular terminals free, and Tom let Hayes put the names into the system. It turned out that the third man was married to Patrick Lynch's daughter.

'Bring up her details,' said Tom.

Holmes 2 isn't the most advanced system in the world, but it is a lot faster than its predecessor. In a few clicks of the mouse, Tom saw the besuited blond woman who had passed something to the steward at Earlsbury Park. 'Show me all the members of Lynch's family.'

Hayes located some surveillance pictures, and he stopped her. 'Look – that's me. Waiting outside the Catholic Church for you.'

'You'd have a long wait, then. What were you doing there?'

'Being nosey – and having my second encounter with Helen. That must be her mother and younger sister going into Mass after Patrick dropped them off.'

There was one more picture on the system tagged as "Family of Patrick Lynch" – a redheaded teenager with a mixed-race man in dreadlocks and a curvy white woman in a bouffant dress. 'Who's that?'

'Let me see … it's Hope King. Patrick's natural daughter and then her mother, Theresa King and Theresa's older son, James King, the one who plays bass for that singer you'd never heard of.'

They both stared at the screen. Tom pointed at the image and said, 'Why has no one said anything in the briefing? Why has no one been pursuing this angle? Patrick Lynch has a teenage daughter by another woman: it happens. But what are the odds that the half-brother ends up dead in a burnt out van? There has to be more to it.'

'I take it you don't want me to enter anything on to the system, sir?'

'No chance. We're going back to Earlsbury Park.'

This time, Tom led them straight through the Hotel and into the Nineteenth Hole, using his warrant card as a shield. They found Butler in his office, and he immediately shot to his feet.

'You can't come in here without an invitation or a court order,' he said.

'Wrong,' said Tom, and passed him the printout from Companies House. 'They set you up, Craig. They let you use your real name, and hid theirs. I've got probable cause to tear this place apart now and see where all the money's gone.'

The steward digested the implications of the list of directors and then collapsed into his chair. 'I had to use my real name,' he said, throwing the paper on the desk. 'I needed to prove my earnings to get a mortgage – the money those bastards on the committee pay me is so pathetic, I couldn't afford a cardboard box.'

'How about a little co-operation,' said Tom. 'Give me the original copy of Griffin's application form to start with, the one in the name of Jack Kirkstone. DC Hayes, can you get an evidence bag from the car.'

The man looked uncertain for a second.

'Don't worry, I'm not going to beat you up while she's out of the room. As you can see from this black eye, I'm not built for unarmed combat.'

Hayes left, and Butler gave in. He flicked the incriminating paper back towards Tom and levered himself out of the chair. While he was rooting in a filing cabinet, Tom threw him a casual question.

'While DC Hayes is out of the room, there is one other thing. What did Patrick's daughter give you on Saturday?'

Butler's eyes gave him away again. He looked at one of his desk drawers for a fraction of a second but it was enough. Tom put on some gloves and opened it. Among the menu cards and matchbooks was a mobile phone. Hayes returned with a sheaf of evidence bags, and Tom dropped the phone in one of them. He examined the application form for membership which Butler handed over, and there at the bottom was the name of Griffin's sponsor: *P Lynch (Honorary President)*.

'We'll be in touch,' he said to Butler. 'And remember, any attempt to destroy evidence such as computer files or legal documents will count as Conspiracy to Pervert the Course of Justice.'

Back in the car, evidence stowed away, Hayes asked him if he'd seen the photograph of Butler's family on the desk.

'No, why? Is he married to Lynch's sister or something.'

'No idea, sir. I just wondered what you were thinking of charging him with.'

'That's up to your colleagues in MCPS Economic Crimes. When I'm gone from here, they'll be digging through the records for weeks. Hopefully they'll find enough for a serious money laundering charge and get him a couple of years.'

'In prison? That's harsh. I thought you might let him go as he's co-operated. Even with a suspended sentence, it'll destroy his family – and he'll lose his house regardless of whether you try to sequester it.'

Tom had been about to drive off but he put the car in neutral and turned to Hayes. 'What did you expect? He's just as greedy as any drug dealer, and he's stealing from every honest worker in the country. Does your mother have a job?'

Hayes seemed to think the question rhetorical at first, but when Tom raised his eyebrows, she responded. 'Yes. She's a Senior Care Assistant.'

'Then that makes it worse. I'll bet she works very hard for very little money and pays more tax than she should, because no one's ever shown her how to claim for things properly. Butler, and every other money launderer in the world is just leaching off her back. He wanted something for nothing.'

Hayes shifted in the seat and fiddled with the safety belt. 'Fair enough, sir, but to go after his family as well, it seems…'

Tom interrupted her. 'Hayes, you ain't seen nothing yet,' he said, and put the car in gear.

Patrick was sitting at the kitchen table going through the VAT returns for Emerald Green Ltd. Since last Thursday he had barely touched his legitimate businesses, but a phone call from his accountant had sent him to the office to pick up the paperwork. He wanted to be at home where he wasn't surrounded by Dermot's Wolves posters and looking at the Wolves mug on the desk. He also wanted to be near Fran.

She brought some coffee through. 'Remember I'm going to Stafford soon, so I'll leave you some lunch in the fridge. I don't want you to start neglecting your diet.'

'Would I use this tragedy to start overindulging? Well, I suppose I would. Thanks love.'

The phone rang, and Fran went to answer. He got back to his papers and his finger was poised over the calculator when he heard her voice raised from the other room. He put his pen down and tried to listen for some clue. Could it be Maria? Theresa? Fran didn't sound amused.

When she marched back into the kitchen, she had gone white with fury, and it seemed to be directed at him.

'That was the police. Not the big boys this time, but the custody sergeant from Earlsbury. They've arrested Helen for conspiracy to bribe a police officer. Or something like that. What have you done, Patrick? What have you done to our daughter?'

He had pushed himself upright and was about to answer, when the room swam a little and his chest started to contract. He slumped back on the chair and felt his pockets for a nitro tablet. Fran dashed to the worktop and fumbled open a container. When she came to stuff it under his tongue, he could see that the concern on her face was not for him but Helen.

She gave him a minute for the tablet to take effect and then she sat down next to him. At least she took his hand first. 'It's got to stop, Pat. I don't care what you've done, you know that, but you've got to get Helen out of jail. You've got to go down there and confess to everything. Anything. So long as our daughter comes home tonight.'

Pat held up his other hand for a second and closed his eyes. The tablet finished fizzing under his tongue, and he swallowed the last of the drug. With the relaxation in his chest came a relaxation of the pain in his shoulders, his arms, and his chest.

'I'll go straight there in a minute,' he said. 'I might not come home tonight so there's some things you need to do. The first one is to get in touch with Dave Parkes.'

'Who? The bloke with the music shop?'

'That's him. Go and see him in person, not on the phone. Tell him to get James King to call you. When James calls, tell him to go to the police straight away. He knows what it's about.'

'Okay.'

'There's more,' said Patrick, and he told her where to find a couple of items hidden at his mother's house and what to do with them. Then he got her to drive him into town.

'No comment.'

'I have a witness who says you handed over this mobile phone at Earlsbury Park Golf Club. Did you do that?'

'No comment.'

'This witness says that you gave it to him with the express purpose of allowing your father to communicate without police surveillance. Is this true?'

'No comment.'

Helen was growing in confidence as the interview progressed. She had immediately asked for a solicitor when booked into the custody suite and had obviously taken the man's advice by conducting a No Comment interview. It took guts. Every single question had to be answered with the same two words. It was hard to sit there and be accused of things and not deny them. Tom could see every sinew of Helen's body wanted to deny having anything to do with

Dermot's death, but as they progressed, her responses became slicker.

It also required patience on the part of the detective. When played back to a future jury, any value from the Defendant refusing to answer questions would be lost if the detective became unprofessional. Tom was okay, but he was beginning to worry about Hayes.

Because of the jurisdiction issues, he had told her to be the arresting officer. They had gone to Helen's workplace which was the Earlsbury branch of a national pharmacy company. Although the arrest had taken place in the back office, they had walked her out of the shop, and all of Helen's colleagues had seen her humiliation. And that was the point.

Hayes was clearly very unhappy about this – very unhappy about undertaking a public arrest on the flimsiest of evidence. She had argued on the way to the chemist that they had enough to arrest Patrick Lynch, but Tom had seen the look in Francesca's eyes at the church. This woman had taken her husband back into the fold after his indiscretion eighteen years ago and that could only be for one reason – the children. He had taken a gamble that Francesca Lynch would persuade her husband that co-operation was their daughter's only chance.

'This is a photograph of the late Detective Sergeant Griffin, also known as John Kirkstone. Do you know this man?'

Helen made the mistake of looking at the photograph and giving it away in her eyes. She knew Griff all right.

'No comment.'

'Could you describe the relationship between this man and your father?'

The solicitor decided it was time to intervene. 'Inspector Morton, you have arrested my client not her father. She can't be expected to comment on his business.'

'Oh yes she can, as a witness. Please, Helen, answer the question: how well did your father know this man?'

Helen looked at her brief who shrugged in response.

'No comment.'

The interview room door opened, and the custody sergeant stuck his head in. It was a different man to the one on Sunday, and he didn't seem as bothered by Tom's presence. Obviously not a friend of Griffin's. He had agreed to give a signal when Patrick Lynch showed up. This was the moment Tom had been waiting for.

'Interview suspended. I believe that we can resume after lunch. Say two o'clock?' He looked at the solicitor. 'Gives you a chance to get something else done in the interim. Your client will be comfy enough until then. Oh, and DC Hayes will be re-arresting her on a charge of money laundering.'

'What?'

'Have a look at this.' Tom passed the solicitor another copy of the register of directors for Nineteenth Green Ltd. 'Either your client, or her husband or most likely both of them have been receiving the proceeds of laundered money. You might want to discuss that with her before you nip off for lunch.'

Helen whispered something to her lawyer who didn't bother to whisper when he responded to her. 'You aren't allowed visitors except at DI Morton's discretion. I don't think he will agree, somehow.'

'No, I won't. Enjoy your lunch, Helen, but I'd avoid the curry if I were you.'

Hayes packed up the evidence and followed Tom out of the interview room. The custody sergeant took Helen back to the cells; her lawyer took the papers and disappeared.

Lynch was waiting for them in the main part of the police station. Tom wondered how soon DCS Winters would hear about it all: he hadn't forgotten that Lynch was under 24 hour surveillance.

Tom had watched Lynch being interviewed at BCSS but the video feed didn't do justice to the man. He looked to be in good condition for his age and medical history, and he was dressed in a well cut suit that was almost a match for Brewer, the media relations manager.

'Mr Lynch? I'm DI Morton from London and this is…'

'Morton, did you say?'

For the first time in his life, Tom saw his name strike fear into the eyes of a suspect. He had no idea why.

It clicked in after a second. Of course! Griffin would have told Lynch exactly who was sniffing around the counterfeit money when Tom first went to Earlsbury last month. The Honorary President of the golf club had come here expecting to do a deal with the Major Enquiry Team; instead, Lynch had been confronted by someone who knew exactly what was going on, someone he couldn't lie to about the counterfeit notes.

'Yes, I'm DI Morton; I've been promoted since the last time I was here. This is DC Hayes of MCPS.'

Lynch leaned in close. 'You'll know I've got a friendly ghost haunting me?'

'If you mean the surveillance team, then yes, I do know.'

'If you want to talk, take me to your big new place by the motorway, and I'll show you somewhere private on the way.'

It was legitimate. If they booked him in here, then only the Prisoner Escort service could transfer him to BCSS. There was nothing wrong in Tom taking a witness in his own car. He jerked his head towards the back of the station and escorted Lynch through the custody suite. 'Don't use this as a shortcut, all right?' said the sergeant.

'Sorry. Won't happen again.'

Lynch cast a look at the door leading to a row of cells. 'Is she in there?'

'No, that's the men. Your daughter's round the side. Come on.'

They took him out the back, and Tom was now sufficiently comfortable with the one way streets that he could get out of town without crossing the High Street. No one followed them, and it would take a while before Winters realised that Lynch had left the station. He drove towards the motorway.

'When you get to the roundabout, take the third turning, the one before your police station, and stop in the lay-by,' said Lynch.

Tom did as he was bid and had to squeeze his car in between two lorries. 'Let's go up the hill, there's a quiet place at the top,' said Lynch.

'Go with him, Hayes,' said Tom. 'I'll get the teas in. Sugar, Mr Lynch?'

'I've got sweeteners, thanks. That's very good of you, Inspector. Especially good of you not to make the girl do it.'

'She's Bad Cop,' said Tom. 'She's going to soften you up before I get back.'

Tom reckoned the next time he did something without telling Hayes first, she'd go on strike. His DC looked from one man to the other and got out of the car. She and Lynch walked carefully up the incline at the back of the lay-by.

When Tom joined them with a carryout tray of drinks, he found that the other side of the embankment sloped down to a security fence. It was private and sheltered, and the used condoms lying around suggested that they weren't the only ones who knew about it.

'Not much of a bad cop,' said Lynch. 'She's been asking after me family. Turns out I know her mother as well. Small world, round here, sure it is. Don't drink your tea yet, they're scalding hot those cups.'

Tom put the tray on the ground. 'You're going to jail, Patrick. You're going to jail for bribing Griffin and money laundering. That much I can prove already, now that I've seen the golf club records. The question is this: are you going to let your daughter go to jail as well or are you going to help me catch those counterfeiters?'

'Helen is innocent. She's had nothing to do with Griffin or my little businesses. She's got her own life.'

'Too late, Patrick. You're a smart man, I know, but you're not a criminal lawyer. All I have to prove is that Helen received the laundered money. It's enough to get one criminal record for her and a matching one for your son-in-law. I can have the house, too. If you don't believe me, you can let her take her chances.'

Hayes reached down and took one of the drinks for herself. 'He means it, you know,' she said to Lynch. 'He got that black eye when he took a woman's credit cards off her. It was ugly.'

A gust of wind found its way behind the embankment and blew Lynch's hair adrift. He was developing quite a comb-over. The Irishman smoothed it back in place and picked up his own tea.

'I can't. Not "won't", it's "can't". The guys who sent me the counterfeit notes have cut me off completely, and they've started doing business elsewhere. I don't know who they are or how to get in touch, and if I did know, I'd let Helen, Elizabeth, Francesca, Hope, and everyone go to jail rather than give you their names. They're worse than the Blackpool lot.'

'Blackpool?'

'Yes, Blackpool. The men who shot my nephew are bunch of fellas from Blackpool. I can give you their leader in exchange for laying off Helen. If you go about it properly, you might use him to get at the Rainbow guys because, they're doing business directly now.'

Tom's phone rang; he checked the screen and saw that it was BCSS. He rejected the call.

'Come on, Patrick. Stop talking in riddles. Who are the Rainbow guys?'

'When we started in business together, they said I had to have Green in the name of the company. I thought it was a joke at first, but they've got some other colours, too. One day on the phone, I heard one of them say Rainbow. That's all.'

Tom thought of the piece of blue sky that he thought was a bit of jigsaw. Not a jigsaw, then, but a rainbow. No. He preferred jigsaw. Hayes reached into her pocket and took out her phone. He shook his head at her and she too rejected the call.

'Why you, Patrick? Out of all the bent market traders in England, why did they choose you to distribute fake twenty pound notes? They must have been doing business before that.'

'I think it was Dermot,' said Patrick a little too smoothly. 'He came up with the contacts. Poor lad did a stint in jail. But you'll know all about that.'

Two men walked around the end of the embankment and started to hurry towards them. For a second, Tom thought that Patrick had arranged an ambush, but then he recognised one of the surveillance officers. He had about ten seconds left.

'I want Griffin's private mobile number, and you only tell me, okay? It's that or the deal's off.'

Lynch nodded.

The two surveillance officers arrived. 'Is everything all right, Inspector? We were worried that we'd lost track of Mr Lynch.'

'You're just in time,' said Tom. 'Mr Lynch is about to tell us who shot his nephew.'

'Not quite,' said Lynch. 'James King is going to do that, although it does depend on how good your storage is.'

Tom picked up his cup of tea, now cooled to a drinkable temperature.

'DC Hayes, would you like to caution Mr Lynch?'

'A pleasure, sir.'

'How did you do it?' asked DCS Winters.

Tom shrugged. 'You thought it was about the future. You were looking to see who was muscling in on Dermot's business. I focused on the past and joined up the dots. Not only that, many of your officers saw Griffin as a copper. I looked on him as a criminal.'

'I can see what you mean. Perhaps that's why the Chief Constable insisted on having you aboard. Still, job done.'

Winters tossed some of the files from his desk on to the floor. 'Won't be pursuing them any more.' He looked up at Tom. 'I suppose you're going to want to question him, aren't you?'

'I'm still in charge of the Professional Standards case against Griffin and Hooper, but it seems that it's all rather interlinked.'

'I know. Look, the MCPS Economic Crimes guys are pretty stretched at the moment. They couldn't even afford to lend us anyone for the Major Enquiry – another reason you were ahead of the pack. Would you mind looking into the money laundering as well as the corruption? We need to have something to charge that slippery leprechaun with before he runs away again. Just for the rest of this week – I'll put in a proper request to CIPPS.'

'Thanks, sir. You didn't have to do that.'

'I'm not about to invite you to dinner, Tom, but I'd be stupid not to use a good resource when it's in my kitchen cupboard.'

Tom's imagination boggled at the idea of him being in Winters' kitchen cupboard and, if so, what sort of ingredient or implement he might be. Food processor, possibly? Something that puréed and blended suspects? Maybe not. Winters' shameless use of him to go through Lynch's financials was in their mutual interest, but it hadn't resolved their other differences.

'Fair enough, sir. Two other things, if you don't think I'm pushing my luck. The first is DC Hayes and the second is the question of Griffin's front door key.'

'You can keep Hayes. No one else wants her. I've had a word with my Exhibits Manager, and she does remember you handing it in. She's made a report to that effect. Mind you, that doesn't mean someone stole it – you could have left a spare in the lock or it could have been you that took it.'

Tom nodded. There was no point in being unnecessarily unpleasant.

'Now,' said Winters, 'how did Lynch say he was going to identify the Blackpool mob?'

A DS from the team knocked on the door, and Winters waved him in.

'Sir, sorry to interrupt, but James King has come in and says the man who shot his brother is the same one who shot his father eighteen years ago.'

Blimey, thought Tom, *that's going to take some sorting out*.

Sir Stephen Jennings was sitting by the fire reading Keith Jeffrey's *MI6 – A History of the Secret Intelligence Service*. It was a very big book, and he had been meaning to start it for some time. It was the WI meeting later tonight so he should have a fairly uninterrupted run at it: the best way to approach a new book was to give yourself enough time to get engrossed. If he wasn't enthralled by eight o'clock, it would be going on the shelf for reference.

He heard the landline ringing and left his wife to answer it – almost certainly another of the village ladies asking for a lift or checking who was going to bring the milk. Footsteps approached the library, and his wife passed him the cordless phone. 'It's for you. Calls himself Mr Green.'

Bloody hell. He had forgotten that the Principal Investor in Birmingham knew his home address – and that because of his wife's position in the village, they were listed in the phone book. He took the receiver and said hello. His wife didn't linger.

'Sorry to bother you at home, Stephen, but I've lost your mobile number.'

It was him all right.

'I'm sorry, I don't recognise your voice. Have we met before?' Jennings could hear traffic noises. The man must have gone looking for one of Britain's few remaining call boxes.

'I'm a friend from the old days. You've got my number, and I've got some news for you. I wouldn't have troubled you otherwise.'

There was a hint of neediness in the voice which might indicate trouble to come. Because of the man's connections, Jennings couldn't afford to ignore him; it might even be important.

'I'm a little busy right now. Can I call you in ten minutes?'

'I'll be waiting.'

It took him the full ten minutes to dig out the man's mobile number and find a suitable SIM card for one of his phones. When the other man picked up, it was quieter in the background. Probably sitting in his car.

'What can I do for you?' said Jennings.

'You were right about Morton. He's cracked the case wide open down here, and got Patrick Lynch in custody giving all the gory details. I tried my best to sideline him but he's persistent.'

'I thought Lynch didn't know anything.'

'He doesn't, as such, but there's been a development. One of the victims' brothers has come in voluntarily to identify the Blackpool man as being involved in a cold case. There's a good chance that they'll be bearing down on your new partner in the near future.'

The note of whining had come back when the words *new partner* were spoken, but the man was right – in less than a week, less than four days in fact, Morton had sniffed out the trail better than a foxhound in full cry.

'Thanks for the tip-off. Hopefully things will calm down in your neck of the woods now. Shame about Lynch, though. He's done very well for you over the years. Very well indeed. Operation Rainbow is a business not a charity. I'm sure that you'll find yourself a new partner, and when you do – we'll be ready to do business with you again.'

Jennings disconnected the call and cut up the SIM card. What a waste.

Knowing Morton, he'll be trying to get himself attached to the investigation up in Blackpool. If they broke off with their new partner, Morton would only follow the counterfeit money around the country until they made a mistake – or someone stopped him.

He had heard some news on the grapevine about the Mortons of Throckton and done a little digging. They were clearly a tenacious family, and there must be something in the water at that farm – even though Captain Lonsdale wasn't a Morton by blood, she appeared to share a lot of their characteristics. Judging by the way that she had acted in Essex, she was willing to take risks and was very attached to her cousin; if something happened to Morton, she would very likely pursue it, and there was still the matter of her connection to the late Sgt Jensen.

The counterfeiting was Offlea's project, and it was his decision as to whether to act against Morton – but if he did, then Lonsdale would have to be put out of the picture as well. That was a shame – she was developing into a very useful asset.

Chapter 11

Earlsbury

Friday / Saturday

29-30th October

Every police force pays for some officers to act as full time representatives of the Police Federation. By law, officers haven't been allowed to join a Trade Union since the police strike of 1919. Apart from not being allowed to call a strike or set up a Political Fund, the Federation is otherwise indistinguishable from any other union; Tom was a member and would remain so unless he rose to the giddy heights of Superintendent. He had never needed a Federation Representative (or Fed Rep), and if he ever did, he hoped it would not be the idiot sitting opposite him.

Since Patrick Lynch's arrest on Tuesday, Tom had been up to his armpits in bank accounts and balance sheets as he attempted to straighten out the crooked empire that Lynch had created. Tom was happy to keep a toehold in Earlsbury – they had even given him and Kris a desk at BCSS.

The bulk of the detectives assigned to the case had been transferred back to their normal units without further explanation after James King dropped his little bombshell. Winters had briefed only a tiny group of senior officers that they were waiting on a DNA result from an eighteen year old case. Unless there was a *very* highly placed source in MCPS, they might actually have the element of surprise this time.

That left two questions, the most pressing being Ian Hooper. Reports from the hospital said that he was off the critical list but was still seriously ill. *It would be the worst time for him*, thought Tom. He would be out of intensive care, but wouldn't feel any better for weeks – if at all. Abdominal wounds were notoriously unpredictable. Winters had been back for a further informal chat; Hooper had added nothing to his original statement. That meant it would be Tom's turn soon. When the Fed Rep allowed him, of course.

The other question was DS Griffin's mobile. After one of the sessions interviewing Lynch, his solicitor had handed Tom a slip of paper with a mobile number on it. The solicitor had said, 'My client believes this is the last part of the bargain – you let his daughter go in exchange.'

Tom had ordered Helen's release – but only on police bail. He'd told Lynch that until he knew the number was genuine, he needed the option; the Irishman had nodded cheerfully in response. He would deal with that at the weekend, back in London. For now he had to cope with Ian Hooper's Federation Representative.

'Be realistic,' said the Rep. 'Why would DC Hooper have an informal chat with you?'

'Because it's in his best interests to do so.'

'I'm afraid I don't see it like that. You can't interview him under caution until he's been signed off as fit for that purpose – which could be a very long time. And then there's no guarantee that he'll have anything to say. I wouldn't co-operate if I were him, and I'll be telling him so.'

'What does he say about this?'

The Rep recrossed his legs. 'It's my role to represent DC Hooper's interests.'

'You haven't been to see him, have you.'

The Rep didn't dispute the statement.

'I'll save you some work here,' said Tom. 'I've been through all of Hooper's financials, and I can see no evidence that he was in receipt of corrupt payments. Unlike Griffin. However, I need to be sure. There's a nasty smell around all the Earlsbury CID, and until I can get some air in to blow it away, it's going to linger. The sooner Hooper can satisfy me, the sooner I'll leave him alone.'

'It's very, very rarely in an ordinary constable's interests to co-operate with Professional Standards. Hooper's been shot in the line of duty – what more proof do you need that he's a hard working officer who's put himself in harm's way to protect the public?'

'You haven't even read the file, have you, because if you had, you wouldn't be spouting rubbish like that. Griffin was on the take. He was supposed to protect a shipment of counterfeit currency, but something went wrong. I need to know whether Hooper was Griffin's sidekick or his victim.'

Hayes was taking notes. Her opinion of the Federation was even lower than Tom's, because when she reported her colleagues with the working girl, the Fed had closed ranks around the men instead of supporting the whistleblower.

The Fed Rep straightened the edge of the file on the desk between them. It had Hooper's name on the front and CIPPS in big letters. A courier had brought a pile of CIPPS stationery for him on Wednesday, including his new business cards.

'You're right, Inspector, this is a complex situation. How about I review the file for a few days while Hooper continues to recuperate. It's not as if he's going anywhere, is it?'

With that, the Rep stood up and packed his briefcase.

'DC Hayes will show you out,' said Tom.

When she returned, he was on the phone looking for someone. He covered the mouthpiece and said to her, 'Don't get comfortable. We're going out.'

He got the reply he was hoping for and replaced the receiver. 'We're going to have a chat with Erin King.'

'You mean we're going to a lap dancing club.'

'Pole dancing.'

Tom had to use the satnav to find The West Pole. His vague description to Hayes had produced only a curled lip and a muttered comment about male drivers.

'Did you miss a game last Saturday?' asked Tom. 'What did you say? Castle WFC?'

'No. There aren't enough teams in the league to play every weekend. We're back in action tomorrow, unless you need me for something.'

'No, I'm going home to my hired box.' Hayes raised an eyebrow. 'Since the separation, I live in a studio flat in the City. My father said it reminded him of a poem by Philip Larkin. I deliberately haven't looked it up.'

The Friday lunchtime trade at The West Pole was starting to pick up when they arrived; the first dancers were due out in ten minutes.

Tom introduced himself to the manager and asked where Erin was. 'Can you wait until the girls come out?' he asked. 'You can use the dressing room then.'

Tom nodded his agreement and declined the offer of a drink.

There was no fanfare or drum roll to announce the dancers – the music started, and they emerged from the beaded curtain. Erin slipped through the side door at the same time. Hayes picked up her bag but Tom stopped her.

'Let's wait a minute. This is Erin's first day back at work, and she needs to know what's been going on in her absence.'

Hayes sat back down on the stool and, for want of anything better to do, they watched the dancers perform a badly synchronised ensemble. Erin was filming it on her phone. When the music changed, and the girls began their individual routines, Tom and Kris got up and showed their warrant cards discreetly. Erin led them through the back.

'I'm sorry about Robert,' said Tom. 'How are the boys?'

'You came to see me with Ian, didn't you?'

'Yes. I was with the London police then, looking for counterfeit twenty pound notes.'

Erin's chin came up in defiance. The Lynch family had clearly filled her in on the extent of police investigations. Tom moved to reassure her. 'I'm not here about Robert, that's up to other people.'

'Rob. His name was Rob.'

'Of course. I'm here about something else. I couldn't help noticing that you are a friend of Ian's.'

'So what? We've known each other for years. Since school.'

'And you care about him – as a friend. I'm going to put a proposition to you that you can ignore if you want, but I hope you think about it first.'

'Okay.'

'I'm not with the Economic Crimes Unit any more. I'm with Professional Standards now. We are the officers who get called in when another officer is accused of something.'

Erin's gaze flicked from Tom to Kris. 'I'll bet that makes you popular.' Hayes gave a snort.

'DC Hayes is on loan,' said Tom. 'She's trying to decide whether to make the move permanent.' Hayes treated him to her best hard stare but said nothing. 'So you can see that Ian isn't going to want to talk to me.'

'Why do you want to talk to Ian? He's the original honest copper and he was even a prefect at school – that's one of the reasons we split up.'

'He told me about that. I like Ian too – but that's not enough. I need to know what he was doing at the Goods Yard, and until I do, there's going to be a big question mark hanging over him. If I arrest him and interview him under caution, I'll have to do a full investigation, look into every detail, make a note of his visits here – and I bet the manager will tell me everything. I might find something really trivial that I can't ignore. Something that loses his pension. If he has to retire on medical grounds, he'll be on benefits without that pension.'

'What do you want from me?'

'When you go and see him – and I'm sure you will – tell him that he should invite me into the hospital for a chat. Nothing on the record, just a chat. I promise.'

Erin bounced on the soles of her feet. 'He said you were a good bloke. If I speak to him, will you promise he won't get into trouble?'

'No, because he might – just might – be guilty. If I see him for a chat, I promise I'll give him the benefit of the doubt – nothing on his record at all. He can recuperate in peace.'

Tom took out a card and passed it to her. 'Just give him that and tell him to think it over.'

She took the card and slipped it into a pocket.

'You've got some work to do on those dancers,' said Hayes to lighten the mood.

'Tell me about it. You'd think I'd been off for a month, not a week.'

'Do you run classes?' asked Hayes.

'Not yet, but I'm thinking about it. Have you got a card too?'

She passed one over, and it joined Tom's card in Erin's pocket. The detectives headed for the emergency exit where Tom had caught his fleeting glimpse of Rob King. 'Kris, are you thinking of a change of career?'

'No, but there's the Castle WFC Christmas Party to think of. That should get them going.'

Tom was summoned to a meeting in the BCSS conference room after lunch, just when he was thinking of trying to beat the traffic back to London. The top table from last Saturday was there, minus the Chief Constable: DCC Nechells, ACC Khan, Brewer from media and DCS Winters. The other surviving DI from the original enquiry was there too, along with a middle-aged woman in a smart suit who identified herself as Evelyn Andrews, the Chief's personal assistant. The man himself was apparently in Liverpool for an ACPO meeting, but wanted to know immediately what was said.

The only outsider was a smooth man with public school hair combed over his forehead and a muted but colourful tie. Nechells was the last to arrive, and he took the chair.

'Mrs Andrews, Gentlemen, thank you for coming on a Friday afternoon. I won't keep you long, I hope. This is Mr John Lake from Security Liaison. His job is to act as first point of contact between police forces and various security services in matters *not* related to terrorism. John, over to you.'

'Thank you. I should clarify that – it's matters not related to islamist terrorism, actually. What I'm going to talk about today is very much related to terrorism, but nothing to do with Al-Qaida.' Lake opened his slim briefcase and took out a paper. Across the top was something like a barcode. 'My office received a flag this morning from the National DNA database, which was triggered when you put in a request. DCC Nechells has filled me in on the details, so I'll cut to the chase. The man you want in connection with the death of Solomon King in 1992 and also with the current investigation has been known to us for some time. He was in the IRA.'

All the officers around the table looked at each other, but none of them spoke. Lake continued, 'When the peace process was concluded, a lot of people had their sins forgiven. Murderers were released, files were closed, and records were destroyed in the name of community relations. However, the message was given to the IRA high command, in no uncertain terms, that this was a one shot deal. Any crimes committed *after* the peace process began were going to be pursued as normal.'

It was Winters who interrupted first. 'Does that mean we have to lay off him?' The whole room could hear the unspoken subtext *two of our own were shot here and two others as well*.

'I'll tell you now, the CPS will never prosecute for the Solomon King murder. Not in the public interest. Since then, this man has kept his nose clean, and there is no official record of his DNA, but there's nothing to stop you beginning an operation from scratch.' Lake pushed the paper into the middle of the room. 'May I introduce you to Benedict Adaire. This man has killed more people than anyone I've ever come across. Be careful.'

Lake nodded and left; Nechells took over. 'Preliminary work by Nigel has put Adaire in Blackpool with a registered minicab business. A discreet word with our colleagues in Lancashire & Westmorland hasn't revealed any active enquiries with him at the centre.' He paused and picked up the piece of paper left behind by Lake. 'This is a delicate situation. Our witness only shows that Dermot Lynch was talking to a man who may or may not be Benedict Adaire, and that Robert King *believed* him to be involved with his father's death. I'm going to liaise with my opposite number up north and put a strategy in place. Until then, this goes no further. Understood?'

The room nodded collectively, and Nechells followed Lake out of the door along with Khan, Brewer and Evelyn Andrews. That left Winters, Tom, and the other DI who said, 'Can you tell us anything, sir?'

'No,' said Winters. 'Go home, both of you. There's nothing to do this weekend.'

Kate was used to jet lag. Flying to Iraq, and especially to Afghanistan, messed with your system, and Hong Kong was even further. She was ready to drop down on the spot and sleep for England. Her boss seemed oblivious.

They were waiting for further instructions to proceed to Shanghai: before they left, they had to collect the hardware for the intercept operation in China, and they had to establish a cover story for themselves as a British technology start-up looking for a manufacturing partner. They would then visit several firms and attempt to install the intercept equipment while they were there. The clock said that it was tea time, but Kate's biorhythms were insisting on bedtime. She asked for a diet cola when the waiter came over: anything to keep her awake.

Her boss, Leach, ordered another scotch and started to play with the new iPad he'd insisted on buying at the airport. Kate wasn't sure whether they'd catch on but quite a lot of the suits scattered around the lobby seemed to have these new tablet computers. They didn't seem very secure to her.

The waiter returned with drinks and the house phone for her boss. He conducted a very brief conversation in English and hung up.

'Slight change of plan. We're to pick up the hardware in Hong Kong rather than Shanghai. Apparently it's less risky on an internal flight.'

'Any news on whether we've got an appointment with the suppliers?'

He shook his head, and Kate picked up her book.

Tom arrived at the Lambeth office on Friday afternoon in a sour mood. The news from the DNA results had delayed his departure, and he'd had to cope with the half term getaway before he could check in with his new employers. No one in CIPPS except Samuel Cohen had a clue who he was: when he arrived at the office, they wouldn't let him in.

'Assistant Director Cohen has got away early. There's no record of you on the system.'

'But I've been with CIPPS for a week. Surely there's been a memo or something. See, I've even got my own business cards now.'

He handed one over, and the receptionist looked at it dubiously.

'I suppose I could contact Human Resources at the Yard.'

What Tom really wanted to say was *yes, I suppose you could if you thought that doing your job was a good idea*, but if he were going to be with CIPPS for a while, he couldn't afford to annoy the receptionist. Instead, he said, 'That would be very kind of you.' For all her flirting, his relationship with Elspeth Brown at City had been the shortcut to many favours. He'd never get any messages here if he got off on the wrong foot with the admin staff.

He retreated to the one chair designated for visitors and waited. Thankfully, there was someone at Scotland Yard who confirmed his new status and, after a close examination of his warrant card, she issued him with a temporary door pass.

'Now I know who you are, I'll organise a proper one. I suppose you'll be wanting a desk, too.'

'Let's not get carried away,' said Tom. 'I'm expecting some documents. Where do you think they might be?'

'Post Room's third on the left.'

He thanked the woman, and found a young man locking the Post Room door. 'Have you got anything for DI Morton in there?'

The lad examined his pass and warrant card, and then his face lit up. 'I said it wasn't a joke. Tracy wanted to send it back to the Yard, but I said no, it belongs here. Hang on.'

He unlocked the door and disappeared into a room full of photocopying and printing equipment. Thirty seconds later, Tom had an Authorisation for Seizure of Records on Griffin's mobile phone. He took it back to reception where the woman was putting on her coat.

'Sorry to bother you, but if I come back here tomorrow morning, will I be able to get in, and will I be able to use one of the terminals?'

'You looked like someone who'd work weekends, so while you were gone I did these.' She handed him a permanent security pass and a UserID for the CIPPS system.

Tom was fulsome in his thanks and made his way, finally, to Horsefair Court.

The next morning he returned to Lambeth and found himself alone in the office. He chose a desk at random and Sellotaped two A3 pieces of paper together while the computer was booting up. He logged on to the CIPPS system and accessed Griffin's phone records. He started to write them on to the blank paper by time of call, by frequency, and by cross-checking against other records from service providers. He also included Griffin's other phone, the police issue one. When he'd finished, he drew around two boxes in red: one of them was a group of calls that pointed towards a Pay As You Go number that probably belonged to Patrick Lynch. The other box was from the night of the shootings and had two calls listed.

Tom had identified the call that Griffin made to Hooper, exactly when Kelly said it was made. The other call was an incoming one which Griffin had received two minutes earlier. It was from a landline registered to a hotel in Birmingham, and it was the call that sent Griffin to his death.

The Authorisation for Seizure had been arranged by Cohen who had pinned a handwritten note to it. The note gave him another deadline: *You can have three more days in Earlsbury, and unless you make an arrest, I've got something else for you.*

Chapter 12

Earlsbury

Monday

1st November

Tom made good time on Monday morning and was early enough to collect Hayes from her mother's house. 'Did you get a result at the weekend?'

'You don't strike me as a footballer, sir.'

'Never played, except on the beach. Mine was a rugby school. And cricket in the summer – proper game, that.'

'We lost. I could tell you about the failings of our midfield and their inability to make a tackle, but if you don't know your 4-4-2 from your 4-3-3, I won't bother.'

'What about you? Striker or defender?'

'Right back.'

They queued at the roundabout, and Tom told her what he'd discovered from the phone records. 'I've got to go to a briefing this morning about something new that's come up. The phone number belongs to a big place near where I used to live in Edgbaston – The Victoria Hotel. I'd like you to go out there and find out, if you can, what was happening at the hotel on the night of the shootings. Find out what sort of telephone system they've got. Push them a bit, but don't get aggressive or threaten. We can always get a warrant later if they won't volunteer the information. Oh, and don't put this into HOLMES 2 until I tell you.'

'Do you really think that there's someone in the MCPS who's helping out?'

'Yes. Someone on the force is watching us. As soon as they realised we were following the golfing angle, they hightailed it round to Griffin's house to remove any evidence from his golf bag. We would have tracked him down to Earlsbury Park eventually, but I'll bet there was a score card in that bag with someone's name on it. All we know is that it wasn't Hooper.'

'Okay. Can I take your car?'

'No problem. I know you'll take care of it.'

There was a line of cars heading into BCSS, and Tom parked near the entrance. He handed the keys to Hayes along with a printout of Griffin's phone records. She drove off cautiously, and he had to remind himself that she didn't own a vehicle of her own. Ah well, never mind.

The same group of senior officers that had met John Lake on Friday was gathered in the same conference room and sitting in the same seats. Had he actually gone home for the weekend? The only differences were that Evelyn Andrews was missing, and that Winters took the chair.

'I'm pleased to say that Lancashire & Westmorland have been very supportive about this. They're willing to provide a surveillance team for a week to support our investigation.'

That was good news. With England's many separate constabularies, co-operation was always a tricky issue. There were forty three separate police forces, and with Britain's extensive motorway network, it was normal for suspects to come from a different force area. The rule of thumb stated that the force where a crime was committed took the lead in the investigation and, subject to notification and agreement, the force where the criminal lived would provide support.

Winters continued, 'We will be sending a team of six up there to conduct the enquiry, led by our DI.' He nodded towards the other Inspector, and Tom felt the ground pulled away from underneath him. He had no authority to demand a place on the team, and it looked like he was being cut out. Winters confirmed it.

'DI Morton has been given another three days to wrap up the charges against Patrick Lynch and will be based here. Tom, do you think you might be able to give us a verdict on Ian Hooper by then?'

'I hope so.'

'Good man. This stage of the operation is on a strictly need-to-know basis, and of course,' he nodded towards Brewer, 'we need a complete media blackout.'

It was a struggle for Tom not to rush from the room and beat the wall in frustration. He waited until the top brass left and followed in their wake. He was so angry that he left the building and walked all the way to the burger van in the lay-by to buy himself a cup of tea and some thinking time.

It was going to go wrong again. He knew it. No matter how secretively the operation in Blackpool was carried out, their target would get wind of it and go to ground like a fox who hears the hounds on its tail. Except that in this case, there was no huntsman to stop the earths or dig it out when the quarry was cornered.

He ran through the last week since he had forced Patrick Lynch to confess: he already had more than enough material against him for a strong case of money laundering and for bribing Griffin. Lynch would go to jail for that, but the ebullient Irishman didn't seem too bothered. Granted, Tom had already established that his family home was untouchable, but Lynch was a not a well man. His heart condition could easily deteriorate in prison and he would have no assets afterwards except the home: he had given up everything in exchange for his daughter's freedom. Why?

His old boss, Pete Fulton, had a mantra for any crime involving cash – *Follow the Money and Find the Felon*. During the *PiCAASA* investigation, Tom had discovered this wasn't true. He had followed the money around London and Essex for some time and got nowhere. Now that he was a DI himself (albeit a rather specialised one), Tom had decided he needed his own mantra. He sipped his tea and rolled the words around in his head. Eventually he came up with *the Proof is in the Paperwork, but the Answer is in the Person.* Not brilliant, but it would do as a start.

He headed back to BCSS and took out his sketch of Lynch's operation. All that Lynch had confessed to so far was money laundering, but he hadn't said much about where the money came from. Tom knew that the counterfeit money was quite recent, but Lynch must have been breaking the law for years. He checked back and found that there was unaccounted income going back at least five years. The source of this had been identified as Dermot Lynch – who was quite young when he died, and according to his record, he had been in jail for some of the time.

Even if Dermot was running things, Patrick must have set them up, must know where all the bases were. He went into the video archive of HOLMES 2 and brought up the interview tapes where the other DI (the one going to Blackpool) had questioned Lynch about the Wrekin Road fire.

The DI had begun by showing Lynch pictures of his cremated nephew. The Irishman winced with unfeigned pain.

'We know you didn't shoot Dermot or Robert,' said the DI, 'but what happened at the workshop? Why did you burn their bodies rather than leave them for us to find?'

'How could I do that to my nephew – or Hope's brother, come to that? I know nothing about any Wrekin Road or any fire. I've never been there.'

'There was a substantial quantity of counterfeit goods in that workshop – cigarettes and vodka. You were dealing in these goods.'

'Not directly. That was Dermot's operation. I've never been there in my life. You can check CCTV for miles around – no sign of my Jaguar anywhere. I was at home with an angina attack, brought on by the worry.'

That was it. The DI wasn't expecting it, so he hadn't noticed it, but Dermot Lynch had just overplayed his hand. *No sign of my Jaguar anywhere.* So he must have used another car.

The dedicated bank of computer monitors had gone, but all the CCTV footage was still online. Tom picked the streets nearest to Wrekin Road and started looking for a car matching the description of Francesca Lynch's vehicle. It took him an hour, but he found it.

Hayes telephoned and said she had some news. She sounded worried but Tom wasn't bothered about that. 'Meet me at the Lynch house,' he said, 'I'll get a lift from uniform.'

Apart from the sense of owning a little piece of England, another benefit of Sir Stephen's woodland was that it harboured foxes. A keen huntsman in his youth, Jennings was determined that he should do his bit to keep the way of life going that had shaped so much of the countryside around where he lived. The season would be starting in a couple of weeks, and with the clocks going back last night, the foxes were looking for their winter lairs. Not that the foxes took notice of the clocks, of course.

He walked the woods at dawn, looking for tracks, fresh earth or bones. Satisfied that one or two might have moved in, he returned to St Andrew's Hall for breakfast. There was a message waiting for him on the mobile phone he had reactivated.

Since the disturbing news from their Green investor, he had decided to reopen a channel of communication. This morning's situation update said that all activity should cease because there was about to be a joint police operation crawling all over Blackpool. When Jennings read the name of the target, he sat up with a jolt: that name brought bad enough memories for him; what would it do to Offlea?

Sir Stephen told his wife that something had come up and drove towards Oxford, where he lost himself in the suburbs to avoid leaving too much mobile data near his home in the sparsely populated countryside. He sent a text message to Offlea and waited for the call.

When it came, he gave Will a concise summary of the information about Adaire. As he had feared, there was an ominous silence at the other end. Jennings waited.

'My God,' said Offlea, 'I never expected to hear that name again.' To hear him speak, you would think he'd never left Belfast. 'And to think I've been doing business with that murdering bastard. I'm going to take a wee sabbatical, sir, if that's all right with you. Don't worry, I'll get myself well out of Red Flag first.'

'What about Morton and Lonsdale?'

'Leave him to me. Where's his cousin?'

'Hong Kong with Leach. They're on their way to Shanghai.'

'I can sort that as well. I'll be in touch.'

Hayes was waiting for him down the road from Patrick and Francesca Lynch's house. He couldn't help himself – he gave his BMW a quick once-over. No damage. Hayes got out. She had a worried look on her face.

'I've got them.' said Tom.

'Sir, there's something...'

'I can connect them to Wrekin Road. I'm sure of it. Come on, Kris, I was nicey-nicey to them on the phone, but they said they're going out soon. I want to get into their house before anyone at BCSS starts following my tracks.'

He accepted the car keys from Hayes and walked up to Lynch's house. 'I want you to look in the garage at Francesca's car. Check the number plates carefully for any sign that they've been removed and look in the drawers or cupboards for false plates. It's a long shot, but if we don't check, we'll never know.'

He rang the bell, and Patrick answered. He didn't invite them inside but he stood back to allow them past him. Through the kitchen door, Tom could see Francesca giving lunch to their youngest daughter. Of course, it was half term. Even better.

'Sorry to trouble you,' said Tom. 'I'll be as quick as possible. You have been arrested in connection with money laundering and Conspiracy to Commit Misconduct in Public Office.' Patrick nodded. 'You gave us permission to search this property in connection with those offences. There are a couple of areas I'd like to look at again. Do I still have your permission?'

'What are you looking for? You went through everything yourself last week.'

'Not quite everything. In fact, not much at all. I don't want to do an invasive search – floorboards and plasterboard – I just want to look in a couple of places.'

'And you promise you'll be quick?'

'If I don't find anything, yes.'

'If you must.'

Patrick went through to the kitchen, and Tom followed. 'Do you need to look in here?' said Francesca with a frown. 'We'll go next door if you want.'

'Could DC Hayes have the key to the garage? I'd like to do an accompanied search of Elizabeth's room.'

Patrick looked alarmed, but Tom couldn't tell whether it was because of the garage of Elizabeth's room. 'Do you think I'd put anything in my own daughter's bedroom. Jesus, Mary and Joseph, what sort of a father do you think I am?'

Out of the corner of his eye, Tom saw Hayes' nostrils flare at the use of the Holy Family for an oath. He noticed that Lynch hadn't commented on the search of the garage. The outrage could be genuine or not. 'Perhaps you'd like to accompany my colleague outside, and your wife and daughter can come with me.'

'No,' said Francesca. 'Elizabeth doesn't need to be involved in this.'

Tom looked at Elizabeth. She was thin and pale, but her eyes had been flicking around the conversation intently. She looked worried but she wasn't looking worried in his direction. Tom addressed his comments to her. 'My younger sister got arrested once, you know. She was only just older than you. When the police came to search her room, she was more worried about what our mother would see than what the cops might discover. I think you should come with us, then you can open the drawers and stuff, and your mother can watch from the doorway.'

Elizabeth flicked her eyes to Francesca and then back to him. She nodded and pulled her long hair back behind her head. She took a scrunchy from her pocket and pinned it in place, then led the adults upstairs. The way that Francesca protected the young girl made it unlikely she would allow her husband to hide things in Elizabeth's bedroom, but that was only part of his aim. He wanted to split them up, and show that he was willing to stick his nose anywhere.

Elizabeth started in the wardrobe, pulling her clothes aside and lifting out shoes to show there was nothing to hide. Hanging at the right hand end were several white shirts, a skirt and a green blazer with Gothic lettering on the breast pocket. 'Which school do you go to?' asked Tom.

'St Mod's.'

'Never heard of him.'

'Her. It's short for St Modwenna. She was one of the few female saints who lived in Staffordshire. Our school's run by nuns who have a convent near Burton on Trent.'

Tom pointed to the chest of drawers and watched her eyes flick nervously towards a pile of DVDs under her television. He let her rattle through the drawers and noticed that she turned her back to her mother when showing him one of them. Francesca noticed too and craned her neck to see what was being concealed. Tom couldn't see anything incriminating in the assortment of neatly folded tops and underwear, but he wasn't a parent. He guessed that Elizabeth would have some explaining to do later.

'Could you open those for me,' he said, pointing to the DVDs. This time Elizabeth looked at her mother.

Francesca reached down and sifted through the cases until she found a blank one. She fumbled open the clasp and showed him a blank disk with the words *Twilight – Happy Birthday Lizzie* written on it. 'There. See? We bought her a pirate DVD for her birthday. You can take it.'

Tom looked at the posters of Robert Pattinson adorning the walls and believed her. He took the disk anyway. 'I'll have a quick look to make sure that's what it is, then I'll throw it in the bin and forget about it. Show me the others.'

The rest of the stack were all hologramed authentic copies. Tom was about to move on to the bed (and whatever was underneath the mattress) when he heard Hayes calling up the stairs.

'Thanks, Elizabeth,' he said to the girl, and was rewarded with a smile. Francesca was torn between missing the action downstairs and investigating her daughter's chest of drawers, but she reacted to the more threatening tone from below.

Hayes and Lynch were waiting in the hall. Kris was gloved up and holding an evidence bag which she raised for his examination. It contained a set of blank number plates, and adhesive letters. Lynch was going purple with anger, and a lot of it seemed to be directed at his wife.

'What's going on?' said Francesca.

'Let's talk in the lounge,' said Tom, and led them into the through room, closing the door behind him. He took out a piece of paper and unfolded it before passing it to the Lynches. They had taken up a defensive position in front of the fireplace and they stared at the image on the paper. It was a CCTV printout of a car matching Francesca's, but with different number plates. From purple, Patrick started to go white.

'I spent some time working the camera data this morning,' said Tom. 'I found that there were several vehicles clocked on the ANPR system with no matching number at the DVLA. There are more than you would think. I checked them all and *this* vehicle,' he pointed to the picture, 'was tracked from a location near here to a location near Wrekin Road. The occupants are wearing concealing clothing but, Mrs Lynch, those cameras are good.' He had his phone ready and went to take a picture of Francesca. She instinctively turned her head away from the lens, but he snapped her regardless and examined the picture. 'Thank you, Mrs Lynch. I've got a good shot of you wearing the same earrings today as in that picture.'

'So what?' said Patrick. 'It could be anybody in that car, and even if it wasn't, you've no proof it was here or at Wrekin Road.'

Hayes held up the bag again. 'I found these in an old chest. There was an empty space in the toolbox exactly the same size, and I'm guessing that you threw the others away but forgot this one. I checked the car; there's considerable wear on the number plate screws which shows they've been removed several times.'

'I want a lawyer,' said Lynch.

'Too late,' said Tom. 'I've got enough here to hold both of you on arson, destroying evidence and several other crimes. I brought you in here because I didn't want Elizabeth to hear this conversation. You can tell her yourself that she's being taken into care.'

'What?'

'No!'

'Sir…'

Three voices assailed him but Tom didn't flinch. Elizabeth Lynch and her school uniform were going to be packed off to Social Services for protection straight away. 'The thing is,' he said, 'your middle daughter is away in London, your oldest daughter is on police bail, and no other relatives would be suitable. It's the only option. Unless you can persuade me otherwise.'

'Wait there,' said Francesca. She stormed towards the french windows in the conservatory and, on his signal, Hayes followed her.

Tom looked at Lynch who was starting to sway gently. 'Mr Lynch, I think you'd better sit down.'

'Thank you, I will.'

The Irishman collapsed on the settee and closed his eyes. Tom waited.

Francesca returned with soil on her hands, her clothes and in her hair. She was crying. Hayes was two steps behind her and opening another evidence bag.

'Here,' said Francesca, 'I don't know what it means, but it's important.' She thrust out a shopping bag with a Manchester United beanie hat inside it. 'Tell them, Pat. Tell them what it is or I swear by St Michael that I'll never speak to you again.'

Hayes took the hat and dropped it into the evidence bag. Lynch had sat up and put his hand to his chest. 'Me pills, Fran. Quick.'

Francesca shot into the kitchen and returned with a tablet. 'I'm only doing this so you don't ruddy die on me. Put it in your mouth and start talking before I strangle you meself.'

Tom gave him a minute. He stood as impassively as he could with all this going on around him; he was more worried about Hayes than Lynch. Her eyes were wide with alarm, and she was watching Lynch as if ready to start CPR any second. He wanted to put his arm on her shoulder and calm her down, but if he did, not only would it be a sign of weakness to the Lynches, she'd probably hit him.

'It was in the van,' said Patrick, mumbling slightly over the pill under his tongue. 'When I went to look, it had fallen under the passenger seat. I'm thinking that one of them took it off for comfort because it was sopping wet when I found it.'

'Could it not have been Dermot's?' asked Tom.

'For the love of God, no. He wouldn't be seen dead with such an ungodly thing in his possession. He was Wolverhampton Wanderers through and through. That hat was worn by his killer: I'd stake my life on it.'

'You are,' said Francesca, 'because if they don't get some DNA or something off it, I'll be after you.'

'We'll leave you in peace,' said Tom. He handed Francesca a card. 'When your husband is ready to make a statement, give me a call directly on that number. I agree with you about one thing, Mrs Lynch: there had better be something to find or we'll be back. If you want me to hang fire on Social Services, I need a result. I'm not bothered about the arson or the counterfeit goods, but I need something that puts one of their mob at the scene. This should do nicely.'

Lynch piped up from the couch, 'Excuse me, Inspector Morton, but how can you tie that hat to the van without putting me at the scene as well?'

'A good question. Hopefully I won't need to answer it, but I've given you my word and I'll stick to it.'

He let himself out, and Hayes stripped off the gloves on the walk to the car. Shock had given way to fury on her face, and Tom had a feeling it was directed towards him. He popped the boot, and she slung the evidence bags inside. 'There's a park down there,' said Tom. 'Let's go and see if they have a café.'

She followed him mutely around the corner and through the restored wrought iron gates of Queen Victoria Park. He was casting about for somewhere to get refreshment, and thought Hayes was doing the same.

'No one can see or hear us, sir, and I'm fed up of you and your cups of tea.'

'Get it off your chest, then.'

She walked over to a bench and stood behind it looking at the bandstand. 'It's always the women that suffer the most,' said Hayes. 'The men go to jail where they get fed and looked after, the women have to go into B&B hostels or leave the area and find themselves with nothing left. Or in this case the old man has a heart attack prior to his kid going into care.'

She turned round. 'Did you take it out on Lynch's family because of your divorce?'

'That's way out of order, constable, and you know it.'

'That's what ACC Khan told me. He said that you were getting divorced, and that I had to watch out in case you tried it on with me. He only said that so he could twist the knife and tell me that "I'm sure you know how to report a case of sexual harassment, Kristal." That's why I wasn't very happy when we first met: Khan had done his best to put me off you. He wasn't to know that the Fraud Squad are firm believers in the Nuclear Family. Or should that be *Nuke the Family – guaranteed results every time*. Have you got it in for married, dependent women just because one of them's taken you to the cleaners in a divorce settlement?'

Tom thought about swearing, just to wind her up. Instead he turned in the opposite direction, where the park sloped down to the west. The autumn air allowed him to see almost to Wales, he supposed, and he focused on a distant hill before he spoke.

'My mother trained to be a lawyer, but gave it up to marry my father; next year she's going to be Lady Morton when he gets his knighthood. My grandmother was a pioneering woman barrister who fought against prejudice all her life. My *great* grandmother was a suffragette who went on hunger strike for the vote. The thing is, Kris, that during the Great War she started handing out white feathers to men who weren't in uniform.'

'So? What does that prove?'

He turned to face her. 'I don't know. I'm a cop and a lawyer, not a historian or a sociologist. I'm also a man, so I guess that means I'm confused. What are you going to do?'

'About what?'

'About what you've just said to the only policeman in the whole of Staffordshire who's been nice to you and wants to work with you. I can do without you now that we've nailed Lynch. Can you do without me? Now that you've seen the reception you get from every male officer on the force, and most of the female ones as well, do you want to go back to Divisional CID or do you want to join Professional Standards and wear the Mark of Cain like me? That's if they'll have you. If you talk like that to all your bosses, I wouldn't touch you with a barge pole. You can find your own way back to BCSS from here. Let me know what you decide.'

He left her, outlined against the bandstand, and went back to his car.

If you have the time, Hong Kong can be a beautiful city. If you're in a rush, it is crowded, ugly, and exhausting. Kate had the time.

The Army would have found her something to do. One of an officer's responsibilities is to make sure that their men and women don't sit around and get bored, so they find them jobs to do. The infantry have a saying: *Don't sit around doing nothing, run around doing nothing.* But there was no one telling her to run around.

They had visited several Chinese middlemen, and pitched their non-existent product, looking for recommendations. The first agent said, 'Why don't you go to Shanghai yourselves? You will find many more people to help you.' The next three gave much the same response until they lowered their sights and found someone more venal and corrupt. For an up-front fee, he said he would provide introductions to his third cousin in Shanghai who had a contract with a small electronics factory.

After that, they just had to wait. Kate finished her book and signed up for several tours. She was having the time of her life, and after today's boat trip she had been invited to a second cousin's restaurant. Even Tom would have enjoyed the food.

The Chinese men she had encountered were very deferential, and she couldn't help wondering if this was because she was taller than most of them. There was a really sweet waiter at the restaurant who became silent and tongue-tied every time he served her, and then cast glances from the kitchen door. His English was excellent, and she was trying to find out if he was married. After the fourth glass of rice wine she was about to proposition him directly when her phone rang.

'Where the hell are you?' It was Leach, sounding even tetchier than usual.

'Having dinner.'

'I've had a call. We've to pick up the equipment.'

'Now?'

'No, in a couple of days.'

'Okay. I'll see you tomorrow. Don't wait up.'

She sat back and pushed away the empty plate. The waiter reappeared.

'What time do you finish tonight?' she asked.

'Very late, very late,' he replied, and removed the plate without making eye contact.

When the next course was delivered, he slipped a note into her hand. It said *Take taxi to this address at two o'clock. Here is my number...*

The Man Utd hat was in his drawer, and Tom was going to have to make a decision about it. He had been back at

BCSS for an hour, and there was no sign of Hayes. He hadn't even thought about ringing her. He doodled the chain of evidence on a notepad:

?Who does the hat belong to?
?Who can check the DNA for me?
?Will the DNA be on the system?
?What is the relationship between the wearer and Benedict Adaire?
?What do I do when I find out?
?How can I admit it as evidence and keep the Lynches out of jail for arson?
?What if it belongs to Dermot's friend and not to the killer?

He crossed out the last one. The rain had been so heavy on the night of the shootings that anyone outside would be soaked. He could see Dermot driving the van, and his passenger taking the hat off for comfort and simply forgetting it.

Tom was working on the assumption that Griffin, Hooper and Rob King had been shot at the same time, at the Goods Yard. Dermot Lynch had been shot in the back of the head and dumped at Wrekin Road. The visitors wouldn't know where it was, so Dermot must have driven them there, probably with King's body in the back, and there were only two seats. To shoot a man in the back of the head in cold blood is a deeply serious thing. Tom couldn't do it, of that he was certain.

Therefore, the killer must be inured to violence, and the chances of him not being on the system were slim. He crossed another question off the list.

Winters wouldn't let him go to Blackpool, but that didn't mean he was out of the loop completely. He doodled for a couple of minutes, and Winters returned to his office with a drink in hand. Tom dived in before the SIO could settle down to something else.

'Sir, have you got a second?'
'Sit down. What is it?'

'There's no obvious link between anyone in Earlsbury and Adaire in Blackpool. I just wondered if Adaire had any associates it might be worth tracking.'

'Have a look at this – but you can't take it away.'

He passed a folder to Tom and logged on to his computer. Tom opened the folder and found the beginnings of a report into Benedict Adaire. He flicked through the pages and found some surveillance photographs that had been taken this morning. Well, at least Lancashire & Westmorland were keeping their side of the bargain. His colleagues from MCPS were probably still on the motorway.

Adaire had a shaved head which made it difficult to judge his age, and he had been photographed coming out of a substantial detached house. Tom noted that a large fence surrounded the property, and he could see several security cameras on the walls.

He flicked through to a list of other people – Adaire was married (second wife) and had four known children. There was a list of all the directors and employees of his companies, and even of his minicab drivers. Only a couple of the drivers had criminal records and they were both for minor drugs offences some years ago. Neither of them were candidates for potential hit man.

'Thanks, sir. I've made a mental note.'

'Leave it on the desk.'

Tom did as he was bid and returned to his own workstation. His phone rang with an unknown number. Could it be Hayes?

'Hello?'

'Is that Detective Inspector Morton?' The voice was local and female. He confirmed his identity. 'I'm Ian Hooper's mother, and I'm calling from the hospital. He's not allowed to use the telephone so he asked me to ring you.'

'Thanks for calling. How can I help?'

'He says "Could you come and see me during Wednesday's afternoon visiting?" I don't know what he wants, though.'

'Of course. What time?'

'Three o'clock. He says not to show your warrant card or you'll never get in.'

There was still no news of Hayes. He made a decision.

Stuffing all the papers into his bag, along with the hat, he stuck his head back into Winters' office. 'Something's come up in London, sir. Can I work from there until Wednesday afternoon?'

'Fine.'

He left BCSS and headed for London. It was time to call in a favour from the Met.

Chapter 13

Earlsbury / Hong Kong

Wednesday

3rd November

The High Dependency Unit had been noisy, but Ian was beginning to miss the attention now that he was in a private room. It had been wonderful having doctors and nurses a few feet away instead of down the corridor. The HDU doctors were also more generous with the painkillers.

He tried to relax the muscles in his abdomen. What was left of them. He could already feel the skin hanging around his arms where his biceps had shrunk from lack of use. Maybe he could get the physiotherapist to lend him some weights.

'Hello Ian.'

DI Morton was standing at the door. Ian waved him in and pointed to a chair. The inspector looked even worse than Ian felt – he was thinner, if that was possible, and a yellow stain round his eye pointed to some serious action. Morton had noticed him looking at it.

'Your DCI gave me this,' he said, pointing to the black eye. 'Defending your honour or something like that. How are you?'

'Bad. I can't do proper physio for another week, and I'm going mad with boredom. That's one of the reasons I wanted you to come in.'

Morton had placed his coat on a plastic chair and made himself comfortable, but he hadn't taken out a notebook. This was promising.

'Can I get you anything before we start?'

'The WRVS trolley will come round soon. You can buy me a coffee.'

'What's the tea like?'

'Better than Earlsbury nick.'

Morton smiled. 'That's not saying much, is it? Well, I'm here in a completely informal capacity but I have to ask if you've spoken to your Fed Rep.'

'He's a tosser. Gives the Federation a bad name.'

'I agree, but he's right. You don't have to talk to me today, and nothing you say is admissible. Fair enough?' Ian nodded. 'Tell me if I've got it wrong so far. You knew nothing about what was happening at the Goods Yard. DS Griffin was too drunk to drive, and he rang you up for a lift. You followed him in to see what was going on. How am I doing.'

Ian wasn't going to commit himself to anything unless he could help it. He chose to remain silent for now.

'I'll come back to what happened in a minute, but I have another question for you. Why did England lose to France and Ireland in the Six Nations this year?'

What the hell was the man on about? Morton had said nothing about being a rugby fan the last time they had met. Mind you, he hadn't said much about anything. The inspector was waiting patiently, and Ian had the choice of talking or sending him packing. Why rugby? He shifted in the bed, and a knock on the door signalled the arrival of the tea trolley. Morton got the drinks in and settled back down. Ian left the coffee because it would be too hot to drink, and moving over would be painful. He'd wait until it cooled then finish it in one go.

'Too cosy,' he said to Morton. 'Martin Johnson's coaching team need shaking up because they've been together too long. They keep rotating the squad, but the coaching team aren't afraid of losing their jobs. The lads played well in France, but otherwise, it's too stale and predictable. That comes from the top.'

'I agree. They should have lost to Wales as well. Tell me, Ian, why did you get shot?'

Morton sipped his tea, and Ian lay back on the pillows. Was this guy some sort of psychologist? Griff had said he was a bean counter from the Fraud Squad, but Ian knew he'd been cornered. He'd answered the question about England because he thought it was meaningless, but now he could see that Morton was expecting some sort of analysis.

Ian rolled carefully over and drank his coffee, even though it was too hot.

'Because Griff was on the take. Because he was doing someone a favour and because he was out of his depth. Because he'd stopped being a copper. I don't know. Maybe it's because I didn't follow procedure. Maybe it's because I didn't stay in the car like he asked me to.'

'It's a start,' said Morton. 'I think you've got some more reflecting to do yet if you want to come back on to the force, but it's a good start. Have you given any thought to that – to whether you want to come back?'

'Can I come back?'

'Medically? I've no idea. Psychologically, you might find that you bottle it the first time there's any confrontation. Or you might overcompensate and take too many risks. That doesn't interest me. It's the spiritual dimension I'm worried about.'

'I'm not religious.'

'I didn't say you were. Even atheists have a spiritual dimension although some of them call it "morality". Where's your loyalty, Ian?'

Morton crossed his legs, and Ian tried to remember what they called his question – that was it, *rhetorical*. Morton had asked him a rhetorical question.

After a suitable pause, Morton continued. 'Griffin was only loyal to himself. He was greedy and bent. You're not like that. I've seen your relationship with Ceri, and I know you care about other people. But what about the police?

You're a good rugby player so you know all about loyalty to your team. What about loyalty to the game as a whole?'

Ian stopped him. This was getting too hard. 'How can you be loyal to a "game"? And what does it have to do with the police?'

'You're not stupid, Ian, so I'll try not to patronise you. If your team fields an ineligible player or takes steroids, you're letting the game as a whole down. Your team might benefit in the short term, but the game as a whole suffers. It's a short step from doing that to bribing the referee. The same with the police. If you let loyalty to your team come first, the whole force is undermined. When you've decided where your loyalty lies, I'll know you're fit to be recommended for duty. I've already decided you weren't involved in the counterfeiting.'

That was news. So Griff had been up to it all along.

'Describe the man who shot you again.'

Ian drew a breath. 'He was quite tall, he …'

'Bollocks. He was short, bald and Irish.'

Ian could feel himself flushing, and the pain in his side throbbed. 'If you want to get rude, perhaps you should go. I've told all this to Winters and I don't recognise the man you're describing. He showed me a picture and I've never seen it before.'

'Cut the crap, Ian. We're going to catch him. You can go to jail with him or help us. It's up to you.'

'Are you married, sir?'

'Divorced. No children.'

'Sister? Parents?'

Morton didn't say he was an orphan so Ian assumed the man had both. 'And there's no secret tape recorder?'

'No.'

'Would you swear to that on your sister's life? Would you swear on her life if you knew that I'd kill her?'

Morton uncrossed his legs but didn't reply. Ian had to lie right back down and tried to move away from the pain, but it followed him across the bed. Morton cleared his throat.

'Are you telling me that Adaire threatened you?'

'Is that his name? Adaire?'

'Yes.'

'He knew which school Ceri teaches at.'

'Dermot must have told him. He saved your life, you know. Twice.'

'How come?'

'He must have talked Adaire out of killing you, and then he rang for an ambulance. Maybe that was what got him killed.' Morton put the empty paper cups in the bin. 'I'll leave you alone if you describe to me – honestly – anyone else you saw.'

Ian weighed it up. Morton could ruin his life, but this Adaire bloke could kill him or worse still, he could kill Ceri and leave him alive. On the other hand, they were already on to Adaire so it wouldn't hurt to co-operate a bit.

'There really was a thin bloke there. He ran away when the shooting started, and I tried to arrest him, but I didn't have any handcuffs. He had a bit of a beard and a Lancashire accent. Blue eyes, I think.'

'Hair colour?'

'He was wearing a Man United hat. Typical United fans – out thieving instead of watching the match on TV.'

Morton seemed both pleased and troubled by this information. He looked at the window for a second then picked up his coat. 'Thanks, Ian. I'll leave you to think about what you want from life when you get better. I'm sorry it's going to be a long time.'

That was a very good question. What *did* he want from life?

The plan was to change hotels for one night. Kate and her boss checked out of the moderately luxurious one in town and checked into a budget place at the airport. She was beginning to see that the quality of the decoration had little to do with price in Hong Kong: the fixtures and fittings weren't any shabbier than the other place but it was a lot smaller: in Hong Kong, wealth was measured in space more than in possessions. She had been studying the London property market a little as she debated whether to settle there permanently, and she had discovered that it was booming so quickly that she wouldn't be able to afford to live there unless jobs like this one came along very regularly. She wondered whether, during her lifetime, London would become as cramped and crowded as Hong Kong. Probably.

A taxi took their luggage away in the morning, and it was returned to them that afternoon with fulsome apologies for the delay. Her boss seemed reluctant to let her take it to her room.

'It'll look really suspicious if we check it in to reception,' she said. 'Besides, do you want someone else looking through it?'

He flannelled for a bit and let her go. She heaved the enormously heavy case on the bed and, shuffling around the narrow gap between the bed and the cupboard, she unzipped it. Underneath her clothes was the equipment for the Shanghai job.

It was broken down into components which were capable of assembly into a variety of legitimate configurations and which were quite appropriate for her cover story; they had been added while the cases were en route to the hotel. She felt underneath and came up against something hard.

Carefully taking out the intercept equipment, she lifted the final layer of clothes. At the bottom of the case were three 18v lithium ion batteries. What were they doing in there? They didn't need them and they hadn't ordered them.

Kate sat on the bed and stared at the grey aluminium cases. Something didn't add up. Someone had buried them at the bottom of the case, so it wasn't an accident or oversight. Leach had been reluctant to allow her access to her luggage, which could be a coincidence (he seemed to have an issue with women showing initiative), or it could be that he wanted them for his own purposes. In which case, why weren't they in *his* luggage? She couldn't trust the man, that was for certain.

She had the note in her pocket still. When the waiter had invited her to his place the other night, she wasn't so drunk that she had accepted. Instead, she had written on the back *You get the taxi to my hotel. Bigger bed.* She had been awoken at one thirty in the morning by the receptionist. 'Miss Lonsdale, there's a man here called Li Wei who says he has a note from you.'

When Wei arrived at her room, he handed over the note like a private handing over a holiday pass. If he really was the sweet, kind young man he seemed to be then she could be signing his death warrant by getting him involved in her problems. She had no commanding officer any more, no chain of command that would back her in any situation. She was on her own.

Tom walked out of the hospital after his visit to Ian as if he were in his own world, which basically he was. He now had confirmation from Hooper that the red beanie hat had been at the Goods Yard. Thanks to a favour from London, he had a name, too. Tom had only handed in one hair for DNA testing because he couldn't enter the whole hat as evidence without alarm bells ringing everywhere.

The report included the subject's criminal record – GBH, ABH etc. Exactly what he would have expected. Unfortunately, the name had not appeared in Lancashire & Westmorland's report on Adaire. Their links must be well hidden. So now what did he do?

He drove back to BCSS and checked his desk. There was an A4 envelope with a handwritten direction and no stamp, which he assumed would be an internal report. He opened it without thinking, and inside was another envelope addressed to him and marked *Personal*. There was also the copy of a printout from the hotel where he had sent Hayes on Monday.

She had never returned to BCSS. He had received an email from ACC Khan on Tuesday which said: *I understand you are in London. DC Hayes has phoned in sick. Please let DCS Winters know if you need further support from MCPS.*

Tom opened the letter and scanned the signature. Hayes' handwriting started neatly, but by the end of the letter, it was looking distinctly out of breath.

Dear DI Morton,

I don't think I am well enough to continue working with the Midland Counties Police Service and I will be talking to Human Resources about this. My doctor has signed me off for a week to start with.

However, I could not go without telling you about what I had discovered at the hotel.

Their switchboard records details of outgoing calls and I was able to track back and find the extension from where the call was made to DS Griffin. It was a hotel phone in the lobby outside the Lickey Hills Suite. No one else had access to that area because the key was given to the person who booked it. I have attached a printout from the reservation system.

I have learnt a lot from working with you and I hope that you make an arrest soon.

Yours sincerely,

DC Hayes.

His first response was *coward*. She was entitled to her opinion about his methods, but she wasn't entitled to speak to him like she had done at the park. If she didn't like the way the police force did its job, she could resign or she could suck it up and apologise to him. To go on the sick like that was taking the easy way out, and she hadn't seemed like that to him. Maybe she had spoken to someone who told her there was a case for constructive dismissal. He liked her and he was sorry to lose her, but that's life. His opinion changed when he looked at the printout.

This hotel had a number of conference rooms and facilities. The report contained the record of bookings for the Wednesday that Griffin was shot. The Lickey Hills Suite had been booked out for the whole day to MCPS, and the booking had been made by the Chief Constable's Personal Assistant. No wonder Hayes had run off: he felt like doing the same.

He breathed slowly for a few seconds to calm his nerves and tried to think straight. Tom didn't suspect the Chief Constable because the man had been in post for only a short period. This went back years. That didn't mean his PA was innocent though – and the first question he needed to answer was the nature of the meeting and who had attended.

He was wondering how much of a gamble to take when Winters shouted from his office. There was no one else around – it was already dark outside. Tom shuffled the letter and printout together and put them in his jacket pocket.

'Sir?'

'I've just had word from the hospital that a certain Thomas Morton paid a visit to Ian Hooper. That wouldn't be your father, would it?'

'No, sir.'

'When were you planning to tell me?'

'It's late. I was going to write up the report at the hotel and present it to you first thing tomorrow before I head back to London.'

'Tell me now and email the report when you've finished it.'

'One second.' Tom fetched his notebook, and was grudgingly invited to sit on his return.

'It's a difficult one,' he said. 'Hooper's memory is returning slowly, and I believe that he might recall further details of the night in question, but that's not my prime concern in his case.'

'It isn't. Anything he remembers should be told to me.'

'Understood. At this moment, based on lack of any evidence to the contrary, and supported by statements from Ian's girlfriend and from Mr Kelly, I believe that Hooper did not know what was happening before or during his visit to the Goods Yard. I believe that he was induced to go there by DS Griffin, and that Hooper was an innocent victim on that night.'

'I can sense a "but" coming.'

'It's more of a "however". If the Chief Constable wants to be sure that Hooper is innocent, I need to know why Griffin chose him. Not just why he rang Hooper that night, but why he chose him for CID. We're all loyal to our bosses.' Winters snorted at this suggestion. 'Well, we are. Up to a point. For some officers, the loyalty stops at a very low level – when the boss is a woman, for example, some men have very little loyalty.'

'Sad, but true.'

'Yet, for other officers and other bosses, the loyalty goes all the way – in Hooper's case, his loyalty took him to the edge of death. I want to know whether that was based on naivety or something else, something that the Chief would not want back on the force.'

'How long will it take to decide that?'

'Until I can interview him under caution, I won't know for sure. And that will take weeks. On the other hand, I can clear the rest of Earlsbury CID immediately and will do so in my report. Clean bill of health, end of pariah status. If anyone else in that team was bent, he or she would have been in the car with Griffin instead of Hooper.'

'Good. That's good to hear, Tom.'

'There is another "but", I'm afraid. I will be recommending that after DCI Storey has passed on the good news to his team, he is given additional leave. Three weeks. That man is on the edge of a nervous breakdown.' Tom pointed to his black eye. 'And if he won't go away voluntarily, he should be forced to go. For his own good, and that of the team.'

Winters grunted an acknowledgement. 'The other ACC won't like it. That team will be three officers short if we do that, but you're right. Thanks. You can go home and save the taxpayer another night in the hotel.'

'I'll be in touch.'

Tom cleared everything from his desk. He wouldn't be coming back to BCSS for a while although he had no idea what he *was* going to do. He hung on to his security pass, just in case, and headed out to the car park.

He loaded up the boot and climbed in with some difficulty. He must have knocked the courtesy light into the off position.

'Good evening Inspector,' said a voice from the back of the car. 'Don't turn round.'

So, what are these batteries? thought Kate. *An actual bomb or something else?* She stood up and retreated from the suitcase. That was completely pointless because if they were a bomb, six feet would make no difference.

She needed to get well away from here.

She stuffed some outdoor clothes into a small rucksack and took her passport and all the cash, but left her cards, phone and laptop behind. She hopped from one foot to the other, staring at the fake batteries. They were the only proof that something had gone wrong, but if she took one with her, she might be carrying a bomb around. In the end, she stuffed one into her rucksack and headed down to the bar. Her boss was talking to an obvious hooker.

Kate put her rucksack down out of sight and caught Leach's eye. She made sleeping signs with her hands next to her head. He nodded back, and the hooker half turned round to see what he was looking at. Kate retrieved her rucksack and was out of the hotel in seconds. She hoped the prostitute turned out to be a man. Unless of course that's what her boss wanted. In which case, she hoped it was a woman.

She found a neglected planting of shrubs in a raised concrete bed. Dodging out of CCTV range, she buried the battery. Safe enough.

Keeping close to the walls, she weaved her way to Departures. A stream of people were being dropped off by taxis which lingered only for a second before roaring off into the traffic. She stopped one at random and climbed in the front.

'Harbour,' she said.

The driver understood that much, and with gestures, signs and a twenty dollar bill, she convinced him to lend her his phone.

She dialled Wei's number and caught him just before his shift at the restaurant began.

'Kate. I thought you leaving tonight.'

'Slight change of plan. I'm in a taxi. If I put you on to the driver, can you tell him to take me back into town and drop me at a shop which sells phones for cash?'

'Of course. Are you alright?'

'I think so. I'll text you when I've got a new phone.'

She passed the receiver to the driver and sat back.

He first took her to a little shop whose female owner spoke good English. Kate left with with a selection of handsets and SIM cards, and a very small laptop. Then the driver took her to the hotel in which she was now holed up and considering her options.

When she had discovered the fake batteries, she experienced a feeling she had never felt before. All her life, someone had covered her back: first her family, then her adopted family – the Army. She thought that Skinner's outfit would do the same, but it seemed that someone wanted to stab her in the back, not cover it. Kate was no James Bond. She couldn't deal with this on her own against the world; she needed help.

She needed someone who was both in the correct hemisphere and who was tricky enough to come up with a suggestion for how to get away. She knew just the right man, but unfortunately she had no idea how to contact him. Well, there was one person who should know.

She opened the laptop and tethered one of her mobiles for a data connection. She found what she wanted on a public database – his mother's phone number in Gloucestershire. Kate made the first call.

Tom tried not to panic, but it was very difficult. He'd seen this trick on the TV enough times to have got bored of it, but when a real live person magically appears behind you, it's very, very scary. He glanced at the mirror, but saw only shadows. He breathed twice and put his hands on his knees.

'How did you do that? I didn't think anyone could copy these remote keys.'

'I didn't need to. I just watched you approach with all your bags and slipped into the back seat when you had the boot open. There's a blind spot.'

The voice was cultured and clipped and a little high. He'd recognise it again.

'I'm not pointing a gun at you, or anything melodramatic. I just want to put proposition to you.'

When the man used longer words, the accent stumbled just a little. Just enough to suggest this wasn't quite his normal speaking voice.

'Go on.'

'Everyone's entitled to his opinion, of course, but that doesn't mean they're in the right. John Lake, for example, is of the opinion that the peace process is more important than justice for Benedict Adaire's victims. We disagree. We'd like to see Adaire go down for a very long time, and we'd like you to be the one to do it.'

'Why me?'

'Because you're desperate to catch those counterfeiters as well as nailing Adaire. And his murderous associates. It's like this, Inspector. Tomorrow, John Lake or one of his friends will tell Adaire that he's been rumbled. He will go to ground, and the counterfeiters will move on. You'll never get them. If you act tonight, you'll get Adaire, his friends, a shipment of Euros and the courier. You'll even get the weapons they used on Griffin and company.'

'How on earth do you know that? Are you part of this operation?'

'Hardly. Like you, we uphold the law but we also have GCHQ at our disposal. We've been tracking mobile signals near Adaire since Thursday night. The computers they have down there can see patterns it would take me days to figure out. Once we'd identified the numbers, we listened in. Adaire is going to take first delivery of some Euros to go to Ireland tonight.'

Tom's hands were sweating and he wiped them on his trousers. He needed thinking time. 'Lancashire & Westmorland already have Adaire under surveillance. He'll lead them straight to the handover.'

'They're good but they haven't put enough men on it. Adaire always takes elaborate precautions involving a nightclub. He'll give them the slip without even knowing they're there. He's like that. So what do you say? Are you up for it or are you going to let them get away again? You won't get a better offer.'

'Okay, I'm in. Do I follow you or meet you up there.'

'Good man, Inspector. We'll take your car. Pass me your phone first. I don't want to have to explain myself to anyone except you.'

He might lose his job. He might be arrested. He might end up like Hooper or Griffin. All of those outcomes were undesirable, but Tom was more certain than he'd ever been: if he let them get away again because he bottled it, he would regret it for every day of his life. To show willing, he passed his phone over his shoulder, started the engine and headed for the motorway.

'As you pointed out, these people are not shy with guns. How am I going to arrest them?'

'We'll get backup when we're there. Don't worry.'

That was the least reassuring thing he'd heard since Caroline told him their marriage was as secure as the Rock of Gibraltar.

Chapter 14

Kabul / Hong Kong / Blackpool
Wednesday
3rd November

The helicopter simulator was more expensive than a real helicopter, but cheaper in the long run: it saved lives and money. Conrad Clarke's students would have worked their way through several million pounds worth of kit, and would be dead many times over if they'd been let loose on the real thing.

Mind you, he thought, *it won't be long before they're suiting up for real.* He didn't know whether to envy them their youth and health or pity them because he would go home to England, and they would go out to fight the Taliban.

In between sessions, he heard a shout across the hangar from the office. Someone called his name and waved him over. He limped across the floor and saw an ex-Marine Corps soldier in the uniform of an American private military contractor outside the squadron office. It was the personal bodyguard of his loathsome American boss. Clarke had no idea whether the PMC was equally loathsome because he had never heard the man speak.

'Afternoon, soldier.'

No response.

Well, it didn't hurt to be polite. Inside the office, his boss was looking at the orders pinned to the wall. Clarke collapsed into his chair and rubbed his leg. The surgeons had warned him that it would be sensitive to cold. 'Tea!' he shouted, and the squadron servant began to scurry about. He was distantly related to one of the pilots, and Clarke paid his wages out of the allowance he had been given for his own bodyguard. He couldn't care less about his own safety, but he cared a lot about having hot tea on demand and someone to look after him. The man had only one hand after an encounter with the Taliban.

The servant put two mugs down on the desk and left them alone. Clarke lit a cigarette.

'You can't do that in here,' said the American. Clarke pointed to a sign that said *Non-smokers should stand in the doorway*. The American started wafting his hand, but gave up and opened the office door before sitting down.

'Congratulations are due. I think.'

'I think so too,' said Clarke. 'My squadron won the Stage One simulator competition hands down. Beat your lot into a cocked hat.'

'The ones that survived did very well. Shame you had so many fall by the wayside.'

'Change the rules, then. That's what normally happens when Americans lose something. To what do I owe the pleasure?'

The American's lip twitched ever so slightly. He wanted Clarke to call him *Sir* just as he'd tried to call Clarke *Captain*. Clarke's response had been, 'Neither of us has a commission from the Afghan Airforce. Until we do, I don't think ranks are appropriate.'

'We're due a break soon. Progress has been good, well up to target. I've had orders from Washington, though. We've to give your squadron ten days furlough with immediate effect. Not you, though. You're going to get new orders.'

Clarke groaned. He was just getting used to life in Kabul. He didn't want to be jetting off again. 'Thanks. I suppose.'

The American went to leave, and Clarke said, 'You're welcome.'

'What for?'

'The tea. It's considered rude in Afghanistan not to take hospitality when it's offered.'

The American left and his bodyguard fell into step behind him.

The office phone rang, and the servant answered it. Most of the calls were local, and Clarke needed a translator. He didn't notice at first that the servant had switched to English until he shouted over to him.

'There's a lady on the line, Chief. She says she's your mother, but I think she's too young.'

Who on earth? He picked up the phone and said hello. The caller actually *was* his mother. His first thought was that something must have happened to his father.

'Is everything alright?'

'Yes, dear. We're all in the best of health. I've had a call from someone who claims to be an old friend. I've sent their contact details by encrypted email. I can't stop, this call is costing me a fortune. Are you okay?'

'Fine.'

'Good. I'm sure you'll be in touch.'

Clarke passed on the good news about the ten days leave to his squadron, and they high fived each other as if they were extras from Top Gun (which many of them thought they were). He wrapped up the session and headed back to his quarters.

He expected the email to be from an old flying comrade. Probably someone looking for work. When he saw the name he took a sharp breath. What on earth did Kate Lonsdale want? His mother had included a note saying that it seemed urgent. He looked up the Country Code and saw it was for Hong Kong. Good grief. What on earth was she up to? He dialled the number, and she answered immediately.

'Hello, Kate. Why has the Army sent you to Hong Kong?'

'Haven't you heard? I left the Army and I'm freelance now. Listen, Conrad, I know this is a bit cheeky, but I'm in a spot of bother and I need your advice.'

Was she really in trouble? She could easily be laying a trap for him if she were still pursuing Jensen's death.

'Why me?' he asked. 'I wouldn't have thought I was your favourite person after what happened to Vinnie.'

'You weren't my first choice, but you're sneaky and you're on the right continent.'

'What's happened?'

'I was about to fly to Shanghai, and someone, possibly my boss, planted something in my luggage.'

'What was it and where is it now?'

'Three lithium batteries. Big ones. I'd rather not say on the phone where they are.'

'Describe them.'

'Grey metal cases. Sealed. Connectors at one end. All the labelling is in Chinese except for the words "Disposs of carefully." That's "Dispose" but spelt wrong … Hello? Conrad? Are you there?'

'Yes. How long have you got?'

'I'm supposed to be on a plane in the morning, our time, so about eight hours.'

'I'll call you back in less than an hour. Promise.'

He lit a cigarette and studied the picture of Ganesha on the lighter: it was decision time. If it had been anything else, he might have helped her or he might have left her. He didn't know. But this was different.

He'd seen those batteries – and the spelling mistake – before. Lots of times. They were a sideline of his shadowy employers, and he knew what was in them. The question was this: why would they be giving Kate Lonsdale three canisters full of pure, refined heroin? Presumably to get rid of her into the Chinese justice system. Should he let them get on with it or not?

Ganesha stared at him, broken tusk in hand. He flicked it on to the back and focused on the little engraving of the fish. Mina. He carried her name in his pocket everywhere.

Could he ever look Mina in the eye if he sent Kate to prison as his bosses clearly wanted? If he helped her get away from China, would he be able to keep his job and his life?

He rolled the lighter round and round in his hand looking first at the god and then at the fish.

God, fish, god, fish.

He snapped his fingers closed around it when his phone rang.

He had only heard this voice twice before – when he was told to sort out a problem in England, and afterwards to thank him for his work and send him to Afghanistan. As far as he could tell, it was the voice of the Commanding Officer, the man in charge of the whole Rainbow of operations – Red Flag, Green Light, Blue Sky. Well, Clarke called him the Commanding Officer in his head.

'Clarke?'

'Sir.'

'Get to Hong Kong and await further instructions. We have a situation there that you need to sort out. Kate Lonsdale has gone AWOL with some of our merchandise, and she needs to be dealt with.'

'Sir.'

He disconnected the call and rolled the lighter around again. This didn't sound good at all.

The journey to Blackpool was conducted in silence. The man in the back had begun and ended the conversation by saying, 'Don't make small talk. Or ask questions.'

They had to stop to buy diesel, and to allow Tom to go to the toilet. Instead of the motorway services, he was directed to a small garage off Junction 27. He also needed a drink because he couldn't remember his mouth being this dry. His passenger seemed unaffected by such minor things. When Tom went to fill the tank, he simply lay down on the back seat and disappeared. Tom made a point of not looking, but when he was queueing to pay, he could feel the man's eyes on him every second. He didn't try to make contact with anyone.

At the end of the M55, he was told to put a postcode into his satnav, and the electronic voice directed him to a deserted street well away from the hordes of families driving into town to enjoy the Illuminations. Tom had never seen the lights, nor had he ever wanted to, but he promised himself that after tonight he was going to make a pilgrimage along the Prom to remind himself how stupid he was being.

'Pull up here.'

Tom parked the car and switched off the engine.

'Open the boot and put your hands on the dashboard where I can see them.'

His passenger's tone had changed from invitation to command. Perhaps it was how the man was used to dealing with people. Perhaps he had made a special effort to talk Tom into joining him. Perhaps not. The most likely explanation was that the man had Tom exactly where he wanted him, and couldn't be bothered to ask nicely.

He did as he was told, and the man got out. Tom checked his watch; it took the man two minutes to return and put something in the boot. The lid was slammed down and the back door opened.

'We're going to wait for an hour and twenty minutes. Make yourself comfortable.'

Tom did just that. He took off his seat belt and twisted his legs to take the pressure off his back. He closed his eyes and tried to focus on what he knew for certain, and to ignore what was speculation.

The passenger had connections with the security services. That was for certain. He knew who John Lake was and what he had said. This didn't mean he was actually a member, just that he knew people who were.

He had got close to Adaire's operation as well. The telephone intercepts showed that the man had very good intelligence indeed. A hundred things were bothering him, but one stuck out from the others: how did he know about Adaire's habit of dodging into the nightclub to avoid detection? Had they followed him before or did they have a source inside Adaire's team that they weren't going to admit to?

The darkness and the motorway driving took their toll. Tom had no obligation to keep watch, and so he let his passenger do the worrying. Tom fell asleep.

'Wake up, Inspector. It's ten o'clock.'

'Right. Okay.'

He ached. All over.

'Get out and go for a walk to the end of the street. You'll be stiff, and the cold air will wake you up.'

Tom didn't argue. He took his time and stretched his arms. His right leg had almost gone to sleep. He was more awake when he got back in but he was more worried, too. Something was about to happen.

Hong Kong's night life was in full swing and it took Kate a few minutes to find a relatively quiet corner in a bar to wait for Conrad's call.

Of all the six billion people in the world, why had she rung Conrad Clarke? She had other friends who had left the Army, but she had lost touch with all of them after they handed in their uniforms. Clarke wasn't even a friend – she knew him, yes, but he was also the man who had organised the flight which killed her fiancé. Only Vinnie hadn't really been her fiancé, because he had never proposed.

She wore the ring around her neck, the one that Vinnie had obtained from Conrad, the one he had been carrying in his pocket when the chopper plunged into the mosque killing him and the pilot.

She didn't even know what Conrad could do to help, but there had been all sorts of rumours about him when he was in the RAF. He was the one who could be relied on for illicit booze or dope if you were organising a party. One night, a junior officer had told her, in all sincerity, that Clarke owned an antique shop in the Cotswolds where he sold historical artefacts smuggled out of Afghanistan and Iraq. Her phone rang.

'Hi Kate, everything okay?'

'So far.'

'Where are the batteries? I need to know if I'm going to help you.'

'Two are still in my case at the airport hotel. The other one is in a safe place.'

'Good. That's very good. Listen, I've taken three days' leave, starting tomorrow, and I'm flying out of Kabul tonight. Trouble is, I can't get a connection to Hong Kong until tomorrow morning. I'm due in at 1530 your time.'

'No. You can't do that. I just wanted someone to talk to. Someone who's been in a few sticky situations themselves.'

'What are you trying to say about me? No, it's the least I can do for you.'

'I'll have to pay your air fare and expenses.'

'I was hoping you'd say that because the flights are rather expensive. When I get there, I'm going to be your middleman and I'm going to cut you a deal.'

'Why?'

'Because you're up shit creek, old girl.'

She heard the rasp of a Zippo lighter. Conrad hadn't given up smoking, then. Maybe that's why he was back in Afghanistan. They didn't have a smoking ban there. Except for women, of course.

Clarke sucked in smoke and continued, 'They were using you for something. I don't know what, but they were. You can't just walk away from a situation like that. I need to work out a solution that pleases everyone, but I haven't decided what that might be. I'll see how he reacts first of all. Have you got somewhere safe to hole up until I get in?'

Kate looked around the bar and checked her watch. If she could trust Conrad Clarke, she could trust Li Wei.

'I'll find somewhere.'

'Pick me up from the airport tomorrow.'

She picked up her rucksack and took Wei's note out of her pocket. He'd have a nice surprise when he got home tonight.

When Tom got back to the car, he had an enormous sensation of impending doom. He felt as if the door to the vehicle was the door to a cliff edge, and that getting inside would be like jumping off into the dark.

He opened the door and stood back.

'Look, I'm not going any further unless I know there's backup in place. I was at Bet with Burton and Four Ashes Farm when these people last tried to sort out a problem. I don't want to be any closer to them than this without support. Preferably armed.'

'I agree. But there's got to be an exit for me. I have as much desire to be alone with your colleagues as you do to be alone with Adaire. Here.'

The man held out Tom's phone, and he took it out of the gloved hand. The sleeve on the man's coat had risen up when he extended his arm, and Tom caught the glimpse of a red tattoo in the streetlight. There was something familiar about it.

Before he could catch the fragment of memory, the man spoke. 'Get in and call 999. Tell the control room to notify the surveillance team that Adaire will be at the Emerald Green warehouse on Preston New Road in fifteen minutes. You can tip them off when to go in.'

That sounded a bit risky to Tom. He would have preferred to ask for an Armed Response Vehicle to be on hand but that would stop his mission in its tracks. He wasn't going to order any arrests until he was sure that officers were safe, that's for certain. He dialled the Emergency number and asked for the police.

'This is Detective Inspector Morton, Metropolitan Police Warrant number 5512358, on attachment with Midland Counties Police Service. You are surveilling Benedict Adaire, repeat Benedict Adaire. I have reason to believe that he has given your team the slip and will be at the Emerald Green warehouse on Preston New Road in fifteen minutes. Officers should maintain their distance and await notification of crime in progress.'

He disconnected the phone and switched it to *silent*. They would be calling him back, but they would also be checking his details. Depending on where the surveillance team had gone when they lost Adaire, they should be in position.

'Do you know the way?' he asked.

'End of the street, turn left then right at the junction. Pull in to the old pub car park on the left. I'll get out there and give you the final instruction.'

Tom started the engine and drove off. They left the gloomy back street, arriving on a slightly busier road as he followed the directions. He slowed down and saw a boarded-up, burnt-out shell set back from the road. Worried about his tyres, he drove carefully on to the front.

'Let me out, there's a good chap,' said the passenger. Tom flicked the central locking switch and then realised: *You don't need to do that to get out of the car.*

Before he could relock it, the other doors were opened, and two men slipped inside. He found himself sitting next to Adaire's right hand man, the one who had killed Dermot Lynch and left his beanie hat in the van. He was also looking at the gun which had done the damage.

'What's this about?' said the new man in the back. He had an older voice and his accent was Northern Irish: this must be Adaire himself.

Tom felt his spine go rigid when his other passenger, the one he had driven up from Earlsbury, replied in the same accent. 'I think you boys have got some talking to do. I'll leave you to it.' The door opened, and the passenger got out, slamming it behind him.

The man's accent triggered Tom's memory of the tattoo: *It was a Red Hand in the symbol of a Loyalist paramilitary gang.*

And then he remembered that the man had put something in his boot. *It's a bomb.*

From the back of the car came Adaire's voice. 'Who the fuck are you?'

Tattoo man had to get clear of the car before he triggered the bomb.

I'm going to die in five seconds.

'I'll drive,' he said, and put the car in gear.

Four seconds.

He slipped the seatbelt out of its holder and accelerated towards a concrete bollard at the end of the car park.

Three seconds.

The man next to him raised the gun towards him, and Tom slipped the car out of gear with one hand and started to open the door with the other.

Two seconds.

The car hit the bollard, and he thrust the door open as the man chopped down with the gun, missing his head by a fraction.

One second.

He hit the ground and started rolling away from the car as fast as he could. He heard the rear door open as Adaire started to get out. He rolled again and put his hands on his head.

Now.

MARK HAYDEN

The End

The Operation Jigsaw trilogy concludes with "In the Red Corner".

Author's Note

Thank you for reading this book; I hope you enjoyed it.

I would normally include a sample of my next book at this point - but as you've noticed, it finishes on something of a cliff-hanger. If you've bought the paperback, and you're desperate to know what happens next without forking out for Volume III, you can go to Amazon, search for *In the Red Corner* and 'Look Inside', but I'd prefer it if you just bought the book…

In this book, all the characters are fictional, and so are most of the places: the whole town of Earlsbury exists only in my imagination - and yours, of course.

Both sides of my family, for many generations, came from the Black Country, and I wanted to give a flavour of what it's like to live there - the people, the attitudes and the accent. If you think I've not done it justice, let me know.

Hong Kong, London and Kabul are real enough but as they're only bit-part players in this book, they don't count.

Both CIPPS and the MCPS are fictional.

To find out more about the books, please visit:
www.pawpress.co.uk

About the Author

Mark Hayden is the writing name of Adrian Attwood. He lives in Westmorland with his more famous wife, Anne.

Adrian has had a varied career working for a brewery, teaching English and being the Town Clerk in Carnforth. He is now a part-time writer and part-time househusband.

The first of his books, the *Operation Jigsaw* trilogy, have now been published on Amazon, and so has the first successor book.

Printed in Great Britain
by Amazon